Bubble o

Book 1 of Lyonnesse Tales
http://www.lyonnessetales.co.uk

Original Copyright © 2013 R.J.Trivett
This edition Copyright © 2014 R.J.Trivett

All rights reserved.

Cover art by Tom Roberts
http://www.tomrobertsillustration.bigcartel.com

Book design by R.J.Trivett

No part of this book may be reproduced in any form or by any electronic or mechanical means including information storage and retrieval systems, without permission in writing from the author. The only exception is by a reviewer, who may quote short excerpts in a review.

This book is a work of fiction. Names, characters, places, and incidents either are products of the author's imagination or are used fictitiously. Any resemblance to actual persons, living or dead, events, or locales is entirely coincidental.

Acknowledgement

I would like to thank all those who have helped with the creation of my Lyonnesse.
To my first wife Jan, for her encouragement to write the first draft.
To Brian and Libby for their *hard* edit.
And to Jen for proofreading.
To Tom Roberts of http://www.tomrobertsillustration.bigcartel.com for the cover artwork.
And, of course, to my beautiful wife Dawn for putting up with me and just for being there.

Dedication

For Kerry, Toby and Aaron,
Children of my heart

And to you dear reader for taking the time to read it.

[To show my appreciation my personal comments for you and you alone are scattered throughout and indicated thus, in square brackets. If you do not wish to interrupt the flow then skim over them.]

Devon Dialect.

Much of the dialogue in this book is written more or less as it sounds in a strong Devonian accent or at least a westcountry accent. When I was growing up *[cue violins playing Hearts and Flowers]* people didn't travel the way they do now and it was still possible to hear good local accents. In those days you only had to travel from one village or town to the next and the sound of the accent changed as did the dialect words that were used. It was quite easy to place someone within ten miles just by listening to them speak. Sadly, with the ease of movement and the mixing of people from across the whole country and the wonders of television, that has gone. It is rare now to hear someone with a Devonian accent, and rarer still for a local one. I have tried to keep some of it alive in my books so you will have to read it with a Deb'm *[Devon]* accent. There are greater authorities on it than me and I make no claim to be an expert in anyway. John Germon is one such and his Devonian alphabet follows.

Pronunciation:

R's are long and often rolled as in butturrr – butter

S's are hard and often sound like a Z zummer – summer

O's a pain because it varies from place to place but is often a U or OA or A buy - boy

F's are usually V's vull – full

The is shortened but to a soft th' rather than the hard t' of the north of England

H's are often dropped altogether 'az – has

D's and G's tend to be dropped off the end of words ol' – old, 'appenin' – happening

Lastly most pronouns are replaced with either 'ee or 'er or uz and me tends to replace my.

This is by no means all or a definitive guide, it is just a guide. If you are interested in learning more, then the books by afore mentioned John Germon are helpful. "Zee 'ee Dreckley" is a good place to start.

I've had some stick for using the word "lad" instead of "buy" *[boy]*, and I understand their criticism. "Buy" is more commonly used in most of Devon when a male younger than the speaker is being addressed. "W'ere be to buy?" "Wha's on buy?" etc. etc. However, where I grew up in East Devon "lad" was more commonly used. Not the hard northern "lad" of the Yorkshire moors, but a much softer "laad" with a drawn out "a" so beloved of pirate films. This was probably due to my proximity to Somerset and Dorset, growing up where the three counties meet. Brace yourself and listen to the Wurzels for five minutes. As I mentioned at the start of this piece, accents and dialect were extremely localised, but it's my story, so I've written it how I want to. So there!

Where I have used dialect words in the text a translation usually follows in the square brackets.

A Devon Dialect Alphabet

Reproduced with kind permission of John Germon from his book "Zee 'Ee Dreckly"

A	Apple	As red as a rawze (rose)
B	Bule	With a ring droo 'ees nawse (nose)
C	Cow	Vull o' 'ees own charm
D	Dumplin	Deb'm volkoo won't do 'ee no harm
E	Edification	Make 'ee wise at 'th end o' 'th day
F	Finniky	Zome maid oo dawn't like rompin' 'n 'th hay
G	Granfer Grigg	With 'ees bandy ole legs
H	Hen	A layin' thikky eggs
I	Ivery whips 'n while	Meanin' now 'n agaan (again)
J	Junket	Like mother maaks, 'twill never be 'th saam
K	Kitty Tope	A Jenny Wren gatherin' grub
L	Leery	Why not git a pasty 'n a pub
M	Mump Aid	'Ee got 'th brains 'o a brick wall
N	Nort	Meanin' nothing at all
O	Osses	Worrited be vlies
P	Pigs	Layin' down 'n thicky sty's
Q	Quaazy	Veelin' really unwell
R	Rawze	Kin' 'ee call t' mind 'th smell
S	Scrumpy	'Th West Countrymans Liquor
T	Teddy Caake	'Twill make 'ee graw thicker
U	Upitty	Tempers grawin' quite large
V	Varmer	'Th aid man 'n charge
W	Want Nap	Place fer piskies 't squat
X	?????	Tiz fer zomethin' but I'm blawed if I naw what
Y	Yokel	A bloke 'o 'th land
Z	Zummer	When 'th countryzides grand

Preamble

Imagine a meteor hundreds of miles in diameter, a real earth-shattering end of the world type rock, hurtling through space. After millions of years it finally begins to spiral down through the orrery of our solar system. Past the small brass balls of the outer planets and on towards a small blue-green planet with a single moon that most of us know so well. Watch the stunning special effects as it leaves a fiery trail through the exosphere, the ionosphere, the chemosphere (with its little known hydroxyl layer), on through the somewhat patchy ozone layer in the stratosphere and finally through the cloud layer in the troposphere.

White hot and half-molten, it impacts upon the planet. Not with an earth-shattering mushroom cloud accompanied by orchestrated thunder and lightning of the disaster movies, instead a dull thud and a fizzle, as the now pebble-sized rock lands in a muddy ditch.

Well, so much for dramatic special effects.

Rewind the film a short way and imagine the view anyone riding the meteor would have as it plunged earthwards. *[Provided they found a way to disregard the heat, lack of oxygen and no way of getting off before impact.]* Wide expanses of dark blue oceans, the grey-green of the land, tipped in places with white caps of snow. As our non-cynic closes in, details emerge. A small island in the Northern Hemisphere, criss-crossed by roads that our friend might recognise as Britain. Closer still and the proverbial patchwork of fields and hedges become visible, as the meteor heads towards the elephant's trunk shape of the Southwest of England.

Now freeze the picture there. Below, clearly noticeable, are the counties of Devon and Cornwall but... if you eat a *really* hot chilli-pepper, accidentally squirt lemon juice in your eyes and sort of squint to one side, the landscape changes and a third county is visible out if the corner of our watering eye. The shape alters from an elephant's trunk to an elephant's trunk with a bun, a very large bun, stuck on the end.

Thud Fizzle...

Chapter 1.

It was Sunday, and since his girlfriend was away visiting her brother for the day, Dave Unwin was partaking of his second favourite pastime, riding his motorcycle around the myriad of country lanes in Devon. It was early spring, and for once the weather was co-operating and he had not been forced to don his waterproof over-suit. It was still rather chilly so, in addition he was wearing a multitude of layers under his leather jacket and quilted ski trousers over his leather jeans.

If Dave was a stereotypical biker, as the media like to portray them, then by rights he should have been mugging little old ladies, robbing petrol stations, participating in illegal road races, or generally causing trouble. However, he was simply riding for the enjoyment of riding, and the thrill of exploring the largest network of roads of any county in the country. Nor was he travelling at high speed, far from it. Most of the unclassified roads were too twisty, and the road surface too poor to travel safely at speed. And besides the potholes, loose gravel, lines of tar around old patches, fallen leaves, and mud, there were also the hazards prevalent in a rural setting, like organic landmines left behind by herds of cows, and psychotic pheasants with a death wish. No, Dave was content to ride at a sedate pace, and absorb the world around him. Occasionally he would stop by a gateway or pull in to a lay-by where there was a break in the high hedges and take a drink of coffee from his thermos whilst admiring the view.

It was a beautiful day with hardly a cloud in the sky. The hedges were in their first flush of vibrant green, growing for all they were worth before they would be trimmed back later in the year once the birds had finished nesting. A sign by the side of the road understated the Hairpin bend ahead, but having ridden this way many times before he was ready for it.

What Dave was not ready for was the imposing bulk of a big red tractor pulling a trailer coming the other way as he went around the bend. Immediately he applied the brakes, the result of which was to lock up the back wheel, causing the bike to skid on the loose gravel and mud on the road. The tractor coming the other way also braked, skewing itself and its trailer across the width of the road, making it impossible to get past.

In the meantime, Dave released the brakes and steered into his skid to bring the bike back under control. Even from the low speed he had been doing there was no way he was going to be able to stop on such a loose surface before he hit the tractor. By the side of the road was a gap in the hedge. By a democratic majority of one, Dave voted to head for this gap. It seemed to offer an altogether less painful option than sliding into the tractor. *[Though with hindsight it would probably have caused far less mental pain.]*

If he had been able to or had the time to stop and explore exactly why there was a gap between the hedges, then he might possibly have found the remains of the broken sign that was in the ditch next to the gap. He might then have scraped off the lichen and the fungus growing on it, and been able to read what was left of indented lettering, which said:

DANGER!
FOOTPATH CLOSED!
KEEP OUT!

It could have referred to the vegetation but it didn't, for the gap between the hedges quickly converged. The footpath was more than overgrown - it was undergrown as well. Brambles and dog roses criss-crossed the path like organic barbed wire. Nettles and docks fought between themselves for space amongst the knee-high grass in the middle, and the blackthorn hedges didn't just loom on the edge of proceedings, they met and exchanged gossip in the middle. A panicked dab of the brakes and a sliding rear wheel informed him that the surface was even more slippery than the road had been and braking was not a good idea. There also appeared to be no room to turn around, not even a gateway or stile, which would mean that even if he could stop he would have to push the bike out backwards through the vegetation, so with no other option forthcoming he kept going.

Dave's knuckles were white inside his gloves as he gripped the handlebars, whilst nature tried its best to get to grips with him and dump him on the ground. The dog roses and brambles ripped and tore at various parts of his protective leathers, trying to get at the vulnerable bits underneath. Inside his black helmet, his face was as white as a sheet, his green eyes bulging with fear, as he tried his best to stay in the saddle during that nightmare ride. A part of his brain, that was obviously not up to speed with current events, noticed what a wonderful smell the freshly broken vegetation gave off as he careered through it.

It seemed to last forever. Perhaps it was his lot to spend the rest of his life riding down through that footpath choked with weeds, when without warning the foliage gave way in front of him. It parted to reveal another road. Heaving a sigh of relief, Dave managed to bring his bike to a halt. For a moment he just sat astride his bike panting. Somehow he had managed to get through it more or less in one piece. Which was more than could be said for his jacket and ski trousers. They were ripped and torn in several places, with the odd thorn sticking right through and into him by the feel of it.

After putting the bike on its stand, Dave pulled off his gloves and helmet, letting his shoulder length brown hair drop down around his ruggedly handsome and clean-shaven ace. Freed from the confines of his helmet, he began to take in his surroundings.

The road he had discovered had the traditional trappings of all little used country lanes. However, the grass down the middle of it appeared to be meticulously manicured and the potholes had a curiously symmetrical shape to them, but otherwise it resembled any other road long forgotten by the authorities. Carefully he placed his gloves and helmet on the ground and after a brief pause to pull out some of the more painful thorns, Dave reached into the tattered remains of his leather jacket and took out the map he always carried. He had acquired the habit of carrying it for those odd occasions when, through no fault of his own, he found himself directionally challenged *[or hopelessly lost]*.

Opening it up, he quickly found the road he had been on and the hairpin bend. The footpath was not marked, nor, as far as he could make out, was the road he had emerged onto. This rather annoyed him. The map was a good quality one printed by the A.S. (The Ammunition Survey Group) and had been quite expensive. It was the kind of map favoured by ramblers and only covered about twenty square miles but showed every farmhouse, barn, and milking parlour, outside loo, rabbit hutch, and dog kennel. Those people who had been unfortunate enough to have stood still for too long when the survey had been conducted were also marked on the map as well, but what it didn't show was where he was.

Vexed by his maps apparent inaccuracy and still shaking from the journey between the hedges, Dave began to swear to relieve the tension, not only turning the air blue but as many other colours of the rainbow as he could. Finally, when Dave began to repeat himself, he let out a philosophical sigh and looked again at his surroundings. Behind him, sandwiched between the two carnivorous hedges, was the footpath.

In front, on the other side of the road, was a patchwork of fields and hedges, and disappearing off on either side was the road that did not appear on the map.

A spark of inspiration struck him and he pulled out his mobile phone. Dave could ring his network service provider, Green, and get directions from them. *[The mobile phone company had named themselves Green, to reflect their fresh new image. Dave, like many others believed that they were named Green after one of his mother's favourite saying "I ain't so green as I be cabbage looking." Meaning she wasn't as stupid as she looked.]* After all, it was one of the many useless functions that Green had spent millions of pounds advertising on the television. All he had to do was phone the number listed somewhere in the bowels of the phone's memory and they would triangulate his position and give him directions. Or they could if his phone had a signal, which of course it didn't. The little aerial icon on the screen was flashing red and had no signal bars next to it.

Dave didn't like mobile phones, and never had. To his mind there was nothing wrong with CB radios. They didn't charge you extortionate prices to contact someone and ask them what they had just had for dinner, and what they were going to do next. And for any information that wasn't so important and could actually wait for more than ten minutes before it had to be shared with someone, you could always tell them the next time you saw them. Dave could see the usefulness of mobile phones. For example, they could be very useful in emergencies, for keeping track of errant teenage children, for mechanical breakdowns *[Which is why he had the phone and carried it when he was out.]*, and for when you were hopelessly lost. That is of course provided that there is actually a signal to allow you to make that emergency call. More swearing.

Retrieving his flask from the bikes panniers, he helped himself to a coffee to try and steady his already tattered nerves and sat down on the ground to endeavour to think his way out of the situation. As far as Dave could see, he had four options. He could go back down the footpath, he could go left, or right along the road, or he could sit there until a car came past that he could flag down and ask its driver for directions.

Unfortunately, not a single vehicle had gone past in the ten minutes he had been there, so remaining where he was to ask direction seemed pointless. He considered going back up the footpath, but facing that nightmare once was more than enough for anyone, and he wasn't sure that there was enough left of his leathers to survive another journey along the footpath. That left the road. Helpfully, there was an old fashioned signpost half buried in the hedge on the other side of the road. Or rather it wasn't.

Dave strolled over and read the sign, and then consulted his map again. None of the names on the signpost were marked on the map. The signpost said Shoton 4, Penhampton 23. The map continued to say that there were no such places. Not one to give up, he checked the index part of the map, which no one normally bothers to read, but it too said that the places named on the sign didn't exist. Little warnings were starting to prickle in the back of his neck. *[Although that could have been another thorn, they seemed to have gotten everywhere.]* He was starting to get worried.

The map covered just twenty square miles, in the middle of which was the town where he lived. A quick check of the mileometer on his bike confirmed his suspicion, he was no more than seven miles from home. His subconscious was screaming *"I'm lost seven miles from home!"* His conscious self said "Oh $&%£#!!!" and filled in the rest of the colours he had forgotten earlier.

Until now Dave Unwin had led what he and most would consider to be a fairly normal if unexciting life. He had had a reasonably normal schooling, normal college, normal parents divorcing whilst he had been at college and being stuck in a grotty one-room bedsit and sharing a bathroom with four other bedsits and their occupants. After college he had been employed in a rather normal, if mind-numbing, job as a clerical assistant for a small firm with big ideas and a boss who though he was an aspiring business tycoon. In fact the only thing that could be called a high point in his life (besides discovering motorcycles as a teenager) had been meeting his girlfriend Joanne at an aromatherapy evening class six months ago. At least the evening class had been a success, in a way. He may not have learnt much apart from the basics but the whole point of going to the class had been to meet girls in a calmer more relaxed atmosphere, and on a one to one basis instead of in flocks in which they travelled in for a night on the town.

That reminded him, he had a bottle of lavender oil he carried in his pocket for emergencies instead of antiseptic. He took it out and dabbed some of it on the worst of the scratches to stop them getting infected and speed up the healing process. Unfortunately, its warm and normally relaxing aroma did nothing to soothe his nerves. He had often heard it banded about on the radio and television that everyone reaches a metaphorical crossroads in their life and that nothing is ever the same afterwards. Dave was beginning to get a sneaking suspicion that his normal if boring life was about to change, whether he liked it or not, and not just metaphorically.

It was time to make a decision; he couldn't simply just sit there. He didn't have much coffee left for one thing, and even though he had managed to give up smoking some time ago, his present predicament was bringing on the familiar cravings for a cigarette.

However, rather than just rush headlong into a decision, he thought he should approach the problem in some sort of logical way, regardless of how illogical his current situation actually was. So, he consulted the sign and his map again. He read the sign. He read his map. He read the other side of the signpost and he read his map upside down to see if it made a difference. It didn't. There seemed to be no other choice other than to head to the nearest place indicated on the signpost, in this case Shoton, and ask for directions. So he donned his helmet and gloves and set off.

After a few miles Dave could see the village a short distance ahead of him, and it was then that the tarmac road gave way to a cobbled surface, which was slightly alarming. As far as he knew, Clovelly was one of the few villages in Devon that had cobbled streets. Shortly after, houses began to appear, dotted along the road. Not the modern, built in a day, flat-pack, PVC doll's houses which make up virtually all housing developments that smother towns and villages, these were of a *reasonable* size and had gardens that were larger than a postage stamp. But no sooner had he taken this in, when he found himself in the village itself.

It wasn't a large village, it was more of a crossroads with a church and attitude. He pulled up by the green, a square of neatly cut grass in the middle of the village, and looked around. There was the church and churchyard and a butcher's shop with garlands of rabbits and pheasants hung outside, and a greengrocers on one side of the square, a post office and general stores, an ironmongery and blacksmith's combined and the ubiquitous village pub on another side. The faded and peeling paint on the sign outside the pub proclaimed it to be the "S oat and Fe ret". Cottages occupied the third side of the square and on the last side of the square was a field occupied by grazing sheep.

Now where would be the best place to ask for directions?

Dave contemplated that question as he opened up the panniers on his bike. He had long ago discovered that the image of bikers as portrayed by the media, however erroneous, has a profound influence on people. Many's the time that he had stopped for a drink, food or other service and been turned away because he was wearing a leather jacket and carrying a helmet. He could never understand why. Like most of the bikers he knew, they cause less trouble than the average business suited, short back and sides business executive going out for a drink on a Friday night after work. However, having been turned away from the only hostelry for fifty miles when you are gasping for a drink of water necessitates that something has to give. And since small-minded people rarely change their minds, it was him that gave. As a result he had taken to carrying his suit jacket in the panniers and wearing a white shirt under his leather jacket.

So after divesting himself of all his "biker" trimmings apart from his leather jeans, and wearing his white shirt and suit jacket, Dave headed towards the Post Office. It seemed the most logical choice. What was a little unexpected, was that as he divested himself of several layers to reveal the shirt underneath, he noticed that it felt a good deal warmer than it had done earlier, and that there was no real need for all that warm clothing.

Although many village, and indeed some town Post Offices had been shut down for economic reasons, and those that are still open are only open because of something like "affirmative action planning", this one seemed to have been overlooked.

As Dave opened the door and went in, the small brass bell on the back of the door tinkled and fell off. The inside of this Post Office appeared to have been overlooked as well, but by time and modernisation. The interior looked more or less like the interior of a Post Office he has visited at a heritage museum. It was not a large shop, with a dark polished wood post office counter in one corner and the shop counter next to it. The rest of the shop was crammed full, floor to ceiling with shelves bowing under the weight of packets, tins, boxes, jars, and bottles. Anything you could possibly want to eat, cook, medicate yourself or animals, clean, polish, or disinfect with was there on those groaning shelves. Somewhere.

One small shop managed to do what so many supermarkets the size of several football pitches always fail to do, supply the customer with whatever they needed, or something that would do the same job. It did not try to con the customer into buying something totally useless and unwanted with multimillion-pound marketing scams, psychological and sociological ploys or by wafting the smell of freshly baked bread, rotisserie chicken, or freshly brewed imitation coffee around the air-conditioning system.

There was, however, one slight difference between this particular shop and other village shops that Dave was familiar with *[besides the fact that it was still open]* and that was the way the goods were packed or rather their packaging. Right alongside the high-fibre, low-fat, polyunsaturated, shrink-wrapped, best before goods of today were the tooth rotting, artery hardening, high cholesterol goods of yesteryear, which people had lived and thrived on for generations. He had only ever seen some of the labels in museums. And the pungent smell of carbolic soap reminded him of visiting his Nan's house on washdays.

"Can I help you," barked a sharp voice from behind the counter. And, after a pause "Sir?"

The voice had a tone that could crack walnuts, probably from a distance and it certainly drew his attention away from the mixture of antique and modern labels.

"Err... Sorry?" he managed to stammer, as he spun around trying to locate the owner of the voice.

"I said, can I help you?" repeated the voice irritably.

Behind a counter piled high with never to be repeated, once in a lifetime offers, Dave spotted a short cone shaped woman. She was dressed in a harsh tweed suit of indiscernible age and colour. Her grey hair was arranged into a large tight bun and attached to her head by an arsenal of hairgrips and pins. She was also wearing a pair of half-moon spectacles, the glass in which was so thick it was probably bullet-proof.

"I've lost my bearings and I was wondering if you might be able to help me out with directions?"

"Humm!" She didn't look best pleased with his request, focusing the full force of her stare on him.

"Or perhaps you might have a map that I could buy?" He continued, trying to placate her.

For a time the old woman continued to glared at Dave over the rim of her spectacles. Her silence and that withering stare made him feel uncomfortable. The intensity of her stare was unnerving enough, but she also reminded him of a particularly nasty primary school teacher he had suffered. The one that all the other teachers had avoided like the plague and managed to find all sorts of other important things to do elsewhere, like marking tests papers or cleaning the blackboard rubbers, when she had entered the staff-room. Dave was beginning to feel that he should have done some homework so he could hand it in, or at least have a very good excuse why he hadn't done it. Although probably nothing short of a broken neck would count as a valid excuse to this woman.

She continued to wilt him with her stare for some time before finally looking at her watch and then back at him again.

"What year is it?" she said at last.

Dave couldn't for the life of him understand the relevance of the question. He wanted directions, not a history lesson but he told her anyway.

"And what's the date?"

Why did she want to know that? This was getting more and more confusing. Dave didn't understand why this village didn't appear on his map, or the other destination that had been on the signpost for that matter. All he was after was a simple "turn left at such and such, then take the next…" What did the date have to do with it?

"Err, the twenty seventh of March. Or at least it was this morning. Why? Does it make a difference?"

"Just a bit laddie, and no I can't give directions. Every time I gives directions people gets more lost than they was to start with. It causes all sorts of problems. I remember the last time, some bloke comes a lookin' vur Cornwall, or was it Cromwell? Terrible mistake, terrible, someone ended up losing his 'ead."

Dave didn't understand her answer any more than he had understood her questions. Perhaps she wasn't firing on all cylinders? He started to back away slowly towards the door.

"Hang on a mo." She said, and ducked down to rummaged under the counter for something. Muttering to herself as she did so.

"So, that's where that went. Damn, Mrs Fuller was in here the other day an' wanted one o' those."

Finally she stood up covered in dust and evicted spiders.

"No, no map neither, least ways not one'd be any use to you. Can I interest you in somethin' else? Some razors? I've got some cutthroats 'ere someplace." she continued.

That was enough for Dave, he quickened his pace towards the door.

"Or what about…" she began and stopped suddenly in mid-sentence. Her expression hardened even further, if such a thing was possible.

"'Ere, you don't work vur the government do you? You ain't a taxman?"

"No! No, I'm nothing to do with…" Dave tried to protest. But it was too late; she was already in full flow

"Only I don't 'old with taxmen coming around and sticking their noses in where they don't belong. I sends my books off regular I do. You got no cause coming…."

"Honestly, I don't have anything to do with…" He tried again, but she wasn't listening.

"…around 'ere, frightening little old ladies and bullying them into showing 'em their books. I remember when I was a gal we never 'ad..."

Dave never found out what it was they had never had when she was a "gal", he'd already sprinted the remaining distance to the door, kicked the bell out of the way, opened it and closed it behind him as he left. Inside he could still hear her shouting at the top of her shrill voice what she thought of taxmen.

So asking for direction in the Post Office hadn't been such a good idea. So much for logic. On the other hand, perhaps because of the fact that this village didn't appear on the map, it was an isolated community and was therefore likely to be a little strange. It might be the case that the only time they ever saw anybody in a suit jacket it probably was the taxman.

Ten minutes later Dave headed towards the pub. His suit jacket had been stuffed back into the panniers, and he was again wearing his leather jacket. He was trying to look as un-taxman like as possible. The rips and tears in his jacket, along with the odd protruding thorn, went a long way towards this goal. He hoped it was enough.

Tentatively Dave opened the door to the Stoat and Ferret. A thick cloud of vapour hit him between the eyes. It was that peculiar kind of haze that is found in pubs and bars throughout the world, particularly if there is sawdust or straw on the floor. There was sawdust on the floor.

The vapour consisted of one part tobacco smoke, one part spilt beer, one part distilled spirits two parts pine resin and one part how many sweaty people can you crowd into a room already full of smoke, spilt beer and spirits, and with sawdust on the floor. It had a reassuringly comforting familiarity to it. There was also the whiff of cooking in the air, so presumably this pub also did food.

Dave peered through the haze and looked around the room. The bar itself was unremarkable. It consisted of one large "L" shaped room arranged with tables and chairs. On the far side a semi-circular bar surrounded a door that led through to the kitchen, and presumably the landlords living accommodation. The only other door from the bar was marked "His 'n' Hers". Large open fires burned at either end of the room.

The bar had been decorated, as many country pubs used to be, with whatever farming and craft implements that had come to hand. Rusting gin-traps were hanging next to broken ploughs, rakes, forks, scythes, and axes.

If a gang of lager-louts ever came in here to drink and got drunk in this place, then Dave thought it would be odds on that after a few pints their hair wouldn't be the only thing that would have a crew cut.

On the other hand if a gang of lager-louts came in here, they were likely to be very disappointed. It wasn't the sort of pub that was likely to sell a lot of lager. This looked more like an ale pub.

Glancing at his watch, Dave saw that it was just after eleven o'clock so presumably the pub had not been open very long, and therefore relatively deserted. But men were crowded around the bar and groups and couples occupied most of the table. There was, however, still plenty of standing room.

Behind the bar stood a traditional looking barman, who would have long since been replaced in most pubs by a far younger and trendier manager. He was about six-foot tall, six foot across and six foot around the middle. His face had the permanently happy grin of a man who enjoyed his job. His cheeks were flushed and crisscrossed with capillaries, suggesting that here was a man that not only enjoyed his job but enjoyed sampling his wares as well.

He gave Dave a cheerful nod of acknowledgement as he approached the bar, but continued speaking with an elderly gentleman, so Dave stood patiently, inadvertently overhearing their conversation.

"You mark my words Fred." Said the elderly man. "We 'ad a terrific amount of weather recently." He continued, shaking his head to make his point. "No good will come of it. Just you mark my words."

The barman smiled. "Zack, we always 'ave a lot of weather, tiz only natural t' 'ave a lot o' weather. Uz gets it every day." The barman leaned in closer. "The time to worry is when we don't get any weather." He said with a wink, before turning his attention to Dave.

"Now, what can I do vur you young sir? Can I get 'ee zummet?" he asked.

"J…j…just a coffee thanks." Stammered Dave. He was still feeling a bit shaken after his experience in the post office, and thought it might be an idea to actually buy something before asking for directions. "And, if it's not too much trouble, I could use some directions as well please. I seem to be lost."

The barman handed him a coffee and turned to shout back into the kitchen, making Dave jump and spill some of his drink.

"Suzan, Suzan would you be good enough t' come yere an' serve whilst I talks to this gentleman?"

"Ah, sorry 'bout that lad." Said the barman apologetically. "I take it you've already tried the post office then? Judging by the state o' yur nerves."

"Um… yes." Dave replied. "I'm Dave, Dave Unwin. I don't want to put you out. I'm afraid I have already upset the woman in the

Post Office. For some reason she seemed to think I was a tax inspector."

"Ah, you don't want t' go worryin' about 'er, she thinks every stranger's a taxman, does our Aunt Agatha."

"Now then, 'tiz awhile since we 'ad any strangers round yere. Let's zee if' I can 'elp. Oh, by the way, I'm Frederic Dray the landlord, but most people just calls me Fred or bar-steward." Said Fred with a chuckle. As if that wasn't the first time Dave had heard that particular joke.

"Now, what date is it?" he continued.

"Funny thing, the woman in the Post Office asked the same question. Wouldn't 'where do you come from?' be more helpful?" He ventured.

Fred turned and gave Dave a strange look before resuming his normal good-natured smile.

"I waz forgettin' for a mo that you're not from round yere. And yes, tiz very important. Could be very embarrassin' if you were t' go back to the wrong time."

Dave still didn't understand the relevance of the question, but he still needed directions home, even if it was only eleven miles away. So he decided to humour the man and told him.

"An' where's you from?" asked Fred.

"Tiverton."

"Which Tiverton?"

"Tiverton in Devon."

Frederic Dray considered this for a time, did a few calculations on his fingers, and then, without warning, shouted across the bar to a shorter and even more portly gentleman at the counter, and making Dave jump again.

"'Ere, Albert! Tiverton in D'em, present day? Out past Lord Timber's place?"

"That's right Fred." The man replied. "Next turnin' past Lord Timber's place on the Hunton road."

"Thanks Bert."

"Lord Timbers? Hunton?" Asked Dave.

He could feel the few nerves he had left beginning to unravel. He was, after all, only a few miles from home, and hopelessly lost. He had narrowly missed ploughing into the front of a tractor, survived a nightmare ride down a carnivorous footpath, and been accused of being a taxman. Suddenly getting up that morning seemed to have been a bad idea. He could have stayed cocooned in bed, wrapped in a nice warm duvet and spent the day relaxing and watching the mindless rubbish on television. But he hadn't, and now he was having difficulty dealing with the consequences.

"Ee's Lord Woods really, but everyone calls 'im Timber. An' Hunton is a village about five miles north o' yere. There's three villages in a sort o' triangle. There's this one..."

"Shoton." Put in Dave, trying to be helpful.

"Aye, that's right. Hunton to the north an' Fishin over to the south-west."

"I see. Hunting, shooting and fishing."

Dave took a swig of his coffee, wishing it was something a lot stronger. Why oh why had he got out of bed that morning?

"Now you leaves the village out past the smithy," said Fred, apparently not noticing Dave's discomfort. "An' carries on 'till 'ee reaches the crossroads this side o' Hunton. Then you takes the right fork. It'll take 'ee right out passed Timber's. Next sign you'll zee says road closed. Stop there. Wait 'till exactly one o'clock, ignore the sign, and ride on.

"Oh! You'd better set your watch by that clock on the wall." Said Fred, nodding towards the clock. "Make sure 'ee set the seconds too. You'll come out just outside Tiverton.

"You must o' come down that ol' footpath on the Penhampton road. Didn't 'ee zee the warnin' sign?" continued Fred conversationally.

"No. I didn't see a sign." Said Dave with a shrug. "Then again, I was um, preoccupied at the time and it was more of a spur of the moment decision to go down the path."

Dave had the directions he needed. As far as he was concerned, the sooner he got home the better. There was something very strange about this place and all the people in it that he couldn't quite put his finger on. Unfortunately, curiosity got the better of him.

"Thank you for the directions." Said Dave, doing his best to smile politely. "But I don't understand, why do I have to wait at the sign until one o'clock?"

Fred leaned across the bar towards Dave in a conspiratorial fashion. "Well, you've crossed the county border. No, no," put in Fred, holding up a finger and forestalling Dave's next question. "I don't mean the Devon, Cornwall border. You've crossed into the county of Lyonshire; at least that's what uz calls it now. Years ago they use to call it Lyonnesse. No, don't look at me like that, 'tiz true."

Unfortunately, Fred had chosen the exact moment that Dave had taken a swig of his coffee to impart this gem of highly improbable information.

Fred had to pause and slap Dave on the back a few times and help him get his breath back after choking on his coffee and spraying the rest of it across the bar.

"Tiz like this yere." Continued Fred, still wiping coffee from the front of his shirt. "A long time ago, when th' Romans first invaded, the Druidhs wanted to hide, coz they could zee what was acomin'. They wanted to still have a place o' their own, but somewhere where they wouldn't be seen. So, they hid what was a whole kingdom. Well tiz nort but a county now, but back then it were a kingdom. Anyroad, they hid it where no one would find it, that's why tiz not on any map." Said Fred, tapping the side of his nose knowingly.

"With the roads out 'o this county, 'tiz not so much a question as where they goes but when, coz they hid it in a bubble o' time."

Dave was feeling so overwhelmed and stunned that he couldn't even make a run for it. He was seriously regretting having any curiosity at all. And just how much of this rubbish did Fred really expect him to believe?

He put his empty cup back on the bar. Obligingly, Fred refilled it.

"You know Nessy?" whispered Fred. "Nessy the Loch Ness monster? Well, she wandered into Penhampton one day, frightenin' the life out 'o people. She'd come from somewhere in the cretaceous period, just strolled the wrong way and wham! Well, she lives in a lake t'other side of Penhampton now, but there's this path out o' the lake that comes out near Loch Ness." He left Dave to fill in the obvious blanks.

"She only does it for the attention mind." Finished Fred with another chuckle.

It was then that Dave did manage to find the energy to make a run for it, but his legs wouldn't co-operate and felt like they had turned to some sort of gelatine-based product. He didn't understand any part of what Fred was talking about. Why hadn't this man been carted off to some sort of secure institution? And where was the nearest one so he could check himself in? Worst of all, Fred didn't seem to be getting tired of talking.

"Can be a lot o' fun and very educational too. The schools around yere don't teach history, they gets taken out on field trips to zee it! I did a bit o' travellin' too, in my younger days. In fact, when ol' man Gripes ran this pub an' I was just 'is apprentice, 'ee took me on a tour to zee how things used to be done an' how beer ought to be brewed, mead too. Then 'ee took me forward so I could zee how things should not be done. Ha! On that trip I drunk so much that I'm still waitin' vur the hangover to catch up!" said Fred with a wink.

"Mind you, there are rules. Well, there 'ad to be really. Stop people messing up the time continuum. Stands to reason."

"What are the rules then?" Asked Dave before he could stop himself.

Fred gave Dave that slow wink that people tend to think is a subtle, all knowing sign and gestured for him to lean in closer.

"There's three of 'em," began Fred. "First, an' most important, no interfering with the course o' nature. You can't stop someone from dyin' and such. Or change history. *[In fact it is possible to interfere with time without causing a paradox that will destroy the universe. For instance, if you travelled back and brought the poor dodo into the present in an effort to prevent their extinction, some strange disease or other problem would make them extinct again. If you stopped the bullet that killed JFK then he would die of a heart attack or meteor strike. And if you went back to try and shoot your own grandfather, the gun would misfire, your grandfather would duck, or your hand could drop off. Time is very resilient but you can't stop someone from dying. Well, almost...]*

"Second, no using time vur profit. No nipping out an' findin' who won the Derby and nippin' back an' puttin' money on it. Causes all sorts o' problems. Although," Fred conceded, "Aunt Aggie does her best t' bend *that* rule. Buying stock thirty years ago an' sellin' it at today's prices.

"An' third," Fred leaned in and whispered in Dave's ear, "third, no using time vur practical jokes!"

"What?!" Exclaimed Dave. He couldn't believe this was happening. It had to be a set-up. He started looking around for a man wearing a false beard and moustache wielding a microphone. There had to be a television crew hiding behind a pot-plant or table-lamp somewhere. This was part of one of those cringingly awful television shows that set people up to deliberately make them look stupid.

But nothing happened.

And Fred wasn't smiling anymore. He actually looked very serious.

"Tiz true." He said, his voice full of sincerity. "We 'ad a devil o' a time a vew years back. Poulter the butcher went back a couple o' days an' pulled a stunt on Tinny the smith. So Tinny went back a bit a' fore that an' got one over on Poulter as 'ee was settin' up the first stunt on poor Tinny. After that it gets a bit complicated, an' some o' the bystanders got in on it as well. After three weeks and lord knows how many gallons o' whitewash and a heap o' other stuff, they was all exhausted an' up to their necks in primeval ooze. If they'd kept goin' back any further they'd have ended up floatin' in space."

And still a film crew failed to appear from behind anything.

Dave sat down heavily on a nearby stool, which had recently been vacated. He was now so confused that he would readily have sworn that black was not only white, but also it was possible to find an honest politician. It was the mental equivalent of an art historian who suddenly spots a digital watch on the Mona Lisa but is then presented with archaeological evidence to show that they actually had mobile phones in the Stone Age.

"Well now, I have seen a pig with wings." He muttered to himself under his breath.

"They 'ave, or at least they did once, I've seen 'em." Said Fred conversationally. "Never really got off o' the ground though."

"Ere, you'd best be makin' a move or you'll be late!"

"What?" was all Dave could manage in his dazed state.

"I said, you'd better be makin' a move or you'll be late." Repeated Fred.

"But you said to cross over at one o'clock, and when I looked at my watch just now it was only eleven thirty."

"Ah, but you've been in yere vur sometime." Explained Fred, pointing at the clock on the wall behind the bar.

It was informing the world in general that it was twenty past twelve, and not being in a fit state of mind to argue Dave adjusted his watch accordingly and left the pub.

He walked back his bike in a state of total and absolute befuddlement. No one had jumped out from behind anything and exclaimed, "You've been pictured!" *[This and similar phrases are the third most feared type of phrase in the world. It causes normal rational people to check under their beds, in drawers, cupboards, the office, garden, up other people's trouser-legs and behind blades of grass for camera crews, hidden microphones and above all men wearing silly disguises.]* That would have been easier for him to accept. What he could not accept was that Fred had been so sincere. And then there had been all that stuff on the shelves of the Post Office. Perhaps he had ridden into a theme park by accident, and this was some kind of total immersion experience.

Dave reached his bike and unlocked his helmet from the helmet-holder and put it on. It had a comfortable, reassuring smell and feel about it. You knew where you were with a good glass-fibre crash helmet, even if you didn't actually know where you were, so to speak.

The bike started first kick and rumbled gently beneath him.

There was also something reassuring about a five hundred cc single cylinder motorcycle ticking over gently.

Dave now had a choice, he could follow the directions he had been given towards Hunton, or he could ride around aimlessly and try and find his own way back. He opted for following the directions.

It did not take him long to reach the crossroads the landlord of the Stoat and Ferret had indicated, and even less time to reach the sign.

As per his instructions, Dave stopped by the road-closed sign but left the engine running. However, he didn't have a clock on the bike so he had to take off his glove so he could look at his watch. It was ten to one, ten minutes to wait. He switched off the engine and looked around.

The road had taken him up a slight rise, at least it was too small to be called a hill, and he could see around him to what must be the villages of Shoton and Hunton. In the distance he could just about make out the church tower at Fishin silhouetted on the horizon. All three villages were nestled in a broad flat valley. His hillock was roughly in the centre of it.

To his left the ground dropped away slightly steeper and he was able to look over an eight-foot high red brick wall that stood a short distance from the road. It was the kind of wall favoured by the rich and the gentry to surround their estates, and interspersed with regal looking gatehouses and pillars covered with statues of stags, eagles, and boars *[probably the owners]*. It was obviously designed to keep the 'wrong sort' out and prevent the gentry from feeling any pangs of guilt if they accidentally saw how miserable the peasants really were. Of course it could be the other way around, and the walls could be there to stop the gentry seeing how happy the peasants were and realise once and for all that money can't buy happiness.

"That must be Lord Timber's place," Dave said to himself. "a big house and estate like that."

From his vantage point he could see as far as the manor house. There seemed to be a lot of activity going on down there at the moment. There were several cars of various ages as well as a number of horse-drawn carriages, including a hearse pulled by six black horses. There was also a police car of questionable vintage with its blue light flashing.

Dave glanced at his watch again. #@%$£"%!!!!! It was a few minutes after one. He'd missed the time he had been instructed to cross. Oh well, a few minutes couldn't hurt, could it? He pulled his glove back on, started the bike, rode past the sign, and almost crashed in the darkness.

It was more than dark, it was pitch black. More to the point, it was night. He could see the stars shining and the moon glowing just above the horizon.

After an initial moment of panic, he switched on the headlight and rode until he reached a junction. Praise to the powers that be, it was a junction that he recognised. It was, just as Fred had said, not far from his home in Tiverton. Ignoring the temptation to look back over his shoulder, and the fact that it had suddenly changed from day to night in a nanosecond, and the temperature had dropped by a good ten degrees, he rode home. Deliberately he shoved all thoughts of what had happened to the back of his mind until he could sit down and think about it calmly and logically.

Dave rode around to the car park behind a small row of shop units and parked up his bike under a flight of galvanised steel steps that led up to his front door. His small flat was above a barber's shop. It was comprised of a kitchenette, a bathroom, and a bed-sitting room. It was all Dave could afford on his meagre wage as an office clerk or as it had recently been re-classified, data analyst.

With shaking hands, it took him a moment to get the key in the lock and open the door. Then he had to push his way through, past a drift of junk mail and newspapers that had built up behind the door. Without even taking any notice of this pile, he switched on the lights, dumped his helmet on the hall table inside the door, and made his way through into the kitchen. Acting entirely on autopilot Dave filled and switched on the kettle, and went through the complicated routine of making fresh, ground coffee. Once the kettle had boiled, and after a brief pause to wonder why the milk he had bought yesterday had gone off, he finished making the coffee, and went in search of an armchair and the open bottle of scotch he had on the side.

The bed-sitting room was neat and tidy. It had one of those double beds that folded up into the wall when it wasn't being used, so Dave tended to just chuck any dirty washing on to the bed and simply folded it all away. It saved time.

He switched the telly on, took his jacket off, and sat down. Over in the corner, the light was flashing on the answer-phone, indicating that someone at least had tried to get hold of him. He ignored that as well. Instead, he drank his black coffee, sipped at a glass of scotch, and began, slowly, to analyse what had happened.

Life had seemed hard enough to cope with before, but now, well...There were Druidhs, time travel, day becoming night right before his eyes *[In an unnatural way, i.e. driving up a road and one minute it is lunchtime and the next its bedtime. As opposed to the perfectly ordinary way that day becomes night every single day of the year.]* and worst of all there was Aunt Aggie! The thought of that grey-haired little old lady made him shudder. And why was there such a large pile of junk mail behind the door? It was Sunday and there were no deliveries on a Sunday. Presumably someone thought it was a laugh to push large quantities of unwanted offers for things he had no use for, through his letterbox.

Eventually Dave drifted off into a fitful sleep in the chair.

Chapter 2.

Something awoke Dave with a start and he leapt out of his chair. The initial disorientation of waking up in an unfamiliar setting hit him full force. Who was he? Where was he? What was he? And why had he just spilt cold coffee all over his lap? Slowly his faculties began to return. Wow, what a weird nightmare! There was a familiar noise, what was it? Eventually he realised the phone was ringing and that was what had roused him from his slumber. The phone stopped as his answer-phone cut in.

"Hello, this is Dave's phone. I am unwell, unable, or unwilling to come to the phone right now. Please leave your message or silence and heavy breathing after the tone." Beep!

"Unwin!" it was Dave's boss on the other end of the line and he did not sound best pleased. "Unwin! Where the hell are you! You've already missed one week's work without any explanation and you're late this morning. You'd better have a damned good reason why or you can start looking for another job!" Then there was the sound of a phone being slammed down.

What was going on? Why was his boss ringing up complaining that he'd missed a week's work? He never missed work and hardly ever took any time off for illness either. Dave glanced at his watch. It informed him that it was six-thirty in the morning. He wasn't due to start work until nine o'clock. Why was his boss ringing so early? Like most managers, Dave's boss didn't really need an excuse to shout and blame others he just did it anyway. But it was unusual for him to ring up two and a half hours before work was due to start and shout at him down the phone. Normally his boss had the courtesy to wait until he was actually at work before he started shouting. It had to be some kind of joke.

Yes, that was it. It was one of his boss's ill-conceived, sadistic jokes. Like the day he had come out of his private office and announced to the personnel in general that the company was going into liquidation and that everyone was going to be out of a job without any redundancy money. A couple of the staff had fainted, and several more had burst into tears because how were they going to pay their overpriced mortgages? That $@#%*!!! had made them wait until lunchtime before he gleefully informed them all that it had just been a joke and the company was in no danger of going bust.

"Practical Jokes." For some reason that phrase made Dave feel uncomfortable, but for now he had enough to worry about wondering what his boss was up to. So Dave decided to ignore it. He was still feeling dazed from his rude awakening, and a large part of his brain seemed to be fixed on the bad-dream he had been having. At the moment he couldn't even remember what happened yesterday. He could recall setting off for a ride, but after that it all got mixed up and confused with his nightmare.

Since he was up and awake so early, and there was no danger of him being able to get back to sleep for an hour, he might as well go and have a shower. He needed to wash off the spilt coffee anyway. Then he could make himself a leisurely breakfast as well. Perhaps a fry-up would be in order.

Unfortunately, once the warm water started to cascade over him and revive the rest of his mental faculties, Dave began to remember his nightmare more clearly. Had it all been a dream? It was certainly one of the most vivid and surreal dreams he could remember. And what had happened yesterday? Why couldn't he remember? Perhaps he had eaten something that seriously disagreed with him and that had given him the nightmare. But he couldn't even remember eating anything, let alone what he had eaten. What if it hadn't been a dream? He didn't even want to begin to explore that possibility.

Having finished his shower and dressed in clean t-shirt and jeans, it was far too early to put on his suit, Dave made himself a fresh coffee and again wondered about the rapidity of his milk turning. It was at this point each morning that he would habitually go and retrieve his newspaper and harbour the vain hope that amidst the usual pile of junk mail there might actually be a letter, a card, or something addressed to him that wasn't trying to sell him something he didn't need or want. Of course there never was anything except offers of double glazing, car insurance, satellite TV, home insurance, never to be missed credit card deals, and electronic stair-lifts. But at least the newspaper gave him something to scan through each morning over breakfast.

Without even registering that it was far too early for either the post or his paper to be delivered, Dave headed to his front door and saw the large pile of newspapers and junk mail he had pushed his way past the night before. Fear began to take a grip of Dave's innards. No, it couldn't possibly have happened! Such things didn't happen! Desperately trying to find anything that would dispel his fear, he began to work his way through the pile. The junk mail went straight into the recycle-bin. The newspapers were another matter entirely. There were six daily newspapers and one Sunday paper, a week's worth of newspapers. Dave's stomach did a somersault. It couldn't be true. Could it?

Scrambling across the room as fast as he could, Dave switched on the television and reached for the remote. Pressing all the wrong buttons in his haste, he eventually managed to hit the red button, and instantly wished he hadn't.

There, clearly displayed on the screen, it said ten fifty-six and twenty seconds, on the fourth of April. A week later than it should have been.

It took some time for Dave to regain composure. It hadn't been a surreal dream after all. It had all been real, all of it! Either that or he had been asleep for over a week. But no, now that he was no longer in denial, he could see the scratches he had on both his arms, and there on the floor where he'd dumped it he could see his tattered leather jacket. It still had a few thorns protruding from it.

What was going on? This sort of thing just didn't happen! Piecing together the previous day's events, events he had thought could only be a nightmare, Dave was engulfed by a wave of panic and confusion. How could he go out for a ride, and accidentally…?

A thought struck him and he rummaged through his bookshelf, pulling out his road atlas. Quickly he flipped through the pages until he found the road he had been on. It didn't show the footpath or Shoton. It didn't show Hunton, Fishin, or Penhampton either. He flicked to the index at the back and thumbed his way down the lists of place names. They weren't there either. He had been to places that didn't exist, at least not as far as the world in general was concerned.

Dave sat back in his armchair to try and think through the situation. Somehow he had visited a village that didn't exist, returned home and woken up a week after the day he had left. He knew he hadn't slept for a week, so where had the week gone? Suddenly Fred's words came back to haunt him: "they hid it where no one would find it, that's why it's not on any map." "With the roads out 'o this county, 'tiz not so much a question as where they goes but when."

Could it be true? Could the mythical county of Lyonnesse really be hidden in a bubble of time? It sounded ridiculous, even in the confines of his own thoughts, but what other explanation was there?

Where could the week have gone?

"Oh my god, Jo!" He exclaimed out loud.

He had arranged to go out with his girlfriend Joanne a couple of evenings this week, or rather last week. Dave shook his head, trying to dislodge some of the confusion caused by the sudden need for trans-temporal thinking. Jo would think she had been stood up. At the very least she would be furious. And it was going take a lot more than flowers and chocolates to make it up to her.

He dived across the room for the answer-phone, hit the message button.

Beep! "Unwin, where the hell are you? Are you ill?" that was his boss. "Are you coming into work or not?"

Dave skipped forward to the next message.

Beep! "Dave? Are you there Dave? Pick up the phone." It was Jo's voice and she didn't sound happy. "Where were you last night? I stood freezing in the rain for over an hour outside the cinema waiting for you. You'd better have a damn good reason for standing me up again."

Beep! "Dave? Where the hell are you?" It was Jo's voice again. "That's two nights in a row you've stood me up, and I'm sick and tired of your broken promises! I've had enough! Do you hear me? I've had enough. As far as I'm concerned we're through. Do you understand me? We're through!" and then there was the sound of the phone being slammed down.

Dave stopped the machine. There was little point in listening to any more. He sagged back into his chair. His girlfriend had dumped him. The one person in the world he really cared about and she had dumped him. Oh, and his boss was out for blood. But his boss could go and do something physically impossible with his own anatomy. It was Joanne that mattered.

He could always try explaining it to her, but why should she believe him? Why would she believe him? He didn't believe it himself and it had actually happened to him. And what was he supposed to say? Provided of course that she would actually let him get close enough to explain things. *"It's really simple dear, I went for a ride on Sunday morning, and arrived back twelve hours later and a week after I'd left."* Like that was going to make a difference.

Dave retrieved his mobile from his bike jacket. He'd had it on silent whilst riding so he hadn't heard it ring last night. He worked his way through a number of voice messages that corresponded with those on his landline, and through a number of increasingly irate texts from Jo which concluded with Jo recommending that Dave do something physically impossible with his anatomy.

He took another swig from his mug, only to find he had already finished off his drink. Perhaps another coffee would help him wake up and come up with some way to get himself out of a situation he was well and truly up to his neck in.

Whilst Dave waited for the kettle to boil again, he discovered that not only did he have no milk, but also he'd finished off the last of the sugar. He began to scour the kitchen looking for more, opening and closing cupboards and drawers and rummaging through their long forgotten contents. There were usually a few sachets of sugar picked up from various service stations knocking around somewhere. His desperate search didn't turn up any sugar but he did find an aged pouch of tobacco.

He had given up smoking a couple of years ago, but as part of breaking the habit he had kept the tobacco as a kind of negative temptation. As long as he had tobacco to hand, the reasoning went, he wouldn't crave it so much. It had been something like that anyway, he was fairly sure that was what his therapist had told him. Or was it reverse craving?

No one in their right mind would smoke, especially if they had managed to give up the habit once. Unfortunately, the one thing Dave didn't feel was being in his right mind so he rolled himself a cigarette. His unease caused his hand to shake wildly, scattering the dry and dusty tobacco liberally around the kitchen. The end result of his efforts, a very tatty cigarette that seemed to have more humps than a camel, proved impossible to light. Nervous sweat from his hands had saturated the cigarette paper.

He threw the retched thing into a corner, wiped his hands, took a deep breath, and started the whole process again. Eventually, after a couple of false starts with the lighter, he inhaled.

Over the years, many attempts have been made to describe the early morning cough of a smoker. They usually start at the point when the knees buckle and the body crumples in an effort to draw breath. Then they describe how the tremor works its way up through the body, building in intensity as it does so, before finally exploding out through the nose and mouth, catapulting any loose teeth and bits of food across the room and causing the knees to buckle again, ready for the next cough.

None of them came close to describing the way Dave coughed after inhaling tobacco that had had several years to dry out, and plenty of time to gather all the bits of hair, dust, biscuit crumbs, and other detritus that accumulates in the long forgotten corners of kitchen drawers.

He gulped at his sugarless coffee, leant against the sink, and tried desperately to breathe without coffee coming back out of his nose, and for the bright lights to stop flashing in front of his eyes.

Perhaps smoking a cigarette hadn't been such a good idea after all. But perhaps that was it! He had been trying to think his way rationally out of an irrational situation. It was not possible to go down through a footpath and find yourself in a county that people didn't know existed. Maybe irrational thinking was the way to go. So, if he was going to approach this irrationally, what would be the obvious way out of the situation? Just ignoring it wasn't going to help. If he tried to explain it to anybody then he would find himself in the nearest secure mental institution, wearing one of those jackets with the nice long sleeves.

"Of course, if I go down the footpath again," he reasoned to himself out loud, "and this time I keep a closer eye on the time and cross back at the right time, then I should get back last weekend and everything will be sorted out."

Dave had put on clean clothes after his shower, but after the morning he'd had so far, he made a quick check, just in case he'd stripped himself naked whilst he hadn't been looking. This done, he pulled on his boots, grabbed his jacket and helmet and ran for the door, before he could talk himself out of it, and slammed it behind him.

A minute later the front door to his flat opened. He'd left his bike keys behind on the hall table.

With his motorcycle rumbling away beneath him, Dave wound his way through the country lanes considerably faster than he had the last time. Before there had been no sense of urgency, he had been purely riding for pleasure. Now there was a need for expediency. He followed the same route as he had before, which to him seemed like just yesterday (which, in fact, it was) but was last week as far as the rest of the world was concerned.

He had stopped en route, before he'd left town, to fill the tank with petrol. It had not gone well. He'd stopped at the petrol station, only to find he didn't have any cash on him and that heir card machine was out of order. That meant he was going to have to ride back into town and prise some money out of his bank account via the ATM. That meant negotiating the one-way system and pedestrianised areas that towns are afflicted with. By the time he had found somewhere to park and walked to the bank, it would have been quicker to have left his bike at the garage and walked back into town.

And then there had been the bank, or rather the supposedly convenient ATM. The first time he had entered his pin-number, the cash machine had refused to serve him. Dave kept calm. Perhaps, in his haste he had entered the wrong pin number. He tried again and got the same uncooperative response from the machine. On the third attempt, the machine had eaten his card and eventually he'd had to give up hitting the thing and go into the bank and cash a cheque.

After a brief argument with the bank clerk, Dave had learned that his cash point card had been out of date and his new one was, even now, sitting amongst the junk mail he'd dumped in the bin back at his flat.

Once he was on his way, Dave didn't bother with admiring the countryside, and it did not take him long to reach the sign that warned and belittled the approaching Hairpin bend. He rounded the bend and, this time as was usually the case, found a total absence of large farm machinery blocking the road. But the footpath was still there, that at least hadn't moved in a week. Some of the brambles and other foliage had been cleared from this end of the path and a new sign had been erected.

Danger! Keep Out!

The red and white paint was still slightly damp. Someone from the other side had obviously decided that outsiders were to be discouraged.

Dave ignored the sign and rode down the path for a second time. This time nature showed less inclination to try and get to grips with him. Mostly because it had been flattened or torn when it had tried to tear him out of his saddle on the previous trip. Nevertheless, it put up some resistance and tried to unseat him and shred whatever it could.

Eventually Dave emerged onto the road at the other end and headed, without stopping, towards Shoton, and made a strenuous mental note to avoid the Post Office. The thought of Aunt Aggie made him break out in a cold sweat and he doubted whether he had drawn enough money out of the bank to escape from her without losing his shirt and most of the rest of his clothing as well.

Shoton looked very much the same as it had when he'd left it. He had intended to ride straight through the village, out the other side and wait until one o'clock and ride home again. But the church clock said quarter past ten and his stomach reminded him that he hadn't eaten since yesterday morning and that had been over a week ago. It strongly suggested that the empty feeling would be considerably reduced if it had something to occupy itself with.

Dave noticed the sign outside the pub. It stated, in somewhat smudged lettering that food was now being served.

He gave in.

What else was he going to do until it was time for him to cross over? If being a few seconds late crossing over last time had resulted in him arriving home a week late, then crossing over several hours before he was meant to could result in him going home whilst he was at primary school, or possibly even before he was born. Besides, if he went into the pub he could ask the landlord if his idea was actually going to work or not, or whether he was just going to make the situation worse and compound his mistake.

The usual cloud of smoke and alcoholic fumes *[although they were seeking help from a good counsellor]* hit him as he opened the door and walked into the pub. It was more than apparent that food was not only being served, quite a lot of people had been served as well, mostly with something intoxicating.

The first thing that Dave did was take careful note of the time on the clock behind the bar and adjust his watch down to the second. If this hare-brained idea was going to work he had to follow it through properly, and if that meant following instructions to the second, then he was going to follow it to the second. His relationship with Joanne and his sanity depended upon it after all.

Fred the landlord was not at his usual place behind the bar, instead he was occupying several seats at a table. He was reading the morning paper, though Dave wasn't sure which morning the paper related to. In Fred's hand was a quart sized pewter tankard. It was steaming so presumably it held something less inebriating than those most of the customers were holding.

Dave approached the table.

"Ah," said Fred looking up from his paper, "how did 'ee get on? Did e' get back alright? Do 'ee want a drink?" continued Fred, not letting Dave get a word in. "Suzan! Suzan, would you be a dear an' get this yere gentleman a large coffee, and not the muck we serves to the customers."

Obediently Suzan brought over a mug of coffee. Somewhat taken aback, Dave accepted the drink and managed to give Suzan a confused smile.

"S' like I said," continued Fred, "'tiz not very often we gets visitors anymore. Least not visitors from the outside. Well, not ones you'd want to talk to or ones you can talk to if you gets my meanin'." Continued Fred, hardly drawing a breath.

"So, tell me, how did you get on? Huh? Get 'ome alright did 'ee?"

"Well, I got home but I was a week late." Replied Dave, his

voice trailing off. Despite his agitation, he couldn't help noticing the front page of Fred's paper.

Fred followed his gaze and turned the paper over.

"Ah, that's the vuss over Timber's place. Tiz terrible, terrible."

"I saw a lot of activity going on up there while I was waiting by the sign. That's why I was late home. I didn't keep an eye on the time. I was watching what was going on." Said Dave miserably. "When I did get home I found I had missed a week. My boss has fired me for not going to work, but the worst thing is that my girlfriend Joanne has dumped me because she thinks I stood her up!" He blurted, desperation creeping into his voice. "That's why I've come back, I thought if I went around again I could get back to where I started from, but I don't know if that will work. What do you think?"

"Humm?" replied Fred, his attention focused on his paper once again.

"Will it work if I go around again? I mean will I get back to the same day I left originally?" Said Dave impatiently.

"Should do." Replied Fred, in an offhand manner. "Bad business that was. Bad business."

Why was Fred dismissing his question in such an offhand way? This was important, his sanity and his relationship with Jo depended upon it! On the other hand, perhaps he was being self-obsessed. He had seen a hearse outside Lord Woods' manor house, which would indicate something fairly serious.

"Was there some problem?" he asked Fred.

"Problem? Well you could say that. T'waz certainly a problem vur ol' Timbers, he'd died you zee. Apparently 'is dog attacked 'im. Real mess it was. Course, we didn't 'ear about it vur a couple o' hours. Then Albert, you saw 'im in yere the other day, and the coroner from Penhampton went back and watched what happened. They couldn't step in and stop it o' course, but they 'ad to check the facts vur the inquiry. You know, make sure that there was no foul play. No one doin' 'im in an' tryin' to make out it was the dog and such." Fred replied.

Dave half listened and half read the paper whilst Fred talked, letting the words wash over his ears and eyes at the same time, while his brain was occupied with the more important business of getting home to the right time. He rubbed his chin. It was covered in stubble. He realised he'd come out in such a rush that he'd forgotten to shave.

"So what's all the fuss about if they know how it all happened?" he asked.

"Well now, 'tiz Timber's Will zee. 'Ee was a rich man, that 'ee was. I don't mean money or gold, nort like that. We can get any amount o' that stuff so it has no real worth. We uses it vur buyin' things but 'tiz more vur passin' around than vur its value. Mostly we barter.

"No, tiz 'ee's land what I'm referrin' to. You can get any amount o' money but there's only so much land in Lyonshire. S' like me yere, I own the pub an' the bit o' ground that goes with it. But I got it from the previous landlord. He'd never married an' 'ad no kids or relatives to pass it on to. So, 'ee left it to me. I'd spent years workin' vur 'im an' 'ee taught me all 'ee knew. That's the way things work round yere.

"Ol' Timbers, well, he was rich. 'ee had that ruddy great 'ouse an' all the land that went with it. But with 'im 'avin' no kids and what with 'is Will having been mislaid, there's an argument as to who gets what."

Dave sat and thought about it for a while, happy to let the conversation distract him from his own problems. A quick glance at the clock behind the bar informed him that he still had plenty of time, so what was the harm in having a discussion with Fred? "So who has the best claim on the house?"

Fred smiled, "There's no problem with the house, that goes to Mr an' Mrs Windsor. They was Timber's butler and housekeeper. Their family has looked after the Woods family vur generations, scrubbin' floors, washin' sheets an' cookin' meals. No, it's what 'appens to the rest o' the land an' the shop 'ee 'ad in Penhampton."

"What kind of dog was it?" asked Dave out of curiosity.

"That's one o' the reasons they went back to check." Replied Fred pointedly. "It were a Labrador. *[It is an astonishing fact that more people are killed by terriers and other small dogs than by Alsatians, Dobermans, and other large dogs. But then journalists don't consider that "savaged to death by a Pekinese" makes a good or believable headline.]* I mean, you could understand it if it'd been an Alsatian or such, but a Labrador? They 'aven't got enough brain-cells t' rub together an' light a fire. If you watch 'em walk along, they 'as a job to work out whether 'tiz their 'ead or tail they's s'pposed t' wag!"

Fred stopped to drain whatever it was he was drinking from his tankard and wandered out to the kitchen to refill it.

Dave's stomach growled audibly, reminding him that a relaxing friendly chat was all very nice but food was more of a priority. It was, after all, what he'd come in for. There was also the matter of the mouth-watering smells drifting out from the kitchen.

On the wall by the bar was the obligatory blackboard, covered in the barely legible scrawl of someone who finds writing difficult but never the less is forced to do it. It listed several alternatives in the food department. Some of which Dave recognised like steak and kidney pudding. Many of the others were less familiar, badger ham and chips, oryx steak, roast guinea fowl, and baked gurnet.

He decided to have the steak and kidney; you knew where you were with steak and kidney pudding. He went up to the bar and ordered it and a glass of orange juice.

"Oh," said Fred, sticking his head out of the kitchen, "'tiz the coroner's inquest s' a'ternoon, you fancy goin' along? There's a spare bed vur'eeyere. You could come along with me, stopover vur the night an' go back tomorrow, to any time you like." *[Most people would expect to go back **at** any time they liked, but the time bubble surrounding Lyonshire means that you can go back **to** anytime you like.]*

~~~~~

Chalky White was primarily a blacksmith in Penhampton, and a prosperous one. His father had been a blacksmith; his grandfather had been a blacksmith. His great-grandfather had made leather under garments for discerning customers. Chalky's family didn't like to talk about his great-grandfather.

Chalky had cut an imposing figure when he had been a small boy, but now, after years of growing up in and around the smithy, bending bits of metal for a living, imposing was no longer an apt or large enough description. He stood about six foot two in his leather trousers and apron, six foot across the shoulders and tapered to the waist.

His forge was situated on the corner of Market Place and Smiths' Row. It was a prime position close to the cattle market, and not far from the town square. His grandfather had been the youngest of seven brothers *[Chalky's great great-grandfather had been very popular with the ladies for some reason.]* and had been apprenticed to the then blacksmith. When the old smith had died, he had inherited the forge and had passed it down through the family to Chalky. It had a large covered yard next to the forge itself, which made it an ideal, and warm, sheltering place in wet weather and a handy place to meet and have a natter. Consequently it was always crowded and Chalky had plenty of work to keep him busy.

Chalky's work was held in high regard. Added to which he was a blacksmith, a job that has always been thought of as slightly mystical. So, it had come as no surprise when Chalky had been asked to be one of the retained advisers to the court in Penhampton. Especially when it had anything to do with metal fragments and the like.

On the whole, being a retained adviser was an undemanding job.

Murder was unheard of. There was always a witness and if there wasn't then someone could be sent back in time to become a witness. But it was annoying to have to leave the forge and go to the court every time someone died in an accident, because he was obliged to go and sit on the advisory panel whether his expertise was needed or not.

He had to go in this afternoon for the inquest of some bigwig from the north of the county, and since he had a few errands to run as well there was no point in getting the forge up to its working temperature. He closed the vents down on the forge, topped up the charcoal, and scattered ashes over the top. Soon the fire would be nothing more than a dull red glow but it would stay in until he got back.

"Never let the forge go cold." Chalky's father had always said. So far he never had.

He strolled along Butchers' Row, which was sandwiched between the cattle market and the town centre. Like most of the streets in Penhampton, Butcher's Row was still true to its name and occupied solely by butchers' shops and slaughterhouses. But because Lyonshire's economy was based on bartering *[much to the annoyance of accountants, estate agents, banks, and insurance salesmen]*, every shop had, in addition to its own wares, a variety of goods for sale. Apothecary Street was full of chemists, herbalists, and practitioners of the healing arts. Goggle Street was full of opticians, Sole Street was cobblers, and blacksmiths filled Smith Row. But inside the opticians there were shelves lined with vegetables. In front of the chemists, rabbits were hung on hooks. Outside the smithies sacks of potatoes waited to be traded.

Many from the more rural areas of Lyonshire thought of the county town as a bustling hive of activity, but Chalky, having once visited the outside world and been astonished and dismayed by the hectic pace of life people endured, enjoyed the relaxed pace of life in Penhampton. How were they going to enjoy life and the wonders each new day brought if they were too busy running around trying to get things done by yesterday. In Penhampton, unless it was a real emergency, things were done d'reckly.*[Many would assume that when someone says they are going to do something directly that they mean they are going to get right on to it. However, in the westcountry when we say we'll do something d'reckly, we mean we'll see to it later on, sometime, or eventually. Perhaps.]*

~~~~~

In the Stoat and Ferret, Dave sat in a bloated stupor and pushed his empty plate away across the table. He had, of course, had steak and kidney before. First the dreaded snake and pygmy at school, which had pastry you could use in the woodwork classes, lots of watery gravy the odd trace of stringy meat in amongst the bits of tube and gristle. *[This is one of the many closely guarded recipes uses by school cooks. Who buy the finest ingredients their meagre budget will stretch to and still come up with watery potatoes, vegetables boiled to a universal shade of yellow and something grey or brown and wobbly lurking in the corner of the plate.]* He had often eaten it at his gran's, and hers had been far better than the best the school could manage. Being a bachelor, he had tried many of the pies and puddings sold by supermarkets, both frozen, fresh or tinned but these tended to taste more of soyabeans and monosodium glutamate.

They were all, not only left standing, but repeatedly run-over by the steak and kidney pudding he had just eaten. The only mono anywhere near it were Dave's monosyllabic grunts as he held his stomach and groaned.

"Umm! Ooh! Ah!"

Fred reappeared from the kitchen, his tankard firmly welded to his hand.

"Enjoy yur meal lad? Chef ain't bad at makin' a good pud. 'Tiz one o' my favourites is that."

Dave let out a long sigh and loosened his belt several notches. He was feeling rather uncomfortable. He didn't make a habit of stuffing himself, but that had been one of the nicest meals he had ever eaten, and leaving food on his plate would have been disrespectful.

"I'm stuffed. I've never eaten so much or such a delicious meal. I just couldn't stop eating. Even after I was full I just could not stop. How much do I owe you?"

"Well lad, 'tiz like I said before. I need t' get t' the inquest s' a'ternoon and I was hopin' you'd give me a lift." Replied Fred a bit sheepishly. "Albert's already left an' well..." Fred left it hanging and nervously wiped his hands on his apron.

Dave sat in a stunned silence; he thought Fred had been joking earlier.

"You zee," Continued Fred after a while, "what I didn't tell e' was that by rights some o' ol' Timber's land should pass t' me. 'Ee promised it to me coz it's good ground vur growin' hops. An' in return, I delivered a barrel o' S.O.D. that's 'strong ol' dark', to 'im every couple o' weeks.

"That why 'tiz Bert that's the witness an' not me. 'Tiz my job really but what with me 'avin' a personal interest, it's fallen to Albert.

Especially since 'ee's nearly as rich as ol' Timber's was anyroad."

For the time being Dave chose to ignore Fred's request, and addressed this amazing revelation. "What Albert? The rather rotund, scruffily dressed gentleman that was in here yesterday; I mean last week? The one who helped you give me directions?"

Fred smiled. "Like's 'is beer does Albert. An' don't go in vur snappy dressin' unless 'ee 'as to. No, 'ee leases out all o' 'is ground t' different families. Then they gives 'im a portion o' the stuff they produces each year t' 'im in payment. 'Ee gives me hops an' barley and a few other odds an' sods an' I gives 'im zummet t' eat an' drink when 'ee comes in.

"No, Albert inherited from 'is father who was a right snobbish ol' bugger. Thankfully Albert don't take a'ter 'im. He lets 'is tenants get on with their lives while 'ee gets on with 'is. Course, there's still a fair bit o' organisin' vur 'im t' do, 'specially if there's ort 'ee wants."

"You mean you exchange goods and services with each other instead of buying and selling?"

"That's what I was tellin' 'ee earlier, money 'as no real value. We don't exchange; we barter. There's only a few that uses money, like Aunt Aggie. She goes out an' gets stuff that can't be growed or isn't made in Lyonshire and then barters or sells it on to those that wants it.

"So how about it then lad? You gives me a ride into Penhampton and I'll feed 'ee and give 'ee a bed vur the night."

There it was again. Dave glanced at the clock. He was going to have to make a decision soon. So far the last twenty-four hours had been, if not the worst in his life, then certainly the most confusing. Didn't Fred understand that? He had lost a whole week, his girlfriend, and his job. Not that his job really mattered. He had travelled to a county that the rest of the world was totally unaware of, and the only reason he was here now was so that he could rectify things and get his life back.

"If you're worried about missin' work or yur girlfriend, you can go back 'ome t' last week tomorrow just the same as you were goin' to t'day." Put in Fred.

But where was the harm in staying and helping Fred out? Especially since he could, as Fred had said, go back home tomorrow and still get there a week ago.

Whilst Dave sat in contemplation, Fred began to smirk and then to laugh.

"What's so funny?" snapped Dave. It was hard enough to think about the situation and what Fred was asking, without him laughing.

"'S not you lad." Apologised Fred.

"I was just rememberin' the last time I rode on a bike. It were a while ago now, when I last travelled into the future. But what a bike it were, a SlingShot 2000 with an anti-Volvo cannon on the 'andlebars. *[Any observant motorist comes to recognise what, in the latter half of the twenty-first century, will be known as Volvo syndrome. It is similar to road rage, only in this case, the ragee knows that the box around him/her is virtually indestructible and therefore does not care if they hit anything or anybody else because they themselves won't get hurt. (A syndrome most commonly suffered by dentists.) Other drivers in the late twenty-first century have decided to get their own back and frequently equip their vehicles to deal with the problem.]* I 'ad to change me drawers a'ter the first time I rode it an' broke the sound barrier. But it was worth it vur the experience. 'T was some years a'ter they tried to ban motorcycles from the roads." Fred grunted. "Stupid politicians didn't realise that they could make it illegal t' ride motorbikes, but they could never take the bike out o' the bikers. So many people broke the law that they 'ad t' reverse it, and that led t' a new breed o' bikes.

"I still got the helmet an' gloves yere somewhere."

Fred leaned in closer and tugged on Dave's sleeve, his voice barely a whisper.

"I don't think Timbers' death was an accident." He whispered. "I think 'ee was done in." Fred leaned back.

"But you said Albert went back and saw the dog..." Dave began but Fred waved him into silence.

"Keep yur voice down lad!"

Dave continued in a whisper, "How can it be murder if the dog did it? I mean, it's not like he was shot cleaning his gun. Easy enough to put a charge in the breach and then sit back and let someone kill themselves cleaning it. But a dog? How do you kill someone with a dog?"

"I don't know lad. I really don't know. 'Tiz just a feelin'. But you can't become a successful brewer an' not be able to smell it when zummet gone sour. Otherwise instead o' beer you ends up with four hundred gallons o' watery vinegar that's no use to anyone."

"I see," said Dave, trying his best to think his way through the situation. "I think that you don't just want me to give you a lift, do you? You want me to find out how someone was murdered with a loaded dog? Am I right?"

"Well I didn't like to come right out with it an' ask, but now you've brought it up."

Dave drank his orange juice and sat quietly for a while pondering recent events. He'd had a narrow miss with the tractor and escaped from Aunt Aggie without losing his shirt. He'd gone home a week late, been fired from his job, and dumped by his girlfriend. And now he'd come back in an attempt to rectify the situation, and eaten a meal that a food critic could only dream about. Now he was being asked to play Miss Marbles by a publican from a county that the rest of the world thought of as a myth.

As an experiment, he picked up his fork and jabbed it at the back of his hand. It hurt and left a line of four prong marks, so presumably he was actually awake and this was real. It didn't in reality help him with his dilemma, but at least Dave knew that he wasn't asleep and dreaming it all.

"Why not?" He replied at last. "I've got nothing left to lose except my sanity and I'll probably wake up in a minute and find out that this has all been one of those really annoying dreams in which you think you're already awake. There is just one thing I don't understand though."

"Go on." Put in Fred encouragingly.

"Why, if Albert went back to witness the death, couldn't he go back a bit further and simply ask Lord Woods what was in his Will?"

"'S like this, it comes under the headin' o' interferin' with the course o' history because it involves a death. It'd be like going back an' killin' the dog first. History would run right over it and Timbers would die o' zummet else an' we'd be none the wiser."

~~~~~

Albert felt empty and out of sorts. Normally by this time in the morning he would have consumed a few pints and the world would have begun to swing into focus. Today he had only drunk tea and was feeling hard done by. Being a court witness had some serious drawbacks.

He brushed the few remaining grey hairs on his head back out of his fading blue eyes and ran his finger around the collar of his clean and freshly starched white shirt. Wearing a clean shirt and his best suit was making him feel even more uncomfortable, and reminded him of his father and his strict regime of snobbery. Albert's father had been a man who considered other people to be beneath him and everything had to be just so. He had been a land-grabber, endearing himself to landowners, estranging them from their families, and inheriting the land himself. It had taken Albert years to sort out his legacy, returning as much of the land as possible to the families concerned, and undoing his father's greed.

Albert was tramping around Penhampton for something to do. He disliked Penhampton at the best of times but normally he was cushioned with beer before having to dislike it. Sober and freshly starched, Penhampton did nothing to improve his mood. He had purposely had the court car pick him up and bring him into town early to avoid the temptation of the Stoat and Ferret, and Albert was now at a loss for something to do.

He'd bartered more than he should for a new cap at a shop in Haberdashery Road, visited several cafes and, as a consequence, several public conveniences. Haggled with a wheelwright about the price of wagon-wheels and was now bored. What made it worse was, he was bored, irritable, and sober.

Eventually he found himself outside the courthouse. He stared at it for a while. It didn't move or do anything interesting, so he went in.

Something almost human in a uniform blocked his way. It could only be considered human in the same way that say the missing link is human. *[Persons of this nature are known to exist throughout the world. Their natural habitat is lurking in doorways, usually outside discos or nightclubs. Their function is to prevent the wrong sort from entering. This usually means turning away anything that is not female and over the age of twelve, male and over the age of sixteen, anyone that looks less human than they do, or simply wearing an unfashionable pair of trainers. Scientists once considered them to be the missing link but changed their minds after all the apes in their laboratories went on strike and sued for slander.]* Buttons on its uniform strained to keep the material together. In places the stitching had given up the struggle entirely and bits of the lining were showing through.

"What you want here?" it rumbled.

"I'm yerevur the coroners' inquest 's a'ternoon. I'm one o' the witnesses." Replied Albert slowly and clearly. He hoped it was slow and clear enough for the guard to understand.

Its pre-neolithic brows creased with audible strain before it continued in a monotonous monotone, as if repeating something it had rehearsed an innumerable number of times.

"You carrying any concealed weapons, recording or photographic equipment?"

"No." Replied Albert. Things were beginning to look more interesting,

"You got a handbag what I got to search?"

"No. Now can I go in?"

"Then you may pass." It rumbled, did what it thought of as a salute, and trudged off into its cubby-hole.

Albert strolled on into the courthouse. It was the first time he had ever had occasion to come into the building. All of the disputes he had ever been involved in had all been settled in a congenial manner over a few jars in the pub.

A high vaulted ceiling soared above him. Stone pillars lined the walls. In between the pillars carved marble busts lurked like dismembered waxworks. Beneath them, inscriptions boasted of who they were and what they had done to suffer petrified decapitation. Bench seats had been arranged to allow parties of people to conspire together. The seats themselves had been designed to be as uncomfortable as possible. Like pews in a church, they offered only a place to make people look tidy and stop them cluttering up the floor.

A vending machine was skulking in a corner and distributing brown muddy water, regardless of what selection was actually chosen, even orange juice. And served it at a temperature which melted the plastic cup to your hand as you held it.

Albert set his bulk down on a bench.

People were rushing around in black gowns. Some of them even wore horsehair wigs. It wasn't apparent why, the hair hadn't looked that good on the horse to begin with. Occasionally one of them would shout something like "Is Mr Kean here for the Baker case?" or "Call Mrs Lemon." seemingly at random and without reason. No one ever answered but the gowns were too busy to notice and had already rushed off.

Albert, much to his own surprise, began to find he was enjoying himself whilst still sober and wearing, what he considered to be, his worst clothes. For some reason the phrase "headless chickens" kept going through his head as he watched the gowns at work.

A couple of barristers, they had to be barristers because they were the ones with the silly wigs on, came out of one of the courts and leant against the wall close to where Albert was sitting. If he strained, he could just about make out what they were saying. They were arguing. Apparently it was something to do with the wording of a statement. Minimal force, what did it mean. Albert leant over as close as he dared and tried to eavesdrop.

"Look, all she did was open the door and usher him through it."

"Ah! But that's my cusp, my apex, my, my point! If as he claims, he didn't want to go in, then minimal force could mean she had to hit him over the head with a frying-pan and carry him in unconscious."

"You never said anything about her hitting him with a frying pan!"

"I never said she did. What I said was..."
"Yes you did! I just heard you."
"No I didn't!"
"Yes you did!"
"Didn't.
"Did."
"DIDN'T!"
"DID!"

Albert listened with interest to this exchange of technical legal dialogue.

"YOU DAMN WELL DID!"

"Look," said the other barrister irritably. "I was merely trying to illustrate the point that your client stated she had used "minimal force" and that minimal force could mean anything."

The other barrister thought about it for a while.

"You're right. I see what you mean. I suppose we had better go and ask the judge for an adjournment to try and get to the bottom of this and define what minimal force really means."

"He won't like it. And it'll be expensive."

"Yes. Paying for an expert to examine the words. Independent committees. Working lunches."

"Well that can't be helped. This is a complex legal conundrum and there is no other way of sorting it out."

The two barristers headed back into the court to tell their judge the good news. Albert grabbed a passing gown.

"Excuse me? Could you tell me what the case in that court is about?" he asked.

The gowned figure looked down at Albert over the top of his half-moon spectacles and glared.

"That, my man, is the case of Sorbic verses Sorbic. It is a very serious case and has been going on for weeks."

"I'm not surprised." Muttered Albert under his breath. And then asked out-loud "A divorce?"

"No, no. Mrs Sorbic is accused of maliciously and without due care and attention forcing Mr Sorbic to have a bath against his will."

It was all too much for Albert and he could hardly contain his laughter as he thanked the gown for his help.

Clearly annoyed, the gown strolled off in a huff. He was probably upset because Albert had been poking fun at the well-oiled wheels of justice as they turned, however creakily, before they flew apart and spun off in all directions.

Once he had managed to regain control of himself, or at least enough that he was fairly sure he wouldn't start laughing again, Albert decided to try his luck with the vending machine, make himself as comfortable as possible on the bench and watch the floorshow. *[It is interesting that drinks vending machines not only fail to supply a drink with a recognisable flavour, but also manage to heat water well above its natural boiling point. And the plastic cups either melt to your hand or let the superheated water scald your hand as you pick it up. Vending machines are also strategically placed where there is an absence of handy coffee tables, shelves or sideboards and thus force their victim to either hold the cup and risk further injury or put it on the floor for someone else to knock over.]* Evidently the idiocies of bureaucracy and small-minded people had found their natural place in Lyonshire in the only way they could in a county without a government or council. They had ensconced themselves in the legal process, or mans' interpretation of it.

Chapter 3.

"#$£&%!!!!" Swore Dave as he knocked the skin off of another knuckle.

Things were not going well. Against all reason and his better judgement, he had agreed to give Fred a lift to Penhampton and stay for the night. That had seemed simple enough. But things had begun to go downhill from then on.

He had gone to visit the 'his 'n' hers' before leaving the pub and had left his tattered leather jacket on the back of his chair. His ablutions finished, he had returned to the table to find his jacket had gone, replaced with what looked like a new one. When he mentioned it to Fred, the landlord took very little notice and simply shrugged it off, and indicated that in the absence of his old one Dave should wear the new one. Unsure about this but with little option except to do as instructed, he had put it on. When he did so, he found that all the bits and pieces that had been in his jacket pockets were now in the pockets of this new one.

Not entirely comfortable with the situation, he had gone outside to start his bike and let it warm up whilst he waited for Fred to get ready.

When Fred had finally emerged, his attire had startled Dave so much that he had taken a step back, tripped over on the unfamiliar cobbles and landed heavily on his rump. Dave had seen similar outfits before, but not normally in the street. He was more used to seeing outfits like Fred's in sci-fi horror movies. The kind with clinically clean computer print text titles and credits, and usually involved killer robots and heavy weapons fire.

Fred was wearing a black one-piece suit. It was probably made out of leather but had the look of black body armour in the heavily muscled style of classical statues. The boots were of the Frankenstein variety and the platform soles made Fred look about seven feet tall. But worst of all was the helmet. It had an insectoid appearance. Two bulging 'eyes' instead of a visor, fins and vents all over it, and a short antenna on either side.

They had gone just over six miles when Dave had been forced to bring them to a skidding halt when the rear tyre had punctured.

Dave had rummaged around under the seat and found a can of puncture inflation foam he carried for just such an emergency. Unfortunately there was a thorn in the side of the can and all the propellant had leaked out. After more rummaging, the bike's toolkit had been found along with a traditional puncture repair kit and Dave had set about fixing the tyre.

Fred sat on the grass bank of the hedge, his insectoid helmet on the ground next to him. He was chewing a blade of grass thoughtfully, content to let Dave carry on unaided.

However, the offending wheel refused to budge, partly because it was being stubborn, but mostly because the nut had rusted into place.

Dave lent against the hedge and sucked his injured knuckles while Fred strolled over and inspected the bike.

"You could use a drop o' penetratin' oil. It would loosen things up a treat. 'T would help get the nut off as well." Said Fred glancing at his watch. "We'll be late too if we don't get going soon."

"How pray are we going to do that?" Dave asked. *[How pray is not a good way to start a question. Several wars, not to mention uncountable vendettas have been started by a "How Pray" in the conversation.]* He was not in the best of moods and seriously regretted being stupid enough to have got involved. Why had he agreed to Fred's proposal? Why hadn't he followed his original plan and simply gone home at the allotted time? If he had gone home he could have woken up tomorrow morning and things would have been back the way they were a week ago before all this had started.

"There's no need t' take that tone with me lad. I was only makin' an observation. Besides, there's other ways o' fixin' a flat tyre."

"How?" Snapped Dave. Fred's calmness irritated him all the more. "Make it feel inflated with its own self-importance?" He threw the spanner he had been using on the ground.

Fred ignored the remark. He had not run a pub and been a successful landlord for as long as he had by losing his temper every time a customer got stroppy.

"Well, that's one way o' doin' it, but altering things a bit 'ud be easier."

"I thought that's what I had been trying to do." Said Dave testily.

"Ah, but you didn't let the tyre know did you."

Fred huddled up to the offending tyre, muttering under his breath, his eyes closed. Then he stepped back and kicked it.

"What the hell..." Dave began. The very idea of someone kicking his bike was outrageous. But as he looked at the tyre, it began to inflate itself.

"How the..." Dave reverted to some of the more colourful aspects of his vocabulary.

"Well," began Fred, "you know I told e' that Lyonnesse was hidden by Druidhs? A'ter a while they found out that the myth about sex interferin' with magic was just that, a myth. Many o' them 'ad descendants an' passed on their secrets. There aren't that many o' what you'd call powerful Druidhs left now, but most o' us in Lyonshire 'ave a bit o' talent."

Dave was flabbergasted. Not only had he wandered into a mythical county, he had wandered into one full of wizards. After a few false starts he managed to find his voice.

"You're a Druidh? But Druidhs and magic don't exist. They're just a bunch of strange people wandering around Stonehenge in bed sheets, and magic is just sleight of hand, misdirection, and illusions. There's no real magic."

"Ah," said Fred, tapping the side of his nose with a finger. "There's no magic in yur world because the church didn't approve. They burned anyone who could so much as read tealeaves an' people burnt at the stake don't tend t' 'ave descendants. Prevents the spread o' subversive ideas and makes the population easier t' control. Then there's the scientists, they're always poking about with zummet and claimin' that there's a scientific explanation vur everythin'. Ha! They can't even explain how dowsin' works!

"But yere we've 'ad none o' that. Zee there's this Trinity, spirituality, technology, and magic. They're all part o' one an' the same thing, nature. Separate 'em an' deny the existence o' one o' 'em, an' you're in real trouble. That's why the world's so messed up.

"There's magic in most things zee. Whether it's forgin' iron, brewin' beer or raisin' crops. They all need a bit o' magic vur it t' work right."

Dave had a thought. "Is that what happened to my jacket? I mean did you twiddle your finger, or whatever it is you do, and repair it?"

Fred's already ruddy face turned a slightly more crimson colour as he blushed.

"You caught me out lad. I thought it was the least I could do, an' repairin' yur jacket was easy. I wasn't an' wouldn't o' told e' if it hadn't been vur that blasted tyre. Now, we'd best get goin'. That is if you're ready?"

Chalky hefted a sack of potatoes onto his shoulder, and set off towards the court. *[Although heft and shoulder are perhaps the wrong words. Because of his blacksmithing they could be replaced with tossed and huge knot of muscle where his arm met his body.]* He stopped once on his way in Goggle Street to drop off the potatoes and pick up his new reading glasses from an optician.

Outside the court the guard stepped forward to block Chalky's path, took one look at Chalky, thought better of it, and retreated into his cubby-hole. Two hundred pounds of muscles that bend bits of iron for a living do not need shoulder-pads to look intimidating.

Chalky nodded to a few of the gowns that were rushing around and went through the door marked "Private. Advisers Only."

~~~~~

Dave pulled up in the car and wagon park next to the cattle market, waited for Fred to dismount, and got off himself. He was visibly shaking, and now absolutely convinced that he had made probably the worst decision of his life by agreeing to stay in Lyonshire.

After Fred had repaired the punctured tyre, he had been worried about being late, so he had also 'fiddled' with the engine before they'd ridden off. Unfortunately, after Fred's magical revelation, Dave had been in too much of a confused state to object. Besides, what harm could it do? It would take a major overhaul and a significant redesigning of the engine internals to increase its performance.

How wrong he had been. When they had pulled away from the side of the road, the extra acceleration had caused the bike to wheelie, so he had brought the bike back under control and continued on their way. Taken aback by the extra power his bike now had, Dave rode gingerly to begin with, but once he'd become accustomed to the increase in speed it had been fun. But that had just been in first gear. As far as Dave was concerned, that was plenty fast enough, but Fred had kept yelling into his ear to change up. Reluctantly, he had given in to Fred's nagging and clicked up into second.

The speedo was designed to read well past the bikes actual top speed; it read up to one hundred and twenty miles an hour. The needle had snapped off long before the bike had stopped accelerating in second, and Fred had stopped nagging him to change up again.

"N, n, n eed aa ddrink k." Stammered Dave after a few moments.

Fred helped Dave remove his helmet and slapped him on the back hard enough to knock the wind out of him.

"Now that were more like it! Said Fred happily. "You did well ridin' at that speed. Isn't it strange how everythin' slows down a'ter yur reach the double ton?"

Fred glanced at his watch again.

"Come on lad. The court's this way." He said and manhandled the stunned Dave towards their destination.

The guard at the court heard footsteps approaching. This time he wasn't taking any chances and peered cautiously around the corner. The sunlight hadn't been blocked out so he stepped forward and blocked it himself.

"What you want here?" he boomed.

"We're yere vur the coroner's inquest." Replied Fred. "Ere, 'old these will 'ee. There's a good chap."

Fred handed the guard their crash helmets and ushered Dave through into the courthouse.

The guard stood where he was for some time, looking down at the helmets in his huge hands. He had not been trained to deal with helmets. He had been trained to ask people questions and relieve them of weapons, cameras, and tape-recorders, by force if necessary. He enjoyed it when force was necessary.

He continued to stare at the helmets whilst other people filled past him unchallenged into the courthouse.

"Hello Fred." Said Albert rising from the uncomfortable bench he had been sitting on. "Managed t' get the lad t' come then I zee?"

"Alright Albert. You been yere long?"

"Just a couple o' hours Fred. Why's the lad shakin' like that?"

Both of them looked at the ashen-faced Dave.

"Well Bert, we was runnin a bit late, so I tinkered with 'is bike a bit a'ter we 'ad t' stop an' fix a puncture."

"Ah." Said Albert, catching Fred's gist.

"Best if I gets 'im a coffee a'fore we goes in. 'Ere, 'old 'im vur me a mo." Continued Fred.

He wandered over to the vending machine, inspected it for a while, and hit it. A plastic cup dropped into the slot, closely followed by various powders and a jet of superheated water. He picked it up and sniffed it whilst the cup began to melt in his hand. Disgusted, Fred dropped it straight into the bin, hit the machine a few more times, and swore at it. The machine made an apologetic beeping sound and dropped an already full cup into the slot. A little of it splashed onto its stainless steel grill and began to corrode the metal.

Fred picked this cup up and sniffed it. It wasn't good but it was a marked improvement on the last one. He went back and thrust it into Dave's unresisting hand.

With some help, Dave managed to take a few sips without spilling too much on the floor.

"YOU $£%@~!!!" He said as the liquid began to do its job.

"What did you give 'im Fred?" asked Albert, shocked by Dave's language.

"S' just coffee Bert, but coffee the way I likes it. Sets 'ee up vur the day it does."

"D' you think 'ee can handle your coffee?"

"I should think so Bert, 'ee managed t' ride the bike ok. I reckons there's more than a touch o' natural magic about 'im. 'T would explain 'ow 'ee managed to get out o' the Post Office with 'is shirt on at least."

"DON'T YOU EVER DO THAT TO MY BIKE AGAIN!" Continued Dave, as the other two talked over him.

"Now lad, it weren't that bad." Began Fred, but he was interrupted.

"Will all those here for the inquest into the death of Lord Woods please go into court one." Cried one of the gowns officiously.

"That's us." Said Albert, stating the obvious.

Still ignoring his protests, Fred and Albert each grabbed one of Dave's arms, and the three of them headed into the courtroom to find a seat.

"So how come the inquest is being held in a crown court? I thought that normally a magistrate's court or village hall would do for an inquest?" Asked Dave.

"Ah, well lad, in Lyonshire there are very few crimes, because it is all too easy t' go back in time an' zee who committed 'em." Replied Fred. "So, the courthouse is used vur inquests, small claims an' generally settlin' domestic squabbles."

"That's right." Added Albert. "Likewise the solicitors an' barristers 'ave adapted t' take on cases of someone short changed on a sack of swedes or whose dog did what on whose lawn, rather than dealing with drug-dealers and murderers. An' the judges themselves 'ave taken intensive weekend or day release courses in mediation, counselling, and cookery. Their ruling is still final but tiz generally only as a last resort that they gets involved. The most vicious crime a judge in Lyonshire is likely t' zee is a case of selling without due care and attention or playin' so called music with a dance, house, acid, or jungle beat."

~~~~~

Chalky was sat on the adviser's bench between the adviser on mammals, a short little man that always smelt of horses, and the adviser on needlework. She was a very rotund woman with a big round smiley face who always looked flushed and had a nasty habit of placing her hand on Chalky's knee. But then, he was one of the most eligible bachelors in Penhampton.

It had long ago been decided to have a number of the independent advisers actually in court because this saved time and meant everyone could get home in time for afternoon tea. The other advisers included experts on optics and glass, electronics, medical matters, engines and modern vehicles, plants and nature, land boundaries, and for some reason yoga.

To Chalky it looked like being another afternoon of dozing off and carefully removing stray hands from his knee. Apparently, according to the brief the advisers had been given, the dead man had been killed by his dog. The only reason there was an inquest at all was something to do with the redistribution of his estate. There was nothing to do with metal or carts at all. Mind you, thought Chalky, the court was quite crowded so it might be worth staying awake after all.

Carefully he removed an unwanted hand from his knee.

~~~~

Fred looked around the courtroom. There were quite a few people from Shoton and the surrounding area, all with various claims to the land. He could even see Aunt Aggie elbowing her way towards the front. As far as he knew she had no claim on any of the estate. She was probably there to see if there were any bits no one else had a claim on and then claim them for herself.

There were also a lot of people that Fred didn't recognise. That did not really mean anything; they could be left over from the last case or simply be following the crowd in the hope that where a crowd was gathering, something interesting must be happening or going to happen. And generally when a crowd as large as this was crowded into such a small room, something interesting generally did happen. Even if it was someone stepping on someone else's foot, a punch being thrown, and finally a free for all.

"Please be upstanding for his honour the coroner, Lord Justice Hammond." Intoned one of the gowns.

The coroner entered from the judges' chambers, absent-mindedly carrying a glass of sherry he had been drinking, and sat down.

"Court be seated." Said the gown. Having discharged his duty he disappeared into the canteen, replacing his gown with a chef's hat and apron as he went.

The coroner cleared his throat before he spoke. Unfortunately it did nothing for his speech impediment.

"Hallo *h*Albert. *h*Alright?" he began when he noticed Albert in the crowd. "Now, Lord Woods death was witnessed by me, Jim Hammond coroner *h*of this county *h*and *h*Albert Strange *h*a resident *h*of Shoton. *H*it *h*is not *h*in dispute that Lord Woods was killed by his dog.

"Right, now that's *h*out *h*of the way, that leaves the matter *h*of his will, *h*or lack there *h*of. How many *h*of you have some claim *h*on the land?"

Nearly every hand in the court was raised. Many of their owners had never heard of Lord Woods, but where there was land going begging, and well, there was always a slim chance.

"*h*Oh, right. *h*I see. Well *h*if you'd be so good *h*as to give your names to the court *h*usher *h*on the way *h*out. *h*I here by *h*adjourn this court *h*of *h*inquest for *h*one week so *h*all claims may be considered."

So saying, he brought down his gavel and rapped it on the desk and wandered off to get another sherry.

Caught out by this sudden turn of events, the court usher had been forced to rush back from the canteen, hastily don his gown over his apron and stood in the doorway wearing his chef's hat. Looking thoroughly harassed, he took the names and addresses of all those who thought that they had some claim, however tenuous, on the estate and brief details of why. All in all it took some time for the courtroom to empty. But once this was accomplished, the gown went off to type up the list. Again it took him quite a while. He had to weed out the names of all those who thought it had been a petition, a works outing or all those who had simply given their names because that was what everybody else was doing. Next he went in search of the court adviser on land boundaries.

~~~~~

Dave, Fred, and Albert watched as the gown left his office.

"Quick Bert!" whispered Fred, "He's gone!"

Albert walked across the court waiting room as nonchalantly as he could. The trouble was that Albert wasn't good at nonchalance and as a result he walked with so much forced casualness that it was impossible for him not to look suspicious.

He listened for a moment outside the office door and went in. It wasn't because he shouldn't have been there, being an official witness he had every right, it was just that as far as Albert was concerned subtlety and intrigue only happened to other people.

He found the newly typed list the gown had left, ran it through the photocopier, and carefully replaced the original back exactly as the usher had left it.

Then he made a run for it.

"H, h, h, it's n, n, n, no good Fred," puffed Albert, trying to catch his breath, "I'm not cut-out vur all this subturfugee. I need a drink!"

Fred nodded and led them out of the court, pausing only to retrieve their helmets from the guard who was still standing as they had left him, wondering why he was holding two crash helmets.

Once outside they headed across the square and into the pub on the corner of Market Road. Just walking into a room full of smoke and alcoholic fumes did wonders for Albert's unease. He stopped shaking, his eyes came back into focus, and the vacancy sign seemed to have been removed from his forehead. He took the shortest possible route from the door to the bar, totally oblivious to the cries of protest from those patrons unlucky enough to have been sitting at the tables that had been in the way.

"He hasn't had a drink all day." Explained Fred as he helped up the fallen.

Several of them nodded in a sympathetic fashion. Others mumbled things like "poor man" or "know how *that* feels!" One even offered to buy them their first round.

By the time Dave and Fred reached the bar Albert had pulled his tie off downed his first pint and had ordered his second.

"Ah! I needed that." Said Albert as he drained his glass. "Right, what do you two want? You grab a table an' I'll bring 'em over."

Albert ordered two more pints and an orange juice, and made his way over to the table by the window where the other two had seated themselves. He set down the tray gave Dave his orange juice and Fred a pint.

"Between you an' me Fred, I don't think much o' this beer." Said Albert, setting the other pint down in front of himself. "It's all fizz an' no substance. 'S more like that gnats water the Americans drink if you ask me. An' not a patch on yours."

"Ok Bert." Said Fred, calmly ignoring the slight to a fellow brewers art. "Lets 'ave a look at that list. Zee who else is layin' claim to ol' Timber's estate."

Despite his confusion, and the bizarre circumstances that Dave found himself in, he was finding events intriguing and crowded around the copied list with the other two. There were twenty other names on the list besides Fred's. Seventeen were tenant farmers who had been promised their farms. They were not subject to dispute and could probably be discounted. The other three however were more suspect.

Fred pointed. "Look. That's Hatchet the butcher from Hunton. Reckons 'ee was promised thirty acres an' the shop Timber's owned yere in Penhampton. An' Poulter the butcher from Shoton wants the same land an' the shop. Ol' man Fetlock claims the stables, which aren't in dispute, an' again the thirty acres."

"Which bits of land did he leave you then Fred? Asked Dave as he sipped at his orange juice.

"Well, there's twenty acres down by the river, ideal vur growin' barley, which no one else is claimin', an' ten acres o' the thirty that everyone's a'ter. That's higher up an' better vur growin' hops."

"So the problem is the thirty acres and the shop." Said Dave, summing things up.

~~~~~

Once back in Shoton, Fred got off and opened the huge iron reinforced doors that led into the yard. Dave rode his bike into the yard behind the Stoat and Ferret whilst Fred closed the doors behind him and shot the bolts home.

Dave was surprised at just how large the yard was, and the extent of the buildings that belonged to the pub. On one side he could see the stables and next to them was the shed where the dray was kept. Further on was the barley store and the huge maltings shed and finally the brewery itself. There were also neat stacks of barrels all around the yard. They were a mixture of traditional wooden barrels and more modern aluminium ones in various stages of being cleaned.

Fred led the way in through the back door, across the kitchen and out into the bar. He poured a couple of pints of S.O.D., gave one to Dave, and returned to the kitchen to organise some food.

Dave found himself an empty table near the window, sat down, and stowed his crash helmet. Now that he had no further riding to do, he was finally able to sample Fred's beer for the first time. He took a few swigs. It had a rich dark full flavour, with a pleasant sweetness about it. He pulled out his pouch of aged tobacco and absentmindedly started to roll himself a cigarette. After a moment he realised what he was doing and wondered why he was being so stupid after all the trouble he had gone through to give up. He screwed up the pouch and the half rolled cigarette and chucked the lot onto the fire. Feeling pleased with himself, he settled back in his chair, absorbed some of the ambience of the room, and thought about recent events.

The journey back from Penhampton had taken considerably longer than the one going. Dave had managed, after a lot of arguing, to persuade Fred to un-fiddle with the bike's engine. It had made it a lot slower again but it had seriously reduced the terror factor as well. It also meant that he had been able to appreciate the countryside on the ride home and not just a green blur.

"Hallo lad." Said Albert slapping him on the back and derailing his train of thought.

"Oh. Hi Albert." Dave managed once he'd got his breath back.

"Hang on a mo lad while I gets meself a drink."

Albert moved his bulk over to the bar and ordered himself a couple of pints from Suzan. He drained the first one at the bar and then came back to join Dave at the table.

"Fred out the back?" Albert asked.

"Yes. Yes he's getting something to eat I think." Replied Dave awkwardly.

He had only been introduced to Albert at the court and already Albert seemed to be treating him like an old friend. Although that could be because they had conspired together and stolen court papers.

"Ah, food vur thought no doubt." Said Albert happily. "We've got a fair bit o' figgerin' to do if we're going t' zort all this out."

"Got back then I zee." Said Fred as he approached and set down a couple of huge platefuls of food on the table. "Fancy a bite t' eat?"

"Don't mind if I do Fred. I was just sayin' to the lad yere that we've got some figgerin' to do."

Fred wandered back into the kitchen, fetched a third plateful, and set it down on the table before sitting down himself.

"Ere we go." He said. "Tuck in lad, Albert."

Dave looked down at his plate, although tray would have been a more apt description. Basically it was bread and cheese. Complicatedly it was white bread, brown bread and granary bread, half a pound of butter, various crackers, crisps and biscuits, a dozen types of cheese and enough pickles, chutneys and relishes to cover a football pitch.

He set about reducing the pile.

"So lad, what do 'ee make o' all this?" asked Fred, prodding at the copied court paper with his knife.

Dave smiled but didn't look up as he continued to pile cheese and chutney onto a buttered cracker. He'd been waiting for Fred to say something.

"Well, to be honest, I think giving you a lift to Penhampton was just an excuse to keep me in Lyonshire for a while." He paused to take a bite out of his cracker, and noticed with some satisfaction that Fred was looking extremely uncomfortable.

"Umm, delicious chutney. I think the real reason you want me to stay is so that I, as an independent outsider with nothing to gain from the situation, can snoop around and try and find out what actually happened. Am I right?" he asked and stuffed the rest of the cracker into his mouth.

Fred choked on the mouthful of food he was chewing, his normally ruddy face flushing with embarrassment.

"Steady Fred!" said Albert with concern, giving his friend a few hearty slaps on the back.

Fred took a sip of his beer and cleared his throat. "Thanks Bert. Well lad, you've caught me red 'anded. I was goin' t' build up t' it, but yes, I was 'opin' you'd investigate. Like I said earlier, you can go back *to* any time you like *at* any time you like. An' you being an outsider means you've nort t' gain from it an' you'd be totally impartial. You might find out ort or nort but I'd like to know vur certain what 'tiz all about.

"You can have board an' lodgings yere regardless o' what 'ee find. 'Tiz up t' you lad."

Dave smiled again. He'd had a hunch that there had been more to Fred's offer than was at first apparent. Thoughtfully he chewed on a hunk of bread and butter, savouring both the taste of the bread and the rich creaminess you only get from unadulterated farmhouse butter.

"If, as you say, I can go home to any time I like, then I can't see that I have anything to lose by staying here to help." Dave replied, waving his knife in the air. "Certainly not my sanity. That's already gone out window. Until I went down that footpath I had never done anything unusual or out of the ordinary in my life. So far today I have woken up a week late, been dumped by my girlfriend, sacked by my boss, had my jacket resurrected from the dead, watched a punctured tyre repair itself, ridden at over two hundred miles an hour and eaten food literally out of the known world." So saying he crunched a pickle.

"Good on you lad, good on you." Said Fred happily. "I was 'opin' you'd agree but it 'ad t' be your choice."

"So how do 'ee want to go about it then?" asked Albert. "You can't just go a pokin' around and expect folks t' answer a strangers questions."

Dave sat in silence for a time, munching his way through the feast of food before him, and pondering Albert's question. What valid reason could he use to ask people searching questions, without raising too much suspicion? Who could ask impertinent questions and get away with it?

"I've had an idea about that. You have newspapers don't you? I saw you reading one this morning Fred."

"That's right lad, the Hunton Times" I gets it every mornin'." Replied Fred. "But I gets all the papers an' puts 'em on the bar in the mornin' vur customers t' look through."

"So if I pose as a journalist I would at least have some pretext to go and see people and ask questions without arousing suspicion. I can probably find out more that way and I could start with Lord Woods' servants."

"You're thinkin' of posing as a hack? You're braver than I thought." Put in Albert. "Journalists is viewed in much the same way as taxmen."

"You like to read the papers though." Said Dave defensively. He wasn't particularly fond of journalists himself, but it was the only reason he could think of that had the slightest ring of plausibility to it. "And you need journalists to write the papers. Besides, from what I've seen they can't exactly be the sensationalist doom-criers I normally read. I mean there's not much crime here, you said so yourself."

"Ah, but it don't mean people likes 'em pokin' around an' diggin' up personal stuff." Blurted Fred amidst a spray of crumbs and bits of pickled onion.

"Well I can't think of a better excuse to go around and ask people questions and I need some pretext to be able to do it. But, if either of you can come up with a better idea..."

"I zee what you mean lad." Said Fred getting up and rummaging around under the bar. "'Ere yur go, The Penhampton Daily news, The Fishin Gazette an' the Hunton Times." He handed over the papers.

Albert looked across the table at Dave, waving his knife as a pointer and scattering chutney across the table. "Penhampton News is more regional an' 'as been round askin' questions already. The Fishin Gazette don't bother with news as such, 'tiz more hatches, matches an' dispatches, an' buys, sells an' wants. The Hunton Times is your best bet. I could 'ave a word an' get 'ee a job. Just on a temporary basis. An' the editor owes me a favour."

"That would be great!" replied Dave enthusiastically. "Especially if you can arrange for a press-pass. And you could promise the editor the exclusive story in return for the favour. What do you think?"

Fred and Albert both nodded.

"Seems reasonable to me." Said Fred.

"Me too." Agreed Albert. "I'll get you your press-pass a'fore I comes in tomorrow mornin'"

They continued their meal in silence, putting all their effort into reducing the huge piles of food in front of them.

Chalky White was out for his evening constitutional. It wasn't that he didn't get enough exercise working in his forge all day. It was just, well, he'd read somewhere that regular exercise was a vital part of a long and healthy life. Jogging was out of the question. He had also read that all mammals have virtually the same number of heartbeats over their lifetime and it seemed stupid to waste them on something as pointless as jogging. So he went for a six-mile walk every evening after dinner instead. And, being a man of deeply rooted habits he always followed the same route. He would walk out as far as the lake behind Penhampton, feed Nessy a few mints and stroll back into town for an early night.

Chalky chewed thoughtfully on a mint as he walked along Butchers' Row and headed back towards his smithy. Whilst walking he reviewed the day's events.

It had been a fairly normal day at court, the various petty squabbles, and a coroner's inquest. He wondered as he wandered, which of the experts would be replaced by the land and boundaries adviser when the inquest reconvened. Chalky hoped it would be needlework and textiles. She always made him feel uncomfortable and kept calling him "sweetie". He strongly suspected that she was trying to get friendly with him, and then there was the matter of having to remove stray hands from his knee.

Just thinking about her made him shudder.

Besides, with her ample proportions she took up most of the seats on either side of her. He always had to sit on the edge of his chair or he would be sitting on her lap or part of it. There was just so much of it.

He shuddered again.

Of course it could always be the lady who did yoga that was replaced, but rumour had it that she was a close personal friend of the coroner. The funny thing was that Chalky couldn't remember why she'd been included as an adviser in the first place. Anyway, she always sat in unusual positions on her chair, which frequently made the coroner blush.

An open doorway further down the street brought Chalky back to the here and now. He could see a light flickering around inside.

Like all other streets in Penhampton, Butchers' Row was just that, a row of butchers' shops, but they differed from most of the other shops and businesses in town because there was no living accommodation above them. They were all single story shops used mainly by farmers from out of town as a dust free environment from which to sell their meat. At this time of night they were normally dark and quiet.

As Chalky approached, the flashing light looked like the beam of a torch moving about inside the only unoccupied shop in the row.

He peered in through the grimy windows. He could see the silhouette of someone inside. He walked through the open doorway and was blinded as the torch swung around and shone in his face.

"Who's that?" demanded a male voice.

"I'm Chalky the smith. Who are you an' what are you doing in here then?" Replied Chalky as the torch was directed away from his face.

It never occurred to him that this could possibly be someone up to no good. That sort of thing just didn't happen in Penhampton, or in Lyonshire for that matter.

"I was just lookin' around the place." Replied the man. "The shop's mine now so I was 'aving a look, sort of thing."

"Then why the torch? You could've turned on the light." Chalky reached for the light-switch and turned it on. "See, the electric is still connected."

"Well I... I didn't want to disturb anyone." Replied the stranger with hardy a pause and blinking in the bright light.

"That's alright then." Said Chalky. "I'll be gettin' along an' leave 'ee to it then. I'll pop in and see you when you're open. Cheers"

Chalky wandered off back towards his forge, his curiosity satisfied. It wasn't that Chalky was stupid, he was in fact quite intelligent, but you don't have to be a lightning thinker when pounding or bending bits of red-hot metal into shape. And who would be up to something nefarious in Penhampton? It was all too easy to for someone to go back and catch you at it.

In the shop the man swore under his breath and switched off the light.

"Damn. Damn. Damn. Damn! I should have been more careful. He saw my face. That smith is going to complicate things now."

The stranger left the shop, locked the door and put his torch and set of lock-picks back in his pocket. That nosy blacksmith had complicated matters. Now he'd have to deal with him as well, and fast.

Chalky reached the door to his forge and looked back towards Butchers' Row. He could no longer see the light so the man must have gone.

A thought shunted into his head. That shop had been empty for some time, ever since the last tenant had passed away. Lord Woods had never rented it out again. Come to think of it, it was the same one they had been arguing about in the coroner's court that morning. But the inquest had been adjourned. Perhaps they had sorted it all out after he'd left.

Chalky made a mental note to check with one of the gowns at the court first thing in the morning. He opened the door to his forge, checked the fire would stay in for the night, and went up to bed.

~~~~~

Dave sat back and drained his glass. His stomach was complaining again but his taste buds said it was well worth a little discomfort. Somehow the food in Lyonshire seemed to taste and smell foodier, more substantial, more real. He said so.

"That's 'cause it's all growed naturally, no chemical fertilisers or pesticides. An' 'tiz not picked six months before its eaten, stored in gas filled cold-stores t' stop it from rotting, an' transported 'alfway round the world in containers. 'Tiz all growed local, and picked or packed when it's actually ripe or ready to eat. 'S like home-grown stuff. It always tastes much better, even the meat. An' we can't be doin' with none o' that pasteurised rubbish around yere." Replied Fred. "Fancy another drink?"

"No, no thank you." Dave was already feeling a little muzzy headed, due more to the surreal situation that he found himself in rather than too much of Fred's beer. That and feeling a little tired. "I think it's time I turned in for the night. There's a lot to do tomorrow and I want to be ready to get started as soon as Albert brings me my press-card in the morning."

"Fair enough lad. I'll show 'ee where yur room is." Said Fred with a smile. "Sure 'ee don't want another to take up with 'ee?"

"No thank you. See you in the morning Bert."

"Night lad." Replied Albert.

Fred led Dave up to his room and then came back down to join Albert.

"So what do you think o' the lad then Fred?" Albert asked.

"Not yere Bert." Said Fred quietly and then raised his voice to make sure others in the bar could hear. "I've got a new batch down in the cellar Bert, an' I'd like your opinion."

"Right oh Fred. I'd be glad to give 'ee my opinion." Replied Albert, raising his voice to match Fred's and further illustrating how useless he was at any kind of subterfuge.

The two of them crossed the bar and went through the door that led to the kitchen. In the short passage by the stairs, Fred reached down and pulled open the trap door to the cellar. He walked down the first few steps and switched on the single un-shaded bulb that illuminated the cellar. He stood back and allowed Albert to go down. Then he closed the trap door as he followed.

They sat on a couple of empty barrels *[although a great deal of Albert sagged down on either side]*, a third in-between them with a short plank nailed to the top to act as a table. Fred filled a couple of handy tankards and set them down while Albert produced a packet of nuts out of his pocket. There just happened to be a handy bowl on the table for him to pour the nuts into. All in all, it was a well-practised routine. It was practised every time they fancied a quiet chat or every time Fred tried a different recipe in his brewing. In fact it was so well practised that the barrels on which they sat had long since been worn smooth and splinter free.

"Well, what do 'ee think o' the lad then?" enquired Albert as he chewed a couple of nuts.

"Ee seems alright to me Bert. 'S like I said earlier, I reckons 'ee's got a bit o' natural magic about 'im."

Albert nodded his agreement. "He's unbiased too. Got nothin' to gain out o' it all. Asides free board an' lodge that is."

"You're right there Bert. That's why I hoped the lad would stay because 'ee's completely impartial."

"You been readin' the dictionary again Fred?"

Both of them laughed. They spent the next couple of hours chatting about this and that. Occasionally one of them would get up and draw off a couple of pints just to check that the beer hadn't gone sour in the last hour or so.

Two floors above them Dave slept soundly. He dreamt strange dreams of schools, being chased and, for some reason, elephant sized mice.

In the past Dave had read a book about dreams and what they meant. It had been a birthday present from a previous girlfriend. In a small rational corner of his mind he analysed his dream whilst he was dreaming. Schools meant something to do with learning, lessons in life and that sort of thing. Being chased could mean a lot of things and mice well... *[What the dream actually meant was learn not to eat large amounts of cheese before going to bed because it tends to give you weird dreams.]*

Chapter 4.

Dave awoke to the sound of banging. Normally he awoke to the incredibly annoying blare from his alarm clock, which he could hit and switch to snooze mode. It would wake him up again ten minutes later, but at least it gave him the impression that he had stolen an extra ten minutes in bed. Fighting through the terror of waking up, Dave quickly shook off the disorientation of waking up in a strange bed. He was in one of the spare rooms above the bar in the Stoat and Ferret. Being in the countryside, he'd expected to be woken by a cockerel crowing or even the blinding glow of early morning sunlight playing across his face. But not banging.

He heard it again and managed to work out through his confusion that someone was knocking with some enthusiasm on the door to his room.

"You awake lad? I've brung `e a coffee." Said Fred opening the door and walking in.

He was carrying a tray which held a small glowing oil lamp and, next to it, a large mug of steaming coffee. It seemed to a bleary eyed Dave to be steaming in a menacing way.

Slowly Dave fought through the remaining panic associated with waking up. He was in the Stoat and Ferret, in a county that didn't exists after going out for a bike ride and somehow losing a week. It was something like that anyway, wasn't it?

"What time is it?" he managed at last.

"Tiz almost five an' twenty t' six. The sun 'll be up soon but I thought I' let `e lie in a bit."

"Oh. Thank you." Replied Dave automatically, as he tried to work out what Fred had said and took the coffee from the tray. "Twenty five to six! Lie in! Wha..." he exclaimed once his brain had finally comprehended what Fred has said.

"Well it all depends on how you sleep zee." Explained Fred. "If you sleeps fast you don't need so much o' it. `S like sergeant majors. To a squaddie they never seems to sleep. What they actually do is sleep fast.

That way they're always around when there's shoutin' t' be done."

Dave stretched his neck carefully in case his head fell off. The brief period of probation that waking allows was over. The lamplight was hurting his eyes, and the banging started again, only this time it was a lot louder and on the inside of his head.

Fred noticed the signs of temporal displacement and put his hand on Dave's shoulder.

"Ave a sip o' the coffee lad. You'll find it will do `e the power o' good."

Dave sipped cautiously at his drink, despite of the continent submerging tidal wave of nausea from his stomach. His throat felt as if it was welded shut and he couldn't swallow. But the hot tar like coffee began to seep through. *[Ninety seven percent proof caffeine has a strange and wonderful effect on temporal distortion and kills all known germs.]* He managed to swallow and took a larger sip.

The banging in his head began to recede to a dull thump and his eyes no longer felt as though they were melting.

Fred noted Dave's first steps on the road to recovery and walked back towards the door.

"I zee you're feelin' a bit better already. I'll leave `e t' get dressed. Breakfast 'll be ready soon." With that he departed, leaving the lamp burning on a shelf by the door.

With his next swig, Dave drained his mug. Under the onslaught of that much caffeine the after effects of his temporal displacement gave up. He roused himself from the bed and drew back the curtains. It was still dark outside. The sun had obviously been permitted to lie-in a bit longer than he had.

There was a sink in his room, and a towel and soap had been provided. However, he had no toothbrush, no clean underwear, and no razor. Well, a wash would have to suffice. He could see about the rest later, but that would probably mean having to go into Aunt Aggie's shop, and that was not a pleasant thought at any time of the day, let alone this early in the morning.

He performed his ablutions and dressed. Much to his surprise the sink had both hot and cold water. The soap also surprised him. It had left his skin feeling revitalised and had a pleasant herbal smell. Finally he took his comb from his pocket and did the best he could without a brush, picked up the lamp and made his way downstairs.

The bottom of the stairs came out into the short passage that led from the bar through into the kitchen, and Dave was standing on what must be the door to the cellar. A quick glance around the bar found it devoid of life apart from a scruffy elderly gentleman with a blanket thrown over him, who was quietly snoring away on one of the settles. A shout from the kitchen informed Dave where Fred was to be found.

He had only glimpsed the kitchen the night before as he passed through after parking his bike in the yard and his first impression had been that it was huge. He knew something of pub kitchens from long hot summers spent washing dishes and scrubbing burnt pots as a student. Those kitchens had been nothing like this one. They had all been small, hot, stuffy, and cramped, and the proverbial cat would find it hard to find a place to stand, let alone be swung.

In contrast, this kitchen was huge and occupied most of the rear of the building. Various ovens and hobs lined one wall, grills and spice racks lined the back of the wall to the bar, and on the opposite wall a large picture window let in light and afforded anyone working there at the sinks a good view of the yard. The fourth was covered in groaning shelves and a door, which lead through to a larder and a walk-in fridge.

But it was the table that fascinated Dave. It obviously served as a preparation area and worktop, but when empty could double as an all-weather football pitch. It stood foursquare in the centre of the room. It was made of well-scrubbed solid pine in a Victorian style with turned legs the size of tree trunks. There were drawers at each end that could hold enough cutlery to feed the five thousand. *[Although this is true from a certain point of view, the five thousand probably ate with their fingers so basically an empty pea-pod would hold enough cutlery to feed the five thousand.]* Above it hung several cast iron pot-hangers. From them hung numerous pots, pans, herbs, utensils, and drying laundry.

Dave could see Fred working at one of the ranges on the far side of the table as he walked into the cavernous room.

"Alright? Feelin' better now?" asked Fred. "There's more coffee in the pot over there." He continued, indicating a brown stained enamelled coffeepot on a hot plate. "Breakfast 'll be ready soon."

Dave helped himself to another mug of tar from the pot, pulled up a stool, and sat down at the table. Gingerly he sipped at his coffee whilst Fred clattered around behind him, preparing their repast.

Dave let out a philosophical sigh. He had made his decision to stay in Lyonshire, and now he was stuck with it. If the previous days' events were anything to go by, then it was going to be the weirdest and most adventurous time of his life. He was still not convinced about this magic business, even though he had witnessed it first-hand. On the other hand, perhaps there was something in what Fred had said, after all, historically the church had gone out of its way to burn or drown anyone that was even rumoured to be a witch or wizard. Even recently, anyone that could so much as divine water had been regarded as a pagan heretic.

When he was a child of perhaps six or seven, he could remember being taken to see a distant aunt on his father's side of the family. She had lived in a rundown cottage at the end of an overgrown dirt track, on the outskirts of a small village. He had been fascinated that the inside of the cottage had seemed so much larger than the outside. When he had pointed this out in a naive way to his father, he had been hushed into silence.

Everywhere he looked in her cottage there were clocks. There had been grandfather and grandmother clocks ticking away and chiming on the quarter hour. There had been clocks on the mantelpieces and clocks on the tables as well. He had been taken to see her because he had had, as children often do, several warts on his hands, and she was supposed to be able to "charm warts". Dave couldn't remember exactly what she had done, but he could remember she had rubbed a piece of raw liver over the warts and then got him to bury the meat in the garden. Sure enough, the warts had disappeared after a few days, but every time he had shown his mother, he had again been hushed into silence and told never to talk about it.

A hand slapped him on the back, causing Dave to almost choke on a mouthful of his drink.

"There you go lad," said Fred enthusiastically." 'Tiz porridge an' there's eggs an' bacon to follow."

Fred placed a bowl in front of Dave, who was still gasping for breath, before pulling up another stool and seating himself.

As far as Dave was concerned, porridge was something that was inflicted upon other people. He had been force fed it as a child and had never plucked up enough courage to eat it since. He recalled that it had always been either thick and salty or watery and tasteless, and depending on which it was, it could either be used as wallpaper paste or for sticking more substantial items together, like tanks or prefabricated concrete buildings.

Cautiously he stirred it with his spoon.

"Eat up lad, there's work aplenty vur 'ee to be doin' today." Said Fred cheerfully.

Dave looked at his bowl. The porridge was neither too thick nor too thin. Gingerly he lifted a small amount on his spoon and tasted it. It was definitely porridge, but edible porridge. He took another spoonful. It tasted of cinnamon and nutmeg, and had been sweetened with honey. He still wasn't convinced, but without a choice of cereals, it would have to do.

Fred finished his quickly and set about frying eggs. Dave took a sip from his mug and pushed his empty bowl away. As if on cue, Fred half dropped, half placed a large plate on the table in front of him.

It did indeed have bacon and eggs on it. It also had fried bread the size and thickness of a paving slab, sausages, a ring of black pudding, mushrooms, tomatoes, fried potatoes and that wonderful westcountry delicacy hogs or white pudding. *[A thick sausage, spiced with pepper and generally made from bits of the pig that the pig didn't even know it had, excluding offal. Usually sold boiled and air dried. It is then sliced into rounds or lengthways and fried.]*

Dave could feel his arteries hardening and his heart murmur in panic just looking at the food in front of him. He took another swig of coffee to settle himself and set about clearing his plate.

"Where did you get that helmet from? It's quite impressive." He asked Fred conversationally between mouthfuls.

"Well lad, t'waz a while ago now. I were feelin' a bit restless, so I left the pub vur a time and went awandering. Course, I 'ad a lot more places t' go than you, zeein' I could go anywhere as well as anywhere." Fred paused to devour a sausage before continuing.

"I went back a few times, saw the ice age, the dark ages and even the first Roman invasion fleet stranded on the shore at low tide. 'T'waz a bit borin' really. So I went forward an' 'ad a look around your time. Stayed in a B 'n' B vur a while, an' saw what a mess the politicians had made of the world. Then I went on a bit further, into the next century."

"Oh?" said Dave, a mushroom halfway to his mouth. "What will it be like?"

"S lot better. No war vur one thing." Replied Fred, waving his fork in the air.

"How do they manage that then? There is always a war going on somewhere, some lame excuse or other"

"Well, it's quite simple really. First they threw out all the politicians an' introduced a system where everyone gets t' vote on things. If tiz a local issue, then the locals vote, an' if it's a national issue then the whole country votes. An' then they banned religion on religious grounds. Trouble is that nearly all religions believe that their god or gods is in the people who worship them. After a particularly nasty conflict, some bright spark declared that he could show people the face of god. He issued statements to the press giving a time an' place. Anyroad, when the day came there was a huge crowd gathered where it was all supposed to happen. This chap jumps up on a stage an' tells everyone to "Behold the face of god!" an' yanks a rope which pulls the cover off o' a ruddy great mirror."

"What happened next then?" asked Dave, enthralled by the story.

"There was a riot an' no trace of the bloke was ever found. 'T'waz then that someone else noticed that the crowd was made up of people from all religions. Then everyone shook hands an' went 'ome happy. An' that was the end of religion."

Fred paused for a moment to devour more of his breakfast.

"A'ter that someone else pointed out that all the wars, whatever the cause, were always settled in discussions around the table, an' perhaps 't would be a good idea t' do that *before* hundreds, thousands, or millions o' people 'ad been killed pointlessly."

Fred set about his breakfast again with great gusto.

"You were telling me how you came to get your helmet." Said Dave as he wiped his plate clean with a piece of bread.

"Ah, I were weren't I?" replied Fred, his mouth half full of fried bread. "It was a bit a'ter that that I hired a bike. It was a Slingshot 2000." Fred's face glowed in the warmth of what was obviously a much-cherished memory. "Top speed o' just o'er Mach 2. Widdled meself the first time I broke the sound barrier. I 'ad some marvellous times with that bike. Anyway, I got the 'elmet and leathers at the same time an' I kept 'em as a souvenir."

Dave pushed his empty plate away and drank the rest of his coffee to the rhythmic sounds of Fred's industrial grade chomping. Things were decidedly on the strange side and getting stranger all the time. Shortly he would have to go and interview people he had never heard of until yesterday. And *that* was the easy bit.

"How long before Albert gets here?" he asked Fred.

Fred glanced at his watch. "He'll be here in a minute or two. Just you watch this." He said with a smile.

Fred left his empty plate on the table, picked a clean pint pot, walked through to the bar, and set it down on the counter. Next, he unbolted the front door, despite the fact that it was still only half-past six. He gave Dave a knowing look and went back to the bar, picked up the glass again, and began to draw off a fresh pint.

The glass was half full when the door burst open and Albert stumbled in for his breakfast.

"There you go Bert." Said Fred as he set the full pint down on the bar. "I thought you weren't goin' t' make it. The glass was 'alf full afore 'ee opened the door. You not feelin' well?" he looked at Albert.

Albert was puffing and blowing like a marathon runner.

"No, I'm fine Fred." He managed between breaths. "I was zeein' the editor o' the Hunton Times." He took a long pull from the glass. "Ah! That's better. Doesn't do 'ee any good t' start the day on an empty stomach." He looked at Dave. "'Ere you go lad, there's yur pass an' badge to say you works vur the Hunton Times."

He handed over the press card and ID badge, downed the rest of his pint, and slapped the glass on the bar in a meaningful way.

"Thanks Albert." Said Dave as he examined the badge. "I suppose I had better be making a move then."

"You get togged up lad," said Fred as he poured Albert another pint, "an' I'll come an' open the gates for 'ee."

~~~~~

Chalky opened his eyes. The clock by his bed said it was exactly six thirty. He was one of the very small group of people who go to bed, close their eyes and are immediately asleep. Likewise, when he opened his eyes in the morning, he was wide-awake. For Chalky White there was no moment of dread when he awoke. There was no "who am I? Where am I? And why do I have a traffic cone glued on my head?" He didn't have anyone else or anywhere else to be. Besides, he didn't get invited to that sort of party.

He got out of bed and dressed before going downstairs to the forge. He inspected the forge itself. The fire was still in, and he could see the faint glow amongst the coals. He raked it over, emptied the ashes, placed a shovel full of coal onto the fire, and pumped the bellows a time or two until flames erupted in a cheery blaze.

He rubbed a soot-covered hand over the stubble on his chin and crossed to the water pump in the corner. Most houses in Lyonshire had running water, but Chalky had never seen the need. A few pumps on the handle were enough to fill his huge kettle, which he placed on the forge. When the water boiled he could brew himself a pot of tea and fill a bowl to wash and shave in.

While he waited he gave the bellows another pump. Before long the kettle would boil and he could pile charcoal onto the blaze, ready for the days' work. He glanced at the forge as he thought about the work he had to do and noticed something odd about one of the lumps of coal. It wasn't burning. As he leaned closer he saw that it wasn't a lump of coal at all.

"How on earth did you get in amongst the coal?" He said as he picked up a pair of tongs.

Carefully, so as not to upset the kettle, he lifted out the bent lump of metal and crossed to the window to get a better look at it in the weak early morning sunlight. Clearly it had been painted; he could see where most of the paint had peeled away in the heat. A short length of string was hanging from it. It was hissing. It was also getting shorter. In fact it was rapidly getting shorter.

Chalky was not a fast thinker, but for once he was able to leap to a conclusion quite quickly.

"Oh bugg ..."

After the explosion, small pieces of Chalky's smithy rained down over a large area of Penhampton. On what was left of the forge the kettle boiled over and put out the fire.

~~~~

Dave rode towards Lord Woods' estate, trying his best to ignore the small irritating voice in his head. It was pointing out that all these wonderful meals went against everything the medical profession preached. The stress this was causing was actually doing more damage to his cardio-vascular system than the meals ever could. Unfortunately, it was difficult to ignore years of social conditioning and he could still taste that wonderful breakfast. He was also trying to ignore the much larger voice in his head that was screaming at the top of its lungs, and pointing out that everything that was going on was totally ridiculous.

Ahead of him he could see the estate and the gatehouse that stood at the head of the drive. Large wrought iron gates barred his way. He looked towards the entrance of the gatekeeper's house.

No one appeared to open the gate.

He honked the horn a few times in the shave and a haircut rhyme, which has long since ceased to be amusing.

Still nobody appeared to open the gates.

Dave could see smoke rising from the chimney, so presumably the gatekeeper was at home. So he honked the horn again.

Nobody went on appearing for quite some time.

At last, his patience exhausted, Dave switched off his engine, put the bike on its stand and walked over to the lodge and hammered on the door. Again, nobody appeared. Perhaps there was no one home after all.

He was about to walk away when he heard the sound of breaking crockery inside, followed by somewhat muffled but very blue swearing. He pounded his fist on the door as hard as he could and stepped back.

After a moment the door opened. It revealed a short skinny elderly man wearing a dirt encrusted vest and a pair of trousers held up by stripy braces.

"Did somebody knock?" the gatekeeper asked squinting and holding up his hand to shade his eyes.

"Yes." Replied Dave. He was beginning to feel impatient. "I want to go up to the house. Can you please open the gate?"

"What? What? Speak up Miss I can't hear you."

Dave ignored the "Miss" and tried again. "Can you open the gate please?" he asked again almost shouting.

The old man thought about it for a while.

"Yes, I can open the gate. See," he said, holding up a large iron key, which hung on a string around his neck. "I've got the key. That's what it's for, opening the gate that is." He finished with a self-satisfied smile but made no move towards the gate.

Dave found himself tapping his foot. He stopped himself. Words like "patience of a saint" crossed his mind. "Mad as a hatter" seemed appropriate too. He tried again.

"I want to go up to the house." He shouted.

"No need to shout!" snapped the old man in an offended tone. "What business do you have up at the house? The master's dead you know."

Dave's foot stamped a military tattoo. "I know Lord Woods is dead. I'm here to speak with his butler and housekeeper. I'm from the newspaper."

"Newspaper?" said the antique. "Yes, ..."

Dave slumped with relief.

"Yes, I've got it here somewhere. Just finished reading it. Load of rubbish if you ask me." Continued the gatekeeper, looking around for his paper.

Dave lost his temper, snatched the key, breaking the string, and stormed off to unlock the gate himself. All the while the gatekeeper continued mumbling about what he thought of newspapers in general. Dave placed the key back in his hand. He didn't even appear to notice it had gone.

As Dave rode through the gate and on up the drive, the gatekeeper stopped mumbling, squinted around and wondered why he was outside. After a few moments indecision, he walked back into his lodge.

"Strange," he said to himself as he settled back into his chair. "I could have sworn I heard somebody knocking."

Dave rode up the drive. It was as typical as a drive to a stately home can get. It wound its way through carefully landscaped fields with iron railings lining the road. Closer to the house it straightened out, the grass on either side becoming manicured lawn. An avenue of beech trees stood like an honour guard down through either side, restricting the view to a vista of the house itself. People with money like you to know they had money before you arrived.

The tarmac gave way to gravel as Dave rode closer. The honour guard of trees ended and the formal gardens began, a mixture of mixed bedding and knot gardens. Right in front of the house was a wide turning circle. The circular lawn in its midst was immaculate. At the centre of the lawn was a hexagonal pond with a fountain, topped off by a statue of some long forgotten but probably heroic Woods. *[This kind of statue is an essential part of any stately home. It provides something to climb and swing on during one of those "hilarious at the time" moments associated with aristocratic parties. This is the "rich" equivalent of the side-splitting office party trick with the sticky-tape, a stapler, and the photocopier.]*

Dave pulled up by the front entrance. It was definitely not a front door; it was far too aristocratic. Having put his bike on its stand and taken off his helmet, he walked up the steps to the entrance and knocked the knocker.

After a moment he heard slow measured footsteps inside and the door opened.

"Yeesss?" droned the butler, looking down his hooked nose at Dave.

Dave fumbled in his pocket for his press-card.

"Hello. I'm Dave. I'm here to interview you and your wife for the Hunton Times." He said, waving the card.

Nonplussed, the butler demeaningly regarded the card. He was outfitted in the outfit of a stereotypical butler, complete with tailcoat and a black string bowtie.

"I sseee. Thee tradespersons entrance iss rround thee rhear." With that, the butler stepped back across the threshold and closed the door.

Dave felt rather miffed. He'd already had a belly full of the gatekeeper. Perhaps this journalist idea hadn't been such a good one after all, but he was stuck with it now. Shaking his head, he trudged off to find the tradespersons entrance.

The gravel drive had an offshoot that headed around the side of the house. As soon as it was out of sight it became cobbles and entered into the world of stables, coach-houses, and outbuildings. Dave followed it around. Eventually, amongst the various sheds and outhouses, he found the backdoor. Compared with the one at the front, this was just a poky rectangular hole with bit of hinged wood filling it.

He knocked.

"And the door shall open!" he mumbled irritably under his breath.

In response the door opened. It was the butler again, but this time he was minus his string tie and tailcoat and his collar stud had been removed.

"Alright mate? Come in. Come in. Sit yerself down and 'ave a cuppa."

Somewhat bewildered, Dave entered into the world of below stairs.

A warm rosy glow and the smell of baking filled the butlers' pantry as Dave was ushered into it, and seated in an overstuffed armchair. He was even given a footstool to rest his feet on. The butler had transformed and was now an attentive host. Shortly, his wife entered the room carrying a tray containing the alchemy set needed to perform the ritual of serving tea.

"'Ere you go. You must be froze. 'Tiz a bit nippy out 's morning and what with you riding that motor-bicycle an' all." Said the woman. "Corr, there's me forgettin' me manners too. I'm Elsie an' me husband's Samuel but everyone calls 'im Shem."

"How do." Said Shem with a warm smile and a nod of his head.

Elsie was a large dumpy woman. She was large enough for two women. Her face had the rosy glow of the truly contented. She was wearing a floral dress of the tent variety; much favoured by more generously proportioned women, and gathered at the waist with a belt. Her hair was short and permed in loose curls. Her whole ensemble was completed with a large white apron and a generous dusting of flour.

Her husband was completely the opposite. He was tall. Dave stood six-foot but Shem was a head and shoulders higher. He was also terminally thin, as tall people often are. However, here, below stairs, he was stoop - shouldered. Gone was the vertical correctness with which he had opened the front door, along with the superior attitude.

"Fancy a cake." Offered Shem, proffering a tin. "'Tiz Elsie's baking. Best yere abouts."

His wife giggled, blushed from head to foot, and gave Shem a playful ding around the ear.

Dave took a bun from the tin. All the while he couldn't help staring at Shem.

"What, if you don't mind me asking, happened to the "Yeesss" and all the rest of it?" he asked.

Shem laughed. "Well, you've got to keep up standards in case 'tiz someone important callin'."

"But I thought the house was yours now?"

"That it is lad. That it is." He said mournfully. "But his Lordship always said that standards is standards. Besides, he's not long gone an' 't wouldn't be right to take on airs and graces." Replied Shem, sitting himself down.

Elsie continued to fuss around like a broody bantam as they talked, bustling in and out as Dave asked the two of them questions and made notes in his notebook. Occasionally she refilled the teapot, passed biscuits around, or tried to persuade Dave to eat "just one more bun" as they chatted.

Eventually she declared it was lunchtime and Dave glanced at his watch. It was indeed one o'clock, and the three of them went through to the kitchen for a light lunch.

On the table was a huge steaming bowl of boiled potatoes oozing melted butter, three more bowls of salad, and what looked like an industrial sized pork pie. When Elsie cut into it, it turned out to be a traditional cold game pie, with large chunks of rabbit, venison and duck meat suspended in a rich jelly.

Elsie dished up the food and passed the plates around.

As they ate and chatted, Dave found that he was enjoying himself enormously. Shem and Elsie were the perfect host and hostess, homely and welcoming. He soon forgot all about his role as a journalist and the surrealness of even being in Lyonshire.

After lunch they took him on a tour of the house. They took him through the grand staterooms, with all their equally grand antique furniture, and their own more modest quarters in the servants' wing. Homespun, unpolished, a place to live and work in, not entertain. Then on, out into the grounds and outbuildings.

Their tour led them past a small, unmarked grave.

"It's the dog." Said Elsie, wiping away a tear.

"Poor thing." Added Shem, his smile gone, his head bent.

"Never so much as bared 'is teeth. Then for no reason 'ee suddenly turns into a killer. Soppy old thing, 'ee was part of the family."

The small grave reminded Dave why he was there. A lump caught in his throat. It was time for him to be a journalist again.

"How old was it?" he managed after clearing his throat.

"He was nine." Replied Shem. "Not old for a dog. An' right after he killed his master, he just dropped down dead."

"I'm sorry to have to ask," said Dave, noting the tears in Elsie's eyes, "but what happened? Did he just turn or was he unwell beforehand?"

"Ee just turned." Replied Shem, putting his arm comfortingly around his wife's shoulders.

"No 'ee didn't Shem." Put in Elsie. "You remember, he was moping about vur a couple of days."

"That's right, I was forgettin'. 'Ee Took his time eating his food. Wouldn't touch it straight off, he'd just sniff at it an' walk away. Ee'd waited till he was starving before actually eating it."

Dave made a note.

"What did he normally eat? Biscuits? Meal? Tinned food? Raw meat? He asked.

"T'waz tins and biscuits mostly. Although he did 'ave the odd pound of steak now and again." Replied Shem. "Mind you, it weren't none o' that cheap processed tinned food. His Lordship used to buy tins that one of the butchers made." He said with just a touch of snobbishness.

They continued on around the gardens for a time but the mood had been spoiled. Eventually, Dave made his goodbyes and promised to call again as a friend and not a journalist.

Dave rode back towards Shoton in a sullen mood. The death of their master had badly shaken the Windsors. Both Elsie and Shem were lost without someone to look after. They still maintained the routine that had dominated their lives for years, only now it was the routine of an empty house.

However, this was not at the forefront of Dave's worries. What he needed was a toothbrush, toothpaste, a razor, and a change of underwear. That meant facing Aunt Aggie. He shuddered.

He rode into the square and through the open gates into the yard behind the pub. Leaving his helmet on the ground by his bike, he walked back out into the square and headed towards the post office.

The small brass bell on the back of the door tinkled as he entered, but did not fall off again. And, as if by magic, Aunt Aggie appeared behind him.

"Ah! It's the young man who's lost." She crowed.

Dave found himself stammering his reply. "Llet mme m make it qu quite clear, I'm n nothing to do with taxes."

"Oh, I knows that." Replied Aunt Aggie in an offhand way. "You'm stayin' over at the pub. Bin doing a bit o' pokin' around vur that Fredrick Dray."

"Who told you that?" he asked with surprise.

"No one tol' me. I don't need to be tol'. I just keeps me mouth shut an' listens. Now, what can I do you for?" she asked.

"Well, I need a razor." Dave thought about Aunt Aggie for a minute. "A safety razor, not a cut throat."

Aunt Aggie vanished and re-materialised amongst the groaning shelves.

"And a toothbrush and toothpaste, and..."

"I've got a special on toothbrushes, buy twenty and get the next 'alf price." She said, interrupting Dave in mid-sentence.

"No!" He blurted "I mean no thank you. I just want one."

"Humph! A body don't know when someone's tryin' to do 'em a favour." She mumbled as she flitted through the shelves.

Dave crossed to the counter, being very careful not to knock over any of the stacks on the way. There was already a packet of disposable razors on the counter, along with a cutthroat. Aunt Aggie appeared behind the counter and set down a toothbrush. She peered at him through the thick glass of her spectacles and patted her hair. Probably to make sure the arsenal of hairpins were still in place.

"The toothpaste is on the shelf over there." She directed him to a pile between a stack of armour polish and a box of rattraps.

Snap! Snap!

"Mind them traps! I've set some of them to show that they works." She warned, too late.

Prizing a trap from his injured fingers, Dave selected a brand of paste he recognised. Well, he recognised the name; the packaging was totally unfamiliar. It was either before or after his time. He hoped it was after. He did not relish the prospect of cleaning his teeth in the morning, only to find he had to clean them yesterday later. He put it on the counter.

"Is that the lot?" sniffed Aunt Aggie.

"No," Dave had been dreading this bit most of all, "I need some socks, a shirt and some undergarments." He replied as politely as he could.

"Oh. Is that all?" She replied disappointedly. But every penny counted.

She rummaged under the counter, and much to Dave's surprise, took out a packet of the white sports socks he normally bought. They were the same brand and everything.

"What kind of underwear do you want? Longjohns? Shorts? Y-fronts? Thongs?" She enquired, much to Dave's embarrassment.

"Um. Y-fronts please." He managed to mumble between blushes.

"I ain't got no shirts. Most people gets their shirts made in

Penhampton." She said, placing half a dozen pairs of pants on the counter.

"Everyone buys tailored shirts?" Dave was amazed. "Isn't that expensive?"

"No, not really. If you're goin' t' trade vur a shirt, it might as well be a good one."

"Oh." Was all Dave could manage.

"Mind, I've got some white short-sleeved vests. A lot of the kids wear 'em as T-shirts." Never one to miss out on a sale, she held one up for inspection.

"Y yes, I'll take two please and a bottle of aspirin."

"There you go. That'll be five shillings and six pence." She said with a smile.

"I'm sorry, but I'm afraid I've only got decimal money." Said Dave apologetically.

The smile vanished from Aunt Aggie's face. Drawing herself up to her full height, she took out a scrap of paper and began to reckon up the price in decimal coinage.

"In that case," she said, looking down her nose at him, even though he was taller than her, "it's twenty eight pounds and sixty pence."

Dave was unsure whether he had been diddled or not. *[But the entire country had been unsure whether or not they had been diddled when decimal coinage had come into use.]* On balance he realised he probably had been, but he was in no mood for a fight so he handed over the money.

"Have you got a carrier-bag I could have please?" he asked politely.

"That's another ten pence." The smile began to reappear on Aunt Aggie's face.

"I think I'll leave the carrier." Said Dave, as he gathered up his acquisitions in his arms and headed for the door.

It took him a while to balance his shopping in one hand and open the door with the other. Aunt Aggie offered no help. Helping someone out of her shop was against her religion, but holding the door open so they could walk in was different. *[If it didn't break the conditions of her probation, she would quite happily lock the door and not let a customer out until they had spent all she thought they could afford.]*

Finally Dave made it back to the pub, in through the kitchen and upstairs to his room. There he collapsed on the bed, letting his shopping rain down around him.

Fifteen seconds later, he nearly jumped out of his skin as someone knocked on his door.

Chapter 5.

Someone knocked on Dave's door again. Reluctantly, he pulled himself from the bed and opened the door. Fred was standing on the other side. He was out of breath and waving a newspaper around.

"What's the matter Fred? I've only just got in. Can't it wait for a while?" asked Dave.

"Tiz the evenin' paper!" Puffed Fred. "Just you 'ave a look at the front page!"

He handed Dave the Penhampton Evening News.

"Tiz Chalky the smith!" Put in Fred before Dave had even had a chance to read the headlines. "He's been blowed up in 'is own forge!"

"It says here that it was a gas leak. Gas built up in his smithy and when he lit his forge this morning, it ignited the gas. Nothing mysterious at all." Said Dave once he had had a chance to study the story.

"'Ee was a blacksmith!" insisted Fred. "No smith worth 'is hammer would ever let his forge go out."

"Well, it would appear that he was a bit lax on this occasion. Probably had a pint or two last night and forgot to tend to his forge." Dave argued.

"Yur missing the point lad." Said Fred in an exasperated tone. "Chalky's a respected citizen. As a matter o' fact, 'ee's one o' them experts from the court yesterday."

"From the inquest?"

"Yes! His forge is just along from the shop Timbers owned. If this was an accident then I'll give up drinkin' an' take up needlework!" exclaimed Fred.

"I think I need a drink." Said Dave, sagging against the doorpost.

"I'll make 'ee a coffee then. You've still a bit t' do yet."

"Alright Fred. I'll come down to the bar with you."

Dave gave his bed a mournful look. All he really wanted to do was have a long hot soak in a bath and to go to bed. He still needed a shave and he had a nagging feeling that when he took off his boots, his socks would either have rotted away or they'd crawl off into a corner by themselves.

Reluctantly he followed Fred down the stairs and through into the bar. He helped himself to a coffee and sat down to try and gather his strength. As he sat there he noticed the scruffy old man who had been asleep in the corner since the night before was stirring.

"He's still here I see." He commented to Fred.

"'Ee's no trouble lad. Generally if someone 'as had a drop too much to drink and nodded off, either me or Suzan 'll chuck a blanket over 'em and leave them to sleep it off." Replied Fred.

The old man got up and went through the door marked His 'n' Hers and on into the His. After answering the call of nature, he washed in the sink and pulled an electric razor out from his baggy shirt.

He looked reproachfully at his reflection in the mirror. What an awful state to get into. And at his age he ought to know better.

Having shaved, he went back into the crowded bar. An inviting and recently vacated stool at the bar caught his attention. He glided across the bar, claimed it for himself, sat down, and ordered a very late breakfast.

"Alright Merlin? Woken up I zee." Said Fred to the aged man on the barstool.

"That's right. Just 'avin' me breakfast Fred." Replied Merlin with an almost totally toothless grin.

"You comin' along vur the meetin' tomorrow night?" asked Fred.

"Flippin' heck! It's not that time of year again is it? Already?" Blurted Merlin, almost spilling his pint of breakfast. "I'd completely forgotten about it."

"Sort o' creeps up on 'ee these annual meeting, don't they?" Laughed Fred.

The old man downed the rest of his pint and climbed down off his stool. "Must be goin' Fred. Lots to do before tomorrow night. Oh, the beer is excellent as always. Be seeing you." He said and made his way out the door.

Fred filled two mugs with his own special coffee and joined Dave at an empty table.

"That was the guy, who was asleep in the corner this morning, wasn't it? Enquired Dave.

"Yes, that's Merlin. 'Ee comes in yere whenever 'ee has a problem." Replied Fred.

"What? To think it through in peaceful surroundings and solve the problem?"

"No lad. He comes yere because this is the last place people would look vur 'im. An' most don't know how t' get into Lyonshire so it's relatively safe."

Dave took a sip of his coffee. It was then he noticed for the first time that he was drinking it black, and he had done at breakfast as well. But on second thoughts, milk would probably turn to cheese in this coffee anyway. So really it was a waste of time thinking about it. Besides, something else, something far more important, was vying for his attention. Mental alarm bells were ringing all over his subconscious.

"What was it you were saying earlier about the blacksmith?" he asked, dragging his mind back to the matter at hand and ignoring the alarm bells.

"What I was sayin' was," said Fred, drawing himself up to his full height, "that the explosion was no accident. I mean, I didn't know 'im personally, but I do know several smiths and I've heard of Chalky by reputation. Our own Tinny the smith's always singin' 'is praises. 'Ee's won the bi-annual smithing contest three times running. An' if another smith 'as problems, they goes an' asks Chalky vur advice. 'Ee was the nearest thing the blacksmiths in Lyonshire 'ave or had to a reference library. 'Ee was a master smith was Chalky."

"You think it's got something to do with Lord Woods' death?"

"Well, I don't know if they're linked, all I know is that 'ee was one of them experts in the court and 'is forge is just down the road from Timbers' shop. An' someone 'as covered things up an' given the paper a load of horse apples."

"So you want me to check it out? Sniff around a bit?"

The coffee had made Dave feel a good deal brighter, but in the background there was still a part of him that was shattered. Once the coffee wore off he was going to need to lie down. Fast.

"Somethin' like that lad. Somethin' like that." Replied Fred.

"It'll have to wait till tomorrow." Dave put in. "I've arranged to interview Poulter the butcher this evening."

"What? Our Mark, "where's me bucket o' whitewash" Poulter? He's been deliverin' meat to Timbers' place vur years. What's he stand to gain from doin' 'im in?"

"Just being methodical." Dave replied. "Besides, he's one of the suspects. You and Albert said so." Dave glanced around the bar. "By the way, where is Albert? I thought he spent most of his time in here."

"Oh Albert's got things t' zee to. Rent agreements and so on. 'Ee don't spend all 'is time in yere. I could never brew enough beer vur one thing." Said Fred thankfully.

"Poor ol' Chalky." Sighed Fred. "They say that only two things in life are certain: Death and taxes.

"Certainly all they so-called advanced civilisations has taxes inflicted upon 'em. *[This goes a long way to explain limits of civilised behaviour.]* 'Tiz only those tribes that folk thinks of as primitive that, not only have no understandin' of the concept, but also 'ave no words vur taxes.

"There're tribes that 'ave no mechanical machinery, have never 'eard of 'lectricity an' stress. They gives back as much as they takes from nature, and generally live t' over a hundred." Laughed Fred.

"Their only vices tend to be smokin' the local wow-wow weed and 'avin' the occasional an' often violent tribal dispute with their neighbours. *[Usually when some civilised person has pinched all their wow-wow weed and it is in short supply.]* Both pastimes that no civilised culture would have any truck with!" He continued with a sad shake of his head.

"An' then there's the civilised ones 'emselves. They 'as well-established methods of dodgin' their taxes. Either they puts large sums of money in offshore accounts or they spends most o' the year out of the country. Then they lies back on some sun-soaked beach, 'appy in the knowledge that their money is goin' t' remain their money."

Dave gave Fred a concerned look over the top of his mug of coffee. Obviously, deep down, Fred felt as strongly about taxes as Aunt Aggie.

In the gathering gloom of early evening, Dave strode across the square to Poulter's butcher shop. A man was methodically going down through the road lighting the gas lamps that lit the village. He nodded to Dave as he passed.

Next to the butchers' shop was an alley that led around to the back. Halfway along was the entrance to the flat above it. Dave knocked on the door and ducked to the side quickly. Fred had taken the time to warn him about Poulter. A bucket of water splashed to the ground in front of the door. Dave stepped over it and knocked again.

The door opened just wide enough for an eye to peer through the crack.

"Yes? What is it?" asked the eye.

"I'm Dave." Replied Dave. "The reporter from the Hunton Times."

"Oh yes. The reporter. Sorry about the water. Force of habit."

The door opened to grant Dave admittance.

Dave was led along a dark passageway and up a flight of narrow stairs. At the top was another gloomy passage with several doors leading off it. He was ushered through the door at the end.

"Please forgive the mess. I don't often have visitors." Said Poulter as he showed Dave into the living room directly above the shop.

In contrast to the passageway and stairs, the room was brightly lit and Dave had to shade his eyes whilst they grew accustomed to the light.

The room was indeed in a mess. Poulter, even though he was a butcher, appeared to exist on frozen microwave meals. Food wrappers festooned the furniture and the discarded plastic trays from tv-dinners covered the floor, contributing to the unpleasant smell in the room. Dave knew that rooms often reflect their occupiers, and Dave studied both whilst Poulter cleared a place for them to sit.

Poulter was a thin pale-faced man, almost skeletal. Most butchers were big burly men who could dispatch an ox with a single blow and quarter it with ease. Poulter, on the other hand, judging by his appearance, could probably manage to joint a chicken - if it was very small chicken. His features were drawn and pallid, almost wraith like. He reminded Dave of the weedy kids at school who were either the targets of the school bully or more often the ones that stood behind the bullies telling them what to do.

"Sit down, please." Said Poulter; his face flushed from hurriedly clearing a space on one of the chairs.

Dave seated himself and watched as Poulter sat down in his armchair in front of the television. He noted that the mess spiralled out from what was clearly Poulter's regular resting-place.

It was the first time Dave had seen a television since he had entered Lyonshire. He hadn't given television any thought, and was surprised to see one now.

"Have many people in Lyonshire got televisions?" he asked.

"No. No, they're not very common. Most people are too busy making their own entertainment or out socialising to watch." Poulter replied.

"How come you've got one then?"

Poulter looked slightly embarrassed. "I don't know whether you've heard or not, most have, but ever since I started playing practical jokes I've not been the most popular of people. And as a consequence I don't go out much either." Said Poulter miserably.

"What do you watch? If you don't mind me asking?"

Poulter fished around amongst the cushions on his chair. Eventually he pulled out what appeared to be a very large pocket calculator.

"More or less anything I want. This is a data-base of television programs." He replied, waving the gismo around. "It contains program listings from the start of broadcasting, right up to the time that it went out of use. It also has precise instructions for directing the aerial to pick up the programs. If I miss a program, I simply move the aerial to pick up the program at the time it was broadcast."

Dave sat in stunned silence for a while. Of course the inhabitants of Lyonshire could go anywhen. It simply hadn't occurred to him that they could make use of it in such a novel way. He cleared his throat and came back to the matter at hand.

"Now, I'm reporting about the death of Lord Woods and the mix up over his estate. I understand that you are claiming his shop in Penhampton and thirty acres of ground. Is that right?" he asked.

"Well," replied Poulter, "I've delivered meat to his Lordship for several years. It was on the understanding that I could take over the tenancy of that shop. Unfortunately, he died before we sorted out the paperwork."

"You were going to move to Penhampton? What about your shop here?"

"The shop here doesn't do that well, and I have to buy in carcasses from the butcher in Hunton. The abattoir behind the shop here is derelict, the meat kept spoiling, and I haven't got the money to get it into good order. Besides, because this is a rural area, many people around here keep their own livestock or get meat from Nowle the poacher. But the shop in Penhampton, well, there's nowhere to keep animals in a city and the people have to get meat from somewhere." Poulter had a dreamy faraway look in his eyes.

"I understand it was mostly tinned pet-food that you delivered to Lord Woods' estate." Put in Dave.

Poulter's face changed. His eyes snapped back from his daydream and took on a hard look.

"Who told you that?" he snapped. His whole demeanour had changed. In an instant he had become aggressive.

"The Windsors." Replied Dave, being less than truthful.

Poulter deflated. "Well, I couldn't compete with the prices Hatchet, the butcher from Hunton, charges. But as for the dog food, I don't have anything to do with that. Ask anyone. I don't have anywhere to can it up for a start, let alone a canning machine."

"What are you going to do with this shop if you move to Penhampton?"

"I shall put it up for sale. There are a few debts I have to pay off. And the land I should get from Lord Woods' estate I shall rent out to others in exchange for slaughter animals to stock the shop."

"Right. Thank you for answering my questions." Said Dave as he stood up. "I won't detain you any longer."

"Oh. Oh right." replied Poulter. "I'll show you to the door then. If you think of any more questions, feel free to drop round and ask. It has been nice having someone to talk to."

Dave arrived back at the pub and collapsed on a barstool. The effects of Fred's coffee were wearing off. Exhaustion buffeted him from all sides. He swayed on his stool.

"'Ere you go lad." Said Fred and handed him a pint.

"How did it go with Poulter? Managed t' avoid the whitewash I see."

Dave accepted the pint gratefully and took a swig.

"He seems harmless enough. Rather a sad man if you ask me, but I wouldn't trust him enough to turn my back on him." He said as soon as he was able to talk.

"There's something not quite right about a full grown man who sticks buckets of water over doors." He continued.

"I agree with 'ee there. Most people keeps out o' 'is way. His meat's pricey too." Replied Fred.

"I think I'll skip tea if you don't mind. I'll just go up and have a bath and an early night." Said Dave.

"The bathroom's the next door along from yours. There should be plenty o' hot water an' I put a fresh towel in yur room."

Dave dragged himself off of his stool and headed upstairs, taking the rest of his pint with him. He stumbled on a step and spilt some of his beer.

"Oh blast!" He exclaimed. The wood of the stair tread began to char where the liquid puddled.

In the bar Fred poured a pint. Magically the door opened and Albert staggered in, snatched the glass from Fred's hand, and drained it

He was shaking.

"You alright Bert? You looks like you've seen a ghost." Asked Fred.

"Dddonn'tt wanntt ttoo ttaalk k k aboutt itt. Jjjusstt ppour." Stammered Albert.

"Fair enough." Said Fred, placing another pint on the bar for

Albert and drawing off a third.

By the time Albert was able to talk, a row of empty glasses lined the bar from end to end, and Fred had been forced to go down to the cellar and change the barrel.

"Ah!" sighed Albert at last.

"You feelin' up t' talkin' yet Bert? You look like you've got a bit o' colour back in yur cheeks now."

"I've 'ad a nasty shock Fred. An' that's the truth. I was out ahuntin' with Nowle." Replied Albert between swigs.

"You get ort interestin' or were there nort about?"

Albert settled himself on his stool and adopted, what Fred recognised as, the pose he always used when he was about to recount a story.

"T'waz like this yere. We'd been out vur a couple of hours and not seed a thing. Then all o' a sudden, this ruddy great stag strolls out o' the trees. Bold as brass 'ee were." Albert paused to take another swig.

"So we started acrawlin' through the bracken towards 'im to get a better shot. Got soaking wet we did. There's nort like bracken vur holding the damp. An' we gets as close as possible an' Nowle uncovers that enormous gun o' 'is. You know the one, 's more like a cannon. So 'ee lines the stag up in 'ee's sights. Aiming careful to bring 'im down with one clean shot. An' there's me fair droolin' at the thought o' a nice piece o' venison vur me tea."

Albert paused to take another drink.

"An' what happened next?" put in Fred dutifully, recognising the cue.

Albert leaned in closer. "Well, all of a sudden I veels zummet a crawling up me trouser leg. Frightened the life out o' me, I can tell you. I thought it were an adder or a rat. So I nudges Nowle just, as it turns out, as 'ee squeezes the trigger. His shot goes wide an' fells a tree, an' o' course, the stag bolts vur cover.

"Meantime, I can feel the intruder crawlin' further up me leg so I stands up, hollering all the while to Nowle. Now Nowle is hollerin' and cussin' me cause o' putting 'im off 'is shot, an' I'm cussin' cause there's something crawling up me leg. Anyroad, I starts jumpin' up an' down and Nowle shakes me trousers. Eventually it drops out. An' do you know what it were?"

"No Bert, I can honestly say that I 'aven't got a clue. What was it?"

"T'waz a ruddy vole! A damn vole! And there was me, not thirty seconds before, fair widdling meself. A ruddy vole!" repeated Albert.

"No wonder yur a bit shaken Bert." Said Fred, doing his best to stop himself from laughing. "I hate t' be the bearer of bad news, but Gladys will be yere in a mo. Her singing should 'elp take yur mind off o' things." He finished, and made a dash for the kitchen, unable to contain his laughter any longer.

"NO! Not Gladys!" Albert shouted after him. He downed the rest of his pint. "I 'ope you've taken precautions. 'Er singing turned all the beer last time. An' she broke three windows, not to mention the one across the street in the church."

"Tiz alright Bert." Replied Fred, sticking his head back around the door. "I've rapped the barrels in blankets t' deaden the sound. I've warned the vicar an' 'ee's bought himself an hardhat t' stop himself gettin' hurt like last time." He finished and burst out laughing in the kitchen again.

Upstairs Dave had found the bathroom. The bath itself was a huge enamelled one, capable of holding at least two people and could double as a swimming pool for small children. He ran the hot tap. Steam billowed and filled the room.

As the bath filled, Dave tested the water. It was wonderfully hot; the precise temperature to relax tired muscles and refresh a weary body. *[It is also the temperature that scientists fail to duplicate in the laboratory and is totally unobtainable to those that insist on having a shower instead of wallowing around in their own dirt. Even the best-designed shower will only operate at three temperatures, too hot, tepid, or ice cold.]* Afterwards he would look like a boiled lobster but for now he was looking forward to a nice long soak.

He turned off the taps, undressed, and tentatively eased himself into the water.

"Eech! Ooch! Ouch. Ooooah, aaahhhh!" he groaned as he lowered himself into the bath.

After a moment's contemplation, he rubbed his chin and the two days growth of stubble. He reached for the razor and a small shaving mirror and inspected himself. It was at this point he realised he had forgotten to buy shaving foam. The idea of shaving using ordinary soap did not appeal, nor did the resulting shaving rash and the stinging face he would have afterwards. So he decided to leave the stubble where it was. After all, apart from a little itching it wasn't doing any harm.

He carried on with his ablutions.

Washed, scrubbed and glowing pink, Dave dressed in his clean clothes. Much of his exhaustion had spiralled away with the water as it disappeared down the plughole. His wet hair combed easily and it did not take long before he looked almost presentable.

He practised the international art of dumping his dirty clothes in a pile on the floor in his room, but hung the towel up on the towel rail.

His stomach rumbled. Thoughts of steak and kidney crept unbidden into his head. His stomach growled.

Finally he gave in, pulled on his boots, and headed down to the bar.

"Thought you was goin' t' 'ave an early night lad?" Said Fred as Dave stuck his head through into the bar.

"I was. I am." Replied Dave. "I just fancied something to eat first. Steak and kidney perhaps?" he said hopefully.

"I go an' zee what uz can vind." Replied Fred.

"Hello Albert." Said Dave.

Albert nodded as Dave settled himself on a stool.

"Here did Fred tell 'ee what happened to me 's evening?" asked Albert hopefully.

"No. He said you were probably out attending to things but he didn't tell me what." Replied Dave unwittingly.

Albert smiled, here was someone else he could recount his near death experience to. He took up his recitation pose and began, again, to relate the afternoon's events.

Dave listened with half an ear, and let his gaze drift around the bar. Occasionally he would nod to show he was listening and encourage Albert to continue with his tale. It was a habit he had picked up at work because his boss would often talk at length about nothing in particular. *[This practice is taken up by all those who work, live, or spend time with people who drone on and on about nothing in particular. Parents often use it in self-defence, especially if they have teenage children.]* Over in the corner he spied a strange tableau.

An elderly gentleman, wearing a sequinned waistcoat of indeterminable style and age, and boldly coloured red and blue striped trousers, was setting up a rack of coloured stage lights. The woman accompanying him looked about sixty, but was dressed like a girl of twenty out on the town. Parts of her outfit were letting her out in places in a very unflattering way. She was wearing what could only be a long blond wig, two tons of plaster of Paris like make-up, a low cut very short dress and fishnet stockings. She was wearing spangled shoes with six-inch stiletto heels.

The two of them were busy setting up lights, speakers, and a microphone. When that was accomplished, an aluminium flight-case was opened to produce a small keyboard, which was set on a stand.

"An' what do 'ee think it were?" asked Albert, grabbing Dave's arm and derailing his train of thought.

"Sorry?" he stammered.

"I said, what do you think it were?" repeated Albert.

"I have no idea. What was it?" Dave replied honestly.

"It were a flamin' vole! Said Albert continuing with his story.

Over in the corner the speakers whined and screamed with feedback until a knob was hurriedly turned down.

"ONE TWO. ONE TWO. TESTING, TESTING. ONE TWO." Boomed the speakers.

"'S funny, musicians can never count past two." Said Fred with a smile as he emerged from the kitchen.

"What?" asked Albert and Dave in unison.

"Musicians. They gets as far as two and starts again." Said Fred hopefully.

The other two still didn't get the joke and gave him a blank look.

"Now, where'd I get to?" asked Albert.

"The vole." Dave replied.

"Oh yes. Said Albert. "It was a ruddy great vole."

"Now Bert, even a ruddy great vole is no more 'an two inches long minus the tail." Put in Fred.

"I know that." Said Albert irritably. "But it frightened the sh..."

"GOOD EVENING LADIES AND GENTLEMEN!" Boomed the speakers at an opportune moment and drowned Albert out.

"WE ARE GLAD RAGS! PLEASE FEEL FREE TO ASK FOR ANY REQUESTS DURING THE INTERVAL." Continued the husky voice.

"I 'ave a request." Shouted Albert in reply. "Go play somewhere else!"

Looking around, Dave was surprised to see the husky voice belonged to the woman. A few moments later she began to sing, very, very badly in a shrill and strangled soprano.

"'Ere quick! Put these in!" Shouted Fred over the noise of the speakers, and opened his hand to reveal three sets of earplugs.

All three of them stuffed the earplugs into their ears, although Albert was hampered as he tried to put them in with one hand and down his pint with the other. Dave soon found out why, after plugging his own ears he picked up his pint, only to watch it curdle in front of his eyes.

Fred pointed towards the kitchen door. The other two nodded and followed him out. They could still hear the din from the bar in the kitchen, but the three-foot thick stonewall and a reinforced fire door did much to muffle the noise.

"Who is the singer?" Dave asked.

"What did you say lad?" replied Fred.

"I said, who is the..." he began, and then a thought struck him. He pulled the earplugs from his ears and motioned for the others to do the same.

"I said, who is the singer?" he repeated, once the others had removed their earplugs.

"Gladys. She's Aggie's younger sister. An' the keyboard player is 'er fifth husband." Replied Fred.

"What? Aunt Aggie from the Post Office? It's her younger sister?" Dave couldn't believe his ears.

"That's right." Confirmed Albert. "Younger's a bit misleading. She's Agatha's identical twin. She's only a vew minutes younger, that's all. Although 'er likes t' make out tiz it's a lot more. Mind you, Aunt Aggie won't even acknowledge that they are sisters most of the time."

"But they look nothing like each other." Exclaimed Dave.

Fred smiled. "Well, p'haps tiz better t' say that they *were* identical twins. It often 'appens with twins, they're either so alike that they're two peas in a pod or they's exact opposites. Aggie's still a spinster but Gladys 'as bin married fourteen times."

"'S right." said Albert. "She chases ort in trousers. An' 'll do anything she thinks will improve 'er chances of gettin' 'er man."

"Or kilt." Added Fred. "There was that Scotsman who came through a few years ago."

"That's true Fred. I'd forgotten about 'im."

"I thought you said the keyboard player was her fifth husband? What about the others?" Dave asked. He was beginning to regret coming back down from his room, and the noise from the bar wasn't helping.

"Aye. 'Ee was the only musician she married. He still does gigs with 'er. He's deaf as a post, an' with her singing that's got t' be a blessin'." Replied Albert.

Dave nodded, but he wasn't sure why. Behind him, Fred had got up from the table and was talking to the chef.

He looked across to Albert. "You want zummet to eat Bert?"

Albert replied with a nod of his head.

Fred returned to the table and seated himself. "Chef said it'll be ready in a mo. You two want another pint while we're waitin'?"

Dave looked at the sad remains of his pint he was still holding in his hand. As far as he knew, it was only things like milk, cream, and possibly mayonnaise that could curdle. Looking at the brown, lumpy sludge in his glass, he changed his opinion.

"Could I have a glass of water please Fred," he replied, "and could I have it in a fresh glass?"

"Better way make mine water too." Said Albert glumly and handed over his glass.

"I'll get us zome fresh ones." Said Fred reassuringly.

"So, what 'ave you got planned vur tomorrow lad?" asked Albert whilst Fred was busy.

"Well, Fred asked me to check out the death of Chalky White the blacksmith, and there are a few more questions I want to ask the Windsors." Replied Dave.

"What? Chalky from Penhampton? I didn't know 'ee was dead." Albert was shocked. "I've done a fair bit o' business with old Chalky. Best smith in Lyonshire."

"It was in the evening paper. He was blown up in his own forge. Some sort of accident according to the paper. Mind you, Fred thinks it was another murder."

"Never! Chalky might hit 'ee thumb with 'ees 'ammer on a bad day, but he'd never get 'eself blowed up." Exclaimed Albert.

Fred returned carrying a tray with three glasses of water resting on it. And the chef brought over three plates heaped with steak and kidney pudding, mash, and peas.

Out in the bar, Gladys continued to go through her set, using a mixture of sign language and improvised hand signals to her ex-husband so he knew what song to play next. Those patrons who had previously experienced the oral torture were drinking shorts from brass cups and had brought their own earplugs. The rest were frantically trying to stuff whatever came to hand into their ears and wondering if a very large seagull had just flown over and dropped something into their beer. At least until the glasses shattered under the onslaught and spilled the highly corrosive liquid in their laps. *[Although this would mean an alteration to the dictionary definition of liquid to include slimy lumpy bits.]*

Women put their arms through their partner's or simply held onto them for dear life frightened they might lose them to Gladys. Even single men in the bar huddled closely together, trying not to make any eye contact less Gladys should take it the wrong way. Time might have stolen what looks she may once have had, but it had done nothing to dampen Gladys's ardour.

Fred had closed the wooden shutters on the windows earlier in the evening. He had also taken the precaution of putting tape on the outside of the panes to prevent passers-by from being injured by flying glass. Fortunately the shutters had so far prevented any windows from shattering. Unfortunately, from across the square came the sound of breaking glass.

~~~~~

Over in the church, Father Turner was kneeling at one of the many altars. Contrary to several old wives tales, he had an umbrella open indoors and was holding it over his head. He was also wearing a construction industry hardhat. Fred had kindly informed him that Gladys was singing in the pub and he had taken precautions.

Above him, an aged stained glass window shook under the sonic onslaught. Dust, dead flies and other detritus drifted down on him, dislodged by the vibrations. Enough was enough and the frail glass in one of the windows gave up, shattered, and rained down like a colourful but sharp and pointed snowstorm around him.

Conscientiously he finished his devotions before getting up and shaking himself off and moving along to the next altar.

Father Turner was a meek man in every way, and lived in permanent fear of someone shouting at him - he even cringed at the thought. All he really wanted from life was his share of peace and quiet. It was for that reason he had joined the Combined Churches of Lyonshire in the first place. Few people ever turned up for his services because most of the population were descended from the Druidhs and therefore did not bother much with gods or a god but held nature itself sacred.

However, there were those who had stumbled into Lyonshire over the years and decided to stay. They were few in number and came from all sorts of different religions. So, to meet this need the Combined Churches had been founded. This meant that there was no need for separate churches, mosques, or temples to be built because everyone could worship in the same building. All be it at different times, but each service was conducted by the same person.

As well as being Father Turner, he was Prior, Monk, Lay Brother, Imam, Minister, High Priest, Benedictine, Templar, Trappist, Rabbi, Mullah, Elder, Reverend, Preacher, Revivalist, Lecturer, Spiritual Director, Talapoin, Guru and Fakir Turner. And capable of giving blessings and services in most known religions as well as in some long forgotten ones.

It was just a shame that nothing in his extensive and varied training had prepared him to be rained on by shattered stained glass windows, every time Gladys sang in the pub.

He finished his circuit of the various altars and went into the vestry to get his broom and the boards to board up the window. The temporary boards would have to do until he could get the glazier to repair it. Something the Archbishop, Lama, Archimandrite etc. etc. would take a very dim view of. And he would probably shout as well.

Farther Turner cringed and brushed dust from his robes. They were somewhat unique as robes go, incorporating something from each and every religion and favouring none.

Then there was the matter of the Holy Texts as well. Combining all religions was all very well, but when you put all their religious writings into one volume you needed a forklift truck to move it around. Farther Turner's copy occupied one of the transepts. He had it padlocked to the floor. He tended to conduct services from memory, it made things easier and meant he had been able to sell the forklift, which he couldn't drive anyway.

~~~~~

"Fred, do you mind if I ask you a question?" Asked Dave, as he pushed his empty plate away.

"Course not lad."

"Why do you allow Gladys to sing in your pub? She's terrible and she must frighten off more customers than she attracts."

"Ah. That's a good question." Replied Fred as he set down his glass of water.

"I've always wondered that meself." Put in Albert. "I've just never thought to ask."

Even in the relative safety of the kitchen, Gladys's singing was painful to the ear, and blankets had been hung over the door to the larder to try and protect the food within.

"'Er voice might not be up to much now, but forty years ago she 'ad a wonderful singin' voice." Explained Fred.

"So why don't she sing forty years ago then?" said Albert tersely.

"Now Bert, don't be unkind. As I was sayin' she used to be a terrific singer, an' was as close as it's possible t' get to a popstar in Lyonshire. She had several hit records an' all. She earned her livin' by singin'. People would exchange all sorts o' stuff just t' hear 'er sing. An' I was one o' those lucky enough t' 'ave 'eard her at 'er best." Fred sighed and shook his head.

"Unfortunately, as she got older, 'er voice went and nobody wanted t' 'ear 'er anymore so she started marryin' any bloke that would 'ave 'er an' look a'ter 'er. Course, most of 'em treated 'er like dirt and it would end in a divorce, an' that would leave 'er with no means o' support again."

"I never knew Fred, honestly I didn't know she'd 'ad it so bad." Said Albert remorsefully.

"How could you've known Bert?" said Fred sympathetically. "Anyroad, by the time I heard about it, I was landlord yere. So it seemed only right that I should let 'er sing yere an' get back some of 'er self-respect. I know 'er voice is terrible, but she does 'er best. Besides, most o' my regulars 'as got used to it an brings their own earplugs."

Chapter 6.

The sun crept up over the horizon and announced the dawning of a new day. At least for about five minutes before the gathering storm clouds blotted it out.

In the Stoat and Ferret, Dave was already awake and not in the best of moods. Fred had given him another cheerful early morning call and a cup of his special coffee.

As far as Dave was concerned, early mornings were something that happened to other people. He was far from lazy, but couldn't understand what all the fuss was about. What was the point in getting up early to do something, when you could get up later after a pleasant lie-in and still do the same thing? If he was supposed to get up early then surely his body clock would wake him up early, and he would feel refreshed and alert, and not like someone had just let all the air out of his tyres.

Grumbling to himself, he began to fill the sink with water.

Once his ablutions were completed, he went down into the kitchen for breakfast, which he ate in silence.

"What's the matter lad?" Fred enquired politely. "Cat got yur tongue?"

"Ruddy cat's probably still stretched out fast asleep by the fire." Muttered Dave under his breath.

"What's that?" asked Fred.

"I said I'm tired Fred. Five o'clock in the morning is not a good time for me."

"Oh. I see. Well I didn't want you t' miss anything. You goin' to Penhampton s'morning?"

"Yes." Snapped Dave, more aggressively than he had meant to. "Sorry." He said apologetically. "I thought I'd check out Chalky's forge as you suggested last night. See if anyone missed anything."

"I would've come with e' lad but I've got to clear up the mess from last night, an' get the bar ready vur the guild meeting t' night."

"Guild meeting?" asked Dave incredulously.

"Didn't I warn you?" Asked Fred innocently. "It's The Guild of Seers and Allied Fortune Tellers AGM tonight. They cause more trouble than Gladys does with 'er singin' but they's always very generous an' draws in a good crowd."

"Seers and Allied Fortune Tellers?" muttered Dave under his breath. "I must be stark raving mad to have got involved in all this."

"What was that?" Asked Fred.

"Nothing." Replied Dave. "Do you have something on every night in the bar?"

"No. I let Gladys do her spot once a month or so, an' there's normally zummet on most weeks, but this is an annual event."

By the time Dave was ready to leave, it was raining cats and dogs, or at least it was raining very hard, as opposed to family pets falling out of the sky. Although, as Fred had informed him, in Lyonshire this had been known to happen, along with frogs, nuts, fish, and on one unusual but interesting occasion, winning lottery tickets. *[This mysterious event only came to light because of the court hearing when the lottery organisers went into liquidation.]*

Dave donned his waterproofs, cursed the rain, and rode off towards Penhampton. He was not a fair weather biker, and never had been. It was more often than not the case that he rode to and from work in the rain. He was also well aware that rain made the road far more slippery, especially the carefully placed manhole covers, the lines of tar around old roadworks, and markings painted onto the road. Unfortunately, this knowledge was of no use to him at all when a sheep jumped into the road directly in front of him. After swerving and braking to avoid the animal, Dave found himself sprawled in the ditch.

He picked himself up and started to brush himself off, when a white-hot pain shot up his arm. On closer inspection, he noticed it was pointing in an unusual direction, and one that required an anatomical rethink. The uninjured sheep had bleated a few times and then jumped back over the hedge into its field.

Dave walked over to where his bike had come to rest. With some difficulty, he managed, single-handed, to get it upright and on its side-stand. Most of the damage to it was superficial, mainly scratches and a few minor dents in the paintwork and chrome. However, lying on its side the engine had flooded and it took some persuading to get it started. Eventually it spluttered into life.

He considered his position. He was standing by the side of the road with his arm pointing at an unusual angle. He was not too far from Penhampton and there was bound to be a doctor there. He could stay where he was and wait for help, but as always the roads in Lyonshire were quiet so that could mean waiting for quite some time. Travelling back to Shoton would mean a much longer ride, and he doubted the village had a doctor's surgery. Tentatively, he got back on his bike and, after a few false starts, managed to knock it into gear and pull away without the benefit of a clutch and rode slowly on towards Penhampton.

After stopping briefly for directions, Dave found his way to Leech Street in Penhampton, where medicines of all kinds were practiced and inflicted. He passed herbalists who were happily smoking their own preparations, aromatherapists busy rubbing essential oils on everything, dentists preoccupied with devising new and interesting forms of torture, and confused looking hypnotherapists.

Eventually, Dave opted to go into a building that proclaimed itself to be a chiropractor's. At least he knew what a chiropractor did or was supposed to do, and having his joints manipulated was likely to be able to sort out his shoulder. Inside the front door was an informal waiting room, which looked more like someone's living room. There was a sofa and several armchairs, a coffee table strewn with various magazines and other publications, and a sideboard on which sat a kettle and other necessities for making tea and coffee.

After a few minutes a tall skinny man with red hair, who appeared to be all shoulder blades, knees, and elbows, came through from the back and led him into the examination room. Dave took off his leather jacket and stripped to the waist, something that proved quite difficult and painful to do with his injured arm.

"Please sit up on the table." Urged the chiropractor. "Please call me Ginger, by the way. Everybody does. Now let's have a look."

"Ah yes, you've dislocated your shoulder." Said Ginger, confirming Dave's suspicions.

"Don't worry, it is easy enough to pop back in." Continued the chiropractor reassuringly. "Brace yourself as best you can with your other arm. This won't hurt a bit"

Dave sat on the edge of the couch and held on tightly with his good arm. Without any further warning, Ginger yanked his shoulder back into place.

"ARRRGH!" screamed Dave, and extracted his fingers out of the padding of the couch. He looked at the chiropractor accusingly.

"I thought you said it wouldn't hurt?" He said indignantly.

Ginger smiled and shrugged his shoulders. "Sorry." He replied.

"Well, thank you anyway. It feels a lot better." Said Dave as he swung his arm around experimentally. It still hurt, but not half as much, and at least it was pointing in the right direction now.

"It will take a few weeks for the soreness to go and you will need to be careful." Piped the chiropractor in a high-pitched staccato voice. "Once a joint has been dislocated, it will easily pop out again, so you need to rest it as much as possible."

"$%@#!!!!!" Cursed Dave, as he began to ease his shirt back on. "A few weeks? I've got too much to do to rest it for a few weeks!"

"Well," continued Ginger, shuffling his feet uneasily. "It is possible to speed things up a bit, although it is somewhat unorthodox."

"How?" Asked Dave anxiously. The idea of being incapacitated for the remainder of his stay in Lyonshire was not appealing. He could just imagine Fred fussing around him like an old mother hen.

"Can we settle the matter of my fee first?"

"I haven't got very much money, but..." Began Dave.

"No. No, that won't do at all, I don't accept money." Interrupted the chiropractor.

"Err." Began Dave. He had little money and nothing of his own of value to trade with. "Um, how about a small barrel of beer?" he asked. He wasn't proud of himself for offering up someone else's property, but what else could he do? Fred would just have to add it to his list of expenses.

"I haven't got one with me of course." He continued. But I could promise a small barrel of SOD from the Stoat and Ferret in Shoton."

"A barrel of SOD! Really?" exclaimed the chiropractor, his already high-pitched voice rising several octaves with his excitement. "A barrel of SOD will do nicely."

"Now, how do I speed things up a bit?" Said Dave firmly.

"Oh that." continued Ginger dismissively. "Well it's quite simple really. When you leave the shop, carry on down Leech Street, take the first right then right again into Apothecary Street, and then turn right again back to here. By the time you get back the pain should have gone and your shoulder will be good as new." Replied Ginger with a smile.

"That's it?" Of all the things he had heard so far, this was by far the most baffling and hardest to comprehend. "I just walk around the block? Is that all? How, on earth, is that going to help?"

Ginger just tapped the side of his long nose with a long slender finger.

"You know, I'm getting tired of people in Lyonshire tapping their noses at me!" Snapped Dave.

"There's a continuum convergence around the corner." Replied Ginger with a shrug, as if this explained everything.

But one look at Dave's annoyed and puzzled looking face and he decided that more was called for.

"Time sort of leaks." He ventured.

Dave shook his head in disbelief. "Well, I'll give it a try." And headed for the door.

"Just be careful to go around the block turning right!" Called Ginger as Dave began walking up the street. "Oh dear! I wonder if I should have warned him about the side effects."

Dave left his bike where it was and strolled down the street. He was still not sure what it was meant to accomplish, but after spending a few days in Lyonshire, he had learned to accept people at their word. Not that he usually had any choice. He noticed a warning sign by the side of the road and read it.

Danger!
Continuum Convergence! Unstable Time!

"Aaah!" screamed Ginger, when Dave poked his head around the door to the waiting room twenty minutes later. "Are you feeling better now?" he asked once he had regained his composure.

Dave was not amused. His two-day stubble was now a beard that reached halfway down to his knees and he could use his hair to sweep the floor. Without having to bend down.

On the positive side, his shoulder no longer hurt. But he was still undecided whether it had been worth it. He shot Ginger a resentful look, stormed out, and went in search of a barbers.

Back at the Stoat and Ferret, Fred was moving the furniture around in the bar and sweeping up the last of the glass broken by Gladys's singing. Half the barroom he left as it was, the other half he roped off and rearranged the tables and chairs to form a rough circle. It was for the meeting that evening, but various members of the Guild of Seers and Allied Fortune Tellers were apt to turn up early. Provided that they remembered that there was a meeting at all.

Fred could remember one occasion when all the members had tried to outdo each other by turning up earlier than anyone else. The contest had come to a head when one of them had arrived three weeks early, only to be disappointed and find four of the others had been camping out in the yard behind the pub since the previous year's meeting. Therefore, it had come as no surprise to Fred to see Merlin fast asleep in the bar the day before the meeting.

Hosting the Guild meetings always caused Fred a few problems and more damage than Gladys's singing, but it was usually worth it for the extra trade it generated. The Guild themselves were always generous, and they always drew in a crowd of onlookers from miles around, who would sit and watch the meetings in case anything interesting happened. They were rarely disappointed.

Fred reached into the secret pocket on his ceremonial brewer's waistcoat and pulled out a small brass key. He tapped an otherwise unremarkable part of the bar, which swung open to reveal a keyhole. A quick twist of the key in the lock opened the hidden cupboard.

Inside were the trappings and finery of the Guild. After a quick inspection to check everything was in order and nothing was missing, Fred closed the cupboard, locked it, replaced the secret panel, and put the key back in his pocket.

Satisfied that all was in readiness for the meeting, Fred helped himself to a coffee, unlocked the front door, and strolled back behind the counter to await the first of the day's customers. He didn't have long to wait.

Dave emerged from the barbers' shop carrying three pounds of carrots and a live chicken in a small cage. He was not altogether sure why.

When he had entered the barbers' shop, the barber had squealed with delight, turfed the customer he had been in the process of shaving and still half covered in shaving foam out of the chair and ushered Dave into it.

As Dave sat and looked into the mirror in front of him, he could see that there was a queue of other customers who were waiting for a shave or a haircut beside the chair's former occupant. The barber totally ignored all of them and their cries of protest, and devoted his full attention to Dave.

Almost hysterical with glee, the barber administered a few quick snips and Dave's hair had returned to its normal shoulder length. Five minutes more and his beard had been neatly trimmed as well.

Most of this, apart from the barber's eagerness and disregard for his other customers, Dave could understand. After that it got a great deal more confusing.

The barber had carefully gathered up Dave's amputated locks and carried them with some reverence through to the back of his shop. He had then returned carrying the bag of carrots and the chicken, which he had presented to Dave.

"Your change Sir." The barber said gleefully.

"But I haven't..." Began Dave, but the barber ushered him out of the door and turned his attention back to finish shaving the unfortunate man who had been extricated from the chair when Dave had entered.

So Dave now found himself wandering around the streets of Penhampton in the rain, carrying a caged chicken and a large bag of carrots. However, since this was the first opportunity he'd had to wander around Penhampton, he wasn't going to let a little weirdness, a bag of carrots, or a caged chicken spoil the occasion. Besides, the last time he had been here, he'd been even more dazed and confused after the high-speed nightmare ride when Fred had fiddled with his bike's engine.

Dave took his time and wandered around, soaking up the ambience of Penhampton, and quite a bit of rain as well. His boots were soaking up something else. It was market day and herds of nervous animals had been led through the streets, leaving an extensive trail of organic landmines behind to mark their passing.

Eventually Dave found himself in Tailors' Mile. It was a street of tailors, it wasn't however, a mile long. He remembered his conversation with Aunt Aggie, and his need for a shirt. He bit his bottom lip. He was sure that Fred would not be very happy with him bartering way another barrel of SOD, but he picked a likely looking tailors shop and went in.

He was immediately set upon by a short but stocky middle-aged man with a hooked nose and a tape measure.

"Waat is it you are affter? Jackets? We've got jackets. Trousers? We've got trousers. A dhree piece suit perhaps? Yes?" said the man hopefully. He had a strong accent Dave couldn't quite put his finger on.

"Actually, all I am after is a shirt." Replied Dave.

"A shirt? Is dhat all? Oh well, a shirt is still a shirt. At least your nod just browsing." Said the tailor in a tone of resignation. "Now hold still while I measure you for dha size. I'm Ezra Tailor by dha way." He continued and brandished his tape measure.

Dave removed his leather jacket. It was dripping wet, but the moisture had not soaked through the leather. Once a month he dubbined his jacket to keep the leather supple and to stop rain from soaking through. *[Dubbin is a mixture of natural oils and wax that has been used since medieval times to soften and waterproof leather]* He hung it on a hook behind the door and let it drip.

Ezra measured, pulled a pencil out from behind an ear, and made a note on a scrap of paper. He took another measurement and wrote that down as well. After what seemed like endless another's, he looked at Dave and sucked the end of his pencil.

"It will be reaady in dhree days. I dake id you want white?" he said eventually.

"White would be fine, but I'm only in Penhampton for the morning. I don't suppose you could..."

"Dhe morning?" exclaimed Ezra and cutting him short. "I'm supposed to create a shirt in a morning?"

"Well," Dave began. "I could..."

"It will be reaady at dwo of the clock." Said Ezra flatly, waving his arms in the air. "Now to business. How are you going to paay?"

"I could give you a chicken?" suggested Dave hopefully and held up the stricken bird.

"You whant dhat I work for chicken feed too?" said Ezra sarcastically. "Tell you what, you give me dhe carrots as well and you've got a deal." He said, shaking his head sadly. "Now go! Leave me to create dhe masterpiece!"

Dave donned his jacket and headed for the door, leaving the chicken and carrots behind as payment.

After making a few enquiries, Dave found his way to Smith Road and eventually to the corner where Chalky's smithy had been.

The top storey had collapsed in on the yard next to the forge. Three of the walls to the forge itself were still partially standing. The fourth was missing. The whole area had been cordoned off but there was no sign of a police presence. They had already ambled off elsewhere. *[He was back at the station cutting his toenails.]*

Dave stepped over the barrier and entered the remains of the smithy. He began to sift through the debris, unsure what to look for and whether he would find anything in an area that had presumably been thoroughly searched already. He could see the hearth and make out where the piles of charcoal and coal had been. Various tools and pieces of iron were strewn everywhere.

A bright orange flash of fresh rust caught his eye. He picked it up. It was a small piece of very thin and jagged metal. He brushed at the rust with his fingertips. It came off easily. It was fresh and only superficial. As he studied it he noticed that whatever it had been part of had been painted black. He could see where the scorched paint was peeling. As he held it up for a closer inspection, he caught a faint whiff of fireworks. Carefully, he put it into his pocket and continued his search.

~~~~

After picking up his new shirt, and carefully stowing it in the panniers on his bike, Dave rode back towards Shoton. He stopped outside the Stoat and Ferret, leaving his bike in the road. He would need it later to go to Lord Woods' estate. He had a few things that were puzzling him and he hoped Shem and Elsie could help him with some of the answers.

Inside he found Fred taking his turn to serve behind the bar. Generally this consisted of drinking and chatting with his patrons, but Fred enjoyed it and it passed the time between meals, and gave him something to do when he was not actually brewing or at work out in the malting shed.

But as Dave approached he could see that Fred looked far from his normal cheery self. His face was missing its rosy smile, despite the fact that several members, of what could only be, the Guild of Seers and Allied Fortune Tellers had turned up and were waiting for their meeting to begin. There was already a large crowd of onlookers. In particular, the representatives from the Temple of Vesta were attracting quite a bit of attention.

"Can you stick this behind the bar for me Fred?" Dave asked, handing over the package that contained his new shirt.

"'Ow did it go then? Fred asked. "Find out ort at Chalky's?"

"Well there's not much left of the smithy. And most of that's spread over the street. It certainly looks like an explosion of some kind."

Fred nodded. "It said as much in the paper. D'you find ort that might o' been overlooked?" he continued, his tone a bit sharp.

"Alright Fred. I'm doing my best." Said Dave reproachfully.

"Sorry lad. I've 'ad a bit of a bad mornin'. Nothing personal."

"Oh?" Enquired Dave. "What's the matter? What's happened?"

Fred bowed his head slightly and shook it dejectedly.

"Tiz bad. Terrible bad." Said Fred, shaking his head again and idly tracing his finger around a knothole in the bar.

"Well?"

"I was checkin' the last brew out in the shed. Seein' how it was doin' an' checking the sugar content an' so on. But I couldn't. On account of it bein' curdled. The whole five-hundred gallons."*[A week's supply for Albert.]*

"What caused that?"

"T'were Gladys's singin'. I covered all the barrels in the cellar with zummet t' deaden the sound but I didn't bother with the vats out in the brewery. I thought they'd be safe. And they was. 'Cept for that one. The newest. I only started it last week an' now I'm goin' to 'ave to clear up the mess an' brew two batches this week. I s'ppose it was just at that fragile stage and her singin', no matter how muffled, was enough to turn it." Finished Fred with a sigh.

"I'm sorry to 'ear that Fred." Said Albert. He had entered the pub and come to stand by Dave while Fred was talking.

"Oh, 'allo Bert." Said Fred.

Dave gave Albert a polite nod of recognition.

"You're slipping Fred. I've been stood at the bar for more 'an a minute and still 'aven't got a glass in me 'and." Said Albert with a smile.

"Sorry Bert." Said Fred, reaching for a glass. "The lad yere has just got back from takin' a look at Chalky's place and was tellin' me what 'ee found."

Dave helped himself to a coffee from the pot on the bar and took a sip.

"Sorry to 'ear about the beer Fred." Put in Albert. "Is there ort you can do? You know, a touch of brewer's magic?"

"No." Fred replied. "Tiz too far gone vur me to twiddle me fingers."

Albert looked across to Dave. "Looks like you've 'ad a bit of bad luck too. Judgin' by the state o' yur bike."

"Ah." Said Dave sheepishly. "I was going to mention that. A sheep jumping out in front of me on my way to Penhampton, and I ended up in a ditch."

"Were 'ee alright?"

Dave looked rather awkward. "Err, actually I dislocated my shoulder and had to see a chiropractor. I'm afraid I promised him a small barrel of SOD for his services. He wouldn't take money, and I didn't have anything to trade."

"That's alright lad. Don't you go worryin' about it." Replied Fred, much to Dave's relief. "Which one were it?"

"Ginger something. In Leech Street."

"I've got t' go an' pay some bills in Penhampton in the next day or two, I'll drop one in t' 'im." Smiled Fred weakly.

"Now lad. What did 'ee find in Penhampton then?" Asked Albert.

"I was just telling Fred that there is not much left of the smithy."

Albert nodded.

"But he wasn't connected to mains gas and his oxyacetylene bottles were still intact in the corner." Recounted Dave.

"Ah!" smiled Albert. "So it weren't no gas explosion then." He said, slapping the bar. "Just as we suspected, foul play."

"And," continued Dave. "I found this."

He pulled out the piece of metal he'd picked up and put it on the bar. All three of them stared at it in silence for a time; occasionally one of them would prod it or turn it over.

"I give up lad. What is it?" Asked Fred.

"Probably just a bit o' scrap Chalky 'ad lying around the floor." Said Albert, in a deflated tone.

"That's what I thought at first." Replied Dave. "But then it occurred to me, Chalky was a blacksmith." He looked up at the other two hopefully.

They both gave him a blank look.

Dave sighed. "Blacksmiths don't normally work with thin sheet metal. And never anything as thin as this. So what was it doing there?" He explained patiently.

"So?" said the other two in unison.

"Look at it closely. It looks like a piece of a tin can. And smell it. Go on, smell it." Said Dave. This was going to be harder than he thought.

They leant over and smelt it.

"Fireworks!" said Fred.

"That's right." Said Albert. "It smells o' fireworks."

"Yes!" Said Dave thankfully. "I think it could have been part of a bomb that blew up Chalky's forge. Unfortunately, I have no way of proving it."

Fred grinned and winked conspiratorially at Albert.

"You might not lad, but Albert yere does. Go on Bert, it's your turn to twiddle yur fingers."

"How can you know what it was? Even if it was a bomb?" Dave asked.

"Well," said Albert, with a sly grin. "You might not know what it was, an' me an' Fred might not know what it was, but it knows what it was. Sort of retained memory."

It was Dave's turn to look perplexed.

"Just sit back an' watch lad. Just watch." Reassured Fred.

―――

Out in the kitchen, Halitosis the chef was busy preparing a buffet ready for the guild meeting. *[Halitosis might not be most people's idea of a good name for a boy, but compared to his sister, Chlamydia, he counted himself lucky.]* Although buffet was perhaps an understatement and not the best way to describe piles of doorstep sandwiches, half-ton porkpies, and pig's trotters, several whole cheeses, a couple of sides of ham, and a dozen fresh pineapples.

Behind him the food for the evening bar menu was quietly cooking away on the stove.

Hal, as his friends called him, enjoyed his work immensely;

confident in the knowledge that whatever he cooked it would all be eaten by the end of the day. Sweating away in a hot kitchen had its drawbacks, but generally the work was not over taxing. This was because he followed three simple rules:

One: If it looks like a picture on a plate and the sauce has swirly patterns, then the tablecloth probably tastes better.

Two: No short order cooking. You ate what he had prepared or you went hungry.

And three: Always get someone else to do the washing up.

Hal couldn't be doing with all that fancy cooking and messing about with food. To him a meal consisted of a large plate full of something tasty but substantial. Generally he cooked whatever he had to hand. And he always had plenty to hand.

As with Fred's beer, no one ever paid for Hal's cooking, they bartered or exchanged for it. From the time he came to work in the morning, people would bring him the raw ingredients. Half a pig here, a side of bacon there, a sack of onions, a whole ox, three hundred weight of potatoes and so on. And for those who couldn't or didn't have anything to exchange, there was always the washing up. And it was amazing just how much washing up people were prepared to do for one of his meals.

No one ever went hungry in the Stoat and Ferret. If the hot food was exhausted, then there was always plenty of cold meat, smoked fish, pickles, preserves, salad, and enough cheese in various stages of decay to feed an army.

~~~~~

All the attention in the bar was focused on the fortune tellers. Although it was still several hours before the meeting was due to start, and half of those due to attend had yet to arrive, those that had arrived were already engaged in a fierce argument. So apart from the occasional trip to the bar to refill their glasses, none of the guild members or Fred's patrons were paying any attention to Fred, Dave, and Albert.

"Go on Bert. There's no one lookin'." Said Fred encouragingly.

Albert looked at the object on the bar and concentrated. He closed his eyes and began to mumble under his breath.

A faint glow spread out over the twisted metal as power grew around it. It began to twitch. Creases straightened, it began to stretch and grow, and the rust disappeared and was replaced with black paint. After a few minutes it was no longer a piece of scrap but something whole. Complete with a hissing fuse.

"So it was a bomb!" exclaimed Dave. "It's crude, but it proves that Chalky was murdered."

"Wait a mo Bert. Can you take it back a bit further?" asked Fred. "To before it were a bomb?"

Albert redoubled his exertion and muttered something more.

Gradually the bomb faded and was replaced by a tin can and a handful of shotgun cartridges.

With an audible pop they disappeared as Albert stopped concentrating, leaving the rusty twisted metal that Dave had found on the bar.

Albert let out a sigh and sagged a little. Fred handed him a fresh pint.

"Takes it out of 'ee it does. 'S like riding a bike though," said Albert reflectively, "you never forgets how."

"Well done Bert! An' well done t' you too lad vur findin' it." Said Fred, as he gave Dave a hearty slap on the back. "You'm smarter than 'ee looks."

"Well thank you very much!" Replied Dave indignantly.

"No! I means you looks smart enough, but it were a stroke o' genius spotting that bit o' tin in amongst all that rubble." Said Fred. "I'd never 'ave thought there were ort strange about a scrap like that bein' in a forge. I like the beard by the way."

On the far side of the bar a fight had broken out. Something even Fred could have foreseen happening as some of the fortune tellers fell out about something.

Dave excused himself by saying he still had things to do before tea and rode off towards Timbers' estate.

At the gatehouse there was no sign of the gatekeeper. There was just a note pinned to the door of the lodge that read "Gone Out". Well that much was obvious. Fortunately the main gates were not locked and Dave was able to let himself through.

Shem greeted him warmly at the backdoor. He was still wearing his butler's uniform, but the tie was missing and his top button was undone, so he was off duty. He might own the house now, but some habits were hard to break. He ushered Dave through into the butler's pantry, thrust him into one of the overstuffed armchairs and called to his wife.

Elsie was no less pleased to see Dave. She insisted that he rest himself and eat at least two slices of her rich fruitcake before he moved and drink several mugs of freshly brewed tea. *[This was a cake made to a traditional family recipe; the type handed down from mother to daughter for generations. As well as fruit, flour, fat, and eggs it contained, as such recipes often do, half a pint of cream and most of a bottle of brandy. It is still possible to find such recipes in very old cook books but it is getting harder to find them because dieticians and doctors regularly buy up such books and burn them to prevent such recipes falling in to the hands of the general public.]* Both of them commented on his new beard and said how well it suited him.

"Thank you, and thank you for the cake." Said Dave as he popped the last morsel of cake into his mouth. "That was delicious."

"Would you like some more? There's plenty left and it don't take hardly no time t' make, and only a couple o' hours to bake." Said Elsie happily, offering him another slice.

"There's more tea in the pot too." Put in Shem.

"No. No thank you. I couldn't eat another bite. I'm afraid that I'm not just here for a social call either. There are a few things I need to ask and I'd like to have a more thorough look around the sheds, if you don't mind."

Both Shem and Elsie's expressions hardened slightly.

Dave got up out of his chair too quickly and upset his empty mug. It smashed on the flagstone floor.

"I'm terribly sorry." He apologised.

The change in Shem and Elsie reversed.

"Don't you worry about it lad." Shem said reassuringly.

"No harm done." Said Elsie, dropping back into the role of the happy hostess. "Don't you go touching it, you might cut yerself." She bustled around and swept up the pieces.

"Why don't I show 'ee round the sheds whilst Elsie tidies up?" said Shem.

He led Dave out and around the various sheds, garages, coach-houses, stables, and outhouses. By the time they reached the last and most distant shed, the gathering gloom of evening was descending upon them.

It was at the furthest end of the walled vegetable garden, not very large and appeared to have been disused for some time. Unique species of spiders had probably evolved and colonised its interior since the last time the door had been opened. It took the combined might of Shem and Dave with their shoulders to the door to gain entry as the door fought all attempts to budge it. Eventually they got through.

Inside were the skeletal remains of long forgotten gardening implements. It was the domain of gardeners past. Unused and forlorn, it had been left to fall apart quietly by itself.

"Well, this is the last one. Come on, let's go an' see Ells and get a cuppa." Said Shem.

"We may as well." Sighed Dave. "I could do with a drink to clear the dust from my throat." He turned to leave.

"Wait! What's that?" He asked as something caught his eye.

"It's an old canning machine. It's vur doin' yur own tins o' stuff. It's been unused vur years. Look at the dust on it." Replied Shem.

"And there. On the bench?" Dave pointed with his finger. "Empty shotgun shell yes?"

"That's right lad. Years old too by the look o' them."

Dave took a closer look around the shed. Besides the canning machine and the empty cartridges there were a few unused tin cans and their lids on a shelf waiting to be crimped on.

"You're right." He said casually at last. "I don't think anybody has used this for years."

They walked back towards the house across the gardens in silence. Dave was lost deep in thought. It was too much of a coincidence that there was a canning machine and empty, not used, shotgun cartridges in the same shed. He was sure that whoever had made the bomb that killed Chalky, had made it in that shed, but it must have been made years ago.

"Shem, I don't suppose that there is one of the crossing points in the grounds, is there?" He asked.

"Crossing points?" Said Shem, looking puzzled. "I don't rightly know what you mean."

"Sorry. I don't know what it is that you call them. I mean the places where you cross in and out of Lyonshire. I know there's one up on the road, I've used it myself, and I was wondering if there was a closer one?"

Shem looked surprised. "As a matter o' fact there is. It's in the old orchard. We passed it earlier. It's that bit that's fenced off for safety."

"Humm. I thought there might be one somewhere." Mused Dave.

"How did you know that?" Asked Shem, a hard edge creeping into his voice.

"I didn't." Replied Dave honestly. "I had a hunch, that was all, and wanted to know if I was right."

Dave wished he knew more about these crossover points. It was something he was going to have to ask Fred about, especially now that it appeared someone was using them to murder people. And from Shem's tone, it was plain that he was not keen on talking about someone using part of, what was now, his estate for such malevolent purposes.

When they joined Elsie inside once more, Dave kept his thoughts to himself. He stayed long enough for just one more cup of tea and yet another slice of cake, before making his goodbyes and heading back to the Stoat and Ferret.

~~~~~

Most of the Guild of Seers and Allied Fortune Tellers stopped what they were doing when Hal placed the huge platters, piled high with food, onto their table. The earlier fighting had died down, although several of the guild supported black eyes and other injuries.

After a while Dave had managed to rouse himself from his gloomy thoughts and set them aside for the evening. With so many people around he had been unable to talk to Fred privately. It was something he would have to keep in mind for tomorrow. In the meantime he was doing his best to make some sort of sense of the guild. Fred had already introduced him to several of the fortune tellers as and when they came up to the bar for liquid refreshments.

"See that one sat next t' the High Priestess of Metis?" Said Fred. "That's Nostradamus, that is."

"What? The one that wrote the book of predictions?" Dave asked.

"That's 'im. 'Ee's a nice enough bloke. I think 'ee 'as got as far as the First World War at the moment. 'Ee says the research is easy, the hard part is the time it takes 'im t' make it all cryptic an' mysterious."

"Why doesn't he just write it as it was or will be?"

"Well lad. If 'ee wrote things as they are, 'ee'd be burned at the stake by the church in his own time. If 'ee writes it all cryptic, then 'ee can get away with it 'cause it either looks like the ravings o' a madman, or like a vision. Very big on visions is the church in his time." Replied Fred.

"But I thought he predicted the end of the world in two thousand and one?" said Dave. "It didn't happen and you've been a lot further into the future than that."

"That's right lad. But that's where it all starts. Events in that year laid the groundwork for the eventual downfall o' all religions an' politicians. So in a way it is the end o' one world and the start o' a new 'un." Answered Fred with a smile.

"And who is that sat next to him on the other side?"

"That's a bloke called Robertson. He stumbled into Lyonshire by accident, same as you. 'Ee found out about the Titanic sinkin' and when 'ee went 'ome no one would listen. So 'ee changed the name of the ship and wrote a book about it years before the Titanic sailed." Said Fred knowingly. *[In 1898 U.S. author Morgan Robertson book, Futility, described the sinking of a ship almost identical to that of the Titanic.]*

"By the way, the chef is goin' to dish somethin' vur us t' eat soon so I would grab us one of them empty tables."

Despite the vast number of people that had popped into the pub to watch the meeting, there were still a few empty tables on the other side of the room because they offered no vantage point to watch the shenanigans.

Albert emerged from recycling several pints and came to sit next to Dave.

"I never see what all the fuss is about." He moaned as he sat down. "Bunch o' loonies that lot. I don't see no point in standin' around watchin'. 'Alf o' them don't even speak English." He said as if this was some sort of crime.

Dave nodded and shrugged in a non-committal way. Behind him the door opened and closed as a weaselly man in a brown toga and wooden sandals came in.

"There's another o' the nuts now." Said Albert moodily.

"Now then Bert. They've got a livin' t'make, same as the rest o' us." Said Fred as he came up behind them carrying a couple of groaning plates.

"Well," went on Albert defensively, "you knows what they're like. They comes in yere, 'as a scrap, breaks a few tables an' chairs, an' then clears off vur another year."

Shouting had broken out amongst the fortune tellers on the other side of the room. Snatches of conversation were audible above the general din.

"You take that back this minute! You hussy!"
"I never said no such thing! What I said was..."
"We know what you said..."
"Look! You four eyed pheasant plucker! I said..."

A minor scuffle broke out. Clubs and cudgels appeared from beneath ceremonial robes and accidentally made contact with several skulls. After a general state of concussion had been achieved, things quietened down again.

Albert and Dave turned back to their meals. Fred came back from the kitchen, carrying his own plate and sat down with them.

"You know the last one that came in?" he asked conversationally. "The one in the brown robes an' sandals? D' you know who 'ee is?"

"No Fred. I can honestly say I 'aven't got a clue." Replied

Albert. "An' I don't give a stuff neither."

"Who is he Fred? Anyone important?" asked Dave.

You could say that." Replied Fred. "It depends on how religious you are really."

"Who is he then?" Said Dave, who was beginning to get a little impatient.

"That's John the Apostle that is. Wrote the book o' revelations. 'Ee got a bit carried away with the seven 'eaded monster an' general embellishment an' such. Won a prize vur the most cryptic foretelling though. Fair put Nostradamus's nose out o' joint it did." Replied Fred in a matter of fact tone.

"What? *The* John the Apostle?" Asked Dave, feeling, not for the first time since coming to Lyonshire, slightly bewildered.

"I should concentrate on yur food lad, an' eat up." Said Albert gloomily. "You never knows 'ow long their ceasefire's goin' t' last."

"I don't agree with your fussin' Bert, but it's probably best if we eats up before they gets a bit raucous." Commented Fred.

"What do you mean, get?" Asked Dave will alarm, and concentrated on clearing his plate.

Chapter 7.

Chaos had broken out once more in the bar. A minor argument had progressed, or degenerated, into a scuffle and then an outright free for all. Bits of broken crockery and furniture were flying around the room. The crowd of attentive drinkers were lauding first one side and then the other. Bets were placed and then doubled or trebled depending on who seemed to have the upper hand. Three members of the crowd had already been laid out by accident, mistaken for guild members.

Albert ducked out of the way of a flying glass.

"I've just about 'ad enough o' this Fred." He said, waving his hand around to encompass the melee.

"You knows you could be right Bert. I've got a couple bottles o' me special ginger beer in a bucket of ice down in the cellar, if 'ee'd fancy one." Replied Fred.

"I thought SOD was your special?" Dave began.

He was interrupted by a popping noise loud enough to be heard above the ruckus in the bar. A large cloud of smoke obscured most of the far end of the room, temporarily halting the melee until it cleared.

A shabby and dishevelled figure in robes stood in the centre of the expanding cloud of smoke.

"I was wonderin' when 'ee was goin' t' turn up." Said Fred.

"Who's he then?" asked Dave. "He looks like that bloke who was asleep in the bar the other morning."

"Ee's the worst o' the lot!" said Albert moodily.

"Now, now Bert." Said Fred soothingly. "That's Merlin that is. 'Ee's the most powerful wizard the world has ever known."

"Ee's the most powerful pain in the rear end, that's what 'ee is." Continued Albert, refusing to be soothed.

"He's *The* Merlin?" Asked Dave in disbelief and experiencing momentary deja view. Why was it that every time he thought he had come to terms with whatever eccentricity Lyonshire could throw up, something twice as improbable happened. "The court of King Arthur, the Holy Grail and all that stuff? That Merlin?"

"That's right lad." Replied Fred.

"Bit o' a disappointment isn't it?" laughed Albert.

"You don't really expect me to believe that he's that Merlin do you?" Asked Dave.

"It's up t' you whether you believe it or not lad." Said Fred with a chuckle. "But that's Merlin right enough."

Dave shuffled his chair around for a better look. The purported Merlin did not look happy. Another fight had broken out amongst the rest of the guild members.

"Look! You four eyed, toga wearing..."

"You know what this four eyed toga wearer thinks of you!"

"That's right! Go on! Resort to violence again!"

"Right! You asked for it! I'm going to..."

Wallop.

"You hit me! I'm wearing glasses and you hit me! You..."

Merlin made his way through the crowd of regulars towards the rest of the guild. He was honorary president of the Guild and had been for some years, and it was only now beginning to dawn on him exactly why no one else had wanted the job.

He put his hand into one of the pockets of his ceremonial robe and pulled out a key. He then tapped a seemingly unremarkable part of the bar, which opened to reveal a secret compartment, which he unlocked. He reached in and took out the Guild's ceremonial gavel. It looked to Dave like one of the tiny metal hammers that comes free with large slabs of toffee to break it up.

The effect on those people close enough to see what Merlin was doing in the bar was instantaneous. Both guild members and pub patrons flung themselves to the floor and clasped their hands over their ears. Those next to those people who had seen what Merlin was doing, realised what was going to happen and threw themselves to the floor and so on. The overall effect was something akin to a Mexican wave in reverse.

Out of the corner of his eye, Albert noticed the wave of prostrations.

"Everybody down! 'Ee's going t' use that ruddy gavel!!!" he shouted.

The only people who did not react as Merlin raised the gavel were those members of the guild that were too busy fighting and arguing with other guild members.

The gavel began its downward swing towards the table.

Already on the floor and under the table in the other side of the bar, Albert was desperately trying to beat his record for downing a pint. Dave had followed Fred and Albert's example and was on the floor under the table with his hands over his ears. He didn't know the reason for it, but he'd spent enough time in Lyonnesse to act first and ask questions about the downright weird later on.

The gavel swung down towards the corner of the table like a slow-motion replay.

Merlin was cringing and doing his best to get as far away as possible from his own hand, whilst endeavouring to cover both of his ears with his other arm.

The gavel swung ever closer towards the point of impact. At a certain angle one of the lights in the bar highlighted the delicately carved pattern on the hammer head. The pattern was reminiscent of a lightning bolt.

~~~~~

Over in the church, Father Turner was doing his best to wear out the knees of another ecclesiastical gown, as he knelt at the altar of an obscure religion and mumbled his way through the relevant service.

Occasionally he glanced up nervously at the remaining stained glass windows above him.

This particular service required the sacrifice of twelve goats, three sheep, and an elephant. And although sheep and goats were readily available in Lyonshire, elephants were something of a rarity. True, he could follow one of the footpaths out of Penhampton and onto the grasslands of Africa, but he wasn't quite sure how to go about capturing a six ton bull elephant alive. Besides, he quite liked elephants and they never needed confession, partly because they couldn't fit into the box, but mainly because they never did anything that warranted confessing.

He tipped a small carton of live yoghurt over the altar's sacrificial stone. He knew it wasn't the same, but if this particular god was watching, at least something had been sacrificed; even if it was only part of his lunch.

BOOM!

Above him the stained glass windows shook. Fortunately, dust and a few concussed insects were the only things to rain down on the penitent cleric.

~~~~~

Nowle "powder" Horn had spent most of the day working on his farm. He'd milked his cow twice, tended his crops, dipped his sheep, and generally cussed his way through the day. Now he was sat on an exposed hillside soaking up the last of the day's warmth and patiently waiting to take a pot shot at any unsuspecting animal that happened to wander past.

He wasn't on his land. All the surviving animals on his land had, long ago, either moved as far away as possible or developed highly efficient forms of camouflage in accordance to Darwinian law. He was on a neighbour's land. *[There was the hard-hat hare, which painstakingly hollowed out stones and wore them as helmets. The scrimnet badger, who had taken to making nets out of foliage to camouflage its set and the surrounding area. The displacer thrush, whose plumage refracted light and projected its image six feet away from its actual position, and the more aggressive land mine rabbit, which had taken to digging concealed ditches and small holes just under the surface in a ring around its burrow to twist the ankle or break the leg of trespassers.]*

He checked his monstrous rifle, it was loaded and the safety was on. It was capable of firing small armour piercing rounds and demolishing mountaintops. He'd given up firing at anything smaller than a wild boar. It wasn't worth it. There was never enough left to eat, and in Nowle's view there was no point in killing an animal if you weren't going to eat it afterwards.

A rustling in the bushes to one side attracted his attention. Carefully he sighted along his rifle, waiting for whatever it was to show itself, his finger poised to release the safety-catch.

The bushes parted to reveal a large tusked boar snorting and grunting its way over the ground in its search for food. Without warning, it stood up straight, its bristly mane standing on end, its head cocked on one side listening intently.

BOOM!

The boar bolted back into the woods. Nowle jumped three feet into the air, a remarkable achievement from a prone position. He gave his rifle a perplexed stare. As far as he knew he hadn't fired the single shot. He pointed it at a distant tree and squeezed the trigger. There was a thunderous noise as it fired, but after the deafening boom it sounded more like a popgun.

Half a mile away the tree collapsed.

~~~~~

Aunt Aggie was participating in her third favourite pastime, checking her stock. *[Second was ~~conning~~ selling things to people, although most people unwise enough to have wandered into her shop would assume that this would be her favourite. It is not, counting the money she got from them is.]* Unlike most shopkeepers who only check their stock once a year for tax returns and each day for perishables, Aunt

Agatha checked all of her stock every night. There was never any discrepancy. She always kept a list of everything she had sold during the day and marked it off against the stock. And although shoplifters were not unknown, simply buying something from her shop was a terrifying enough experience that very few were prepared to suffer the consequences of getting caught stealing from her. And stock taking gave her something useful to do with her evenings.

She picked up a tin of peaches in syrup that had been canned in nineteen twenty-six. She could remember going back and buying it three years ago. It had been on her shelf ever since. She gave the can a shake. There was still some liquid sloshing about inside. She licked the end of her pencil and made a note in her book. Then she wrote out a new price ticket, doubling the original price, crossed it out, and wrote the original price underneath to make it look like it had been reduced. *[In the time honoured tradition of chain stores everywhere.]*

Carefully, she reached out to replace it on the shelf.

Boom!

The shelf collapsed, leaving Aunt Aggie standing in the centre of a pile of tinned goods still clutching the can of peaches.

~~~~~

Merlin opened his eyes. Plaster dust was settling around the bar. The larger chunks had already finished their downward journey, bouncing off of skulls and furniture alike. He looked down at the corner of the table. The table leg had been driven two feet into the floor and the rest of the table looked like kindling.

He shook his head, trying to dislodge the ringing in his ears and only succeeding in stirring up a fresh cloud of dust. He put the gavel back into the secret compartment and twiddled his fingers in his ears. That didn't help either. He had been at the epicentre and even with his free hand covering his ears as best he could, the noise had still been deafening.

The rest of the guild lay around the remains of the table. The lucky ones were just stunned, having covered their ears or having had their ears covered by someone else trying to unscrew their head. The others were either unconscious, concussed, or both, but they were no longer fighting and arguing.

Dave, Fred, and Albert crawled out from under their table. Albert immediately headed for the bar and helped himself to a fresh pint to calm his nerves.

"I wish you wouldn't use that bloody 'ammer!" shouted Fred as he wandered over to Merlin.

"Whut? Whut was that?" shouted Merlin in reply, still wiggling a finger in his ear.

"I said, I wish you wouldn't use that bloody 'ammer!" Shouted Fred directly into Merlin's ear.

"'S no good. I can't hear a thing. It's that bloody hammer. I wish I didn't have to use it." Shouted Merlin in reply. "I can't hear a damn thing for days afterwards!"

Fred sagged and shook his head.

"'Ere you go Fred." Shouted Albert as he held a pint out to Fred. "It'll do 'ee the world o' good."

Fred took the glass and, much to Albert's disgust, passed it on to the dusty wizard who took it gratefully.

"I fancies zummet' stronger Bert. I think I'll have a bottle instead." Replied Fred to Albert's unasked question.

Albert gasped. "You don't mean a bottle of ****?"

"Four star?" asked Dave. "You don't mean petrol surely?" After recent events it would not have surprised him in the least.

"No. 'Tiz ginger beer, but not just any ginger beer." Replied Albert.

"Come on you two. Let's retire to the cellar." Said Fred. "We can leave this lot t' sort 'emselves out."

Various members of the Guild of Seers and Allied Fortune Tellers were beginning to stir. Many of them were groaning, clutching their heads, and wondering what had hit them.

Fred led the way down to the cellar and pulled over a third barrel next to the other two for Dave to sit on.

"**** is the special brew we was talkin' about before the fuss started." Explained Albert.

"Oh. I see." Replied Dave "But why is it called ****?" he asked. He was feeling more than a little unhinged and thought it best to go along with things. He could tell from the arrangement of barrels and the makeshift table that this was something Fred and Albert did regularly, and he was being inducted into a select club.

"Well it's not call ****. Not really." Explained Albert. "It hasn't got a proper name. Has it Fred?"

"No. See, SOD is strong old dark. It says what it is. But this stuff..." Fred lifted a small thick glass bottle out of a bucket of ice and handed it to Dave. "Well, we've never found words t' describe it. Least not ort' you could put on a label or write on the blackboard in the bar."

Dave looked closely at the bottle.

"You said it was ginger beer? Ginger beer is a child's drink.

What's so special about this stuff?" he asked, holding up the bottle.

"Careful lad!" Exclaimed Fred. "Don't shake it up!"

Dave quickly handed the bottle back as gently as he could.

"No lad. 'S not a kid's drink." Replied Albert.

Fred opened the bottle carefully, poured it into a very thick glass, and handed it to Dave. The golden brown liquid had a heady cloud of vapour condensing above it, forming a small cloud. It drifted upwards towards the ceiling.

"For Pete's sake don't light a match!" exclaimed Albert.

"You'd better drink it quick before it all evaporates." Said Fred, nodding towards the glass.

There was already noticeably less liquid in the glass than there had been when Fred had handed it to him moments before, despite the fact that the air in the cellar was distinctly chilly to keep the beer barrels cold. However, the liquid in Dave's glass continued to evaporate as he watched it.

He sniffed the glass.

A few minutes later, Fred and Albert managed to help him up off of the floor and back onto his barrel.

"*Whaasf fassa khasssa* **** *ma?*" he managed, trying to blink away tears and persuade his eyes to focus again.

"It's better just to drink it lad." Said Albert sagely, patting Dave on the shoulder. "Sniffing it can be dangerous."

"That's right lad." Added Fred. "If you sniffs it goes straight t' yur head without the intervention and protection o' yur stomach."

"*Saffer raffa ham!* You don't say!" Said Dave as his head cleared a little. "What on earth is that stuff?"

"Well," began Fred cautiously opening another bottle and handing Albert a glass of the liquid. "It's essentially ginger beer, ginger, sugar, lemon juice and water. The only thing that's a bit different is the yeast."

"So what's so special about the yeast?" Dave asked. "I've done a fair bit of home brewing in the past and one yeast isn't vastly different from another. Some are more tolerant to alcohol than others and there is a slight variation in taste, but not much else."

"'S not ordinary yeast." Continued Fred. "An' it don't exactly convert the sugar t' alcohol neither. I reckons I can trust 'ee with the secret. It comes from a planet that orbits the twin suns of Cygnus X-1. In fact, 'tis the only thing that comes from or lives there. It's been banned in three hundred and twenty-seven galaxies as a narcotic *[and used in drinking purification systems in seventy-six others]* an' no respectable intergalactic trader will ship it. However, every once in a while I goes into the future and picks up a container o' the stuff from a bloke I knows."

Fred poured himself a glass and drank it down.

"****!!!!" He said.

Albert pushed his glass forwards shakily for another drink. Fred obliged and poured out another for Dave and himself.

Dave took his glass, and holding his nose, drank a sip of the golden brew.

"****!!!!" He exclaimed.

It tasted wonderful. It was light and not too sweet on the tongue, and slightly fizzy with a refreshing gingery taste. As he swallowed warmth spread down through his system as it headed for his stomach. A moment later he could have sworn that Merlin had just wielded his gavel again as the drink reached his head. But the pain subsided quickly and left him with a warm glow. He took another sip.

"So lad, what do you think?" Asked Fred when Dave's eye's uncrossed.

"It's good. It's **** good!" replied Dave before draining his glass.

Fred opened another bottle and refilled all their glasses. Above their heads the vapour was beginning to form a cloud just below the ceiling. Insects that had managed to remain conscious when Merlin had used his gavel began to drift or drop towards the floor. Their mandibles fixed in a wide vacant grin.

~~~~~

Dave awoke the next morning with a smile on his face. Then he winced, remembering the night before, expecting the hangover to catch up with him at any moment. He waited a few minutes. A hangover failed to appear and beat him viciously about the head. Cautiously, he opened his eyes in case it was lurking elsewhere in the room. It wasn't. Instead the room was brightly lit with the first rays of the morning sun.

He got out of bed and dressed; still no hangover. In fact, he was surprised how bright and fresh he felt. It was the first morning he hadn't had to drag himself out of bed to the sound of Fred hammering on the door. Energy surged through him like syrup of figs through... through other things. He performed his morning ablutions with a spring in his step, combed his hair and beard, and went down to breakfast.

Fred was in the kitchen performing the ancient art of making tea and cooking their breakfast. He appeared to be frying up anything edible he could find in the kitchen. *[Sausages, eggs, a fruitcake, a side of bacon, pork chops, anything that came to hand.]* He nodded to Dave as he entered.

Dave sat himself down and waited for a plate heaped with a dietician's nightmare or wildest dream to arrive. The wonderful aroma of food filled the kitchen and wafted up his nose as he inhaled. In an instant, and much to Dave's surprise, he was ravenous. He felt so hungry that even the table was beginning to look appetising; especially if he could find some mustard.

Fred plonked a mug of tar strength tea on the table in front of Dave and set down two more.

"Who's the other mug for?" Asked Dave.

"Albert 'ad a bit o' trouble gettin' 'is legs to co-operate last night. So 'ee slept in one o' the spare rooms." Replied Fred, turning back to the enormous frying pan.

"I didn't think Albert drank tea, and you usually have coffee as well?"

"We don't normally, especially Bert, except when 'ee 'as to go to court. But we'll all need it s'mornin'. It's the ****, it don't mix well with coffee, an' vur some reason it puts Albert off of 'is beer vur oh... hours sometimes."

"Mornin' Fred, Dave." Said Albert as he walked in and sat himself down at the table.

Dave realised he was absentmindedly chewing his fork and put it down.

"'Tiz a bugger vur givin' 'ee the munchies is ****." Said Albert with a smile.

Fred pulled three tray sized plates out of the rack and dished up the food. There followed thirty seconds of silence, broken finally by the clatter of cutlery as the three of them pushed their now empty plates away. All three of them peered hopefully at each other's plates in case anybody had left anything. But all the plates looked like they had been licked clean.

"By the gods! I needed that!" declared Fred with some satisfaction.

"You're not wrong there Fred." Added Albert.

"I think the table had a lucky escape there." Said Dave.

The other two both looked at Dave who blushed and cleared his throat.

"So, where are you off today then lad?" Asked Fred.

"I thought I'd go over to Hunton and interview Hatchet the butcher. See what sort of claim he has on the land and the shop in

Penhampton." Dave replied.

The other two nodded their agreement.

"And you said Fetlock the stable master lives over that way somewhere?" He continued.

"Aye, about 'alf way between Timber's place an' Hunton." Said Albert between swallows of tea. "Just past the turnin' back t' your place."

"You want to watch yurself though." Put in Fred. "They're a bit strange o're Hunton way. "

"Why's that?"

"Well, you know the Romans invaded Britain some time ago?"

Dave had a vague recollection of his history lessons at school. Usually the teachers who taught history looked old enough to have experienced most of it first-hand. It wasn't a subject that had really appealed to him. Consequently it had never held his attention and he had not been very good at it. He did, however, remember the bit about the Romans. *[Although mostly from comic book stories]*

"Their army was split into legions." Continued Fred. "And each legion had its own standard. During the invasion of Britain one of the legions disappeared, the Ninth Roman Legion. No trace o' them was ever found. D' you recollect any o' this?"

"Yes. I know about the Legion of the Ninth, the supposed elite force of the Roman army. It's one of those myths. Most historians reckon that they were either ambushed by the invading Scots from Ireland or by the Picts from what is now Scotland and utterly destroyed."

"No lad, they never were. They never even saw combat. They might o' been an elite fighting force, but their commander 'ad no sense of direction an' got 'em lost. Eventually they stumbled into Lyonnesse. And, a'ter a few skirmishes with the locals, they set up one o' their fortified marchin' camps where Hunton now stands." explained Fred.

"They make some damn fine pasta too." Put in Albert. "An' the pizzas, oooh the pizzas!"

At the mention of food, three stomachs rumbled in unison, despite the fact that they had just eaten enough breakfast for a dozen people.

There was a general migration in the direction of the fridge.

~~~~~

Feeling somewhat bloated, Dave rode off northwest from Shoton and past Lord Timbers' estate. He passed the road that would take him home and stopped momentarily by the turning. He glanced at his watch. It was ten to eight. After a brief mental struggle, he estimated that if he rode down that road now, he should arrive just in time to witness the birth of his several greats grandfather. He shook the thought from his head and continued on.

Sure enough, he passed a magnificent stable block. Glancing up from the road, he could see several horses being led around a show ring. Other horses had their heads stuck out over the bottom half of their stable-doors. The building itself was breath-taking. It looked like the work of an architect who, forced for years to design housing estates and other box based developments, had suddenly found himself with a free hand to explore his long suppressed talents. Carved stone archways enclosed every doorway; ornate columns supported the second storey gallery. A vast stone relief covered the walls, and cherubs and gargoyles peered down from every corner of the roof.

Hunton turned out to be more than just a Roman village, it was an Italia/Roman community. As Dave rode towards the outer limits of the village, the air became noticeably hotter and more humid, and the landscape changed. Gnarled olive trees and vineyards grew on the gently sloping hillsides. The style of the houses changed, here they were all painted white and had red tiled roofs. Many had had large balcony and/or roof-terraces. Chickens wandered freely across the road. It looked like part of Italy had been transported and dumped in Lyonshire, complete with its Mediterranean climate.

A disgruntled cockerel crowed and tried to peck Dave's leg as he rode slowly into the village. There didn't seem to be a village square or green, or any organisation to the village at all. The buildings were arranged in a higgledy-piggledy ramshackle way, some widely spaced apart and others crammed right up against each other. They might once have been on a traditional roman grid pattern but they had been extended and altered so many times over the years that now the overall effect appeared as if someone had thrown a handful of stones over their shoulder and the buildings had sprouted up where the stones had fallen.

He could see a sign on one of the larger buildings, which proclaimed it to be the home of the Hunton Times. Right next to it was a single story building with a roof terrace. Outside it a generously built, short woman cocooned in black cloth, was herding a flock of chickens for no apparent reason. Next to that was a pizzeria bedecked in red and green stripes, with the compulsory blue checked tablecloths adorning the tables in the street.

Dave parked his bike, locked his helmet away and strode off in search of the butchers' shop.

It didn't take him long to find that the apparent haphazard layout of the village was far worse than it had looked when he had ridden in. Streets and alleyways crisscrossed and re-crossed each other. A wide street would abruptly end in a building, which had apparently been placed at random, leaving a narrow arched walkway through to connect with the rest of the road on the other side. Within minutes Dave was lost and, ignoring male stereotype, had to ask for directions. They didn't help. Whilst everyone spoke English, they all spoke with a very strong accent, part Italian, and part Romano Latin, which he couldn't understand. And those directions that he could understand didn't seem to correspond to the streets themselves, forcing him to simply wander around at random. Frequently around places he had wandered around only moments before.

By the time Dave had passed his bike for the fifth time, he was beginning to give up all hope of ever finding Hatchet's butchers shop. He was feeling the heat too, his black leathers were designed to give protection against gravel rash not Mediterranean sunshine and he was sweating profusely. A cool refreshing drink was called for, and his stomach was beginning to rumble again, demanding to be fed.

He sat himself down at an empty table outside one of the many cafes and began to peruse the menu. Eventually the waiter sauntered over and took his order before disappearing back into the café.

"Excuse me." Called a refined English accent somewhere behind him. "I say? Excuse me."

Dave looked around, absent-mindedly chewing a breadstick. On the table behind him sat two men. One of whom was tall, thin and well groomed, the other was short and stocky with a face like a dried prune.

"Ware wow spiking to me?" he asked spraying crumbs.

"Are you Dave? The young gentleman who is staying at the Stoat and Ferret?" asked the thin, well-dressed man.

Dave nodded.

"Excuse my forwardness, and correct me if I am wrong, but I believe you are looking for my companion." The speaker indicated the stocky man next to him, who flexed his bare arms. Muscles like knotted ropes danced up and down.

"Who are you?" asked Dave hesitantly.

"Please forgive me and my rudeness. My friend is Hatchet the butcher and I am his business partner, Jessup, Bill Jessup. Pleased to meet you I'm sure." Jessup offered his hand.

Dave shook it.

"Whooar hrrre wur surr." Growled Hatchet his words totally

unintelligible.

"What did he say?"

"He says he is pleased to meet you too." Translated Jessup.

"I take it you and Hatchet are not from around here then?" asked Dave hazarding a guess and spitting out raffia. Having finished off all the breadsticks, he had begun to absentmindedly chew the basket they had been in.

"How did you know that?" asked Jessup with surprise.

"Just a guess."

"Whurr do hatterrr wannt?" asked Hatchet

"Sorry?" replied Dave. "I didn't quite catch that?"

"My associate wishes to know, what it is that you want to know." Translated Jessup.

The waiter made a timely arrival, deposited two plates in front of Dave, and relieved him of the half eaten basket.

"Actually, all I want to know is why he is claiming part of Lord Woods' estate, the shop in Penhampton and the disputed land? I'm doing a story on it for the Hunton Times." Explained Dave as he began to shovel food into his mouth.

Hatchet rubbed his large hands over his stubbly chin, making his huge biceps dance as he considered the question. Eventually he spoke at some length. Dave was unable to comprehend a single word and looked hopefully at Jessup for a translation between forkfuls from his second plate of food.

The waiter reappeared and set down another couple of full plates and removed the empties.

"It seems," said Jessup, "that Lord Woods gave my colleague the shop in Penhampton as payment for delivering fresh meat up to the house a couple of times each week. Which he has done for several years and continues to do so at the moment."

Hatchet nodded.

Dave stopped eating for a moment to look at Hatchet carefully. He wanted to challenge his claim because Poulter was claiming the shop for the same reasons but he had the feeling that Hatchet might take it the wrong way. So, he kept quiet and would ask Shem and Elsie.

"But he has no real claim on the land. Apparently he put his name down for that because he cannot stand that horrible, greedy man Fetlock, and simply wanted to spite him." Concluded Jessup with a shrug.

"HURR TURR HUM BRATTLE SKAT!!!" exclaimed Hatchet.

Dave's fork, heavily laden with food, paused in mid-air as the butcher bellowed. And when Hatchet punctuated his next sentence by producing a meat-cleaver and burying it several inches into the table, Dave jumped and accidentally stabbed himself in the chin with his fork.

"I take it that he doesn't like this Fetlock very much?" he asked, dabbing his chin with a napkin.

"Apparently not." Replied Jessup from somewhere under a nearby table. "They are brothers." He continued, as if that explained everything, whilst he crawled back towards his chair.

Hatchet nodded and pulled the cleaver from the stricken table.

The waiter returned with the last of Dave's meal and surveyed the damaged table. With a sigh, he waved his hands over the damage and muttered a few words. Beneath his hands the damaged wood restored itself and the threads in the tablecloth wove themselves back together again.

"Sibling rivalry? Some childhood grudge?" enquired Dave tentatively.

Hatchet spoke a few words and stormed off.

"He says he doesn't want to talk about it." Translated Jessup as he watched his companion disappear into the maze of streets. "I am afraid he gets like this every time someone mentions his brother." He apologised.

"Families can do that to people." Nodded Dave in agreement. "Incidentally, how did you know I was looking for you and not just passing through?"

"Ah," began Jessup, "it was not that difficult. Strangers are rare in Lyonshire as you have no doubt heard, and word has got out that you are looking into this nasty business about Lord Woods' estate. I saw your motorbicycle, another rarity, pull up earlier and concluded it must be you." He gestured towards Dave's leather jacket.

Chapter 8.

Fred and Albert spent most of the morning drinking tea, eating anything they could get their hands on and chatting across the kitchen table. At least they drank tea until the effects of Fred's special ginger beer wore off, and they were able to stomach coffee.

There was no rush to get the pub open, all the regulars knew that after the Guild of Seers and Allied Fortune Tellers had had a meeting, the pub would be closed the following day to allow for renovations and repairs to the furniture, and for the guild members to regain consciousness. Fred had briefly reconnoitred the wreckage in the bar and concluded that even he would not be able to turn the large pile of kindling Merlin had created with the guild's ceremonial gavel back into a table. Removing the table leg that had been driven into the floor was going to be a major challenge on its own.

Throughout the morning, various members of the guild had regained consciousness or reawakened and wandered into the kitchen in search of coffee, painkillers, and a cold compress. When questioned, none of them could remember with any clarity the events of the night before, or exactly what had caused the fight. A brief search had recovered the minutes of the meeting but they were almost as useless as the guild members themselves:

The Minutes of the two hundredth and thirty-ninth meeting of The Guild of Seers and Allied Fortune Tellers.

1: Validation of the Minutes for the previous meeting.

2: Meeting adjourned due to outbreak of fighting over the wording of the Minutes from the previous meeting.

Ironically, the minutes from the previous meeting said more or less the same thing. *[But so did the minutes of nearly all the guild meetings.]*

Fred had seen Merlin disappear in a cloud of smoke, a haze of alcohol and singing rude rugby songs late in the evening, leaving his fellow guild members to their own devices. The few lucky ones had managed to walk out clutching their heads or other injuries and bleeding quietly to themselves. The pubs regulars had lost interest once the fighting had ceased and drifted off in dribs and drabs to recount the evening's events to those not fortunate enough to have witnessed them first hand.

Around midday Albert declared his intention to leave, and wandered off, leaving Fred to survey the damage and try and restore his pub. The damage was no worse and no better than usual, but at least most of the windows were still intact. Tables and chairs were normally easy to repair, and broken glasses were an almost nightly occurrence, but for some reason he always found windows difficult. They were more of a specialised job. Besides, it was almost always impossible to find all the pieces. It was inevitable that shards would get caught in clothing, or someone would walk through the broken glass and it would get lodged in the soles of their shoes or sandals.

Here and there amongst the piles of broken tables, chairs and crockery there were still a few unconscious or semiconscious bodies. The occasional groan gave away the location of those buried beneath it.

As Fred stood behind the bar sipping his coffee and contemplating where to make a start, the door to the His 'n' Hers creaked open shyly, or at least as shyly as it is possible for a door to open. A face peeked out. Fred stood stock still where he was and looked on with interest. This was something different.

The face in the doorway looked like a panda, or at least Nostradamus looking extremely pale and with two black eyes. He didn't appear to notice Fred standing behind the bar, and ducked back through the door. There was a whispered conversation and the door opened wider. This time Nostradamus emerged into the bar, leading a very attractive young lady by the hand.

Fred recognised the woman. She had been one of the Vestal Virgins. 'Had' being the operative word by the look on her face, a mixture of embarrassment and a twinkle of delight. Fred thought it was very doubtful that she would still qualify for her job in the temple anymore.

Nostradamus coughed nervously when he finally noticed Fred. The young lady with him demurely dropped her gaze to the floor and chewed her bottom lip.

"I never saw nothin'." Said Fred sympathetically, and ushered them across the bar and out the door.

One by one, he roused the remaining casualties. It took all his ingenuity, a bottle of smelling salts, several burnt feathers, and a bucket of water, but eventually he managed to evict the last of them. Most went in search of a doctor, or a pub, or preferably a pub with a doctor in it.

Finally, with the last of the guild members gone, Fred was able to set about his work. The first job was to find all the pieces of an object and then convince them that they all wanted to get back together again. As with the windows, there were always a few problem cases resulting from missing pieces. Chair legs and other objects that had been used as missiles or melee weapons, and then tucked without thinking into a pocket or belt for later use, and then simply taken away when that person left. There were also the bits that were impossible to sort from one another, which rather than throw away, Fred would persevere with. The end result would be an amalgam of furniture, such as the barstool with integral fruit bowl, or the table with built in ashtrays and glasses. Generally they had a pleasing effect and as long as they weren't dangerous, he would leave them as curios and conversation pieces.

Dogmatically Fred worked his way through the wreckage, and by mid-afternoon the bar more or less resembled the way it had looked before the Guild meeting.

Albert stuck his head around the door.

"You nearly finished Fred?" he asked.

"Just about Bert. I've only got t' push a broom around and mop the floor an' that'll be it." Replied Fred.

"You want a hand? I knows yur always a bit pushed a'ter they've gone. I could clean the pumps for e' or zummet."

"Ta very much Bert. Cleanin' the pumps would be a great 'elp."

"Oh, by the way Fred, I've been down t' collect me rent from ol' Pennywell o're Fishin way. 'Ee's got some hops left in an' 'ee'll drop it off vur 'ee the day a'ter tomorrow."

"I could do with it too." Replied Fred appreciatively. "After Gladys turned that batch the other night, I 'ad t' use the last o' me dried hops t' start another batch off."

A cloud of smoke filled the bar, stopping both of them from working and distributing Fred's neat pile of sweepings across the floor once more.

Cough, cough, splutter, cough! Came from amidst the cloud.

"Bloody stupid spell! Why the" *cough* "do all teleporting spells have to start and finish in a ~%$£@#!! puff of smoke!" *Cough, cough.*

Gradually the smoke thinned once Fred had managed to open the windows. It revealed the stunted figure of the world's most powerful wizard, with his robes smouldering and his eyebrows missing.

Fred shook his head in despair. Albert was more vocal and far less subtle in his disapproval.

"WHAT THE FRELL ARE YOU DOING BACK 'ERE?" he shouted. "We 'ad enough o' your lot last night, an' you're not due back vur another twelve months."

Merlin shrugged and tried unsuccessfully to put out his smouldering robes. Fred came to his rescue, picking up a soda-siphon off of the bar and dousing the stricken magician from head to foot.

"Why do I always end up soaking wet as well?" exclaimed the sodden mage as he tried to ring out the corner of his robes.

Distracted, Albert pulled himself a pint and took a swig. He immediately spat it out, further drenching the unfortunate Merlin who happened to be standing in the line of fire.

"'S ruddy cleanin' fluid!" explained Bert, wiping his mouth on his sleeve.

Merlin glared at him, trying to decide if Albert had done it deliberately or not.

Albert poured the rest of the pint down the sink and passed a bar towel to Merlin by way of an apology.

"I have come" began Merlin dramatically striking a pose, and waving his arms in the air, which sent a spray of water across the room. "on official business. One of the Vestal Virgins did not return to Rome last week after the meeting, and hasn't been seen since."

"You mean last night's meetin'" Corrected Fred. *[With the ease and frequency of time travel in Lyonnesse with people just dropping in or out, forwards or backwards depending on their whim, it can cause problems for the untutored. Fred solved this problem by simply ignoring whatever they said and substituted his own frame of time reference.]*
"The last of 'em left more 'an three hours ago. I was just getting' ready t' open up again an' Bert was givin' me an 'and."

Albert nodded his agreement. "'S right. 'Sides, what difference does it make to you?"

Merlin pulled himself up to his full height. "I just happen to be an honorary eunuch and advisor to the temple of Vesta. AND YOU CAN STOP THAT RUDDY SNIGGERING!!!"

It took a few moments for Fred and Albert to pull themselves together and stop laughing. In Albert's case he only managed it by shoving his handkerchief in his mouth and biting down hard.

"How did you come to be an *honorary* eunuch then?" asked Fred, doing his best not to start laughing again.

"Never mind that," said Albert, wiping away tears of laughter with his hankie, "what is an honorary eunuch?"

"I happen to be an honorary eunuch, THANK YOU VERY MUCH because only eunuchs and female virgins are allowed into the temple of Vesta and I was asked to be an advisor to the High Priestess and have to go into the temple every so often."

Albert began to giggle again.

"And I am honorary because I have one or two things eunuchs don't!" finished Merlin defiantly.

Albert couldn't help himself and shoved his hankie back in his mouth in an attempt to stop himself laughing again.

" Anyway," continued Merlin, "have you seen any missing priestesses hanging about the place?"

"Like I said, the last o' your lot left several hours ago." Replied Fred.

"And you didn't see any of the girls acting suspiciously?" asked Merlin, pressing the point.

"Well, to be truthful, the last o' the girls to leave was, erm, how can I put this?" said Fred uncomfortably. "Let's just say, I don't think she would qualify to enter the temple anymore."

"WHAT??????!!!!!!!!!!" yelled Merlin.

It was all too much for Albert, his handkerchief flew from his mouth and he collapsed behind the bar in fits of hysteria.

"She," began Fred, "she didn't leave alone if you know what I mean."

There was a crash from behind the bar as Albert knocked over a shelf full of glasses between howls of laughter. "Stop it please! I can't take anymore!" he implored.

Merlin's face was livid, his already flushed cheeks were turning scarlet with rage and his eyes had narrowed to slits.

"Who was it?" his voice flat and toneless with repressed rage. "Who was it? Was it that young lad you've got staying here?"

"No! No." Said Fred defensively. "It weren't 'im. He's been out since first thing."

"It was him, wasn't it?" asked Merlin, pushing the point.

"No it weren't 'im!" snapped Fred. "I told you 'ee'd left hours before they did!"

"So it was a THEM!" said Merlin, jumping on Fred's words. "Who was it then?" A wave of enlightenment crossed his face. "Nostradamus! I should have known." His voice was no more than a whisper, a very sinister whisper.

Fred recognised it; it was the kind of whisper that is far more terrifying than an all-out shout. A whisper to send shivers down your spine, because the whisperer's body is under the full control of his or her mind, and knows that the listener will automatically lean in closer to hear what is said, only to receive the full benefit of the next outburst right in the ear hole. Tactfully he put his fingers in his ears.

"THAT RANDY $£@#*$!!!!! JUST WAIT TILL I CATCH UP WITH HIM!! I'LL SEE TO IT THAT HE QUALIFIES TO ENTER THE FRELLING TEMPLE!"

His tirade over, the diminutive mage slumped.

"How am I supposed to explain to the High Priestess that one of her Vestal Virgins isn't?" continued Merlin unhappily.

Albert had managed to control himself enough to pull his head up over the bar. Tears streaked his face.

Merlin continued to rant and rave as he headed towards the door. Much of what he said was lost in the cowl of his robes; those few words that Fred managed to catch, would never be repeated by the barman in polite company.

When he reached the door, Merlin straightened up and turned, the door half open. "Same time next year?" he asked calmly.

~~~~~

Dave had ridden back as far as the ostentatious stables and, much to the relief of his groaning shock absorbers, parked his bike, and gone to look for Fetlock. He had again been amazed by the splendour of the stables.

After stuffing himself at Hunton he'd had difficulty zipping up his normally spacious leather jacket, and his trouser buttons were on the verge of an all-out strike.

He waddled up to the stables and eventually found Fetlock slapping an errant stablehand around the head.

"How many times must I tell you? Never feed a horse maize before a race!" Snapped Fetlock, cuffing the young lad around the head again.

Fetlock seemed to fit right in with the overly elaborate stables. He had clean chiselled looks and a big nose, reminiscent of classical statues. He stood a little under six foot high in his tight fitting jodhpurs, riding boots and expensively tailored riding jacket. He also had a paisley patterned red cravat neatly tied around his neck.

"Excuse me?" ventured Dave as he approached.

"Oh. I didn't see you there." Fetlock was still clearly angry. "Who are you? And what are you doing here? This is private property you know." He snapped.

"I don't mean to intrude," Dave began, "but I'm doing a write-up for the Hunton Times about the dispute with Lord Woods' estate. I hoped I could have a few minutes of your time to ask you a few questions?"

Fetlock seemed taken aback. In fact he stepped back into something soft and steaming.

"Is it so difficult for them to keep the stable-yard clean?" he asked the world in general, and raising his eyes to the heavens.

"YOU!" He shouted at a passing stablehand. "Come here and clear this up at once!"

"Of course I can spare a few moments for the press. My office is this way." He said politely, turning his attention back to Dave with hardly a pause.

~~~~~

By the time Dave had made a brief detour to see Shem and Elsie, it was early evening when he rode his bike through the huge double doors that led around the back of the Stoat and Ferret. His encounter with Fetlock had been pleasant enough. Once he had learned that Dave was a reporter, Fetlock had gone out of his way to answer all of Dave's questions and been the very model of courtesy. He had even given Dave a full guided tour of the overly elaborate stables, but Dave couldn't help remembering the incident with the stablehand. And it wasn't so much what Fetlock had said, it was more the things he hadn't said. Since coming to Lyonshire long suppressed instincts were beginning to surface, and Fetlock gave Dave the creeps. *[Most people have very good instincts, although they have been suppressed and beaten into submission as a safety reflex to help get through the mire of modern everyday life. It would, for instance, be very inconvenient to get the creeps every time you saw someone wearing a suit, or the need to keep tight hold of your wallet every time you walked into a supermarket.]*

Inside the Stoat and Ferret everything appeared to have returned to normal, whatever that was in Lyonshire. Patrons were arranged in various states of repose, relaxing at the bar or the tables. Those that had been in the bar since Fred had opened were more relaxed than the others and some were quietly snoring into their beer. There was a general buzz of cheery conversation around the room, and fresh sawdust on the floor. Much of the conversation centred around the previous days' guild meeting, but there was also the occasional remark about the latest curios created by Fred's repairs.

Dave headed straight up to his room to dump his helmet and

jacket and freshen up. He had things he needed to discuss with Fred and Albert, questions and half formed theories. After the heat of Hunton's Mediterranean climate he needed a wash and something refreshing to drink. But most of all he needed several spoonfuls of stomach powder and about an hour in the smallest room. He was feeling very decidedly uncomfortable and the normally comforting and reassuring vibrations from his bike had made him feel nauseous.

Sometime later, and feeling considerably lighter, Dave strode into the bar.

"'Allo lad. 'Ow did e' get on?" inquired Fred.

"Not bad Fred." Replied Dave. "I think I've made some progress. In fact, I think I now know who murdered Lord Woods *and* Chalky the smith. But it is only a theory, and I still don't have any proof or any way of proving it." Whispered Dave.

"Sounds like we need to talk in private." Said Albert, again showing his grasp of subtlety by tapping the side of his nose.

"I'll pour us some drinks an' get Suzan t' watch the bar whilst us go downstairs." Said Fred.

"I'd prefer a mug of your coffee Fred." Replied Dave, his stomach still feeling rather delicate.

"Comin' right up lad." Fred retrieved a mug from the kitchen and filled it with dark and steaming caffeine.

Dave gratefully accepted the mug and downed the liquid. Both Fred and Albert held their breath. Fred's coffee was not something that should be downed in one go, too much too quickly was worse than drinking ****. But it appeared to have no adverse effect on Dave. He was still standing. They both eyed him with newfound respect, unaware that his system had been lined with four helpings of paella, pizza, garlic-bread, and chips.

"Fancy a bite to eat?" asked Fred. "There's no hot food t'night, it's Hal's night off, but there's plenty of cold cuts?"

Dave shook his head so furiously, the other two thought he had overdone the coffee after all.

"NO! I mean no thanks. I don't want to eat. Again. Ever." He rubbed his still swollen stomach. The mere thought of food was making it feel very uncomfortable again. And he wasn't sure what effect raffia would have on his system.

The pub door creaked open slightly and in strolled a cat. It was a small ginger tabby, not much more than a kitten, still covered in patches of downy fluff. It strutted across the floor as if it owned the bar, its little pink nose high in the air. It swaggered, full of feline confidence and sure in its own mind that it looked absolutely wonderful. Simply everybody just had to stop whatever he or she was doing and pay it their full and undivided attention.

It jumped up onto a vacant barstool next to Dave and glared at him.

"I didn't know you had a cat Fred?" said Dave with surprise.

"'S not mine. 'Tiz one o' Aunt Aggie's. Can't stand the little furballs meself." Admitted Fred with a grimace.

The cat turned to look at Fred and scowled at him, as if it had understood every word he had said. Then it rubbed its head up against Dave.

"Friendly little fellow." Observed Albert. "It never ceases t' amazes me that she keeps cats. Never comes across as a pet person does Aunt Aggie."

The cat gave up rubbing itself against Dave. It had tried the lovable glare, the affectionate rub and even a pathetic mew, and received nothing in return for its trouble. Not even a scratch between the ears. It was beginning to think that this human was lacking in the intelligence department, when Dave reached out and smoothed its head. It shrugged its shoulders as if to say "at last!" and gave a soft purr of encouragement.

"Seems t' like you right enough." Smiled Albert.

"Nah, you knows what cats are like Bert. The little bugger will 'ave 'is 'and in a mo." Sneered Fred.

The cat smiled and rolled over onto its back to allow Dave to tickle its tummy. Dreamily it stretched all four legs in the air and flexed its claws.

"I think you're bein' a bit hard on it Fred" said Albert. "You're just not a cat person, that's all."

Without warning the cat unfurled its claws and sank four matching sets into Dave's wrist. As an encore it bit down hard on his thumb.

"Ahhh! You little $£%^~#!!!" Shouted Dave, snatching his injured hand away.

"Told you." Said Fred flatly. "Vicious, nasty, self-centred things cats. Especially Aunt Aggie's."

Dave nursed his arm. "Look at that! That was my new shirt! Look its torn and spotted with blood now."

"I should go an' wash it if I were you." Said Fred. "You never knows what they've been up to with them claws. Bert an' I'll meet e' in the cellar in a bit."

A short time later, an antiseptically spotted Dave joined the other two in the cellar.

"So what 'ave e' found out then?" Asked Albert

"You was sayin' you knows who murdered Lord Timbers" Prompted Fred.

Dave sat down on his barrel. "Well I think I've figured out who killed both Lord Woods and Chalky the smith, but its only supposition and theories really. I can't prove any of it. At least not yet."

"But you thinks you knows?" pushed Fred.

"Who lad? Who?" asked Albert.

"Well, first we know for certain that it was actually Lord Woods' dog that killed him?"

The other two nodded their agreement.

"But from what I could find out from the Windsors, he was one of those affectionately stupid dogs that is more likely to lick a burglar to death than actually bite him."

Again the other two nodded.

"So, it seems highly unlikely that it should turn so nasty that quickly, and, for no apparent reason, go for his master." Said Dave, trying to sum things up.

"Yes, but we knows that." Said Albert irritably. "Me an' the coroner went back an' witnessed it."

Dave's stomach growled and popped audibly. He sat quietly for a moment, looking about nervously. Then he clasped his middle, a worried look on his face.

"If you will excuse me for a moment!" he said hurriedly and fled the cellar.

Once he had gone, Albert took a swig of his drink and leaned in closer to Fred.

"Look, I know I've said it before, but are you sure about this lad?" he asked. "'Ee comes across a few quarts short of a hogshead t' me."

Fred smiled and patted his friend on the shoulder. "Bert you have my word on it. There's nort wrong with the lad."

"Just the same," said Albert, he was not convinced. "We only met the lad a few days ago an' know next t' nothin' about 'im."

"I didn't say ort t'other day, but I've met the lad before, though 'ee doesn't know it yet. He helped me out o' a bit o' bother." Said Fred reassuringly.

Albert glanced towards the cellar door to check that there was still no sign of Dave returning.

"When'd you meet 'im then?" he asked.

Fred sat back, a warm smile on his face as he remembered his youth. He could almost breath in and smell and taste the sights he had seen.

"'T were many years ago now, when I was younger an' still full o' wanderlust. I'd travelled into the future a bit an' found meself in a serious spot o' bother. E' recognised me from now an' showed me a bottle o' **** which was top secret in them days and still in development. So I knew e' knew me even though I hadn't met him before at the time."

Albert stared at nothing in particular as he tried to navigate his brain around the mental labyrinth created by travelling forwards and backwards in time as easily as popping down to the corner shop for a newspaper. *[Just because it is easy to travel backwards and forwards in time it doesn't make it any easier to talk about without a common frame of reference.]*

"Let me see if I've got this straight Fred." Began Albert, still trying to drive straight around the corners. "When you were younger, you went into the future an' met the lad, who was older than e' is now, an' he recognised you from 'is past which is now?"

"That's the gist of it Bert. I were ..." Fred was interrupted by Dave's return to the cellar.

Dave heaved a sigh of relief as he sat back down on his barrel. "Pugh, that was close. Never, ever, eat raffia."

The other two looked at him slightly puzzled. Albert tipped his head slightly in Dave's direction whilst he wasn't looking, as if to say 'you sure he's not nuts?' to Fred. Fred shook his head slightly.

"D' you think you could recap an' explain the bit about the dog not killin' Timbers?" asked Fred.

"Sorry." Said Dave, shuffling around on his barrel to make himself comfortable again. "Didn't I make myself clear?"

"No, not really." Said a slightly disgruntled Albert. Despite Fred's reassurance he was still not convinced that Dave was firing on all cylinders.

"Ok. We know the dog killed Lord Woods..." Began Dave.

Nod, nod.

"And we also know that the dog was not normally nasty. Quite the opposite in fact."

"We follow you so far." Said Fred helpfully.

"Right. So what and or who made the dog turn vicious?"

The other two gave him a blank look. This might be harder than he thought.

"From recent personal experience, I can vouch for the fact that having an upset stomach can dramatically affect your mood and make you feel irritable." He said, rubbing his still swollen stomach. "Imagine then, if you will, the effect on your mood if your stomach feels like it is on fire."

"Well you've tried ****!" laughed Albert.

"I mean burning with pain." Snapped Dave.

"Sorry Lad. No offence intended." Apologised Albert. "Just my little joke." He mumbled.

"What if," continued Dave, whilst glaring at Albert. "What if the dog had been given something in his food that made him turn nasty?"

"But surely the dog would go vur whoever fed 'im." Put in Fred. "An' that would be one o' the Windsors."

"No, Lord Woods always fed his dog and cleared up after it." Said Dave triumphantly. "I checked with Shem and Elsie, apparently he insisted upon it. His dog, his responsibility."

"Ah!" Nodded Fred and Albert in unison. They were beginning to understand where Dave was going with this.

"That means the irritant must have been in the dogs food already. Assuming of course that it wasn't Lord Woods that poisoned his dog. Anyway, the dog always ate a mixture of fresh meat and tinned dog food. The fresh always came from the kitchen and was generally the scraps from whatever everybody else in the house was eating."

"It must 'ave come from the tinned food then!" exclaimed Albert excitedly.

"Shut up Bert an' let the lad continue." Said Fred in a flat tone.

"It took me a while to sort out where the tinned food actually came from. Both Poulter and Hatchet denied supplying the dog food and said it must have come from the other. Neither of them has a canning machine either. But the Windsors insist that the dog food always turns up with the fresh meat that Hatchet supplies. However, Hatchet has no delivery wagon, all his deliveries are done by one of Fetlock's, his brother's, stablemen. Even though they hate each other."

Dave paused to draw breath and took a swig from his coffee.

"Don't tell me," said Fred "Hatchet denies supplying the tins?"

"That's right. But guess who the stablehand is that distributes Hatchet's meat? None other than Poulter's cousin, Martin Coope."

"Ok, I'm with you so far." said Fred. "You're suggesting that Poulter is supplyin' 'is cousin with tins of dog food which 'ee then sells on t' Hatchet's customers that 'ee's deliverin' meat to. That seems simple enough, but leaves two very important questions. One, where does Poulter get the tins from because e' don't have a canning machine. And two, why? What's in it vur Poulter?"

"Right." Began Dave. "As far as I can tell no one has a canning machine. Poulter hasn't got one in his shop, and neither does Hatchet. The only one I'm not sure of is Fetlock, because it would be easy to hide one at his stables. However, there is an old canning machine in one of the sheds on Lord Woods' estate, but it looks like it hasn't been used for years.

"But what if whoever makes the tins goes back in time to use the canning machine? That way, if they were clever, they would only have to buy one lot of tins and simply go back a little further each time they used the machine, utilising the same tins over and over again. Not only that, but ARGH!!! Get off you $%£#@!!!!"

It took the other two a few seconds to realise what was happening, but a quick glance revealed a ginger ball of fur affectionately sinking its claws into Dave's leg. Somehow the cat had managed to find a way past the locked trapdoor and into the cellar.

Fred grabbed it by the scruff of its neck, and despite its hissing and frequent attempts to swing around and disembowel him, he managed to carry it up the stairs and eject it from the back door.

"Carry on lad." Said Fred as he returned to his seat.

"As I was saying, not only is there an old canning machine in that shed, but also a lot of empty shotgun cartridges."

Judging by the blank looks on the faces of the other two, this revelation did not have the effect that Dave had hoped. With a sigh, he started again.

"Gunpowder has, at times, been known to be used by dishonest kennels to make dogs more vicious so that they make higher prices as guard dogs."

"So whoever is canning the dog food was puttin' the powder into it. Which in turn soured the dog's stomach an' made it mad enough t' attack its master!" said Albert happily, chuffed that he had managed to follow Dave's line of reasoning.

"That's right!" said Dave with some relief. "And probably the lead shot too."

"Alright." Said Fred dubiously. "But the question still remains, why Poulter?"

"Because he is in debt. In fact he is heavily in debt. He told me so himself, although he didn't tell me how much or to whom. Everything was fine until the quality of his meat started to go down. Eventually he lost the contract to supply Lord Woods and thus lost his entitlement to the land he had been promised in exchange. That left him in debt. My guess is that he hoped the coroner would either honour the terms of Lord Woods' old will or that the coroner would divide up the land equally between all the claimants."

"But why would Poulter want to kill Chalky? It makes no sense." Pointed out Fred.

Dave reached for his coffee to take another swig, only to find a matching set of front claws dig into his hand.

"AHH! I thought you threw it out?" he said to Fred accusingly.

"I thought I 'ad." Replied the confused barman. "I don't understand 'ow it got back in. The trapdoor t' the kitchen is bolted, as is the door t' the yard. There's only the air vent an' that's got a fine mesh o're it t' stop rats an' mice from getting' in."

Dave tried to shoo the cat away but, in true feline fashion, it thought that this was some new game to play and kept trying to swipe at Dave's hand every time he waved it in the cats' direction. Albert had seen the earlier injuries that it had inflicted on Dave and stayed clear. Fred tried to grab it by the scruff again, but it was wise to that ploy and left the landlord with a line of four scratches across the back of his hand.

"See if you can distract it vur a bit while I look vur zummet t' chuck o're it." Said Fred, clutching his injured hand.

Dave pulled a handkerchief from his pocket and dangled it in front of the cat whilst Fred picked up one of the blankets he had used to lag the barrels and deaden the sound when Gladys had performed her set. With a flick of his wrist, he threw it over the cat and scooped the animal up in the blanket. Much hissing and spitting from within revealed what the cat thought of its new predicament. It kept poking its claws out through the material at random, hoping that sooner or later it was going to connect with something or someone. Fred carried the ad hoc sack out of the cellar and deposited the cat out in the yard for a second time.

"Now, where were we?" asked Fred when he returned once more.

"You was askin' the lad why Poulter would want t' kill Chalky." Said Albert helpfully.

"That's something I don't know." Admitted Dave. "All I can come up with is that the bomb that killed Chalky was made from a tin can, so presumably whoever killed one killed the other. Perhaps Chalky saw something? I don't know. But they were both at the inquest."

"Nah." Put in Fred. "Chalky's' death can't be ort t' do with

Poulter. 'Ee were in yere 'avin' a drink t'other night when Chalky's forge blew up. I know 'cos I served 'im. First time 'ee's been in vur ages."

"It wouldn't matter Fred." Said Dave with a smile.

The other two looked puzzled again. Secretly, Dave was quite pleased. He had felt lost and out of control since coming to Lyonshire. For the first time he was in charge and not the one that was repeatedly bewildered.

"Don't you remember when I first arrived? You told me about the rules?"

An even more confused Fred nodded in reply.

"You said the third rule was not to use time travel for practical jokes. You went on to explain that Tinny the smith and Poulter started playing practical jokes on each other, and as a result the third rule was introduced."

Both of them still had blank faces.

"Well, to play the jokes Poulter must have a very good knowledge of when and where to enter and leave Lyonshire to travel backwards and forwards in time with any accuracy. So it is quite possible for him to have planted the bomb and given himself an alibi. You said yourself that it was unusual for him to come in for a drink."

"Tiz true enough." Replied Fred matter of factly.

"On a hunch, I also asked Shem if there was a time gate, or whatever you call them, on Lord Woods' estate."

"And?"

"There is." Replied Dave smugly. "It's in the orchard and fenced off to stop anyone accidentally walking through it."

The three of them spent the rest of the evening discussing the various ins and outs of Dave's theory. Occasionally they would have to stop and evict the cat.

Chapter 9.

Dave awoke a full thirty seconds before Fred hammered on his door. It gave him the advantage of knowing exactly how many arms and legs he had and how they were arranged before he had to deal with anything complicated like holding a mug full of coffee.

As Fred headed off to the kitchen, Dave discovered that not only was he still alive and had the correct number of arms and legs in the right place, but also he was in good spirits. He sipped his mug of tar strength coffee in a more positive way. The feeling of control he had had the previous evening was still there. For the first time since coming to Lyonshire he felt settled. He no longer had to go with the flow, and was beginning to understand how things worked.

Besides, he wasn't stuck in an office all day, doing a job he didn't like, and making money for someone else. Here he was allowed to be his own person, and that made a big difference. He was also beginning to enjoy the splendour of Lyonshire and its non-intensively farmed countryside.

He glanced at his watch. It was a quarter past five. He'd only had five hours sleep, and yet he felt thoroughly refreshed. He sniffed gently and marvelled at the warm rich aroma of Fred's coffee.

Last night they had formulated a plan, or rather he had come up with the idea and, with the help of the other two, had refined it.

He leapt out of bed, dressed, and performed his ablutions. Standing in front of the mirror, he puffed out his chest like a superhero. It was time to make a difference.

Dave grabbed the door handle and went in search of despicable criminals.

And breakfast.

~~~~

Albert strolled gloomily through Shoton. The pre-dawn sky reflected Albert's gloomy mood. Mist had rolled in from wherever mist rolls in from, making the darkness before dawn wet and miserable. He was soaked from head to foot. His clothes stuck to his skin, and what little was left of his grey hair was plastered to his scalp.

Albert glared at the sky, daring it to do its worst. As if in response, a long low rumble of thunder rolled across the cloudy firmament. He stomped across the square and entered the pub. After a brief pause to dry himself as best he could on a couple of bar-towels and drink his breakfast, he continued on into the kitchen.

"Mornin' Bert" said Fred cheerfully.

No reply.

Dave set aside his empty plate. "Are you alright Albert?" he asked, and took another swig of his coffee.

"You don't seem your normal self s'mornin' Bert, anything wrong?" enquired Fred.

"Well who am I then?" snapped Albert.

"Now Bert, there's no need t' get snappy." Said Fred, trying to defuse the situation. "Come on, what's the matter?"

"There! Look!" snapped Albert as he flung the morning paper onto the table.

Fred and Dave both leaned in to scour the front page. It was the first time Dave had had a close look at one of Lyonshire's papers, even though he was supposedly working for the Hunton Times. The broadsheet Albert had flung on the table bore the legend 'The Lyonshire Daily News'.

"Well?" asked Fred. "What is it I'm s'pposed t' be lookin' at?"

"It's there on the front page! Bold as Brass!" Snapped Albert.

"Look Bert, I don't mean t' be rude but I don't see ort unusual." Replied Fred.

"You mean a vicar time looping himself six times to conduct two weddings, three christenings and a funeral simultaneously, and getting so confused that he can't remember which one is the real him isn't unusual?" asked Dave, as he read from the paper.

"No lad, that sort o' thing 'appens all the time." Replied Fred, patting Dave on the shoulder.

"I didn't see nort about no daft bible-basher!" said Albert sharply. "Let me 'ave a look."

Fred passed the soggy paper across the table.

"That's not it!" exclaimed Albert. "It's the wrong ruddy paper!"

"Well that's the paper you flung on the table Bert."

"Oh." Said Albert and sagged in his chair.

After a brief rummage within the confines of Albert's dripping raincoat, another paper was produced. This time it was the Penhampton News, which had very different headlines.

"Inquest into possible suicide of well-known and highly renowned blacksmith today." Read Fred aloud.

"There's nort vur it Fred, us 'as got t' go!" Blurted Albert. "We knows 'ee was murdered!"

"Don't you think it's time we turned all this over to the police and let them deal with it?" asked Dave.

"Fair enough, if we was in yur county." Replied Fred. "But we've got next t' no police force yere. There's normally no need. An' we could do with keepin' what we found out about Chalky's' death quiet, coz tiz all tied up with Timber's death."

"Then why don't the two of you have a quiet word with the coroner, you both know him. Couldn't you ask him to adjourn Chalky's inquest until after Lord Woods'?" asked Dave.

"Tiz so simple!" exclaimed Albert, his mood brightening. "I would never o' thought o' that! The court car's supposed t' be pickin' me up from yere vur the inquest as I'm still on the advisory panel at the mo."

"You reckon we could get a lift with you Bert?" asked Fred.

"I don't see why not. There's plenty o' room in the car as you knows. 'Ee should be yere soon." Replied Albert, glancing at his watch. "'Ee's a bugger vur turnin' up early."

Albert looked longingly at his empty glass.

"I s'ppose I'd better 'ave a cup o' tea." He said gloomily.

The court car did arrive early. The court would convene as usual at ten o'clock. The journey to Penhampton of just over thirty miles normally took forty-five minutes. So, the court car arrived at ten past six.

They made the driver wait.

Outside in the rain.

When the trio finally emerged from the pub, the driver dragged himself from the warm and dry air-conditioned interior of the car and held open the rear door to allow them to get in.

Fred and Albert seated themselves with the minimum of fuss, but Dave stood stock still staring in awe at the car, whilst rain soaked his hair and ran down the back of his neck unnoticed.

The chauffeur, assuming that Dave had never seen a car before, a rarity in Lyonshire, kindly pointed out, "It's an automobile or car Sir."

Dave looked around at the chauffeur. The expression on his face was not pretty.

"I know it's a car!" he said slowly through clenched teeth.

"My apologies Sir." Replied the chauffeur. "I did not mean to cause offence. Now if Sir would kindly be seated?"

Reluctantly Dave got in the car. He did know what cars were, he tried to avoid them as much as possible. They were claustrophobic boxes on wheels; even the ones without a roof. And all of them seemed to have an intermittent fault that prevented their indicators from working, usually as they were approaching junctions. He'd just never seen one quite like this.

This car was all black, apart from the chrome, and there was a lot of chrome. It had a polished radiator grill at the front that looked large enough to cool a playful volcano. The bonnet was about fifteen feet long, with a huge forward-facing air intake. On either side, the wheel arches curved gracefully up and over the small front wheels and swept down stylishly to join the running boards. The windscreen ran almost organically from the bonnet up over the single central driving position, giving almost a hundred and eighty degree forward visibility to the driver. Behind the driver the car flared out slightly to accommodate the limousine style passenger compartment, before tapering to an almost flat fishtail at the back. On either side the running boards widened dramatically and rose up to form elegant arches over the huge rear wheels. Twelve shiny chrome exhaust pipes fanned out from either side. Inside was no less extraordinary, with room to enfold six people comfortably in the deeply padded black leather seats. Polished wooden trim was everywhere.

"Right oh George." Called Albert to the driver, once Dave had seated himself.

The chauffeur turned the key, flicked up the safety cover and pressed the starter button. There was no usual whine of a starter-motor, just a long drawn out hiss as air was drawn into the engine through the intake on the bonnet. An unfortunate passing sparrow was plucked from the air and briefly pinned to the grill over the intake. Then the engine came to life, with the roar of two-dozen big cats, before settling down to a gentle throbbing purr.

The clutch was engaged, a gear selected and the handbrake released. Smoke poured off of the rear tyres for an instant, and then the car was gone. It didn't drive off; it was simply gone. All that remained in the village square was a cloud of atomised rubber, and a thick, tense heavy silence. After a moment, sound returned as the sonic boom shook the buildings.

A damp, bedraggled, and slightly stunned sparrow flew off in search of something to peck.

~~~~~

A black blur whistled along Market Road in Penhampton. A

titanium/kevlar-reinforced parachute billowed out behind the car as George steered the car into the almost empty cattle market car/wagon park and neatly parked it in a vacant space. The parachute folded itself away tidily.

The journey from Shoton had taken less than a minute.

Somewhat shaken, the trio emerged from the car as George held the door open for them. By the time they had caught their collective breath, the car had departed again with another sonic boom.

"S' one o' the advantages o' having next t' no traffic on the roads." Said Albert smugly.

"But that horse and cart!" exclaimed Dave, his face was deathly pale. "We hit it head on! We didn't even slow down!" He was appalled. "There must be little bits of the horse, cart and driver all over the road!"

Fred and Albert laughed.

"I don't think it's funny at all!" He snapped in disbelief. "I really don't understand you two sometimes!"

"S' alright lad." Said Fred soothingly.

"HOW CAN IT BE ALRIGHT?!"

"We didn't hit anything, and the horse an' cart are fine."

"But we hit it! We must've hit it!"

Albert placed a reassuring hand on Dave's shoulder. "No, we didn't. You see we were travellin' so fast that the molecules of the car an' us was so spread out that we went through the cart."

It didn't help Dave feel any better, just more confused. He turned to look at Fred for help.

"The molecules of the car became spread out a bit in time." Explained Fred.

By the look on Dave's face, this didn't help either.

Fred sighed and tried again.

"If you looks at zummet travellin' really fast it looks like a blur?"

Dave nodded.

"Now if e' takes zummet that's travellin' so fast that the front end has arrived before the rear end has started movin', it actually is in several places at once. So when it looked like we hit the cart, the car weren't actually there to hit it."

"So we didn't hit the cart?" asked Dave. Of all the strange things he had had to get to grips with since entering Lyonshire, this was the hardest. "We passed through it?"

"Near enough lad, near enough." Replied Albert.

"Oh." Was all Dave could think of to say. Whilst he waited for his brain to catch up, he glanced at his watch. It was half-past six. There were still three and a half hours to go before the inquest.

"So what do we do now?" he asked.

"Us 'as a stroll round the market t' start and zee about a coffee." Replied Fred with a shrug.

"What market? There's nothing here yet!" Dave swept his arm around to illustrate his point, and sat back heavily on the ground in astonishment.

In the time from when they had arrived to now, a seemingly bustling market had apparently sprung into existence and filled most of the carpark behind them.

"I didn't even hear them set up." Whispered Dave. It felt like life was going on around him and he was continuously running to keep up. Suddenly, spending eight hours a day doing a pointless job didn't seem so bad.

"You brung anythin' t' trade Fred?" asked Albert.

"Just a couple o' bottles o' ****." Replied Fred. "An' there's more 'an a few yere that owes vur me hospitality."

"Come on lad." Said Fred, giving him a hand up off the ground. "Lets 'ave a look round."

～～～～

By contrast, Lord Justice Hammond was exploring the contents of his breakfast tray. His valet had just brought it into him, and opened the curtains before retiring to within hearing distance of his master's bell.

On the tray were a cafetiere of fresh coffee, a large mug, sugar, milk and cream, and three gleaming silver tureens. Lord Hammond poured himself a mug of coffee and doctored it with a couple of spoons of sugar and a dash of milk. He sipped it thoughtfully for a moment before carefully lifting the lid off of the first tureen. It revealed a plate of bacon, sausages and eggs. All of it was covered in the little burnt crunchy bits you get if you don't ever change the fat in, or clean out, the frying pan. The next tureen revealed a plate of hot buttered crumpets oozing cholesterol.

He took several large gulps from his coffee and paused before lifting the third and final lid. He knew what would be under it, it was the same every morning. He smiled to himself. The contents of that last platter made waking up worthwhile, but it wasn't time to open it yet. A little excitement generated by the suspense put an edge on his appetite.

He chewed a crumpet, trying to distract himself from the tureen. No, he'd eat everything else first before he lifted the last lid. So he picked up his knife and fork and began to plough his way through the first meal of the day.

Finally, whilst doing his best to mop up the last of the melted butter with the last remnant of crumpet, he looked at the untouched lid and sighed. His hands were itching with anticipation, although that could have been caused by dripping butter. Cold shivers ran down his spine. But that could have been caused by butter as well. *[Just because he was a judge, it didn't mean he had good table manners.]*

A rogue thought struck him. It struck him every morning but it still worried him. What if it wasn't there? What would he do? What could he do? It was no good, he simply had to know. He closed his eyes and lifted the lid.

Peeking out through partially closed eyes, he let out a sigh. It was there! Carefully he placed the lid to one side and gazed wistfully at the tray. His heart pounding, he drained the last of his coffee and sat up straight to fully appreciate the sight before him.

It was a glass of prune juice.

But not just any prune juice. This was the best. Made from the finest sun dried plums, reconstituted to a secret family recipe, his family recipe, and squeezed to extract every last drop of precious juice. It was then matured in scorched oak barrels for three hundred years and stored in a cool, dry cellar. His cellar.

Every year he took a holiday and travelled back to his family plum orchards. Of course he had to rough it for a few weeks, but then, three hundred years ago they didn't have the same modern conveniences.

He'd oversee the harvest, and even help layout and turn the plums as they dried in the sun. Then he'd monitor the reconstitution and pressing of the previous year's prunes, and sample it for quality as it was put into the barrels to age.

After a month, he would return *home [Or what would be his home in three hundred years]* and place a year's supply of new barrels in his cellar exactly three hundred years ago, and then return home to the present to sample it again. *[Always his favourite part.]*

A good fry-up followed by a glass of the finest prune juice set you up for the day. And kept you regular.

Dave found the market fascinating. He regularly visited his local market at the weekends, and always bought his fruit and veg from it, but other than that it was a bit dull. Usually the other stalls would sell things like clothing seconds, or high street fashion surplus, cheap plastic toys from far away sweatshops and salesmen demonstrating the latest totally useless labour-saving gadgets that it was impossible to live without. All the stalls promised never to be repeated, once in a lifetime offers that would be there again next week. The only high point was the local farmer's market once a month, which offered not only fruit and veg, but also local meat, cheese, fish and a plethora of homemade jams and chutneys.

But, as with everything else in Lyonshire, this market was as far from Dave's experience of markets as possible. Almost everything ever, and to be, invented was here. No money was changing hands, everything was being bartered for. Within a hundred yards it was possible to barter for anything from a cold-fusion powered combine harvester to a Neolithic flint axe from a hairy looking gentleman in animal skins. Meat of every description hung from hooks. Fruit of different shapes, sizes and colours from all over the globe were heaped in enticing piles. Fresh and saltwater fish and shellfish of every kind rested in beds of slowly melting ice. And the smells! A combination of aromas enticed the senses from every direction. Fresh fruit and veg, the fish, and the meat were just the beginning. Newly tanned hides of leather, cut flowers of every colour and description, stalls selling incense, other selling perfume, freshly roasted coffee, spices, newly baked bread and a wide diversity of stalls selling cooked takeaway food from around the globe were all giving the olfactory nerves a good workout.

Dave watched as the carcass of a whole pig was carried through the market by a couple of men who were presumably butchers. It stopped next to a vegetable stall, and a leg was cut off and exchanged for a selection of fruit and veg. Further along it stopped by a woman grinding knives. One of the butchers handed over several knives, which the woman duly sharpened. After checking the blades, another joint was cut off and handed over.

Fascinated, Dave completely forgot his companions, and wandered through the crowd following the carcass. Gradually it diminished in size, and the number of parcels the butchers carried increased until the last pork chop was gone.

Fred and Albert meandered through the busy market, tasting this, stopping to look at that. Occasionally Fred would call in some debt or favour as they went. And by the time Dave caught up with them at a stall selling freshly brewed coffee, Fred had a new pair of boots, a flat cap and a large brown paper parcel under his chair.

"Alright lad?" asked Albert cheerfully, and called across the counter to order another coffee.

"You've been busy I see." Said Dave, nodding towards Fred's

parcel.

"Tiz just a few bits I've been meanin' t' pick up vur months." Replied Fred, shuffling his feet and obscuring Dave's view of the parcel. "What do 'ee think of me new boots then?"

Dave was envious. They were a good quality, hand stitched, serviceable pair of boots that would last for several years, and would have cost him several months' wages at home.

"I wouldn't mind a pair of them myself." He admitted.

Albert looked up at the distant church clock. It was already after nine.

"'Ere, we'd better be makin' a move in a mo. The inquest starts at ten, an' we needs t' 'ave a word with the coroner before han'."

Dave glanced at his watch, Albert was right. He couldn't believe how fast the time had gone. It seemed only moments ago that they had arrived in Penhampton but more than two and a half hours had passed

~~~~~

Keith, the neanderthal like court guard, sat in his cubbyhole by the main entrance staring blankly at the huge clock on the wall. As the hands ticked around to half-past nine it triggered a switch, which in turn lit up a large illuminated sign. The sign flashed in big, easy to read letters: 'Open Door'. Above his beady eyes, Keith's large overhanging forehead creased as he tried to think. The sign meant something. But what was it?

After a minute or two, he worked out the connection, it was time to put his cap on, go and open the door, and stop anyone with weapons or cameras from entering. He stood up, further straining the already overstretched material of his uniform, and splitting another seam. His huge hairy paw grabbed for his cap, crushing it in the process, and slapped the abused millinery on his head. He left what passed for his office and unbolted the doors into the court building.

That was the difficult bit over with. His brow relaxed and uncreased. All he had to do now was to stop anyone entering the court with weapons or photographic equipment. He spread his feet and folded his arms, adopting the pose necessary to remain standing on the same spot all day.

~~~~~

Fred, Dave, and Albert strode towards the court building, with Fred clutching his mystery parcel under one arm.

"D' you bring the remains o' that tin can with you Bert?" He asked gloomily.

"You mean that bomb Fred?"

"I didn't mean a flaming tin of corned beef!" snapped Fred with uncharacteristic sharpness.

Since they'd left the market Fred had become more and more sullen and withdrawn. His usual cheery nature and smile had vanished, replaced by a scowl.

"'Old yur 'orses Fred." Replied Albert, his feelings hurt. "I was only askin'."

"Sorry Bert. I was just thinkin' what a bad business this all is. I can't understan' where all this nastiness 'as come from." Apologised Fred, shaking his head with misery.

They climbed the steps to the court entrance in silence. At the top Keith blocked their way.

"You got any concealed weapons, recording or photographic equipment?" He rumbled.

They shook their heads.

"You got a handbag what I got to check?" Continued Keith, reading from notes on the cuff of his shirt.

"NO!" shouted Fred. "Now get out of the way and let us ruddy well pass!"

"Now Fred." Said Albert soothingly, and placing a restraining hand on Fred's arm.

Albert noticed something out of the corner of his eye.

"Wait a minute!" he exclaimed. "That weren't yere before!" Albert pointed to the wall.

The expression on Keith's face changed as rapidly as his genetic makeup would allow, and eventually lit up in a beaming smile. The three friends were forced to take a step back as his massive chest swelled with pride.

"That thur new hat rack." He boomed. "I made it my self." He rapped his fingers against his chest.

Fred, Dave and Albert looked at it. It was obvious that Keith had grasped the concept of a hat rack, and that sometimes a stuffed stags head was used for this purpose. So, he'd gone out somewhere and purloined a stag. And quite a magnificent one too, with wide, many-pointed antlers. However, having obtained the animal and killed it, he must have been at a loss as to what to do next. Thus confused, he had simply nailed the whole thing to the wall. And it was beginning to smell rather unpleasant. *[Although that could have been Keith himself.]*

"It…. It….err…. looks good." Lied Dave.

For some reason this was the straw that broke the camels' back for the already overwrought Fred. He couldn't contain himself. He burst out laughing.

Quickly, Dave and Albert each grabbed one of Fred's arms and half carried, half dragged him past the offended guard.

The interior of the court was no different than it had been at the beginning of the week, only quieter. Those few cases that needed to be heard before a court were generally sorted out by mid-week or had been adjourned to allow the various solicitors, barristers and independent committees to argue over some point of law or the exact meaning of a word or phrase. The few gowns still floating around were trying to look important, but they had a half-hearted end of the week-ness about them.

Fred had tears in his eyes as the other two led him over to the vending machine. Albert hit it until it disgorged three cups of scalding brown liquid it tried to pass off as coffee.

"Us's got to get into zee the coroner a'fore the inquest." Whispered Albert.

Dave glanced at the clock on the wall. It was nearly ten o'clock.

"We'll have to hurry then, the inquest is supposed to start in a few minutes."

"You don't want t' worry 'bout that lad, they always says ten o'clock but never gets themselves organised 'till half-past." Replied Albert.

"So how are we going to get to see the coroner? From what little experience I have of courts, the judges have private chambers well away from the public areas." Hissed Dave.

Fred was not doing well. His hysteria had degenerated into floods of tears. He had his arms crossed on top of the vending machine; his head nestled in his hands. Tears streaked down his normally cheery face.

Much to Dave's surprise, Albert started to go through Fred's pockets. Fred was apparently oblivious.

"What are you doing!" hissed Dave.

"Relax lad, I knows 'ee's still got one somewhere." Replied Albert, switching pockets.

"Ah! Got it."

"Got what?"

"A bottle o' ****." Replied Albert, pulling the small thick bottle from Fred's pocket. "'Ee brung a few with 'im t' trade."

"I don't think this is quite the right time or place for that." Observed Dave.

Albert ignored him and carefully eased the top off of the bottle.

"Now, we don't want to overdo it." Said Albert.

He wafted the bottle under Fred's nose a few times. Nothing. No reaction at all.

"Well I'll be!" exclaimed Albert. "'Ee must be worse than I thought."

Between them they managed to force a little of the liquid between Fred's lips. The reaction was instant. Fred stood bolt upright, almost to attention.

"****!" Swore Fred, coming back to his senses and knocking the bottle away from his mouth.

The thick bottle bounced once on the marble floor before coming to rest against the wall, spilling the rest of its contents. The marble began to fizz and dissolve rapidly, until the **** ate its way through the floor and disappeared into the basement.

"And we drink that stuff?" asked Dave in disbelief.

"Don't worry lad, tiz perfectly safe t' drink." Replied Fred, his faculties restored. "So what's happenin'?"

"We 'ave to get in t' see the coroner." Said Albert, peering around the corner towards the judge's chambers. "There's one o' them gowns prowlin' around."

"Then we need a distraction." Replied Dave, rounding the corner. "Excuse me! Excuse me?" he called to the gown in the corridor.

"Yes? What is it?" snapped the irritated gown. How dare someone actually approach him?

"I think you've got a problem you should look at." Replied Dave.

"WHAT? What cheek! How dare you imply that there is a problem! Why the very idea that something is wrong is preposterous!"

"I don't know about preposterous, but there's a hole in the floor over there and it could cause a nasty accident." Said Dave.

A panicked look crossed the gown's face as he rushed across to look at the hole caused by the spilt ****.

"My word!" exclaimed the shocked gown. "How on earth could that've happened?" He stood still looking at the hole, apparently at a loss as to what to do.

"Erm, I wouldn't want to speak out of place," began Dave in the most subservient tone he could manage, "and far be it from me to presume to tell you your job, but…"

"Yes?" asked the perplexed gown. "Please, continue. I would value your input."

"Well, if I was in your position, I might be inclined to go down to the basement and see where the hole goes and just how deep it is, and whether or not it has affected anything important?" Suggested Dave meekly.

"Do you think I should?" asked the gown, totally lost in a situation that didn't fit into his normal routine.

"If I was in your place..." Dave left it hanging.

"Yes..." Said the gown tentatively. "Yes." He said again in a more positive tone. "Perhaps I should. It might have damaged some pipes or whatnot. But I will have to wait for one of my colleagues to watch the corridor for me."

"I could do that if you like?" offered Dave. "I mean it could be a while before one of your colleagues comes along, and by then the damage could already have been done."

"No, no I couldn't do that. Could I?"

"I don't see why not, it seems fairly quiet today. It's not like there are any dangerous criminals in here."

"Right!" said the gown, he had obviously made up his mind. "I have an idea. If you would be good enough to watch the corridor and prevent anyone from harassing the judges, I'll go and investigate."

"That sounds reasonable to me. Since you asked so nicely I'll watch the corridor for you and stop anyone disturbing the judges." Replied Dave.

The gown went off to investigate the 'mysterious' hole, leaving Dave, Fred and Albert in the unguarded corridor.

"Well done lad!" said Albert, slapping Dave on the back and almost knocking him off his feet.

Quickly they found the door with the correct nameplate. Albert knocked on the door and went in. After a moment his head reappeared around the door.

"S' all clear, come on."

The opulent surroundings of the judge's chambers amazed Dave. The walls were adorned with wood panelling and carved oak details. The carpet on the floor had pile so deep his feet sank into it. Next to a roaring log fire, Lord Justice Hammond was sitting in an enormous green button-backed leather armchair. The three companions seated themselves on an even larger matching sofa.

"Hello." Said the coroner cheerily.

"This is the lad I was tellin' 'ee about an' o' course you knows Fred." Said Albert.

"So what was so *h*important that you had to sneak *h*into my chambers?" asked the coroner.

"Well," began Albert. For some reason Fred had gone back to being sullen and sat quietly. "Well, you knows that we saw ol' Timbers killed by 'is dog? It didn't sit right with Fred an' me so we asked the lad yere to investigate a bit cos 'ee's an outsider an' 'ad nothin' t' gain from it. Then Chalky ends up dead in mysterious circumstances so 'ee went an' 'ad a look at that too." Said Albert a bit sheepishly.

"There *h*is nothing mysterious *h*about Chalky's death," put in the coroner, "*h*I went *h*and witnessed the *h*explosion myself."

"Ah, not to doubt your word, but did you 'ave a poke around in the wreckage a'terwards? Or find out what it were that actually caused the explosion?"

"No, *h*I didn't see *h*any point, *h*it looked like *h*a straightforward *h*accident to me."

"I'm afraid that, that's where us differs." Said Albert sadly. He fished around in his pockets and pulled out the twisted scrap of metal Dave had found.

"As I was sayin', we got the lad yere t' poke around a bit in the wreckage, an' e' found this." Albert handed over the remains of the can.

"*h*It looks like *h*a piece *h*of scrap metal to me." Replied the coroner in a nonplussed tone.

"That's what it looks like at first glance." Cut in Dave. "But Chalky was a blacksmith and blacksmiths don't normally work with thin sheet metal. That's what drew my attention to it in the first place, it shouldn't have been there."

"So?" asked the coroner. "Perhaps he was doing something *h*outside his normal remit *h*and was working with sheet metal?"

"That is possible, but if Albert would be good enough to …" began Dave.

"Not a problem lad." Replied Albert. "Just set it down on the table well away from ort else."

Dave did as he was told and set the chard and twisted scrap of metal down on the table, and stepped back.

"*h*I still don't see" began Lord Hammond, as Albert began to concentrate on the scrap metal. "why *h*it *h*is *h*important, *h*it doesn't seem to be… *h*OH MY WORD!" he exclaimed, as the twisted metal straightened itself out to the shape it remembered, complete with hissing fuse.

"*h*ALRIGHT *h*ALBERT! That's *h*enough." Screamed the coroner, as the fuse fizzled away. "*h*I'm convinced!"

Albert stopped concentrating and the can reverted back to being a charred and twisted scrap.

"Fair puts the cat amongst the pigeons an' no mistake!" he said.

The coroner mopped his forehead with a hankie and drained his glass of prune juice. He was not naturally a coward, but the thought of little bits of himself being liberally distributed around the local vicinity made him more than a little nervous.

"Yesss," he said shakily, "*h*It certainly puts *h*a different slant *h*on things. What would you suggest?"

"Adjourn Chalky's inquest an' leave the rest t' us. Dave already has an idea of who's behind this nasty business." Said Fred angrily.

"I do, but I have no way of proving it as yet and need a little more time." Replied Dave.

"Lord Woods' *h*inquest *h*is *h*on Monday, *h*and *h*it's Friday today, that gives you the weekend to sort *h*it *h*all *h*out." Said the coroner. "*h*I can't really give you *h*any more time than that without having to *h*answer too many *h*awkward questions."

They all looked at Dave.

"Well lad?" Asked Fred. "D' you think you can sort it by then?"

Dave let out a long sigh, and scratched his bearded chin for a time before answering. "I don't honestly know, but I'll do my best."

"Right!" said Fred jumping up out of his seat. "Now that's all zorted, let's find that blasted car so uz can go 'ome!"

~~~~~

After another hair-raising journey in the court car, Dave and Fred returned to the Stoat and Ferret. Albert decided to remain behind in Penhampton to make certain that Lord Justice Hammond actually did adjourn Chalky's inquest.

Fred bolted from the car as soon as it drew up outside the pub, his parcel tightly gripped under one arm. He had not had a good day, and was desperate to get back to where he belonged behind the bar. He charged in through the door, across the floor of the bar and vaulted all nineteen stone of himself over the bar with apparent ease.

A chorus of cheers and applause went up from the appreciative crowd of regulars, apart from the poor unfortunate Tinny the smith who had been directly behind the door when Fred had entered. But someone helped him back to his feet and the concussion would pass after a few days.

Fred poured himself a tankard full of his own special coffee and, without waiting for it to cool down, drained it in one swift motion, before letting out a sigh of relief. Normally he was unshakeable, but going to the court had been too much for him. It had brought home the fact that even in his normally peaceful Lyonshire, evil lurked just under the surface. To begin with it had been an interesting diversion getting Dave to investigate Lord Woods' mysterious demise. Now it was no longer a game. Innocent people were dying.

Outside, Dave was torn. Did he follow his friend into the bar? Or did he ask George the chauffer to pop the bonnet of the car so he could have a look at the engine? In the end it wasn't much of a contest, as he followed his friend into the bar, just in time to knock Tinny off his feet with the door for a second time.

Chapter 10.

It was dark and slightly chilly as Albert and the coroner waited. But then it had been dark and slightly chilly at five o'clock last Tuesday morning.

Albert shivered. "I wish I'd brung a thicker coat." He moaned, stamping his feet in an effort to keep warm.

After the coroner had adjourned the inquest, both of them had gone back in time to act as witnesses.

"*h*I wish *h*I'd brought *h*a larger flask." Said the coroner miserably as he emptied the last of his coffee from his vacuum flask into his cup.

"You think *h*I've got time to go *h*and fill *h*it *h*up?" he asked Albert hopefully.

"No!" snapped Albert. "'Ere, suck a peppermint." He said irritably, proffering a bag of humbugs.

"Thank you."

Behind them the sun began to rise as it had done three days before. Various cockerels and dogs around the city raised their voices to welcome in the new day. They were followed closely by a rain of thrown boots and shoes or anything else that came to hand, and shouts of "SHUT UP!" or "JUST WAIT UNTIL I GET THE SAGE AND ONION READY!".

"Look!" exclaimed Albert. "He's up."

"Where? *h*I don't see *h*anything?"

"There, see? The curtains just opened upstairs." Replied Albert in a conspiratorial whisper. "Come on! Let's 'ave a peek in through the windows o' the forge."

They traipsed across the road from their vantage point in Butchers' Row and peered in through the grimy windows. Lord Hammond tried to wipe off some of the dirt with his sleeve but most of the grime was on the inside.

Chalky was inspecting his forge, raking it over and emptying out the ashes. Next he put a small shovel full of coal onto it and pumped the bellows a few times until the fire blazed away cheerfully.

"If things go the way they did the other day, an' there's no reason why not, then we're goin' t' 'ave t' make a run vur it in a mo." Pointed out Albert.

"*h*I think you *h*are right Bert." Replied Lord Hammond.

They watched a little longer as Chalky drew off water from his pump in the smithy and set his kettle down on the forge. As he pumped the bellows a couple more times, something caught his eye. Carefully he picked it up with a pair of tongs. It was fizzing.

"RUN!" shouted Albert.

Both he and the coroner were not the fittest of men, especially Albert who was almost as wide as he was tall, but with the threat of the imminent explosion both of them sprinted across the square in a time a professional athlete would have been proud of.

BOOM!

Bits of stone and mortar rained down around them. Once the larger fragments had finished their descent both men straightened up and looked at each other. In the early morning sunlight the drifting dust made them look like a pair of spectral apparitions. By mutual unspoken agreement, they both decided it was time to go home.

~~~~~

Since returning home to his pub, Fred had made a full recovery, and was now happily chatting to and serving his customers, with a mug of his own special coffee welded to his hand.

Dave had kitted himself out, donned his helmet and ridden off to Hunton to write up the first part of his story for the Hunton Times. His problems had started just as he reached the outskirts of Shoton, when his bike engine began to cough and splutter. Changing down a gear, the engine picked up momentarily before gradually petering out altogether.

He knew it wasn't anything major, having ridden a bike since he had been old enough to have a licence, he recognised the symptoms as a lack of petrol. Reaching down under the tank he turned the petrol tap around to reserve and waited a few minutes for the fuel to flow again and restarted the bike. The trouble was that the reserve tank only held enough petrol for twenty miles or so, usually enough to get to the nearest petrol station and fill up. However, since his sojourn into Lyonshire had begun, he hadn't seen a single petrol station and he had more miles to do than the reserve fuel would allow.

There was only one thing for it, he would have to leave Lyonshire and fill up. The turning was not far ahead, and he could go home and pick up some clothes and be back before he left. He glanced at his watch to check the time. It was coming up to one o'clock. So according to Fred's instructions he should end up going back to a time before he'd entered Lyonshire the first time.

Having been caught out before, Dave took the precaution of switching on his headlight as he drove past the barrier. Which was just as well because it was indeed dark on the other side. He didn't know exactly which night he had gone back to, but he knew that it must be before his first visit to Lyonshire, and briefly thought about warning himself. He could also tell himself what he knew about the murders and speed up the investigation, but he wasn't sure exactly what effect this would have. He had read several articles by eminent physicists who had hypothesised that doing such a thing could result in the destruction of the universe. After his experience in Lyonshire he was no longer sure if this was true, or whether eminent physicists simply spent too much time in stuffy universities contemplating their own navels.

Eventually he decided against the idea to be on the safe side. Besides, he couldn't remember talking to himself and so he hadn't. And secondly, the idea of meeting himself would probably give his other self a heart attack. Just trying to think his way through it was enough to give him a headache.

He rode towards his home in Tiverton and stopped at a twenty-four hour petrol station to fill up. The tank filled, he began fishing around in his pockets, and he realised he had left all his money on the dressing table in his room at the Stoat and Ferret. It had been more or less useless in Lyonshire, nothing more than ballast in his pockets so he'd taken it out. He did however have his cash-card, which meant he could get money from the automated machine outside his bank.

Dave walked over to the petrol stations' shop to explain the situation. He left his bike by the pump. There didn't seem any point in moving it, there wasn't a queue at whatever time in the morning it was, and he didn't want to be accused of driving away without paying. As he entered, he could see the man behind the counter was sat on a stool watching a small black and white portable television.

Television! When had he last watched or even thought about television! Briefly he felt a pang of loss and withdrawal, but it quickly evaporated as he realised he'd had a much more enjoyable time not watching television. He hadn't sat down and had his brain sucked out as he watched endless repeats, watching only because it was what people did in the evenings. Hours of reality shows and soap operas that tried to mirror real life but which were really the other way around. Un-funny comedy programs that went for the cheap laugh by demeaning someone else or by swearing profusely for no apparent reason. The only bits worth watching were the repeats of comedy programs that were at least twenty years old or the few defunct sci-fi series.

As Dave approached the counter he picked up a newspaper from the stand. It was dated three weeks before he'd first gone to Lyonshire. He'd stayed at Jo's flat that night. It was the anniversary of when they'd first met. One of the many occasions a man daren't forget on pain of serious pain or being ignored for a month or two. He had taken her out for a meal to celebrate and then gone back to her place afterwards. The memory of that night made him smile.

"Them's yesterdays." Said the shopkeeper, spoiling Dave's reminiscing.

"I'm sorry?"

"I said, them's yesterdays. I've got the new 'ns yere if you want one. I've been meanin' to swap 'em over but got absorbed in the film." He pointed to the screen behind him. "I'll see to it d'reckly."

"No. I am afraid I've filled up with petrol but haven't got any cash on me, only my cashpoint card. But my bank is just around the corner so I'll leave my bike here and go and get some. If that is alright?"

"Normally you've got to fill out a form but if you're leaving your bike you're not actually driving off with the petrol so I suppose it's alright." Replied the bored attendant.

"Thanks." Replied Dave and he wandered off to his bank.

He pushed his card into the slot and typed in his pin-number. The machine apparently didn't like it and told him to enter it again. He tried once more. Again it refused his request. So, rather than loose his card to the three strikes and you're out routine, he pressed the button and the machine spat out his card. It wasn't his cashcard. He remembered that his cashcard had already been eaten by this very same machine, or would be in three weeks' time. This card was his cheque card and quite incapable of extracting any money from a "hole in the wall" at all.

Dave sighed. How was he going to pay for the petrol now? He tapped the card against the side of his hand as he thought. He could go to his flat, it was a bit of a walk from here, and find his cashcard but then he wouldn't have it in three weeks when the machine ate it.

He glanced at his card again and noticed the Estuary logo in the corner. This wasn't just a cheque guarantee card, it was an Estuary card as well and could be used to pay for things and get cash back.

Feeling rather foolish, he ran back to the garage.

~~~~~

It was lunchtime at the Stoat and Ferret. The bar was unusually quiet. Albert still hadn't returned from Penhampton and business was slow. But then it usually was on a Friday. Most of the regulars either had stalls at Penhampton market or went there to shop, so they wouldn't be in until the evening.

Fred sat at a table picking his way through a brace of grouse, gleaning the meat from the bones. Accompanying the birds on his plate were a pound of crunchy roast potatoes, a mound of carrots and a pile in the corner of his plate he was doing his best to ignore; sprouts. *[Of the small number of people on the planet that actually like sprouts, half are in institutions. The other half only eat sprouts because they were force-fed them as children and have never managed to break the habit. Sprout tops on the other hand, the bit that is normally thrown away, are divine sautéed in a little butter and black pepper.]*

Hal was busy in the kitchen, doing what he did best, cooking up the fresh produce Fred received as payment into something mouth-watering. Suzan had gone home as soon as Fred had returned and felt well enough to cope.

It had been a bad day. One of the worst that Fred could remember. Upon his return, he'd checked the various batches of beer out in the sheds and even turned the malting barley, but his heart hadn't been in it. He didn't even fancy pudding, and it was his favourite, spotted dick and custard. He wished Albert and the lad were there to talk to.

The situation didn't get any better when one of Aunt Aggie's feral cats sank its teeth into his leg whilst he was eating.

"Aargh! Get off you little $%@#$!!!"

The cat removed its teeth from his leg and sat looking lovingly up at him with a "Who? Me?" look on its face before raking Fred's leg with its claws.

"Clear off! Go on, shoo! Shoo!"

Fred got to his feet and flailed at the cat with his napkin. In true cat fashion, the intruder thought that Fred wanted to play and swiped a paw at the cloth. Fred flicked it again, and this time the cat caught it on its claws and shredded the corner.

"I don't believe this!" exclaimed Fred. "I'm not even safe in me own pub." He went in search of a broom.

The cat followed, reluctant to give up its newfound toy.

"You're goin' t' get it in a minute sonny Jim."

Fred grabbed the broom and brought it to bear on the malignant moggie, sweeping the cat across the floor towards the backdoor.

The cat soon tired of being pushed across the floor and found it was much more fun riding on the broom. It looked up, pleased with this new game and began to purr at Fred.

"Hal! Hal, open the back door quick."

Obligingly, Hal opened the back door and held it open. The passing cat took a swipe at him.

"That's got to be one of Agatha's. Vicious little swines they are."

"That's easy enough t' work out." Replied Fred. "They guard 'er shop. There plenty that gets on well enough with dugs. But cats... Well they're loyal t' no one."

Fred managed to sweep the cat out into the yard. Hal quickly closed the door behind them.

Now the broom had stopped moving, it wasn't fun anymore and the cat stopped purring. It sneered at Fred and bit a clump of bristles out of the brush and began to chew them with every sign of enjoyment.

Fred had the feeling the cat had just threatened him. He shook it off of the broom and backed away towards the door. He groped behind him, feeling for the doorknob. Carefully, not turning his back to the cat, he opened the door. Once in the kitchen he slammed the door and turned the key to be on the safe side.

"I've got nort against cats, not that I'm fond of 'em mind, but I'm sure 'er cats aren't normal." He said.

"That's true enough Fred." Replied Hal. "I've got a mate o'er Fishin way who's got a pair o' tigers and I'd wager one o' Aggie's cats would rip both o' 'em apart."

Fred sighed, shrugged his shoulders and walked back into the bar to finish his lunch. Hal watched him go and drew off some warm water to bathe the scratches he'd received.

"HAL! HAL! WHERE'S MY SHOTGUN!" screamed Fred from the bar.

Hal dropped the bowl of water and ran into the bar to see what Fred was shouting about. He dashed through the doorway and burst out laughing at the tableau before him.

Fred was staring in disbelief at the table where he had been sitting, and his plate of food. His empty plate of food. *[Apart from the pile of sprouts which was still there.]* Even his bowl of spotted dick and custard was gone, the empty bowl rolling slowly around on the table. A fat, well-fed cat was lying on the table. Another was curled up on the warm patch on Fred's chair. A third was swaggering across the floor towards the door, its distended belly swaying to and fro.

"T'waz acting as a decoy!" laughed Hal. "No wonder it were so determined not t' leave! It was keeping you busy so t'others could sneak in an' scoff your lunch!"

Fred was fuming. He grabbed a soda-siphon in each hand from

behind the bar and let loose a double volley at the retreating cat. He hit it with both jets of water, soaking it from head to foot in an instant. The drenched and startled moggie leapt straight up into the air, its legs rigid, its back arched, its claws at full stretch and hissing for all it was worth.

Its two companions reclining on the table and chair heard its hissing and made a quick dash for the exit. Fred was faster, redirecting the jets of water and soaking both of them. Both of them hissed. One even tried a spirited but unsuccessful attempt to disembowel the offending jets of water.

Those few customers that were in the bar, whistled and cheered as the last cat left the bar.

"Fastest siphon in the west!"

"You showed 'em who's boss Fred."

"Alright you lot." Said Fred. "That's enough. I didn't see any o' you lot doing ort about it. And as vur you Hal, you can stop ruddy laughing an' get back t' work in the kitchen." He snapped.

"I've just about 'ad enough of 'er cats. When Bert gets back I'll go o're an' 'ave a word with our Aunt Agatha."

~~~~~

Dave felt like a fool. He'd had the card for over a year and only ever used it as a cheque card. He didn't believe in credit or debit cards, as they were just a tool used by banks to make more money out of people that couldn't afford it. He hadn't wanted the card in the first place, but the bank had stopped issuing simple cheque guarantee cards, and in his opinion, were trying to get rid of chequebooks all together.

Returning to the garage, he had a quick look around the shop to see if there was anything that he needed. There wasn't, but if there had been he wouldn't have bought it anyway. After being in Lyonshire, everything here seemed insubstantial, false and artificial. There was not one thing there for sale that he couldn't get a better, more decorative or thought-out equivalent in Lyonshire. He'd only been there for less than a week and yet his own world was already beginning to feel so contrived.

With a sigh he wandered over to the counter and paid the terminally bored all night attendant for his petrol with the dreaded Estuary card.

"Do you want a receipt?"

"What? Sorry?" stammered Dave, dragging his thoughts back from Lyonshire.

"You looked like you were a million miles away." Said the attendant. "Somewhere nice I hope? Do you want a receipt?" he asked again.

Dave shook his head in reply, took his card and headed for his bike as fast as he could. With his bike underneath him once more, he felt slightly reassured. It gave him the power to go anywhere and, after his recent experience, anywhen. He patted it affectionately and rode off towards his flat.

The flat was just as he had left it three weeks ago when he'd taken Jo out to dinner; a mess. It was strange, but looking back, he remembered coming home the next day and being puzzled to find it tidy. So presumably he was going to tidy it up now.

After a bit of progressive thinking, he remembered the argument he'd had with the bank after his last statement had arrived with an Estuary payment on it. At the time he knew for a fact that he hadn't ever made an Estuary payment on the card. Now he knew that it was simply a case that he hadn't made the payment yet.

He looked around his flat. Surrounding him was the wreckage of a bachelor trying to dress to impress his girlfriend. He smiled again at the fond memory of that evening, and began picking up discarded clothes, putting the clean ones away and the dirty ones in his bag ready to take to the laundrette.

He opened a window and let out the awful smell of deodorant and aftershave. He scratched his beard thoughtfully, picked up the bottle of aftershave and threw it in the bin. He wouldn't be needing that again. After another moments thought, he threw out the deodorant as well, its artificial scent now smelt more revolting than a dung heap.

Gradually Dave worked his way around his flat, clearing up the mess he'd made several weeks ago. When he was finished he remembered why he was there, grabbed a rucksack and put a change of clothes into it.

As he switched off the light, retrieved his helmet and locked the door, it struck him that he felt more at home in the Stoat and Ferret than he did here. This was just a place to exist; there it was a place to be.

He got back on his bike as quickly as he could and set off to find the footpath that would take him back to Lyonnesse.

～～～

A large quantity of strong drink with the coroner had done little to lighten Albert's mood after witnessing the explosion of Chalky's forge. It had, however, removed all his control over his legs, assuming that they were actually his legs. When George the chauffeur had arrived to take him back to Shoton, he'd had to physically assist Albert out to the car and then into the Stoat and Ferret. Inside he gently set Albert down in a chair and looked around for help.

There wasn't any. The bar was deserted. He called out.

"Hello? Is there anyone about? Hello?"

"'Alf a mo, I've just got t' take this yere pan o' milk off the stove." Came the reply from the kitchen.

A moment later Hal's cheery round face appeared in the doorway. "Can I help you?" he asked. "Only Fred 'as stepped out vur a bit."

Much relieved, George pointed to the inebriated Albert slumped in the chair.

"He's been drinking with the coroner and is a bit worse for wear. I was worried I would have to leave him here alone in that state. I've got other things to do this afternoon."

"Well there's nort new in those two 'aving a drink, they're friends. Mind I can't ever remember seeing Albert in that state before. He's always had enough sense and self-control t' know when he'd 'ad enough t' drink an' be able t' walk out the pub in an orderly manner." Replied Hal in a worried tone.

As they talked Albert slid slowly off the chair and onto the floor.

"Can you do anything for him?" asked George.

"Us could give 'im a drink" began Hal.

"NO!" cut in George. "He's had too much already."

"S' lies." Slurred Albert from floor level, displaying the usual lack of intelligence that comes with drinking too much. "S'never enough."

"I meant," began Hal again, "a drink o' Fred's coffee. There's been a pot abrewin' all mornin' but it should still be safe t' drink. Or as safe as it ever is." He finished truthfully.

"It hasn't got any alcohol in it has it?" asked a concerned George.

"No, no alcohol. It don't need it." Replied Hal, filling a mug.

George sat Albert up so Hal could administer the coffee. A few drops ran down Albert's chin and began to eat through his shirt.

"There, that should do it." Said Hal happily, after Albert had taken a few swallows.

"You think that will be enough?" asked a startled George.

"'Ave you ever tried Fred's coffee?"

"No."

"Ah, well. 'Ow should I put it?" said Hal. "You knows coffee is often labelled vur strength?"

"Yes, there's normally a number between one and five, one being the weakest, five the strongest." Replied George.

"Well on a scale o' one t' five Fred's coffee would rate about a twenty."

"You're pulling my leg!"

"No, straight up." Said Hal honestly. "Last zummer a bloke dropped down stone dead. Fred forced some o' 'is coffee between 'is lips an' ten minutes later 'ee was up and dancin' on the tables."

"That's right, I remember that. I was in yere when it 'appened." Put in Albert.

The other two looked at him in astonishment. Albert was now apparently sober. He appeared to have regained his co-ordination and there wasn't the slightest trace of a slur in his speech.

"Vur some reason I feels thirsty." Continued Albert. "Give us that mug." He snatched the rest of the coffee from Hal's hand.

"I think you can leave him with me now." Hal told George. "You go an' do whatever it is you've got t' do an' I'll look a'ter 'im."

"If you are sure?" Enquired the perplexed chauffeur. With a nod of confirmation from Hal, he headed back to his car.

"Where's Fred got to then?" Asked Albert.

"'Ee 'ad to go an' 'ave a word with Aunt Aggie." Replied Hal solemnly.

"He's a brave one is Fred, an' no mistake."

~~~~~

Things were not going the way Fred had planned. He'd finally managed to evict the cats from his pub. Then he'd bathed and disinfected the claw and bite marks, put on a shirt that had not been shredded, and because he wasn't stupid, he'd gone around to Aunt Agatha's back door instead of going into the shop. He couldn't afford to go into the shop. He was still paying off the instalments from the last time he had gone in there.

After much cursing from inside, Agatha had come to the back door and opened it. Before even uttering a word, she had presented him with a bill for lost revenue because she had had to shut the shop to answer the back door. From then on, things had gone downhill. Not rapidly by any means, but slowly and steadily in subtle ways, so that it had taken Fred a while to notice.

Aunt Agatha had invited him into her parlour, showed him to a seat and even offered him a cup of tea. All without charging him. On reflection he should have noticed the warning signs. She had sat patiently and listened whilst Fred had aired his grievances, and she had not interrupted once. All the time he was there, there had been no sign of any cats. Not so much as a hair on the cushions. Then, once Fred had finished having his say, she sprang her trap.

"D' you see any cats?" she began forcefully. "No? Now there's a surprise, CAUSE I 'AIN'T GOT ANY CATS!"

"But everybody knows you ke…" was as far as Fred got before she let him have both verbal barrels.

"Fancy comin' 'round yere harassin' an ol' woman an' stoppin' 'er from doin' an honest day's work! Makin' false accusations an' inflictin' all sorts o' stress." She paused to glance at her watch. "An' you owes me for one hours consultation." She finished, writing out another bill and thrusting it into Fred's unresisting hand.

It was then that Fred realised his mistake and bolted for the safety of his pub, clutching two new and very expensive bills.

Inside the post office, Aunt Aggie breathed a sigh of relief. It was always so much harder dealing with people away from her shop. If they came into the shop people knew that they were going to lose out before they entered and it was easy to convince them out of their money. But when they came around the back it was a real strain to live up to her vaunted reputation.

She allowed herself a moment to rest in her chair before getting up. She was after all an old lady. She crossed the room to the door that hid the enclosed stairs and opened it. A wall of cats spilled out and onto the carpet and began taking turn rubbing against her legs.

"Now what 'ave you lot been up to? Hey? You're goin' t' get me into trouble one o' these days an' who's going to operate the tin opener then, I'd like to know?"

~~~~~

Dave rode down through the overgrown footpath carefully in the darkness. He'd expected to come out in Lyonshire in the dull gray drizzle he'd left a few hours ago. Therefore, he was rather surprised to find that it was a clear starry night when he emerged on the Penhampton to Shoton road. It was also a lot warmer and far more muggy than he remembered.

Something was wrong.

He stopped at the exit to the footpath and tried to work it out. After a moment's thought he realised his mistake. Whenever he'd gone down the footpath before it had taken him into Lyonshire in the present. This time he had been in the past, so when he had gone down the footpath in the past it had brought him out in Lyonshire in the past too. He was now in Lyonshire a couple of weeks before he had arrived.

He glanced at his watch, which told him it was half-past two in the afternoon, which was clearly not the case. He let out a sigh, which condensed on his visor, making the starlight dance in an attractive way on the droplets of moisture. He watched the droplets slowly evaporate from his visor whilst he thought about his predicament. Temporal thinking was not something he was familiar with, and it took him a while to think it through.

Logically, if going through the barrier out by Lord Woods' estate at one o'clock brought him back home to the time he left the first time, then a few seconds after would bring him out in his present and he could then ride around and go down the foot path which would bring him back here in the present. He hoped.

The first thing he had to do now was find out exactly what time it was here and now. He couldn't go into the pub because that would mean confronting Fred and Albert before he'd met them. The post office was out of the question. That left... Of course!! The church clock at Shoton!

Dave wiped the last of the condensation off of his visor and rode off towards Shoton.

~~~~~

Albert had taken over serving behind the bar in Fred's absence so that Hal could get back to his kitchen, and was in the process of serving a few stray customers when Fred returned.

"'Ow did it go then?" he asked. "Hal tol' me all about it whilst you was gone. You'd never catch me goin' round there to complain."

"You don't want t' know Bert. You really don't want t' know." Replied Fred, shaking his head in stunned disbelief.

"I didn't think 'ee'd get anywhere, but I admire yur bravery." Said Albert sympathetically. "Yere, get yur lips round that." He said handing Fred a tankard of his coffee.

"Thanks Bert." Said Fred, absentmindedly scratching at the bandages on his arm. "How did your mornin' go?"

"The coroner adjourned the inquest 'til Monday right enough, but 'ee wanted more proof than just that bit o' twisted metal."

"So what did e' do?"

"Us went back and watched the explosion an' damn near got ourselves blowed up in the bargain. It was all very depressin'. Very depressin'." Albert shook his head sadly. "So what 'appened with Aunt Aggie then?"

"She's got nerves of steel, I'll give 'er that. I went round the back, so I didn't 'ave t' go into the shop." Began Fred

"Wise, very wise." Observed Albert.

"An' as soon as she opened the door, she charged me vur shuttin' up shop an' loss of trade!"

Albert's jaw dropped.

"Next she denied 'avin' any cats. An' there weren't no sign of 'em neither. Not so much as a whisker. An' she 'as a go at me vur 'aving a go at 'er and then presents me with another ruddy bill vur 'er time!"

"You're not goin' t' pay 'em are you?" Asked the astonished Albert.

"I still ain't paid off the bill from the last time I went round t' complain."

"So any idea what you're goin' t' do then?"

Fred drained his mug. "I'm going t' get a couple of the biggest ruddy dugs I can find." Said Fred resolutely. "That's what I'm goin' t' do."

"I didn't think 'ee were that fond o' dogs either Fred. You've never really been a pet person."

"I've looked a'ter Ferret's dug a time or two. An' I lets 'im bring it t' work." Said Fred defensively.

"Fred you have t' let him bring it t' work, Ferret's dog runs round on the tread mill t' power the extractor fan when tiz hot." Pointed out Albert. "Besides, don't you think you're bein' a bit hasty getting' a couple o' dogs?"

"Not if it keeps them vicious little…. CATS out of yere." Said Fred forcefully, and showing remarkable restraint in the colourful language department.

"So where's the lad then?" asked Albert, changing the subject.

The pub was filling up around them as people returned from Penhampton market. Fred took his customary place behind the bar.

"'Ee's not come back from Hunton yet." Replied Fred as he drew off a pint for a customer.

"You recon it'll do any good 'im printin' that story?" Asked Albert.

"You were all for it last night when we discussed it Bert. Had a change o' heart?"

"No, 's not that Fred. I'm worried that it'll put the lad right in the line o' fire, so t' speak."

"Nah. 'Ee can look a'ter 'imself. 'Sides, we're yere t' look a'ter 'im." Smiled Fred. "What could possibly go wrong?"

"I was afraid you was goin' t' say that Fred."

~~~~~

The church clock in Shoton had informed Dave that it was almost midnight, and since his sojourn home had been to three weeks ago, presumably it was midnight three weeks ago. He parked his bike out of sight, but nearly all the buildings around the square were in darkness so he wasn't likely to be spotted. Even the Stoat and Ferret was all in darkness, which was something unusual in itself.

All he had to do now was find something to do and keep him out of sight for thirteen hours. He had considered knocking on the pub door, but the Fred in the pub hadn't met him yet. He could do with some shelter as well. It was beginning to get really chilly. But three weeks ago it had still been March and spring had not yet sprung. He shivered.

A light flickered behind one of the church's stained glass windows, illuminating an avenging angel from one of the more aggressive religions. As the light moved on inside, the dark angel appeared to leap from the window. Dave felt less like someone had walked over his grave and more like someone was digging it up with a swing-shovel.

He stamped his feet and put his hands on the rapidly cooling engine in an attempt to keep warm. It was almost stone cold, but the residual warmth seeped into his fingers. A thought struck him. The church.

"It'll be warmer in the church, and I'm sure they won't mind giving me shelter." He said to himself.

He pushed his bike through the lychgate and into the churchyard. The door to the church wasn't locked, a quick turn of the huge iron ring on the latch and he was able to push it open. The interior of the church was in almost total darkness, except for a flickering candle flame that was bobbing around on the far side.

"Hello?" he called out.

"Sssssh!!!" Hissed a voice in the darkness.

"Excuse me?"

"Shush! I'm ruddy well praying!" The voice had a touchy edge to it. It suggested a man who had had very little sleep, only to be woken by an alarm so that he could get up again and see to the devotions.

"Oh gods! You've made me swear now!" it snapped again in a slightly more neurotic tone. "Now you've made me blaspheme!!"

Dave thought it best if he sat down on one of the pews and let the priest, prior, brother guru etc. alternately swear, blaspheme, and do penance until he had settled himself. This done, he made his way over to Dave.

"Hello, and what religion do you follow?" he asked.

After many squabbles and several fights, Father Turner had painfully learned to offer a neutral greeting and to enquire what religion someone belonged to before giving his name and title.

"I… I don't really follow any religion." Replied Dave, somewhat confused.

"Well in that case I'm Father Turner." Said Father Turner with a sigh. "What can I do for you?"

"I'm Dave," said Dave lamely. "And all I was really after was shelter for the night."

Father Turner was surprised. "Shelter?"

"Yes." Replied Dave. "Just for the night. I'll be on my way tomorrow. Is that alright? I thought churches were supposed to offer shelter to those who needed it?"*[Provided you are not poor, destitute, or homeless and the church isn't locked outside office hours.]*

"Well yes. I suppose." Father Turner was flabbergasted. "My, my, it's been a long time since anyone has come to the church seeking shelter. Are you a stranger to Shoton*?" [It had been a long time since anyone had been in the church.]*

"No. Not exactly." Replied Dave. "It's just a matter of time really."

Farther Turner nodded sagely. "It all comes down to time in the end."

"So, is it alright if I stay in the church tonight?"

"Oh, yes of course. Shelter is what the church is here for. Would you like me to say a prayer for you?"

"Um, would you be offended if I said no?" asked Dave tentatively.

"No, no. I don't mind. But they might." Said Father Turner, pointing discreetly upwards.

"Well, perhaps just a short prayer them." Replied Dave.

"I have to finish my midnight devotions, but I'll pray for you before I go back to bed." Said Father Turner reassuringly.

"That would be good. Thank you." Said Dave. "I'll just sit here quietly and watch, if that's ok."

Father Turner took a candle out of his multi-denominational robes, lit it and put it in a sconce on the end of Dave's pew before going back to his alters and finishing his rounds.

Dave watched for a time until his eyes became too heavy and he drifted off to sleep with Farther Turner's various chants and prayers in his ears.

~~~~~

He awoke with a start to find the priest gently shaking him.

"Wake up, it's almost noon. I didn't like to leave you to sleep any longer." Said Farther Turner, holding out a mug of tea. "I've made you tea, I hope that is alright. I'm banned from drinking the stuff myself by two different religions." He continued wistfully.

"Thank you." Said Dave gratefully. "I'm sure it will be fine." He noticed the priest looked very pale and weary. There were bags the size of shopping trolleys under his eyes. Religion must be very tiring, particularly if you had to get up every twenty minutes to pray.

"I have to drink it on some religious festivals though." Said the priest wearily. "Half the time I'm fasting for one religion. Then I'm feasting for another. My weight goes up and down faster than a ping-pong ball in a mattress factory."

"What did you say the time was?" said Dave, interrupting the flow.

Father Turner glanced at his watch, the water clock on the wall and a portable sundial. "It's five past twelve."

"FIVE PAST TWELVE? Oh my god, I'm going to be late!" exclaimed Dave. "Here, can you hold this for me?" he continued, handing back the tea, and frantically resetting his watch. "Oh and have this for the collection." He said as an after-thought, fishing around in his pockets and handing over a handful of fluff, sticky sweets and a small ball of string he carried for emergencies.

"Thank you." Shouted Father Turner to Dave's retreating back. He watched as Dave pulled on his crash helmet as he went. Absentmindedly, Father Turner sipped at the tea until he realised what he was doing. "Oh well, I don't suppose it will hurt just this once."

Dave jumped on his bike, flicked the stand up and kicked it into life. He roared off towards the Hunton road, cursing his tardiness.

In the churchyard Father Turner looked down at the trail of grass torn up as the back wheel of Dave's bike had spun. Never mind, it would grow back. Besides, it had been so nice actually having someone in the church besides himself.

An alarm went off in his pocket. With a sigh he pulled it out and switched it off. It declared the time to be quarter past twelve, and time to begin his round of prayers again. From somewhere deep inside himself a spark of rebellion flashed, and he threw the alarm clock against the church wall.

Chapter 11.

Dave completed the loop, coming out of the footpath on the Penhampton road. This time it was daylight, and cold, damp and raining, so presumably he had got the right season at least. He rode off towards Shoton again.

One of the doors to the yard behind the Stoat and Ferret was open, something that Fred did to allow him to ride his bike in and out, so hopefully he had the right week. Another positive sign, but he still didn't know which day it was.

He could go into the pub and ask, but that might worry Fred and he had not been in a very stable frame of mind the last time Dave had seen him. There was the smithy next door, but he hadn't actually been introduced to Tinny. And there was that unfortunate incident when he had knocked Tinny out with the pub door. There was Poulter's butchers' shop. Best if he stayed away from there - and the Post Office. There was always the Post Office. The thought of Aunt Aggie terrified him - definitely not the Post Office.

Dave glanced around again. The church! He could ask Father Turner what day it was. He looked up at the church clock and used it to reset his watch. It was ten to two, a couple of hours or so after the time he had left yesterday. No, that wasn't right; a couple of hours after he had left today; hopefully.

A brief and somewhat confusing conversation with Father Turner revealed that it was indeed Friday, and the correct Friday. All Dave had to do now was go to Hunton and write up his story for the paper.

～～～

"Yere Fred?" began Albert, as he glanced out of the window.

"What is it Bert?" Replied Fred from behind the bar.

"I could've sworn I just saw the lad ride past on 'is bike." Said Albert in a puzzled tone.

"Couldn't 'ave been. 'Ee left hours ago Bert. You must be seein' things."

"Look Fred," began Albert patiently. "I know it's been a bad day, but 'ow many people d' you know in Lyonshire that rides a bike like 'is?"

Fred thought for a moment, whilst he poured a pint for Tinny the smith, who had a bandage around his head.

"No one that I can think of."

"My point 'xactly. So what's 'ee up to then?"

"Gone t' write up 'is story, like we agreed. I don't know. You'll 'ave t' ask 'im when he gets back d'reckly." Replied Fred.

Hal came out of the kitchen. He did not look well. His normally ruddy face was scarlet, and sweat was running freely from his forehead, soaking the top of his chef's whites. He collapsed on a stool, fanning himself absentmindedly with a meat cleaver.

"You alright Hal?" asked Fred with concern.

"Drink. I need a drink." Wheezed Hal. "An' lots of ice."

Fred filled a pint glass with squash and passed it to the chef, along with a bucket of ice from the bar. Gratefully Hal took the glass and downed half of it in one go before up-ending the rest over his head. And instead of putting ice into his now empty glass, he picked up the ice bucket and stuck the whole thing on his head. He held out the glass for a refill.

"I take it you're a bit on the warm side then?" said Fred, refilling Hal's glass.

Hal lifted the bucket up enough to get the glass to his lips, cascading ice down his neck, across his lap and all over the floor.

"It's too flamin' hot in the kitchen with all the windows an' the backdoor shut, Fred." He muttered from under his bucket, once he had finished the second pint of squash.

"I'm sorry Hal." Apologised Fred. "But I thought it best to keep 'em closed t' keep them $£@#$! cats out of yere."

"Fred, I've got two ovens roastin' meat, three others with braised dishes an' casseroles. Most of the rings are goin' with vegetables an' sauces. It's so hot even the dug, Nevel, 'as flaked out an' is no longer walkin' round the treadmill keepin' the extractor fan goin'"

"I'll take 'im out vur a walk in the fresh air." Said Fred with concern.

"You mean take 'im vur a drag. I tried temptin' Nev with a bit o' steak an' 'ee didn't even twitch!"

"I'd better go an' 'ave a look. Bert? Can you watch the bar vur a bit?"

"No problem Fred."

Fred followed Hal out into the kitchen. In his younger days Fred had visited the Amazon rainforest on one of his trips. On that occasion he had gone from the winter snows of Lyonshire straight into the heat and humidity of the rainforest. Walking into the kitchen now had pretty much the same temperature differential. A wall of steamy heat hit him.

"Tiz certainly a little warm out yere Hal, I'll 'ave t' give 'ee that." He said, crossing the room and opening the backdoor.

Anyone watching from in the yard would have been amazed. The hot steamy air from the kitchen escaped into the cool damp air in the yard, it condensed into a small cloud which settled about waist height. As the cloud thickened it began to rain.

Fred lifted the small mongrel terrier out of the treadmill that drove the extractor fan and carried him out into the yard. Very quickly Fred became wet from the waist down as the small cloud continued its precipitation. He looked at Nev, just in case, but he was far too dehydrated.

After ten minutes in the fresh air, the little dog was showing signs of returning to his old self. He had eaten the steak and drained a bowl of water. Fred couldn't close the gates and leave him to run around the yard because Dave would need to get in when he got back. Instead he tied the little fellow on a long rope, so he could choose to stay in the yard or come inside the backdoor if he wanted to.

Hal had also recovered. Several pints of squash, and another bucket of ice for his hands and feet had done much to cool him down.

"Are you alright now Hal?" asked Fred when he returned to the bar.

"Getting' there Fred, getting' there."

"Hal you don't 'appen t' know anyone whose got a couple of big dugs vur sale do 'ee?" Asked Fred.

"No, not off hand Fred. But I'll keep me yeres open." Replied Hal.

~~~~~

Dave's problems had not ended when he had arrived back in Lyonshire at more or less the right time on the right day. He had forgotten to retrieve his press pass from the pub, and after his recent meanderings he hadn't felt like going back and getting it. It had therefore taken much arguing and finally the intervention of the editor, before he had even been allowed into the Hunton Times building by the security guard. *[One of Keith's cousins.]*

He had planned to write up his story quickly, and get back to the Stoat and Ferret for something to eat. It had been over twenty-four hours since he had last eaten, and his stomach was displeased with him.

Unfortunately, he had come up against the typewriter.

In his rather dull job as a clerical assistant Dave was used to typing in general, but not on a typewriter. At work he used a computer with a word-processing package. It allowed him to type quickly and correct his mistakes and his atrocious spelling. Now, faced with a typewriter and its steeply slanted keys he was having real difficulties, and he was having to stop every thirty seconds to trawl his way through the dictionary. The overflowing wastepaper bin in the corner vouched for his progress.

When the editor stuck his head around the door to see how Dave was doing, one look at the scrunched up balls of discarded paper, prompted him to take pity.

"I take it it's not going well?" he asked. "Would you like a secretary to take dictation? It might be kinder on the environment?" he said, pointing to the overflowing bin.

Dave looked from the accursed typewriter to his temporary boss and back again, pulled another badly typed and horrifically spelt piece of copy out of the carriage and sighed.

"I think it would probably be best. It's the only way this story is going to make it in time for the morning paper." Replied Dave gratefully. "Do you mind if I ask you a question?"

"Go ahead lad, freedom of speech and all that is what the press is about." The editor replied.

"Why do you still use typewriters? Wouldn't it make it a lot easier if you bought computers?"

"That's two questions."

Handle Blackthumbs was not naturally an unkind man, despite several decades of working as a journalist and finally as editor of the Hunton Times, but he didn't have a particularly sunny outlook on life either. Even in Lyonshire where most of the stories were often of good news, and bad news stories like Chalky's death were few and far between, working as a journalist still took its toll on a person's humanity.

"Sorry." Continued Handle. "I'll give you both answers. Second question first, yes computers would make it a lot easier. I spent some time away from Lyonshire working as a tabloid journalist and used a computer all the time. Unfortunately, by the time I returned to Lyonshire I was a compulsive liar, and was sued repeatedly for making false allegations. I ended up spending six months in a rehabilitation unit. Anyway, I digress. When I came back to Lyonshire I brought several computers back with me, and even had electricity installed especially.

Unfortunately, every time I switched one of them on it would beep a couple of times and switch itself off again. After repeated attempts, I took them back to the shop where I bought them. They plugged them in and switched them on and they worked perfectly." He said with some sadness.

"Why won't they work in Lyonshire?" Asked Dave.

"It's something to do with the time bubble that surrounds Lyonshire apparently. Or so I learned later. The computers work on pure logic, something either is or isn't. They can't cope with the inability to know *when* it is, and they switch themselves off. Right, now if you have no further questions, and there is no point in asking any because I won't give you an answer, I'll go and get a secretary for you."

With that, Handle stormed off, barked at a secretary, slammed his office door, and searched frantically for his bottle of pills.

～～～

Father Turner peered out of the church, mosque, pantheon, synagogue etc. to see if anyone was likely to come in, well you never knew, and ducked back inside and locked the door. He hated having to lock the door. He hated it when any church locked its door. Religious buildings should be open and providing sanctuary and a place to pray at all times, it was a fundamental part of his many beliefs. But once a month he locked the door. There were some things that had to be done behind locked doors for decencies sake, and this was one of them.

It always made him feel guilty doing it. It was not the sort of thing that a priest of any denomination should have to do, but the Combined Church was always short of funds so he couldn't pay anyone else to do it for him. Every time he did it, he was petrified that someone would knock on the church door and put him off. And there was always the possibility of someone peeking in through the windows and catching him in the act.

Father Turner went out into the vestry, took a key from the pocket of his robes and unlocked a cupboard. At the very bottom of the cupboard, under a pile of out of date hymnbooks was a small wooden chest. Shifting the books out of the way, he took the chest out and, after unlocking it with another key, opened it. If anyone ever found out what he kept hidden in there, he would die of shame. Doing his best not to watch, he took it out and put it on, despite the fact that he looked ridiculous wearing it.

Father Turner let out a resigned sigh. "Well I suppose the pinny keeps the dust off my robes when I clean the inside of the windows." To complete the ensemble, he put on the rubber gloves as well.

He took a couple of rags out of the chest, along with a bottle of stained-glass window polish, picked up his ladder and went back to the main part of the church. He set the ladder up against the first of the huge windows and began to climb up. He was always methodical about the windows, at least those that weren't boarded up, and cleaned them from top to bottom. He caught any spiders and other insects that had made their home there since the last time the windows had been cleaned, and let them go outside once he had finished.

He thought it was a great shame that no one ever came into the church. The windows always looked quite spectacular with the evening sun shining through them once they had been cleaned.

It was a long job, and always took the best part of an afternoon. Father Turner worked his way around the church as quickly as he could, but every time he started to make progress, one of the many alarm clocks he carried would go off. Then he'd have to stop, climb down the ladder and see to whatever prayers needed to be said, before climbing back up once more. Those windows that were boarded up, he gave a coat of varnish. Some of the boards had been used so many times that the varnish was thicker than the wood itself.

As if on cue, when he climbed down after finishing the last window, the late afternoon sunshine broke through the clouds and shone through the sparkling windows. It lit up the interior of the church with a multi-coloured glow. With a contented sigh he took off his pinny. It was always embarrassing having to wear it, but moments like this made it all worthwhile.

Another alarm went off in his pocket and spoiled the moment. As if in response, a cloud hid the sun once more and the ethereal glow vanished, leaving Father Turner to put his cleaning gear away and get back to his normal routine of prayers.

~~~~~

By the time Dave rode into the yard behind the Stoat and Ferret, the sun was already setting. He had hoped to go around and visit Shem and Elsie and warn them on the way home, but the hours spent wrestling with a type writer had put pay to that. He shut the yard gate, dropped the bar into place to lock it and strolled towards the backdoor, pulling off his helmet as he went.

As he passed through into the kitchen, Hal was busy jointing up a side of beef for the following day. Delicious smells wafted around the kitchen, making Dave's stomach growl. The tempting aromas reminded him that it had been twenty-four hours since he had last eaten, and distracted him enough so that he didn't see the rope that Nev was tied to and consequently tripped over it. His helmet rolled away from him towards the bar.

Fred looked down as something came to rest by his foot, and was surprised to see it was a crash helmet.

"Dave's back I see." He said. "You can ask 'im if it were 'is bike you saw earlier. Bert."

"I could." Replied Albert. From his vantage point he could see out into the kitchen. "But I don't know if 'ee will be able to answer, 'ee's just fallen over Nev's rope."

Dave struggled to his feet and glared down at the offending rope. The small mongrel terrier from the treadmill was jumping up and down and yapping on the end of it.

"Sorry about 'im" apologised Hal, brushing Dave down. "But it were a bit hot in yere earlier an' 'ee needed a bit o' fresh air."

"Don't worry about it Hal. After the day I've had, I'm surprised I didn't fall down the cellar." Replied Dave.

"You alright lad?" asked Fred, coming through to the kitchen. "I 'ad t' tie 'im up vur a bit a'ter the ruddy cats got in again."

"He got all hot and bothered chasing them I expect."

"No, 'ee flaked out in the heat a'ter I shut the backdoor." Replied Fred.

"So 'ow did yere day go?" asked Albert. "D' you get yere story written up?"

Fred poured a pint and handed it to Dave. Much to his surprise, Dave drained the glass like a hardened drinker and handed it back.

"Let's just say that the inquest was the high point of my day and the rest went down- hill from there." Replied Dave as tactfully as he could. "Now what's for tea? I'm starving." He said trying to change the subject.

"Albert thought 'ee saw 'ee ride through the square earlier."

"Around lunchtime it were." Put in Albert.

"Ah." Began Dave; so much for changing the subject. "I had a spot of bother… to put it politely." He said, dumping his rucksack on the floor and sitting down on the barstool next to Albert's.

"But did 'ee get the story written up? An' is it goin' t' be printed?" asked Albert impatiently.

"Probably best if 'ee tell it from the beginnin' lad." Said Fred soothingly, trying to appease both parties.

Whilst Dave recounted the day's unfortunate events, Fred and Albert listened attentively. He explained how he had run out of petrol and gone home to fill up. His getting lost in time and having to spend the night in the church, and finally getting to Hunton and the problems he had had with the typewriter.

"I tol' you it were 'im." said Albert smugly when Dave had finished.

"I think it's probably best if we sits down an' draws you a map lad. You were very lucky. You can get into serious bother if you gets lost in time." Said Fred seriously. "Not getting' back can be the least of your problems. There's places you can end up that make the Spanish Inquisition look right friendly."

"An' them's the nice ones." Agreed Albert.

"If you say so." Said Dave. "I'll follow your lead as it were, you know far more about it than I could ever hope to understand. Now where did I put it?"

Dave rummaged around in his rucksack and pulled out a large folded sheet of paper and handed it over.

"Here you go." He said. "It's a proof copy of tomorrow morning's front page of the Hunton Times."

Albert held up the paper at arm's length. Eventually, after much squinting he gave up and reached into his waistcoat pocket and pulled out a pair of spectacles.

"I didn't know you wore spectacles Bert." Said Fred in astonishment.

Somewhat abashed, Albert put on his glasses. "Let uz see." He said holding up the paper again. "The deaths of Lord Woods and Chalky White were not accidents." He read. "Although there is no definitive link between the two deaths, it is believed that both men were killed by the same person. All signs point to Lord Woods being killed in order to generate confusion over the distribution of his estate. It is also believed that whoever the murderer is, he or she has a good working knowledge of the time gates."

"You didn't actually name anyone then?" asked Fred.

"No, I couldn't. I couldn't actually print a name until someone's been arrested." Replied Dave.

"Well you've done everythin' you could t' shake the tree." Said Albert. "It's just a matter of sittin' back an' waitin' t' see who falls out."

~~~~~

The rest of the evening passed uneventfully, or at least as uneventfully as they ever did in the Stoat and Ferret. They ate, much to Dave's relief, the huge plates of food Hal set before them. After the meal was finished, Fred took out pen and paper and drew up a map of Lyonshire with Albert's help. When it was finished, they took great care in marking on the time gates and where and when they went. Quite a few he simply marked with a skull and crossbones.

"Why the skull and crossbones?" asked Dave.

"You see this one yere?" began Fred. "Just along from the footpath you came down?"

"But I've been past there several times." Pointed out Dave. "Twice in the last twenty-four hours, and there is no road there."

"I never said nort about a road. It's only an animal trail now, but it used to be a path years ago. Anyroad, it's there an' if you crosses o're there you'll end up choking' t' death." Said Fred Ominously.

"Right a'ter your feet burn off." Put in Albert.

"Why?" Asked Dave. "Does it come out in a volcano?" he said jokingly.

"This ain't no joke lad." Fred was deadly serious. "You'll go back to the early days of the planet when it was nort but a ball of molten rock."

Dave laughed. "You're having me on."

"No, 'ee's serious lad." Said Albert earnestly. "When the original Druidhs hid Lyonnesse and thus made the time gates to anywhere and anywhen, they had forgot that most o' the times an' places would be…" Albert struggled for the right word, "let's just say unhealthy an' leave it at that."

Dave was shocked. Several questions jostled for attention in his head like "how do you know?" and "who found it out?" but he had learned to trust what he was told in Lyonshire. So instead he pointed to another skull and crossed bones. "And this one?" he asked.

"I haven't the foggiest on that one." Replied Albert. "D' you know Fred?"

"That one's not quite so bad." Replied Fred. "But I still wouldn't give much vur your chances of survival. It comes out in the middle of the Sahara desert in the present, miles from anywhere. There used to be a big city there thousands o' years ago but the desert moved in an' buried it."

"And that one?" asked Dave, pointing to a skull and crossed bones that Fred had underlined and put exclamation marks next to.

"Don't even think about that one!" blurted Albert.

"What's wrong with that one?" enquired Dave innocently.

"Promise me right now that you'll never go that way!" snapped Albert.

"Ok. Ok, I promise I'll never go that way." Replied Dave, trying to placate Albert. "But could you at least tell me why?"

"We don't EVER talk about that way." Said Albert insistently.

"That's right." Agreed Fred. "It causes all sorts o' problems does that way."

Dave had the annoying feeling that they wouldn't give him a straight answer, but their agitated response thus far had prickled his curiosity so he asked anyway. "So what is it then?"

"You're too young to be tol'." Albert was adamant.

Fred looked around the bar. Once he was confident that no one was paying them any attention, he picked up a pen and wrote one word on a scrap of paper.

"NO FRED! Don't even write it!" Hissed Albert, half panicked. "You never knows when they'm watching! An' after the day we've 'ad….."

Fred held up the paper long enough for Dave to read it, then screwed up the scrap of paper, threw it in the fire and watched until it had been destroyed by the flames.

"I tried to warn 'em." Mumbled Albert to himself. *"But do they listen?"* He shook his head sorrowfully.

It took a few moments for Dave to register what it was that had actually been written on the scrap of paper. It took another minute for it to sink in. Eventually it registered.

"Goblins?" He was confused.

"SSSSSHHHUSH!" Hissed Albert. "DON'T SAY IT OUT LOUD! You can never tell when they're about or when they'm listenin'."

If Dave had been asked to write a seven thousand word essay on the theory of relativity and how it related to motorcycles in the modern age, with accompanying illustrations, he couldn't have looked any more confused.

Fred leaned in closer.

"NO FRED!" said Albert so loudly that everybody in the bar hushed and turned to look.

"You know when there's a problem, particularly with ort mechanical or electrical?" he whispered. "An' there's no apparent reason vur the problem? Some might say there's a gremlin in the works?"

Dave nodded, he could follow things so far.

"Well it ain't gremlins, they're actually quite cute. It's the… what I wrote on that paper." He finished.

Fred's explanation did little to alleviate Dave's confusion, but it had reduced Albert to a state of total and utter panic.

"You've gone an' done it now. We'll be infested with the

$%£@#$!!! *Right enough."* He mumbled to himself, shaking his head.

"But aren't they mythical?" asked Dave.

"We've got enough ruddy trouble as it is at the moment. We don't need them makin' it worse."

"Would that be the same mythical that also refers to Merlin an' magic an' time travel?" Pointed out Fred.

"Do they listen to me? After all, what do I know?"

"I see what you mean." Said Dave reflectively. "So what are they?"

"They're humans." Replied Fred, much to Dave's surprise. "Not Homo Sapiens of course, but like the Neanderthals they branched off some ways back an' co-existed on earth vur a long time. Every so often some archaeologist finds a skeleton o' one and says they've found some new pigmy species but what they've actually found is one o' them."

"No good will come o' this, you mark my words."

"When the world got too much vur 'em an' somehow they found their own place t' live. Sort o' a pocket in reality. ALBERT WILL YOU SHUT UP VUR A MOMENT! 'Tiz a bit like Lyonshire. They're more like mischievous children than ort else. But they do cause serious problems." Concluded Fred.

Chapter 12.

Dave watched as the steam gently drifted up towards the ceiling from the mug of coffee on the table next to his bed. He lay on his bed with his hands behind his head, watching it swirl and dissipate. Fred had brought him his morning coffee a few minutes before, and although he had slept well and felt thoroughly refreshed, he was reluctant to get out of bed. It was Saturday morning after all, and the rules of common decency dictated a lie-in on Saturday mornings. *[Other rules of common decency include: Do no harm; Treat others as you would wish to be treated; Enjoy life as you are a long time dead; Be kind to animals and plants as they are living beings too. The rules also include some more unusual things too: Do the washing up when it is your turn; Strictly observe all breaks at work; Don't shoot Volvos out of season; and in the volume especially edited for council workers and civil servants, Never let one person do one person's work when half a dozen people can do it and make a total pig's ear out of it.]* The other reason he was reluctant to get up was because he was waiting for Albert to arrive with the Hunton Times and the story he had written. He was both nervous and excited about the consequences of the story he, Fred and Albert had put together to try and bring out into the open the murderer of Lord Woods and Chalky the smith.

BOOM!

The shockwave and noise from the explosion rolled across the square, blowing in windows.

Dave managed to get the bed covers up over his head as the window shattered, showering splinters of glass across his room.

Father Turner had the customary shopping trolleys under his eyes. As usual he had been awoken numerous times during the night to pray or perform one religious observation or another. He was standing over one of the more obscure altars in his church.

He pulled a matchbox from one of the many pockets of his robe and pushed out the drawer. An ant blinked in the sudden brightness and crawled out of the box and onto the altar. Father Turner began to mumble the relevant chant and waved his hands over a knife on the altar.

The ant began exploring its new surroundings. It was on a stone slab with ridges and grooves on it. The biological spirit level in its tiny brain informed it that the whole slab was sloping slightly along the line of the grooves. It could see that all the grooves ran in the same direction and converged into a shallow dish-like bowl.

Father Turner came to the end of his chant and picked up the knife. He really hated this particular service and had made repeated representation to the Conclave of the Combined Churches but their answer was still lost in the bureaucracy stage. Strictly speaking, he should be sacrificing a chicken, and if he had a live yoghurt, he would be using that, but he didn't.

It was no good; he couldn't do it. Putting down the knife, he ushered the ant back into the matchbox. He would release it outside later. With the matchbox back in his pocket, he continued with the service. The problem was, there was nothing in the basin for him to dip the knife into. So he had to pretend and imagine the blood, and dipped the knife into the empty basin. But even that made him feel squeamish.

BOOM!

The interior of the church abruptly filled with a cloud of multi-coloured fragments of stained glass as all the windows blew in at once. Even the boards on the boarded up windows blew in, crashing to the floor and leaving the church windowless and open to the elements.

Fortunately, Father Turner had had the cowl of his thick and itchy woollen multi-religious robes up over his head for the service he had been conducting. Sharp fragments of glass rained down all around him, counter-pointing the noise of the explosion with the softer tinkling as the glass hit the floor.

Albert was making his way across the damp and chilly square towards the Stoat and Ferret when the explosion happened behind him. The shockwave lifted him off of his feet and slammed him up against the door to the Pub. There was silence and a brief pause and then bits of broken masonry began to rain down around him for the second time in two days, but the porch over the door shielded him from the worst of it.

"Bugger this!" He said, and got to his feet and through the door as fast as his bulk would allow.

Inside the pub it looked worse than it had done after the Guild had left. There was broken glass everywhere.

Albert scratched his head and removed a stray fragment of mortar from what was left of his hair. Unsure what to do next, he simply stood in the middle of the floor shaking violently.

"You alright Bert?" Asked Fred with concern as he rushed from the kitchen into the bar.

"No I'm not alright!" shouted Albert. "You get blowed up and see if you're alright!" he snapped.

"D' you know what it was that exploded?" Fred asked.

""No, I 'ad me back t' the explosion."

Fred peered through the space where until recently one of the windows had been.

"Ruddy heck! It's Poulter's shop." Exclaimed Fred.

Albert joined him at the window.

"Most of 'is shop's gone!" he said. "'Ee must have been makin' another bomb or zummet."

"Come on." Urged Fred. "We'd better go an' help."

"What was that explosion?" Asked Dave coming into the bar, still pulling his shirt on.

"Poulter's place has blown up." Replied Fred en route to the door. "We're goin' t' help, see if there is ort we can do."

They ran across the square, making their way through the rubble. Now that the worst of the dust had settled it was possible to see the full extent of the destruction in the square. Most of Poulter's shop had gone, leaving only part of the front wall still standing. The houses on either side had been badly damaged as well.

"Look." Said Dave pointing to the church. "All the church windows have gone too."

"Along with 'alf the windows in Shoton I shouldn't wonder." Said Albert.

Other villagers were beginning to fill the square. But far from panicking, they were already starting to claw their way through the rubble as Fred, Albert, and Dave joined them. With no tools they were using their bare hands to shift the broken masonry in a search for survivors.

"I wonder if Father Turner is alright." Wondered Dave out loud. "I mean with all that flying glass."

"Why don't you go an' 'ave a look lad, there's enough o' us here." Replied Fred as he tossed a large stone to one side.

Dave ran off towards the church. Behind him the crowd of people continued to sift through the rubble. Tinny the smith had opened the big doors to his forge and was handing out anything that could be used as a crowbar or shovel.

The inside of the church looked like a blizzard of broken glass had passed through it, covering everything from the altars to the pews. Dave could see no sign of life as he began to work his way around the church. With no glass in the huge windows, the church acted like a receiver and he could hear the shouts from outside through the gaping windows, as the impromptu rescuers worked. He also heard what sounded like another explosion off in the distance. Briefly he wondered if he should go and alert the others, but they had probably heard it too.

Eventually he found the fallen priest. He was huddled up in his robes, leaning against one of the many altars. He looked uninjured but was shaking violently. He looked up as Dave approached.

"I think I've angered the gods." Groaned the shaking priest.

"You're alright. It's not the gods. There was an explosion in the butchers' shop." Replied Dave, doing his best to reassure the cleric.

"You, you don't understand!" groaned the cleric. "I had to make a sacrifice and couldn't do it!"

"No, honestly. It was a bomb."

"Are you sure?"

"YES!" exclaimed Dave, his patience was beginning to wear thin. People were hurt and possibly dying outside. "Now come on. We've got to get outside and help the others."

"But my windows! My poor windows." Sobbed the priest. "You can't repair them you know." He babbled

"You can't?" replied Dave with surprise, as he helped Father Turner to his feet and led him outside. "Fred's always repairing the windows in the Stoat and Ferret. He repaired them the other day after the Guild meeting. One of them had this wonderful pattern in the glass, sort of a...."

"No." cut in Father Turner. "It's the stained glass you see. Many have tried and Mister Packer the specialist has only managed to reassemble a few complete windows, but even he can never get the pattern right."

"OH MY GODS!" he exclaimed on seeing the devastation outside.

The rescuers had managed to get out the people in the houses on either side of the butcher's shop. The more seriously injured were being stretchered away and put on carts to be taken for treatment. There was no resident doctor in Shoton and no ambulance service. Most people were able to treat minor injuries and illnesses themselves or knew someone else in the village who could. Horses were backed into the traces, and spells cast over them and the carts to reduce the journey to

Penhampton to a matter of minutes.

The Stoat and Ferret had become an ad hoc first aid station, for those less seriously injured. As he led the cleric through the doors, Dave could see that Hal had swept up the worst of the glass and had pots of hot tea and coffee on the go. Suzan was using her healing talent on people with minor injuries. Those that were too seriously injured for her to treat she made as comfortable as possible and then sent them to join the others on the carts outside. She was busy dealing with everything from closing wounds to healing broken bones. Quite a few of those she was helping were those people who had used their bare hands to claw through the rubble and either torn them on masonry or cut them on broken glass.

Dave sat Father Turner down in a vacant chair in the pub and went back outside to see if there was anything else he could do to help. He met up with Fred and Albert as they were walking back to the pub.

"We've got everybody out lad." Said Fred with a heavy heart. "The first o' the carts should all be in Penhampton by now."

"No one else was killed except Poulter." Said Albert solemnly.

They walked back to the pub in silence, passing the sheet that covered Poulter's mortal remains. Albert tugged an imaginary forelock as a mark of respect.

The pub provided a safe refuge for everyone, but gradually they wandered off alone, or in pairs or small groups to begin their grieving. Suzan was exhausted. The huge energy drain of healing so many had left her barely able to stand, so Fred got one of his regulars to escort her home. Hal had retreated to the kitchen to set about the clearing up; that left Fred Dave and Albert alone in the bar.

Fred washed the dirt from his hands and poured them each a cup of his coffee.

"S'ppose I'd better see t' the windows in a bit." He said, looking at the neat pile of glass Hal had swept up.

They were all stunned. Adrenalin had kept them going through the search for the injured, but now the backlash and shock were setting in. Not one of them could hold their coffee in a steady hand.

"All the upstairs windows have gone too." Said Dave. "At least mine has."

"An' the rest." Said Albert gloomily. "I've said it before, an' I'll say it again, this is a bad business."

"And it's all my fault!" Exclaimed Dave remorsefully. "This has happened because of my story. I should never have written it."

"S' not your fault lad. This 'ad all started before you'd even 'eard of Lyonshire." Said Fred, trying to reassure Dave.

"But Poulter's dead!" exclaimed Dave. "And innocent people have been hurt!"

Albert patted him on the shoulder. "Look lad, we knows Poulter was mixed up in this from the start…."

Albert never got to finish what he was saying. He was interrupted as the door burst open and a young lad collapsed on the floor in front of them.

"That's one o' the lads from Fetlock's stables." Said Fred, knocking over his chair in his rush across the bar to help the lad.

"It's young Andrew. An' you're right, 'ee does work vur Fetlock." Added Albert.

The young man was exhausted, and shaking so badly that he could hardly breathe. His clothes and hair were scorched and covered in dirt.

Fred helped him sit up and held up his coffee to the lad's mouth. A few sips of the elixir were enough to bring the lad round.

"The stables!" he panted. "They exploded!"

Fred gave him a little more coffee.

"None of the horses was hurt, they were already out for exercise, but those of us that were off duty were still asleep in the flats above and many are trapped in the rubble."

"The second explosion!" said Dave. "I'd forgotten about that."

"Is there anyone helping?" asked Fred.

"No! I mean Mr and Mrs Windsor came down from the house and are doing what they can, but there was another explosion in Hunton so there's no one else to help."

"Another explosion in Hunton!" said Albert with surprise. "This is worse than we thought!"

"That's why I rode here. I've half killed the horse getting here and Mister Fetlock is going to have my hide for that, but we need help!" continued the stablehand.

"There's not a flamin' cart left in the village!" Said Fred angrily. "D' you reckon you can carry the three o' us on yur bike lad?" he asked Dave.

"I don't know." Replied Dave. "We can give it a try."

"I think 't would be an idea, it'll take us too long t' walk that far."

"You ain't getting' me on no motorcycle!" put in Albert.

"Come on Bert! This is an emergency." Said Fred with a touch of anger in his voice.

It took a bit more persuasion, but eventually Albert was convinced. It took a good deal longer to get everyone on the bike. Even then, Dave was sat on the petrol tank, Fred on the seat, and Albert's bulk was half on the pillion and half on the luggage rack.

The overloaded motorcycle limped gingerly off, its shock-absorbers hard up against the stops and its tyres looking flat. The damp misty drizzle permeated everything, drenching them as they rode, and making the overloaded bike slip and slide on the greasy roads. But eventually they reached the stables.

It looked like the explosion had gone off right in the centre of the ornate building, blowing out the walls and collapsing the flats above into the stables below. The horses, back from their early morning exercise, were all in the show ring. The grooms and stablehands were already hard at work, clearing the rubble under the watchful eye of Shem. Elsie was doing her best with torn sheets, bandaging the wounded. It had been fortunate that most of the stablehands had been out exercising the horses. If the explosion had happened earlier they would all have still been in their beds.

As they dismounted the bike and went to help, a cheer went up as Fetlock was pulled from the rubble. He had been extricated from the remains of his office, and apart from a few scratches was uninjured.

"'Ow many 'ave you got working yere?" asked Fred.

"There's eighteen. Or there were last night." Replied Fetlock calmly, trying to brush the grime from his clothes as if the explosion was nothing more than a minor inconvenience.

Fred did a quick headcount. Allowing for young Andrew, there were still two unaccounted for.

After another quarter of an hour, they were pulled from the rubble, but no amount of torn sheets and bandages could do anything to help them. Tears ran freely down Albert's dirt encrusted face as he covered them with a makeshift shroud.

Fred stood back and took a moment to survey the destruction. He grabbed a passing stablehand.

"Whose room was in the middle of the top floor?" he asked.

"It weren't nobodies room Sir, it was Mr Fetlock's office." He replied. He was still in shock. His face was pale and the gravity of the situation had obviously not yet sunk in.

"And the lads that were killed, their rooms were on either side of Fetlock's office?"

"Yes Sir. I shared with one of them, but I was out with the horses when it happened." Replied the lad shakily.

Fred patted him reassuringly on the arm and thanked him for the information.

"You 'ad a bit of a lucky escape then?" He said to Fetlock, as he came to where Dave, Fetlock, and Albert were standing.

"The stables have been completely destroyed!" said Fetlock haughtily. "I don't see what's lucky about that."

"Ah, but you were in your office weren't you?"

"Yes I was." Agreed Fetlock uncertainly. "But I don't see what that has to do with it."

"You must o' been right o're the explosion."

"Are you implying that the bomb was meant to kill me?" asked Fetlock with surprise.

"It certainly looks like it, don't it?" Put in Albert.

"Good heavens, do you really think so?"

"Considerin' the lads on either side of you was killed, I'd say you was lucky, yes." Commented Fred. "Very lucky indeed."

"It must have been the new mattresses." Said Fetlock thoughtfully. "Some of the stablehands have been complaining about the old horsehair mattresses, saying they were old, smelly and lumpy. Quite unreasonable in my mind, but to keep the peace I ordered some new mattresses and they turned up last evening. I stored them in my office overnight and was going to hand them out today."

They left Fetlock to his thoughts and helped with the litters for those who needed treatment in Penhampton. Shem and Elsie offered accommodation to the horses and stablehands until something more permanent could be arranged.

Dave winced as he pulled off the tattered remains of his bike gloves. Like Fred and Albert, he had torn and bleeding hands.

"Do you think we ought to go and see if there is anything we can do in Hunton?" he asked.

Fred nodded. "Hal can manage vur a bit longer in the pub, we'd best go and check." He replied as he rubbed the back of his neck with his hand to try and ease the stiff muscles.

"Come on lad." Said Albert. "Get that machine o' yours working again."

~~~~~

Hal was not managing. After returning to their homes, the people of Shoton had decided what they really needed was company and companionship, and that meant the Stoat and Ferret. Consequently the pub was crowded in spite of the fact that it still had no windows. Suzan was still at home recovering, and although the weekend washer up was busy washing up in the kitchen, Hal was rushed off his feet serving customers in the bar. As a result he had already had to pull one burnt pie out of a smoke filled oven.

For the moment at least, everybody that wanted a drink appeared to have one, and Hal nipped out into the kitchen to take a breather. The washer up was hard at work. He was always hard at work, even if there was nothing apparent that needed doing. He was known as Ferret *[One of those strange coincidences that makes the world such an interesting place to live in]*, no one knew what his real name was or even if he had one.

As far as Hal could tell, Ferret's age was somewhere between sixty and ancient. It was difficult to be more precise, he had washed up every weekend since long before Hal had taken over as chef, and didn't seem to be any older now than he had been then. And despite a legendary appetite, Ferret looked like a collection of matchsticks bound up in a shirt and trousers. His teeth had long since disappeared, but he was always chewing something. Whenever he passed any unattended food, he would pick it up and chew it - in some cases for hours.

The little man always amazed Hal when he came in each weekend. As a chef, Hal religiously kept his kitchen spotlessly clean, but when Ferret came in and there were no dishes or glasses that needed washing, Ferret would always find something to clean. And whilst one hand would be scrubbing away, there would be a pint in his other hand, an unlit dog-end in the corner of his mouth, and he would be incessantly chewing on some morsel he had scrounged. No one knew where Ferret lived, or what he did for the rest of the week, or even where he went when he wasn't at the pub.

One Sunday evening, Hal had waited outside to follow him home. At midnight he'd gone back into the pub to see what Ferret was up to, only to find that the little man had already gone. Ferret hadn't left by the front door or out through the gate to the yard, Hal had been watching. Apparently he had been there one minute and was gone the next. *[In any given town, in either a café, a pub, or even a high-class restaurant there is someone like Ferret. No one knows what their real name is, they are always known by a nickname, be it Ferret, Stoat, Weasel, Rat or something similar. Normally they are not related to the owners or managers, but were simply inherited with the rest of the fixtures and fittings when the present managers took over. Estate agents have noticed this phenomenon and have now started listing them amongst the assets in property details.]*

"Anyone serving?" came a shout from the bar. With a sigh, Hal went back to serving.

~~~~~

Dave nursed his bike through the gates and into the yard behind the pub. As if sensing that nothing more was required of it, something in the engine went bang and sprayed a puddle of oil across the yard, both tyres popped and deflated, and the springs flew off of the shock absorbers.

Albert lifted his bulk and dismounted. He had not enjoyed the journey to Hunton and back, and was feeling several pints short of his normally sunny nature. He headed straight through the kitchen and into the bar to remedy this situation, almost running over Ferret in the process.

In the yard, Fred helped Dave to lift the sad remains of his bike onto its stand.

"Don't worry lad, I'll see it gets fixed." He said reassuringly.

Dave looked lovingly at what, even he was prepared to admit, was now just so much scrap metal.

"I don't think it's worth it." He said, a solitary tear running down his face. "It would be cheaper to get another one than try and fix what's left of this one."

It felt strange to be shedding a tear for what was, when all was said and done, a machine, when he had seen so much death and destruction over the last few hours, but when it came down to it, this was *his* bike. Like any true biker, the bike was part of him. He could feel when it wasn't running right. He could tell if the tyres were just a few PSI out. At a very deep metaphysical level, he was connected to the bike. It was also the only enduring link with the world he had left behind. Vainly he hoped he would wake up from this nightmare.

"Come on lad, I reckons we've earned a drink." Said Fred sympathetically.

By the time they had made their way through into the bar, Albert was busy serving customers, and Hal was back in his kitchen, trying to work his way through the backlog of food orders. Even Ferret had been drafted in to wait on tables.

Fred poured Dave a pint and took a moment for himself, drinking a tankard of his special coffee. With the bar crowded with people all seeking solace after the day's tragic events, a few moments rest was all he could allow himself before coming to Albert's rescue, and help him serve.

Dave accepted the pint gratefully from Fred, but unlike everybody else in Shoton and for miles around, he didn't crave the warmth of companionship, and slipped off upstairs to his room to be alone with his thoughts. With the glass in the window still missing, and without the benefit of two log fires and the crowd of people in the bar below, his room was cold and damp. He pulled the curtains closed and lit a couple of extra candles which made little difference, their flickering light only emphasised the draught.

After carefully removing the glass-covered bedding from his bed and sweeping the rest up into a pile, Dave filled the sink full of cold water and began to wash the grime off his hands. As he washed them and scrubbed the dirt away, the water in the sink took on a crimson hue. Until now he hadn't realised just how badly his hands had been ripped and torn in the desperate struggle to shift the rubble earlier. Washing them had opened up the wounds again. He did his best to pat them dry on a towel, staining the white cloth red as he did so. They needed bandaging at the very least, but nothing could salve the pain he felt inside.

Just twenty-four hours earlier he had gone back to his flat and felt homesick for Lyonshire. Now, everything in Lyonshire had gone sour, and people had been blown up because of him or the story he had written. And to top it all off, the most important thing in his life, apart from his girlfriend, was now just so much scrap metal. *[Girlfriends come and go but "The Bike" remains the same.]*

"Dave! Dave!"

He could hear someone shouting his name, but he didn't have the energy or the enthusiasm to reply. Instead, he curled up on his bed, paralysed by his emotions.

"Dave!" The shout was louder this time. "Where are you lad?" It was Fred's voice.

The door to his room burst open, and Fred entered.

"There you are. I was hollerin' vur 'ee." He said.

Dave didn't reply. He didn't even look up. What was the point?

Fred looked on with concern, and noticed the blood-stained towel. With the door open, a gust of wind blew in through the broken window, extinguishing the candles. Fred shivered, relit one of the candles by clicking his fingers, and sat on the edge of the bed.

"I'm sorry I got 'ee into all this lad. I 'ad no idea that t' would ever, could ever, get this bad in Lyonshire." He began, putting a hand on Dave's shoulder. "An' you mustn't blame yerself vur what 'appened t'day. It weren't your fault.

"I've just spoken t' the police investigators, their team popped in vur a drink a'ter they was finished goin' through Poulter's place."

Continued Fred. "They didn't find ort. They've still got t' go t' the stables and Hatchet's shop in Hunton, but it's as if the place blowed itself up. They'll send someone back t' witness the explosion a'ter the weekend, perhaps we'll find out zummet then."

It became apparent to Fred that the conversation was all going one way. The pint he had poured Dave was still sitting untouched on the side. The day's events had obviously taken a heavy toll on Dave, plunging him into a private world of deep dark despair. Life was still carrying on around him, but as far as Dave was concerned, it could carry on without him.

"Let's 'ave a look at yur 'ands." Continued Fred.

When Dave made no move, Fred gently took Dave's unresisting hands in his own, and turned them over to examine the wounds.

"I'm not as good as Suzan is but …" Fred closed his eyes and began to concentrate, vocalising the words of the spell as he did so.

Dave felt a warmth spreading slowly through his hands. The pain lessened, and the wounds began to close over.

"There you go lad." Said Fred in a slightly horse whisper, and cleared his throat. "It'll 'ave speeded it up a bit if nort else. Now, I knows you feels like $%@# an' there seems t' be no point in ever getting' up off that there bed again, but I could really do with an 'and. We're flat out in the bar, an' I've still got all these yere windows t' fix." He shook Dave gently.

Whether it was Fred's words, or whether he had done more than just heal his hands it was difficult to tell, but Dave's depression had lifted a little and he turned to look at his host. Fred's normally ruddy face looked quite pale. He didn't look like he had enough energy to pour a pint, let alone use his talent to repair all the windows.

Dave sighed. "How about I give you a hand to fix the windows? You look done in."

Fred let out a short laugh, which ended in a wheezy cough. "An' just 'ow are you goin' t' 'elp me fix the windows?" he said, once he was able to speak.

Dave shrugged. "I don't know? Perhaps there's some way you can channel energy from me? Cos at the moment I don't think you could fix a jigsaw puzzle, let alone a window."

"Sorry lad, but that can't be done, well not by me anyroad." Said Fred with a slight smile. He was pleased to see that Dave had recovered enough to communicate.

"So how about you show me how it's done? And I give it a go?" replied Dave.

"You?" said Fred with a smile, which brought back a little colour to his face.

"Why not? You told Albert that I must have a bit of natural talent." Continued Dave, much to Fred's surprise.

"Alright!" said Fred with a chuckle. "Why not indeed? There's no 'arm in tryin'. An' if it don't work we've lost nort. So what you do's mostly in yur 'ead. The words are only a sort o' focus an' a way o' releasing the power."

Fred rose from the bed, crossed to the window, and drew back the curtains. "Now this shouldn't be too difficult, most of the glass is still yere. First you concentrates on the way you want's the window t' look. I.e. the way it were before it got broke. Then you pictures in yur 'ead all the bits goin' back together, like a slow-motion replay o' the window breakin' but in reverse. Then you says whatever yur goin' t' say an' releases the power." Said Fred. "Now watch."

Dave watched attentively as Fred concentrated. Although he had witnessed Fred 'twiddle his fingers' on several occasions, this time he could feel the gathering energy and had the tinny taste of static in his mouth. Then, as Fred spoke, he felt the energy released. As he watched, the shards of glass collected themselves together and reformed one of the panes of glass in the window. He took a closer look.

The restored pane of glass wasn't perfect. Dave could see ripples and deformities where the thickness varied and the glass had spread itself out to fill in for missing pieces.

Fred collapsed back onto the bed in a fit of coughing. The colour had drained from his face again.

"I think that's about as much as you can manage, for today at least." Said Dave, handing Fred his untouched pint.

Fred took a sip to settle his coughing.

"I think you may be right lad." Replied Fred, once he was able to draw breath again. "I didn't realise I was so knackered." He sighed. "So are you goin' t' give it a try? Or 'ave you thought better of it?"

"Well it'll either work or it won't." replied Dave. "There's no harm in trying."

Fred caught hold of Dave's arm in a firm grip.

"No lad. It won't work if 'ee thinks like that." He said, gently squeezing Dave's arm. "Think about what you've seen since comin' t' Lyonshire. 'Ow many things 'ave you seen that you thought was impossible?"

"I... I don't know." Dave was taken aback.

"None. Everythin' you've seed *is* possible. You've just 'ad it drummed into 'ee that things are a certain way an' that's all there is to it. Load of rubbish. If that were true, how could 'ee go 'ome a week late? 'Ow could 'ee 'ave travelled around in a time loop? 'Ow could yur bike 'ave travelled so fast when we went to Penhampton? Concentrate on that, not on what is or isn't possible."

Dave drew in a deep breath. How could he have gone home a week late, and that nightmare ride to Penhampton on his return to Lyonshire? He looked at the fresh scars on his hands. He thought about the window, how it had been before the explosion. His body began to tingle from head to foot. He could taste tin in his mouth, and his fillings were tingling like he had chewed kitchen foil.

Fred sat with his hand still on Dave's arm. He could feel the power building.

"Now release it." He hissed quietly into Dave's ear.

"Repair." Uttered Dave under his breath. He felt the energy he had built up surge and leave him. All the strength seemed to go out of him and he collapsed back on the bed shaking.

"You did it lad!" exclaimed Fred in astonishment. "You did it."

Dave felt as weak as a kitten, but he managed to open his eyes. The other pain of glass in the window was intact. True it was opaque and looked more like a pane of frosted glass from a bathroom or toilet window, but it was unbroken.

After a few minutes he felt his strength beginning to return.

"I didn't realise it was so exhausting." He said.

"That's cos it were your first go, an' you drew in enough power t' fix 'alf the windows in Shoton." Laughed Fred. "I ain't ever seed no one from outside Lyonshire do ort like that before, an' I don't know of anybody else who has neither lad. I honestly didn't think you'd do it."

"Thanks for the vote of confidence!" said Dave indignantly.

"I don't mean nort by it lad." Continued Fred, wiping a laughter tear from his eye. "It's just never bin done before."

"Now you tell me!" said Dave, shaking his head. "So why did you let me try in the first place?"

"Well, just cos it's never been done, don't mean it can't be done. That's the whole point!" Replied Fred, with a wink. "Now I'd best get back to 'elpin' Albert behind the bar. You reckon you can do it again? Or did it take too much out of 'ee?"

"I don't know." Replied Dave. "I guess I can do it again, the fatigue is wearing off."

"Right." Said Fred, getting up off the bed. "Give it a try on some o' the other windows up yere. Mind you don't put too much into it, and stop when you've 'ad enough."

Chapter 13.

When Dave came down the following morning, he found Fred clutching a clipboard and inspecting the cupboards in the kitchen. He also noticed that there was an absence of the aroma of frying breakfast.

"I've never seen you do a stock-take before Fred." Said Dave as he helped himself to another mug of coffee from the pot.

"Necessary evil I'm afraid." Replied Fred, moving on to the next cupboard. "A'ter yesterday, an' just about everyone vur miles around all decidin' t' eat yere, there's nort left. I've already put a sign on the door sayin' the pub's closed till t'night."

"So I take it we've got porridge for breakfast then?" said Dave with a slight grimace.

Fred's porridge was good, compared to some porridge he had had it was wonderful, but it was no substitute for a good fry up.

Fred laughed. "Don't worry lad, I reckons there enough yere vur me to scrape zummet together. I've just 'ad too much t' do 's mornin' t' get round t' it yet. We was that busy last night that I never got a chance t' fix the windows in the bar, an' 'ad t' do it first thing. I've never known nort like it, we was still servin' food at gone midnight."

Albert stuck his head in through the back door.

"I tried the front but you ain't unlocked it yet Fred." He said, slightly puzzled. "A'ter last night I reckoned you could do with an 'and 's mornin' so I thought I'd pop in early."

"Thanks Bert." Replied Fred. "There's a fair bit o' clearin' up t' do. Sorry about the front door, but there didn't seem a lot of point in opening' it yet. Now I was just about to start breakfast. You want some?"

"You ever known me t' turn down a fry up Fred?" Chortled Albert.

Fred set down his clipboard and set about cooking breakfast, whilst Albert helped himself to a coffee and joined Dave at the table.

"I saw Lofty the undertaker as I was acrossin' the square." Said Albert solemnly. "'Ee's sorting out the arrangements vur Poulter since he's got no family. An' I thinks we need t' do a bit o' brainstorming. We was all agreed that it was Poulter who killed Lord Timbers an' Chalky. I guess we've got t' start all o're again."

"We'll come up with zummet Bert." Put in Fred, wielding a frying pan.

"Well we'd better come up with zummet fast, the inquest reconvenes t'morrow." Continued Albert. "Who blew Poulter up? An' Hatchet an' Fetlock?"

"If the bomb at the stables was meant for Fetlock then he is extremely lucky." Said Dave. "Especially since those two unfortunate lads were killed."

"Aye." Said Albert. "An' I'll never forget the look on Hatchet's face when we got to Hunton. The poor man was just standin' there staring at the rubble of 'is shop. All 'is 'air an' eyebrows burnt off an' 'is clothes all scorched. 'Ow 'ee survived that I'll never know."

"And poor Jessup, Hatchets partner." Added Dave. "I hope he'll be alright. He didn't look too good when they pulled him out of the rubble, but at least he wasn't killed."

"I'm sure the pair of 'em will be fine." Said Fred, adding something else to the pan. "The healers in Penhampton are very good. Oh blast!"

"What's the matter Fred? Have you burnt yourself?" asked Dave with concern.

"No lad, I forgot t' put out a few crates by the back gate vur them that wants a drink. This'll be alright vur a minute, can you give me an' 'and with the crates?"

Dave helped Fred stack half a dozen crates of quart bottles of beer outside the front of the pub.

"Aren't you afraid people will just help themselves?" Asked Dave.

"That's the whole point lad. This is still Lyonshire don't forget, an' I'll get paid back one way or t'other." Said Fred with a smile.

"I don't think I've ever seen so many quart bottles in my life." Said Dave "Let alone all in one place. And the only ones I have seen have been in museums."

"People around yere can't be 'aving with them piddlely little bottles they sells in your world. All them new-fangled 'alf litre bottles and such." Fred shook his head in disgust. "With quarts you get a couple o' pints out of each bottle, not t'other way around."

"But you use tiny little bottles for the ****."

"Ah but that's vur safety reasons. An' Albert is the only one who has ever drunk a quart o' ****." Fred laughed at the memory. "I shouldn't laugh really, but Bert was so hungry a'terwards that we 'ad t' tie 'im up t' stop 'im eating. An' **** is very unstable. If you puts it in larger bottles, well…. You see that newer lookin' buildin' in the back corner of the yard? I left one batch in the barrel vur too long after it 'ad finished brewin'. Good job it were only a small barrel or it would have destroyed the pub too. Now best get back to that breakfast afore it burns."

Dave joined Albert at the table whilst Fred finished cooking their food. Albert didn't look happy and was tapping his fingers against his mug.

"What is it Albert?" Asked Dave.

"Are we really sure that Poulter was the one that killed Lord Woods and Chalky?" he said with a worried look on his face. "I mean, we was guessin' that he's the one who made the tinned dog food? Though the dog food was actually delivered to Lord Woods with Hatchet's meat, Hatchet denies all knowledge of the dog food. I can't see meself that we're any closer t' sorting ort out than we was t' begin with."

"Ok." Began Dave. "If we take this back to the beginning, we know that it was highly probable that Poulter made the tinned dog food that made Lord Woods' dog turn on him. And that he used his extensive knowledge of the 'time gates', for want of a better term, to use the canning machine on Lord Woods' estate. He was also seriously in debt and had the most to gain from Lord Woods' death. It then follows that he used the same canning machine to make the bomb that blew up Chalky."

"But why did he blow Chalky up?" Asked Albert.

"I don't know why exactly." Replied Dave. "But, and this is important, why else would he have come into the Stoat and Ferret for a drink unless it was to give himself an alibi for the time that Chalky was killed? He hardly ever came in here for a drink. Isn't that right Fred?"

"Hang on a mo, I've just got t' finish turnin' these sausages. There we go. Now, what were you sayin'?"

"I was saying to Albert, why did Poulter come in here at the time Chalky was killed if not to give himself an alibi? You told me that he hadn't been in the pub for ages."

"That's right. He used to come in regular, but a'ter the business with the practical jokes, everybody shunned 'im and 'ee stopped comin' in." Replied Fred.

Albert was still having difficulty getting his head around the problem, and still had a worried look on his face.

"Ok." He said dubiously. "Puttin' aside the fact that all you've got is supposition an' hearsay, an' we take it as read that Poulter was responsible for the first two murders, then who was it that blew 'im up? 'Ee can't of done it 'imself and blowed up Hatchet an' Fetlock?"

"Perhaps he had an accomplice." Put in Fred, getting the plates out of the cupboard and placing them on the shelf above the stove to warm through.

"Of course!" exclaimed Dave. "If he had an accomplice, and that accomplice found out from my story in the newspaper that we were closing in on Poulter, then that would be a reason to kill Poulter, to prevent him from identifying this accomplice once he had been caught."

"So why the two other explosions then? If this yere mystery accomplice was just a'ter Poulter?" Asked Albert.

"Mornin' all." Said Hal cheerily as he came through the door. "Messin' up my kitchen again I see Fred."

Fred rounded on him, waving the fork he had been using to turn the sausages. "Just whose kitchen is this?" he said with mock seriousness.

Hal laughed. "Easy Fred. I've seen the sign on the front door an' since there's nort here vur me t' cook with, what would you like me to do?"

Fred thought for a moment before answering; they really needed some privacy in the kitchen for a while so they could talk freely. He considered sending Hal home, but he was going to be needed if they stood a chance of doing any food when they opened later on.

"I've checked the cupboards in yere." He replied at last, picking up the clipboard he had been using. "If you can make a list of what's what in the cold store out the back. It would be very useful, an' it would give us a chance t' eat our breakfast in peace."

"Ok Fred, I can live with that." Said Hal, taking the clipboard from Fred. "Just give us a mo, an' I'll get to it."

Fred dished up their breakfast and set the plates on the table before pouring another coffee and seating himself.

"Getting back to what we were talking about." Said Dave thoughtfully. "If, as we presume that Poulter was the target, then the other two explosions were just a diversion to throw us off of the scent."

"Could be more to it than that lad." Said Fred sternly. "It's a bit extreme t' kill others just t' throw us off of the scent. Could be that whoever done it did it t' make sure that the way was clear vur them to get Lord Woods' land an' the shop."

"Besides," put in Albert, "them explosions 'appened before the papers were delivered yesterday."

"I don't think that makes a lot of difference." Replied Dave.

"Why's that then lad?" Asked Fred.

"We know Poulter had a good knowledge of the time gates because of the practical jokes he used to play. So wouldn't it follow that whoever his accomplice was, would also have a good working knowledge of the time gates? That way the explosions could have all been carried out by the same person, before the paper came out with my story, and also eliminates the need for complicated timing devices which probably wouldn't work in Lyonshire anyway."

"Ok, but that doesn't bring us any closer t' workin' out who this accomplice actually is." Said Albert gloomily.

Dave set down his knife and fork and rummaged around in his pocket. He pulled out a tatty piece of paper.

"This is the list we got from the court of those that say they had a claim to Lord Woods' estate." He said, unfolding the paper and smoothing it out on the table next to his plate. "If we ignore all those who just put down their names on the off chance, then that leaves us with Fred who is after ten of the thirty acres. I think we can discount him."

"Very generous of you I'm sure." Said Fred in a flat tone.

"Fetlock is claiming the stables which are now his anyway and the land, and Hatchet is claiming the land and the shop in Penhampton."

"That don't give us any clue then." Put in Albert. "But with Poulter out o' the way, Hatchet's goin' t' get the shop in Penhampton vur definite. That just leaves what's left o' the land a'ter Fred 'as 'is ten acres."

"It were awfully convenient that Fetlock just 'appened t' 'ave all them mattresses in 'is office when the explosion 'appened." Said Fred.

"That's true." Added Albert. "'Ee 'ad a very lucky escape an' no mistake."

They sat in silence for a moment, chewing over ideas in their heads and forkfuls of breakfast. Outside the kitchen window a side of beef walked past. Nev, who was lying by the backdoor, sprang up from a position of total repose and began bouncing up and down and yapping. A moment later a small gangly man walked back the other way towards the gate.

"It's Clifford." Remarked Albert.

"You'll 'ave t' excuse me vur a mo." Said Fred, rising from his chair. "I'll 'ave t' go an' check the delivery an' Clifford normally 'as a bone on the wagon vur Nev."

Fred untied the little dog and led him outside.

"'Ere Fred!" called Albert after him. "You was on about getting a dug? Well Clifford knows most o' the dug breeders."

After a minute or two, Fred returned. "Sorry about that." He said.

Nev was carrying a bone that was nearly as big as he was. He laid down by the warmth of the stove and crossed his front paws protectively over his bone. His tongue and teeth were already busy as he set about reducing the bone to something he could swallow without leaving himself bone shaped.

"What was it you was sayin'?" asked Fred.

"Fetlock." Said Albert helpfully.

"I did see him hit one of the stablehands, when I was out there." Commented Dave.

"'Ee's got a reputation as a hard taskmaster." Put in Albert. "But 'ee dotes on the 'orses."

"And then there's Hatchet." Said Dave.

"Now there's a one who's got a temper on 'im." Added Fred.

"He was a little strange when I interviewed him, but the only time he really got angry was when I mentioned Fetlock."

"Why was that then lad?"

"They don't see eye to eye. It goes back to when they grew up together apparently."

"They grew up together?" Albert was stunned.

"Well they would've, they're brothers." Said Dave. "Twins actually. But for some reason they fell out. Or so Jessup told me. And Hatchet only put in the claim for the land to annoy his brother."

"They kept that ruddy quiet!" exclaimed Albert. "Gladys and Agatha are twins but even they couldn't keep stum."

"I didn't find it out from either of them. It was Jessup who told me." Replied Dave.

"That reminds me." Began Fred as someone carrying a large cheese went past the window towards the cold store. "I've got a crate vur 'im."

"Oh?" Asked Dave and Albert simultaneously.

"I gives Jessup a crate of **** once a month but with all that's been goin' on I clear forgot about it." Replied Fred.

"What do you get in exchange?" Dave was curious.

"That side o' beef Clifford dropped off vur a start."

"That wasn't payment for Clifford then?" Dave was intrigued, he still didn't fully understand how the bartering system worked in

Lyonshire.

"No, Clifford's a dog walker. That's how 'ee knows all the dog breeders. But 'ee makes some of me deliveries an' picks up stuff that I can't. I should've given the crate t' deliver, but I didn't think. Shows 'ow messed up my 'ead is at the moment." Replied Fred.

Dave leapt up from the table, banging his knee as he went.

"Argh!" He said, rubbing his leg.

"You alright lad?" Asked Fred. "Only you jumped up rather quick."

"I'm ok Fred. I've just had an idea. And I think I know why the police investigation team didn't find any trace of explosives. I could be barking up the wrong tree, but it's something I need to follow up." Replied Dave thoughtfully. "Albert, are you busy?"

"No, not really. Why?"

"Only I could do with a witness in case what I suspect is the case is actually the case. And since you are on the court advisory panel, your word will carry a lot more weight than mine."

"You're not makin' a lot of sense lad, but if Fred don't need an 'and yere, then I'm all yours." Replied Albert.

"I've finished checking the store Fred." Said Hal cheerfully, coming in from the cold store. "T'waz a bit bleak, but the deliveries are comin' in so us should be able to rustle up some zummet vur t'night's menu. And I'll do us all zummet cold vur lunch. Times getting' on a bit."

"I was just goin' t' say t' Albert that the two o' us can sort things out yere can't we? An' 'ee needn't hang around." Said Fred in reply.

"Well if you say so Fred." Said Albert, taking the hint and giving Fred a rather obvious wink. "I think I might go vur a stroll. What about you lad? Fancy joinin' me?"

"Err, um, yes." Said Dave, slightly taken aback.

"Ruddy' heck!" exclaimed Hal. "Tiz not like you t' take unnecessary exercise Albert. Are 'ee veelin' alright?"

"A'ter what's gone on recently?" replied Albert quickly, much to Fred and Dave's surprise.

~~~~~

Father Turner surveyed the wreckage in his church. Until now he had not worked up enough courage to enter the church since Dave had helped him out after yesterday's explosion. His nerves were never that good at the best of times, but the previous day's events had shaken him badly. Poor Poulter had been murdered practically next door to his church. Such a thing was unheard of in peaceful Lyonshire. It had affected him so badly that he hadn't conducted any services since it had happened.

He looked around the church. Every single window on the church had been blown in. The floor and just about every surface was covered in a carpet of sharp multi-coloured shards from his once beautiful stained glass windows.

With a heavy, heartfelt sigh, he carefully made his way through to the vestry and put on the iron-soled boots that he kept there in case of emergencies. Picking up his broom, he crunched his way across the broken fragments to begin the clear up.

Normally when a window was broken, for example when Gladys was singing in the pub, he could sweep up the broken pieces and when the glazier, Mr Packer, came, he could waggle his fingers and the window would repair itself. *[Even though it was against many of the religions Father Turner represented.]* There were, of course, always a few anomalies, and the pattern could be a problem, but Mr Packer had a collection of odd bits that could be used to fill in any gaps. If all else failed, he usually had one spare window in stock.

Father Turner mournfully shook his head. There was no way that even someone as skilled as Mr Packer could do anything with all this lot, except melt it all down and start again.

Once he had finished sweeping, and put all the broken glass into several steel bins, he began the tedious job of putting up the boards. They were kept in a specially built shed out behind the church. This time he had to make running repairs to the boards that had been blown down as well, and not being good with tools, this resulted in several hefty hammer blows to his thumb. Followed by much swearing, blaspheming, and finally penance.

~~~~~

Aunt Aggie was enjoying herself immensely. She couldn't remember the last time she had enjoyed herself so much. She was counting yesterday's takings again, having taken the money from the tin box under the counter that served as her safe. For security reasons, as soon as she shut the drawer to her till, all the money fell down a chute into the armour plated box on the shelf underneath. After all, she never gave anyone change if she could help it. And, if someone was foolish enough to try and rob her and by some miracle managed to get the till open and stuck their hand in, all they would find would be several razor sharp mousetraps.

She was gloating. In all the confusion yesterday a lot of stunned people had come into her shop for bandages and other items for first aid.

Being in a state of shock, she had been able to lead them around her shop by the nose and sell them all sorts of things they didn't really need. And although actual money was not widely used in Lyonshire, a few people carried a small amount. Those that didn't had left her with a pile of lucrative IOU's promising goods or services. It would be several years before she had to mow her own lawn or weed her garden, and her windows were guaranteed to be spotless inside and out for the foreseeable future.

She reached down and absentmindedly stroked one of her cats as it rubbed itself against her leg. She didn't feel in the least bit guilty for exploiting the terrible events that had shaken not only the village, but all of Lyonshire.

~~~~~

Hatchet was pushing his business partner Jessup through the labyrinth of streets in Hunton. Hatchet himself had escaped with only a few cuts and bruises from the explosion that had partly destroyed his shop. Jessup hadn't been so lucky and was bandaged from head to foot, which was why his partner was pushing him in a wheelchair.

They reached their shop. It wasn't nearly as badly damaged as Poulter's and the explosion had been far smaller than either of the others. In contrast to the almost total destruction of Poulter's shop in Shoton, their shop was still standing. The shop front had been blown in and the room above was open to the elements, but most of it was intact.

"FASSAR GRETEA MULER BAH!" Exclaimed Hatchet.

"It's no good swearing about it." Mumbled Jessup from under his bandages. "And will you please stop waving that cleaver around so close to my head!"

"SURRY." Apologised Hatchet.

"It's alright, I understand you're upset, but it is nothing that we can't rebuild. Aren't you glad I persuaded you to take out that insurance policy? Besides, both of us survived, more or less. Look what happened to poor Poulter."

"FURSE WEUR PLORT BLAH HA."

"Exactly my point. We could both be dead. I feel really sorry for the families of those poor lads that were killed out at your brother's stables."

"HARG! FELDA HARG!" Swore Hatchet.

"Alright, I'm sorry for mentioning your brother, but you have to accept that he is your brother. Besides, if you want to play your silly sibling game of one-upmanship, then with Poulter's death you won't have any competition when it comes to Lord Woods' shop in

Penhampton. It's yours by default now."

Hatchet's face split in a big grin. After a moment he burst out laughing. He had got one over on his brother.

"And will you PLEASE stop waving that cleaver around!"

~~~~~

Fetlock was pacing up and down outside the wreckage of his stables. As many of the horses as possible had been moved up to Lord Woods' house, but these stables had once been the stud for the house and those few stables at the house had been used for working horses. Consequently, there hadn't been enough room for all of them. They had been forced to house the remaining horses in what temporary accommodation they had been able to construct with the materials at hand. They had used the wooden poles from the jumps in the show ring, roped them together and tied tarpaulins over the top.

Those stablehands unfortunate enough not to be staying up at the house with the other horses, were also in temporary accommodation, a collection of cardboard boxes with a leaky old canvas cover.

Fetlock wasn't happy. He had a fixed grin on his face, a sign all the stablehands had come to dread. Occasionally he would flick his riding crop against his bootleg; another bad sign. And worst of all, he wasn't shouting. The stablehands were all doing their best to stay out of his way. There had been a fight amongst themselves to take the remaining horses out for their early morning ride; a very long ride. Fetlock had worked out for himself that his beloved brother was going to get the shop in Penhampton by default. And that really needled Fetlock. The shop was of no particular use to him, although he could've used it to sell tack, but it was the fact that his brother had something and he didn't that annoyed him.

He looked on in silence, as those stablehands that had lost the fight earlier and had remained behind were busy shifting the rubble of the ruined stables. The investigators had pawed over it the night before and apparently found nothing, but there was a fortune buried under that mess and Fetlock was determined to get it back. He stopped pacing.

"Haven't you useless lot found it yet?" He shouted, letting out the full force of his ire.

The stablehands looked at one another with panic evident on their faces. One of them was going to have to give him an answer and he wasn't going to like it. There was a hurried round of 'rock, paper, scissors' as they selected a *volunteer* from amongst themselves.

"N… n… no. Not yet." Stammered the loser, making sure he was as far away from Fetlock as was possible.

"Come on you worthless imbeciles! You know as well as I do that those horses are just so much walking salami without that stud book!" He shouted at them, and threw a stone in their direction.

~~~~~

"So what exactly are we doin'?" Asked Albert as he followed Dave across the square towards where Poulter's shop had stood. The church clock chimed, proclaiming the time to be twelve noon. "The investigators 'ave already been o're this place with a fine toothed comb an' found nort that could've caused the explosion, an' the court is sendin' back witnesses a'ter the weekend."

"And the witnesses will be just as baffled as the investigators were." Began Dave. "They will see the explosion, but still have no idea of how it happened or what caused it. They might spot who did it, but they will have a hard time actually proving any malice."

"Why's that then lad?"

"Because I think the explosions were caused by bottles of ****, and you can't arrest someone because they gave someone else a bottle of ginger beer." Replied Dave.

"Ruddy heck!" exclaimed Albert.

"And if they did arrest anybody for it, that person could always claim that they didn't know that **** was so volatile and that would put the blame back on Fred for selling something so dangerous." Concluded Dave.

"So we're lookin' vur broken glass? 'Ow are we supposed t' find a broken bottle in amongst that lot?" Albert indicated the wreckage of Poulter's shop that had yet to be cleared. "There could be hundreds o' different broken bottles amongst all that, besides all the window glass."

Dave smiled, "That's the easy bit, and the advantage we have that the investigators didn't. They didn't know what caused the explosion because they were looking for traces of explosives. But, if as I suspect the explosion was caused by **** then we know exactly what to look for."

"We do?" Albert was puzzled.

"Once the mutated alcohol has evaporated off, which it would very quickly, what's left?" asked Dave.

"A hole in the carpet usual." Replied Albert with a straight face.

"Alright, I'll put it another way. What is ****?"

"Well it's ginger beer." Albert's face split in a broad grin as he caught on to Dave's train of thought. "Ginger! You'd be left with the smell of ginger!"

"That right!" replied Dave happily. "So all we have to do is sniff around for the smell of ginger and then poke around where we smell it."

By the time they finished their search, it was early evening and Fred had opened the pub. Hal was hard at work in the kitchen, and Suzan had recovered enough from her efforts the previous day to be back at work behind the bar.

Having only had sandwiches for lunch, kindly brought over by Hal, Dave and Albert made quick work of clearing their plates of Hal's steak and kidney pudding before joining Fred in the cellar for a private conference.

"So, did you two find ort?" Asked Fred, once they were safely away from prying ears and propped up on their barrels in the cellar.

Dave carefully removed several shards of glass from his pocket and placed them on the makeshift table between them.

"There you go." He said. "Bottle glass that strongly smells of ****, and something else." He reached into his pocket again and pulled out an old-fashioned screw bottle top. "Albert if you would be good enough?" he said, making a wiggling gesture over the table.

"Oh, right." Replied Albert, who began concentrating and muttering over the broken glass and the stopper.

After a few moments the fragments drew themselves together as the rest of the bottle materialised, complete with its screw top.

"Flippin' heck!" Exclaimed Fred. "It's one of me quart bottles. There's the pub's mark impressed in the glass!"

Albert stopped concentrating and the bottle disappeared, leaving the few broken shards and the stopper on the table once more.

"Our conversation this morning when we put out the crates by the gate got me thinking." Began Dave. "If **** is so unstable that it can explode under its own weight in larger quantities, then it would make the ideal untraceable explosive if you put it into larger bottles. All you would need to do is throw the bottle or drop it from a reasonable height and it would explode."

"Well." Fred was taken aback. "I can't say I'm not shocked. But it's goin' t' narrow it down a bit, there's not many that can stomach **** and fewer still that drinks it at 'ome. 'Alf a mo, an' I'll go get the list."

Fred left the cellar to get his list of customers. When he returned, clutching the list in his hand, he had a worried look on his face.

"Fat lot o' good that's goin' t' do us." He said. "Neither Fetlock or Hatchet 'as **** delivered, an' none o' those that does 'as ort t' do with the case."

"Can I have a look Fred?" Asked Dave.

Fred handed him the list. "I don't s'ppose that anyone wants a bottle of ****?" asked Fred. "No I didn't think so, not under the circumstances."

Dave studied the list for a while. "Jessup's name isn't on the list Fred, but you said this morning that you owed him a crate of ****?"

"That's right lad." Replied Fred. "I owes it t' 'im vur the meat Clifford delivered. 'Is names not on the list cos I just gives 'im a crate now an' again."

"Is there anybody else you give a crate to, or anyone else who has a few bottles now and again?" asked Dave.

"Nope. There's one or two that'll 'ave the odd bottle as payment, like when we went t' the market in Penhampton, but that's it." Replied Fred honestly.

Dave smiled. "In that case, I think I know who Poulter's accomplice is, but again I have no way of proving it."

"So who is it lad?" asked Albert eagerly.

Dave shook his head. "No, I'm not going to say, not after what happened yesterday. I don't want to risk it again."

"But there's no one else that can 'ear us down yere lad." Coaxed Fred.

"You forget that that cat got in here somehow. If it could get in then perhaps someone else can too."

"You're not bein' very fair lad." Said Albert glumly. "You can tell us."

"Nope, besides, I have no way of proving it."

"Well I just 'ope you can come up with zummet afore the inquest t'morrow." Said Fred.

Chapter 14.

Dave was up and dressed the next morning before Fred knocked on his door to bring him his early morning coffee. He had not slept much, and spent a restless night tossing and turning, unable to settle. A mixture of feelings and emotions were swirling around in his head. Today he had to find some way to prove his theory about the murders that had affected Lyonshire so badly, and it was also likely to be his last day in Lyonshire.

He sat on his bed, sipping his coffee and inhaling its rich aroma. He was not looking forward to returning to his flat and the stresses and strains of his pointless job. He had only been in Lyonshire for a short time, but already felt a strong connection to its people and relaxed way of life. His world, what until a week ago he had thought of as the real world, held nothing for him, except his girlfriend Joanne.

Dave spent some time on his morning ablutions, dragging out the time before going down stairs to do justice, if not to Lord Woods and the other unfortunate victims, then at least to the hearty breakfast that would be waiting for him in the kitchen.

When he finally went down, breakfast was a solemn affair. He was not really in a sociable mood himself, and Fred was not his normal cheerful self either. For the most part the meal passed in silence, and as soon as Fred had finished eating he made an excuse and disappeared out to the brewery. That left Dave alone with his thoughts once more.

By contrast, Albert breezed into the kitchen, his face split in a jovial grin, and a pint of coffee welded to his hand.

"You ready to sort this mess out then lad?" He asked cheerfully.

"I don't know, I suppose so." Replied Dave hesitantly.

"Cheer up lad!" said Albert as he slapped Dave playfully on the back. "You'll do just fine, I'm sure. Now, where's Fred got to?"

"He mumbled something about the brewery."

"Good!" exclaimed Albert happily. "Then we can make the court car wait when 'ee turns up."

Outside the Stoat and Ferret, the court car drew to a halt in the square. It had arrived with its usual exaggerated punctuality. As per usual the court was due to convene at ten o'clock so it arrived at half past six. George the chauffeur got out and respectfully tapped on the front door. Tooting the horn was out of the question; he was a chauffeur not a taxi driver.

He waited, for what he considered a reasonable time without an answer, and then knocked again. There was still no reply, and after standing at the door for five minutes he sat back in the car and switched on the radio.

George regretted it immediately, as the strains of a 'new romantic punk garage rap' from the middle of the twenty-first century washed over him, pinning him to the driver's seat. *[New romantic punk garage rap was developed by a group of sound researchers who were investigating the effect of sound on the neurological system. The resultant cacophony of sound is not actually heard by the ears; they shut down after the opening bars. The music is instead heard by nerve receptors in the skin and instantly shut down all the body's motor functions. Thus incapacitated the body itself moves in a series of jerks and reflex action, trying to get away from the noise. Unfortunately, without proper training or the aid of a strong muscle relaxant listening to the music results in total paralysis.]* After a minute or two a deafening crescendo marked the end of the 'song' and the DJ's voice cut in.

Slowly the effects of the music wore off and as soon as he was able move again, George hastily redirected the cars aerial to pick up music from a different time and station.

~~~~~

Hal let himself in through the backdoor to the pub. He had just inspected the cold store and was happy to see that it was almost full again.

"Morning all!" he said to Albert and Dave as he entered. "You knows the court car is waiting vur 'ee out front?"

"We decided t' make 'im wait." Replied Albert.

"Do you think we ought to invite him in for a coffee?" Asked Dave. "It must be a bit chilly sat out there in the car."

"S'ppose you're right lad." Replied Albert as he rose from the table. "I'll go an' get 'im."

"Where's Fred 's mornin'?" Asked Hal, dumping half a pig on his butchers' block.

"Out in the brewery I think." Replied Dave, without enthusiasm. "He's not feeling too chipper this morning."

"I expect 'ee's a bit worried about the inquest." Replied Hal, who swung his cleaver down as he began jointing the meat. "Not one vur showin' 'is feelings is Fred."

Out in his brewery, Fred was indeed far from his normal cheery self. He couldn't remember a time when he had felt more miserable. He was sitting on a barrel in the corner of the maltings. The air was thick with the sweet musty smell of sprouting barley, but he didn't notice it. He was lost in his own private gloomy thoughts.

It had all been a bit of a game to begin with. When he had asked Dave to investigate Lord Woods' mysterious death, it had been little more than a diversion from his everyday humdrum existence. He had never dreamt that Dave would find out anything except that it had been an unfortunate accident.

It had been intriguing to be sure, but then it had all started to go wrong. Chalky the smith had been killed as well, and that had obviously been murder. Then there had been the explosions on Saturday and more people had died, killed with his own ****.

Perhaps Poulter had been responsible for Lord Woods' death, but he still hadn't deserved to die, and neither had the two stablehands. It was all his fault. If he hadn't asked Dave to investigate, then perhaps they would all be alive now. He should have known better than to interfere.

Fred shook his head sadly as he cradled it in his hands.

A small but significant part of his consciousness wasn't having any of it. *[Although it could have been caused by the fumes in the maltings.]* What if he hadn't asked Dave to investigate? The coroner would probably have passed a verdict of accidental death, and the whole thing would have been forgotten. If he hadn't asked Dave to investigate, then a murderer would have evaded justice. The tranquillity of Lyonshire would've resumed, but it would have been tarnished. And having escaped justice once, what would have stopped Poulter and his accomplice from killing again?

Fred began to brighten up. Perhaps with the advantage of hindsight he would have done things differently, but if Poulter and the stablehands had not been killed then they would not have known about his accomplice. Then this mystery accomplice would have got off scot-free and again a murderer would have gone unpunished.

He slapped his hands on his knees in a resolute way and stood up. Sitting around feeling sorry for himself was not going to achieve anything. He just had to hope that Dave knew what he was doing and could bring about an end to all this nastiness.

~~~~~

By the time Dave, Fred and Albert arrived at the courthouse at nine o'clock, it was already packed to overflowing. People were fighting for space and sitting wherever they could, both inside and outside the building. Some had even brought deckchairs. Several of the normally austere gowns were busy rushing around with stepladders, wires, and speakers, trying to rig up a makeshift public-address system so that those who were unable to squeeze into the overcrowded courtroom could follow the proceedings.

It looked like virtually all the inhabitants from the Hunton, Shoton, and Fishin area were there, along with a good number from Penhampton itself. Apparently Fred wasn't the only one who had been disgusted with the detestable way the peace of Lyonshire had been shattered. Even though this was only an inquest and not a trial, they were all determined to find out who had been behind it all.

Those gowns not involved with the public-address system looked very uneasy. Things were not going by the book, and like all officials everywhere, going by the book was everything, even if the book was totally ridiculous. *[It is one of the qualifications for middle management or man management, personnel, sorry, human resources, to have no initiative what so ever, and always go by the book, regardless of how stupid or irrelevant the book actually is. If a situation is not listed or mentioned in the book, then that situation does not and cannot exist.]* There had already been a few scuffles between some members of the public and the extra security staff that had been drafted in at short notice. As a result, the members of the Bouncers and Doormen's Association had been asked to guard the building from outside the exits. All apart from Keith, whose job it was to watch the courtroom.

Inside the courtroom itself people were packed in tight. Sardines would have got up and walked out, demanding more room. Even on the official court advisor's bench things were crowded. There were at least three people for every two seats. A problem made worse because many of the advisors were built on the same lines as the advisor on needlework, and she took up three seats all by herself. There was however, despite the cramped conditions, one empty chair on the advisors bench. In respect of his memory, Chalky's seat had been left vacant. A small arrangement of flowers tied in a black ribbon marking his place.

Dave, Fred and Albert wormed, and in some cases elbowed, their way through the crowded room to the seats that had been reserved for them at the front. Even then, they had to politely but firmly evict people from their seats.

Once they were seated, Dave looked around. He could see

Fetlock and his brother Hatchet. Sandwiched between them, presumably to keep the peace, sat Jessup in his wheelchair. He was still bandaged from head to foot. A little further along, Aunt Aggie sat counting the change in her pocket.

Things were beginning to get restless in the over crowded courtroom, and with so many bodies cramped into such a confined space the temperature in the room was approaching that of a sauna. Combined with the general squeeze and lack of personal space, tempers were beginning, not only to fray, but come apart at the seams as well.

A high-pitched whistle of feedback reverberated around the building, marking the success of the gowns in setting up the public-address system. One of the gowns struggled his way through to the judge's bench, tapped the microphone and began the traditional "one two, testing, testing" routine, deafening everyone in the building in the process and scaring a flock of birds into flight on the lake outside Penhampton. There was a mixture of angry shouts and genteel swearing in protest, and the volume was reduced.

Just as the crowd looked like rioting, the door to the judge's chambers opened and a gown stood up to announce the arrival of the coroner.

"Please be upstanding for his honour Lord Justice Hammond!"

"Oh get on with it!" shouted someone in the press of people.

Lord Justice Hammond calmly took his seat and beckoned for everyone else to do the same, which resulted in several minor scuffles as the large number of people tried to sit down on a limited number of seats.

The coroner banged his gavel on the bench until some semblance of order had been restored.

"Right." He began. "*h*I here by reconvene the *h*inquest *h*into the death *h*of Lord Woods. *h*And *h*I would like to remind you that this *h*is *h*an *h*inquest *h*and not *h*a trial."

There was much booing and hissing from the crowd.

Justice Hammond banged his gavel again. "*h*Any more *h*of that *h*and *h*I will clear the court!" He said angrily. In truth he didn't have a clue how this was going to go, and hoped desperately that someone else did.

"We *h*are here to *h*establish the facts, *h*and not to convict *h*anyone."

The crowd had obviously taken his warning seriously and there wasn't a repeat of the booing, just a general 'rhubarb, rhubarb' of disquiet.

Having opened the proceedings, Lord Hammond was at a loss as to what to do next. Desperately he beckoned Albert to approach the bench.

"Have you *h*any *h*idea what to do next?" he whispered urgently, covering his microphone with his hand.

"The lad knows more 'an any o' us. Why not put him on the stand an' let 'im 'andle it." Replied Albert, also in a whisper.

The coroner nodded and beckoned Dave to come forward.

"*h*If *h*I put you *h*on the stand, can you sort this mess *h*out?" he asked Dave.

Dave looked around the crowded courtroom and swallowed hard before answering. "I, maybe." He began. "I've got an idea that might work, yes. But I will need some time to explain things, and it will mean identifying the guilty party."

"Just so long *h*as you get this *h*all cleared *h*up *h*as fast *h*as possible!" replied the coroner urgently, his voice rising several octaves in his desperation.

The coroner sat back in his seat and banged his gavel to quieten the impatient throng.

"*h*I now call ...." A panicky look crossed his face as he couldn't recall Dave's name.

"Dave Unwin!" Hissed Albert, coming to his assistance.

"*h*I now call Dave *h*Unwin to the stand, *h*as special *h*investigator to the court. He will reveal his findings to *h*us."

Dave flushed crimson as every eye in the room turned to give him their full attention. Gingerly he took the stand and faced the crowd.

"As many of you will know from my story in the Hunton Times, I was asked to investigate the unusual circumstances of Lord Woods' death." He began nervously. "And I can confirm that Lord Woods was killed by his dog. However, his dog was not naturally a violent dog, and was deliberately and purposely poisoned to make it turn nasty, and ultimately kill Lord Woods."

There were a few gasps of surprise from people who had not read the Hunton Times and his story, and a grumbling nod from those that had.

"I found out that the poison had been put into the tins of food that the dog ate, and that these tins were manufactured by Poulter the butcher, using a canning machine on Lord Woods' own estate. I also found out that Chalky White the Blacksmith was murdered with a bomb made using the same canning machine, again presumably by Poulter. This is subject to a court appointed team of witnesses to go back and actually prove he planted it though. However, the tragic explosions that took place on Saturday, that killed Poulter and two stablehands from Mr Fetlock's stables, strongly suggests that Poulter was not working alone and had an accomplice, and that this accomplice killed Poulter to silence him and prevent him exposing the plot. I believe that the other two explosions, the one at the stables and the one in Hunton were designed to be nothing more than a distraction to draw attention away from Poulter's death."

"Never mind all that, just get on with it and tell us who did it!" shouted someone in the crowd.

"*h*Order! *h*Order!" Shouted the coroner harshly, as he banged his gavel.

A mumbled "Sorry" came from amongst the press of people.

Dave was a little shaken. The whole thing was nerve-wracking enough without hecklers. He drew in a deep breath to try and steady himself again before continuing.

"As I was saying, Poulter was responsible for the death of Lord Woods and very probably Chalky as well, but he did not act alone.

"I know from a conversation that I had with Poulter that he was deeply in debt. He had become entangled in a vicious downward spiral. The quality of his meat had declined, and as a result he lost several regular customers including Lord Woods. As a consequence he was only able to get in poorer quality meat and so he lost more customers. In the end most of his business came from making tinned dog food."

The courtroom was deathly quiet; hanging on Dave's every word.

"Because of this, he was hoping to use the land from Lord Woods' estate to pay off those debts, and move here to Penhampton and start afresh from the shop in Butchers' Row. Unfortunately for Poulter, he became too much of a liability once I had discovered his connection to Lord Woods' death, and his partner silenced him permanently."

Dave looked around at the coroner, who gave him a reassuring smile and gestured for him to continue.

"This whole affair revolves around the tins of dog food that Poulter made. He always denied making the tins because he feared that if it became common knowledge it would have an adverse effect on his already tarnished reputation. So he distributed the tins from Fetlock's stables."

"That's a lie!" Shouted Fetlock, rising from his seat and bristling with rage.

"*h*Order! *h*Order! Let the lad continue." Countered the coroner, silencing the protest before it could get out of hand.

Still fuming, Fetlock sat back down.

"It's no good denying it, I found the stack of tins that were stored at the stables when I was out there helping to dig through the rubble in the search for survivors.

"Which left me wondering what Fetlock was doing with all that dog food." Dave turned to address Fetlock directly. "Perhaps you were Poulter's accomplice. Perhaps it was you that Poulter was in debt to and passed on the poisoned dog food to Lord Woods so that Poulter could pay you back what he owed you?"

"I protest!" Snapped Fetlock. "This is just supposition!"

"May *h*I remind you that this *h*is *h*an *h*inquest *h*and not *h*a trial!" Countered Lord Justice Hammond sharply. "We *h*are here to find *h*out the truth behind the case *h*and sometimes supposition *h*is *h*a necessary tool."

"But why would I make a claim for the land if, as you say, Poulter was going to give me the land anyway? And you have no proof that Poulter owed me anything anyway! And don't forget, I was nearly killed in an explosion too!" Shouted Fetlock.

"That *h*is *h*enough! *h*I shan't warn you *h*again! *h*One more *h*outburst *h*and *h*I will have you *h*arrested for contempt."

Reluctantly Fetlock backed down.

"Perhaps you made the claim to be on the safe side." Continued Dave once Fetlock had sat back down. "And as for the supposed attempt on your life, well it was extremely lucky that you escaped virtually unhurt because there happened to be a load of new mattresses in your office, especially when the poor stablehands in the rooms on either side of you were killed."

Fetlock sat opening and closing his mouth in stunned silence, much to his brother's amusement. And as Hatchet sat laughing openly at his brother's discomfort, a wave of disquiet rippled through the room.

"And you Hatchet." Dave pointed at the stocky butcher, who immediately sat bolt upright and stopped laughing. Until his brother had been put through the ringer and given him something to laugh about, he had been sulking because Keith the court guard had confiscated his meat cleaver. He shot Dave a murderous look.

"I found out that the tins of dog food were being delivered by one of Fetlock's stablehands, the same stablehand who delivers your meat for you."

The crowd gasped, switching their attention from Fetlock to his brother.

"Even Lord Woods' butler and housekeeper thought that you

were the one supplying the tins. So, perhaps it was you that Poulter was in debt to. And you also had a lucky escape from the explosion that wrecked your shop. Or maybe you just wanted the shop here in Penhampton for yourself, in which case it would be very convenient that with Poulter's death there is no one to contest your claim on it."

Hatchet was fuming. His face was crimson with rage and he was shaking uncontrollably. His knuckles were white as he gripped and twisted his apron in his hands.

"On the other hand, perhaps there is a more obvious person that Poulter was in debt to." Continued Dave, turning away from the livid butcher. "After all, everyone knows that it is tempting fate and your wallet to go into the Post Office in Shoton."

At the back of the courtroom, Aunt Aggie's shrill voice shrieked with rage. "I runs an honourable shop I does! If people come in an' 'ave nort to pay with it ain't my fault if they gets themselves into debt!"

"Madam! Please!" interjected the coroner. "*h*I will have *h*order *h*in the court!"

"Well 'ee ain't got no right slanderin' my good name." Squealed Aunt Aggie.

Most of the room burst out laughing at Aunt Aggie's reply, further injuring her feelings.

"Please go *h*on Dave." Urged the coroner.

Dave nodded. "So who is the guilty party?" he asked the room in general. "Who was Poulter's accomplice, or more correctly, who gave Poulter the idea and steered his actions? For I believe that Poulter was carefully steered into becoming involved in the plot. Someone knew the extent to which Poulter was in debt and used it as a lever to force him to carry out this evil plan."

There was a hushed silence in the courtroom as everyone took this in.

"It's a difficult question to answer." Continued Dave. "But there are clues if we follow the trail of the tinned dog food.

"Poulter made the tins and stored them at Fetlock's stables, from where they were distributed with Hatchet's meat."

"But all I did was store the tins and see they were delivered!" put in Fetlock.

"HURR FLECK FRATTANUR!" Bellowed Hatchet angrily.

"As my business partner said, he has never supplied anyone with tinned dog food." Protested Jessup on Hatchet's behalf.

"That's right!" Snapped Dave spinning around to face Jessup in his wheelchair; much to the little man's surprise. "Because Hatchet himself does not, and did not know about the dog food."

"*h*Excuse me for *h*interupting." Said the coroner. "But you just said that Hatchet …"

Dave waved him into silence. "I said that the tins were distributed with Hatchet's meat. Isn't that right Jessup?"

Jessup said nothing. He was too busy crouching down in his wheelchair and trying to look as unobtrusive as possible.

"It was Jessup that supplied Poulter with poor quality meat to begin with. Then when his customers started going elsewhere for meat, Jessup was able to make a deal with Poulter to buy tinned dog food from him and supply Hatchet's customers. Hatchet might be a good butcher, but because of his unusual err… speech impediment…"

"Well put lad." Commented the coroner.

"… because of his speech impediment, Jessup is the one who deals with the public and with the orders."

The courtroom was silent. Partly because they were hanging on Dave's every word, but mostly because they couldn't believe that Dave was accusing such a quiet, inoffensive man. Especially when the alternatives were Hatchet, who was known to have a wicked temper, Fetlock who was known to treat others with cruelty and contempt, and Aunt Aggie who was, well, Aunt Aggie.

"It was Jessup who came up with the idea of how Poulter could pay him back what he owed him. It was Jessup that ensured that Poulter was in debt to him in the first place by giving him bad meat to spoil his reputation, because Jessup wanted to run the only butchers' shop in the area. And after Jessup found out from my story in the paper that I suspected Poulter, he killed him and caused the other explosions as a decoy."

"So what if Poulter was in debt to me." Countered Jessup smugly. "And so what if I was supplying the dog food without my business partner's knowledge. You have nothing to link me to the explosions at all. As I understand it, the courts' own investigators couldn't find out what caused the last three explosions, let alone who was responsible."

Dave smiled and reached into his pocket. He pulled out a small package carefully wrapped up in tissue paper. Then, in full view of the courtroom, he unwrapped it to reveal a small bottle. It was instantly recognisable from its size and its nameless label. It was a bottle of ****.

"Here, catch!" He said and threw the bottle towards Jessup.

As if by magic, Jessup's bandages fell away, revealing that he was fully clothed underneath, as the small man bolted, trying desperately to get out of the way.

The bottle clattered to the floor where he had been sitting. The thickness of the glass saved it from shattering.

"Are you mad!" demanded Jessup. "You could've killed me and everyone around me!" He screamed.

"Why's that then?" Asked Dave innocently.

"Because that stuff is highly ex….." Jessup twigged what was going on and stopped in mid-sentence. "You've got no proof that I had anything to do with Poulter's or the other murders." He continued, changing the subject. "All you've got is supposition and hearsay! And this isn't even a court of law, it's nothing but an inquest!" He said defensively.

"No." Said Dave calmly. "I didn't have any proof until now, and congratulations on your miraculous recovery by the way. That bottle contained nothing but water, but of course you weren't to know that. But from your words and actions it is apparent that you know what most in this court don't, that **** is highly volatile and can explode."

"I… I…" began Jessup.

"One bottle on its own is fairly harmless, and will cause a small explosion like the one at your shop in Hunton, but if you use several bottles, or decant several bottles into a larger container, say a quart bottle, it can cause a big explosion like the one that killed Poulter or the lads at the stables. I searched through the wreckage of Poulter's shop with Albert acting as a witness, and found the remains of the quart bottle you used."

Jessup bolted for the door. Unfortunately, his progress was slowed by the sheer number of people in the courtroom and by the time he got there, Keith the court guard, was waiting for him. He spun around, addressing the court.

"Poulter was a fool!" he shrieked, his voice accentuated with madness. "He didn't even realise it was me supplying him with bad meat!!! He thought there was something wrong with his cold store!! In the end he was so desperate, and owed me so much that it was easy to convince him to get rid of that stuck-up toff, Lord Woods. And Hatchet and his dear brother Fetlock were just as easy to manipulate. They were so busy fighting and trying to get one up on each other that I could lead them by the nose."

"But what pray, did you hope to gain from all this?" Much to everyone's surprise, it was Hatchet who asked the question in a crystal clear voice.

Jessup was too consumed with his madness to notice the

difference.

"THE POWER YOU FOOL!!!" He screamed. "You all live your dreary lives in this isolated utopia and think money isn't important, but outside money and power are one and the same! Whilst you are all tucked up nice and safe, I have influence over governments, world leaders, oil producers, and international banks. I buy up global corporations and shut them down on a whim, sacking thousands of workers. I can use time travel to acquire billions on the world's stock markets every day. With their ridiculous commodities markets I can go forward in time to see the outcome of a crop, and then go back and buy 'futures' for that crop, like the entire coffee crop the year after next. I can do whatever I like.

"But the biggest challenge of all is here in sleepy little backwards Lyonshire. You don't use money, so I can't simply buy people off. I had nothing that was worth anything in this miserable county, so I had to start at the bottom. I wheedled my way in with Hatchet and took control of him, and eventually Fetlock and Poulter. They didn't have a clue. I could have built my own private empire in Lyonshire, overseen the reintroduction of money, and controlled all of you."

Dave shook his head. The one thing he had learned since being in Lyonshire was how stupid money really was, how much better life was without it, and how much nicer people were as a consequence.

Lord Hammond rapped his gavel on his desk. "*h*I here by pass *h*a verdict *h*of *h*unlawful killing, both *h*in the case of Lord Woods *h*and Chalky White, *h*and *h*order that Jessup be held *h*in custody *h*and tried for their murders *h*and the murders *h*of Poulter *h*and the two stablehands. Court dismissed."

It was over. Dave collapsed back into a chair, shaking with spent adrenalin, whilst around him the court cleared. Lord Justice Hammond had disappeared back into his chambers, presumably for a glass of prune juice. Jessup had been led away by a couple of the court guards. Dave let out a sigh of relief. His gambit with the bottle of **** had worked.

Fred and Albert joined him and engaged in a round of hugs, handshakes, and hearty backslapping.

"Well done lad. You've pulled it off!" Said Fred, shaking his hand.

Chapter 15.

The rest of the morning passed in a blur. Dave couldn't remember much of what happened after the inquest, or the journey in the court car back to Shoton. The departing sonic boom of the car brought him back to himself, and he was standing outside the Stoat and Ferret once more with Fred and Albert.

Still a little dazed, Dave looked around Shoton. It was still quiet and looked almost deserted. The other inhabitants of Shoton didn't have the advantage of such high-speed transport, and it would be another twenty or thirty minutes before anyone else arrived back from Penhampton.

The door to the Stoat and Ferret was open. Hal had been left in charge in the unlikely event that anyone had wanted a drink or meal, but with most of the village in Penhampton it was doubtful.

"So who's vur a drink and zummet t' eat?" Asked Fred with a beaming smile.

He was feeling much better about things. Justice had been done, his conscience was clear and he could go back to being a fat and happy landlord, brewing probably the best beer in the world.

"I thought you was never goin' t' ask!" replied Albert with a smile.

All three of them strolled gratefully into the pub, and all three of them were flabbergasted by the sight that greeted them as they entered. The inside of the pub again looked like the aftermath of a meeting of the Guild of Seers and Allied Fortune Tellers. Tables and chairs were overturned, some of them were even broken. Shattered glass littered the floor and the sound of breaking crockery was coming from the kitchen. There was no sign of Hal but someone was swearing profusely in the kitchen.

"Bugger off you little ~%$£$!! Go on! Shoo! Scram! Aaahhhh get off!"

"Hal is that you?" called out Fred tentatively.

"Fred? Thank the stars! Aahh! Bugger off!" came the reply.

"Well that's charming I must say." Said Albert.

"I don't think 'ee was talkin' t' us Bert."

The three of them made their way through the wreckage in the bar and peered through into the kitchen. Hal was standing on top of the kitchen table, a broom in one hand and a saucepan lid in the other, doing a fare impression of St George, and trying desperately to keep two-dozen slightly wild and very playful cats at bay.

They were everywhere, biting him from behind, attacking him from the front and sides, in the cupboards, wandering amongst the shelves and knocking things onto the floor, and helping themselves to food from the oven, the fridge and anywhere they could. Several of them were tormenting Nev, the little terrier, who was cowering behind his treadmill.

Hal looked imploringly at Fred. He was bleeding from numerous bites and scratches. His white apron was in shreds, and the rest of his chef's whites were blood spotted and in tatters.

"That ruddy woman an' 'er cats!" exclaimed Fred

Instantly he regretted it as two-dozen pairs of feline eyes swivelled round to look at him. Here was someone new to play with. In fact, here were three new someones to play with. Perhaps one of them would like to be disembowelled?

With the cat's attention on the newcomers, Hal made a dash for it. He jumped from the table and was out through the door to the bar, whilst the cats were still looking at Fred and the others and wondering what to do about them. Hal slammed the door closed and leant against it.

"They got in right a'ter you left!" Panted Hal. "Just a couple o' 'em t' start, but then while I was tryin' t' get rid o' them a vew more turned up. A'ter that they just kept comin'!"

"I'll give that woman what for when she gets back!" Fumed Fred.

"I couldn't do ort t' stop 'em." Continued Hal.

The handle on the door started to rattle.

"They're tryin' t' open the ruddy door!" Cried Albert, pointing to the door handle.

"There's a couple o' packages vur 'ee out in the yard, but I didn't get a chance t' see what they was before all hell let loose." Said Hal breathlessly.

"There is?" Said Fred, his lip curling in a nasty smile. "Is the backdoor shut?"

"Yes, yes it is." Replied Hal. He could feel the cats pressing against the door behind him, and looked down nervously at the rattling door handle. "I reckons it's best if I stays yere an' keeps this door closed."

"Right." Agreed Fred. "Now let's go an' 'ave a look at these packages!"

The three of them took the long way around to the yard. In it were two very large crates. One was more or less six foot square and had a large number of holes drilled in the top and sides, the other was about eight foot long, three foot wide and five feet high.

Fred headed straight for the smaller of the two. As they got closer, they could see that it wasn't a crate after all, but a wooden box with a bolted door on the front. There was the sound of movement inside as they approached, and something was breathing heavily and sniffing.

Fred drew back the bolts and opened the door carefully. Inside was the biggest dog Dave had ever seen.

"Bloody hell Fred!" said Dave with astonishment. "What kind of dog is that?"

Fred let the dog sniff his hand before grabbing its collar and leading it out of the box. It was about the same height as an Irish Wolfhound or Great Dane and easily came up to Fred's waist. But there the similarity ended. Its muzzle and head was more like that of a Bull Terrier or Rottweiler, and it was far more heavily built and thick set. But for all its size and bulk, it had a soppy look about it.

"Tiz a Bearhound." Replied Fred with a really wicked smile on his face. "You don't see 'em very often these days. They was bred t' catch bears when bears still roamed the countryside. They're a bit big vur most people t' look a'ter, which is a shame cos they're as soft as mud." He continued, stroking the dog affectionately. "They're strong enough that two or three of 'em can bring down a full growed bear." Fred's wicked grin turned to an evil chuckle. "An' it just so 'appens that they can't stand cats."

"But you're not what I'd call a pet person Fred." Put in Albert.

"No, I don't suppose I am, but if it comes down t' a tossup between Aunt Aggie's cats and ownin' a dog..." Fred left it hanging. "Now if one o' you would be good enough t' open the back door vur me."

Obligingly Albert opened the back door, making sure he was behind it when it was open and not in a direct line of fire.

Inside the feline miscreants turned their attention towards the movement. Here was something else to investigate, eat, savage, or if possible all three in whichever order they chose to.

They swaggered towards the open door. *[Cats are undoubtedly* the champion swaggerers. They can swagger and flounce in a way that can make the most dedicated supermodel give it all up and go back to stacking shelves in a supermarket. Cats can swagger in a number of different ways, these include the simple 'here I am, aren't I wonderful' swagger, the 'my gods aren't I the sexiest thing on legs' swagger, and the all-time favourite, 'I know something you don't know' swagger. This normally happens right after they have left you a present somewhere on the carpet.]

  Fred unclipped the dog's lead, leant down and lifted one of its huge floppy ears.

  "Cats!" he hissed.

  The effect on the dog was instantaneous. Its floppy ears pricked up, and its somewhat saggy body went rigid as rippling muscles fought amongst themselves for room. It turned to look at Fred, and when Fred nodded his approval it padded silently towards the kitchen door and the curious cats.

  Dave knew it was not possible, but he could have sworn that he saw the dog give a wry smile and a wink as it strolled towards the door.

  Albert had retreated out of the way and was hiding behind Fred. Unfortunately for him, Fred couldn't prevent him from jumping out of his skin when the dog let out an ear-piercing howl and darted into the kitchen.

  Much shrieking, hissing and spitting came from the cats in the kitchen as some inherited instinct kicked in and they realised what sort of dog this was. This was not something they could play with, even if they worked together as a loosely knit feline team, this was something that was going to play with them; probably in new and interesting and, above all, painful ways.

  "I think I'll call 'im Woody." Said Fred over the ruckus in the kitchen.

  "Any particular reason Fred?" asked Albert nonchalantly, having regained some of his composure.

  "In honour o' Lord Woods." Replied Fred. "This whole business started with 'is death, an' now it ends."

  The cats were trying to flee the kitchen and get as far away from Woody as possible. In their desperation and panic, their fur on end, they fought amongst themselves. Occasionally, just to increase their terror, Woody would pick one of them up in his huge mouth and give it a shake. It was not actually hard enough to hurt the frightened animals, but just enough to remind them that it could be.

  Two-dozen cats all tried to get out of the kitchen and escape in a rolling ball of fur and claws. Once outside they fled in every direction, but paid particular attention to avoiding the humans in case additional claw marks would offend the dog in some way.

Once they were gone, Woody loped out of the kitchen grinning like a Cheshire cat that had not only got the cream but the eggs, milk, butter and cheese as well. It jumped up at Fred, easily putting its front paws on Fred's shoulders, and licked his face.

"I don't reckon you'll 'ave any more trouble with Aunt Aggie's cats Fred." Laughed Albert.

"I 'ope not Bert. I 'ope not." Replied Fred, disentangling himself from the dog and retrieving a crowbar from one of the sheds. He handed the crowbar to Dave.

Dave looked down at the crowbar in his hand, unsure what to do with it.

"Go on lad, open the other crate." Said Fred encouragingly. "'Tiz vur you."

Somewhat perplexed, Dave began prying off the planks on the top of the crate. As the planks came off all he could see inside was straw, so whatever it was inside was fragile. As he removed a few more planks, he caught the glint of something metallic and shiny. A thought struck him and he glanced at the corner of the yard where his bike normally stood. It was empty.

Quickly he pulled off the remaining planks and wrenched off the side. A cascade of straw fell around his feet to reveal his bike. Dave stood there dumbfounded.

"Go on lad, pull it out."

Dave pulled the bike out from amongst the straw. It was his bike alright, but it didn't look like his bike. His bike had been second-hand when he had bought it, and although it had always run well, it had been a bit tatty around the edges. This bike shone. The paintwork gleamed, the chrome sparkled, and even the engine glistened. It looked better than a new bike in a showroom.

"I 'ad a word with a friend o' mine 's mornin' a'ter the inquest, 'ee owed me a favour. I asked 'im t' pick it up last night an' give it an overhaul." Explained Fred. "What d' you think?"

"It... it... it looks like new." Was all Dave could manage.

"Why don't you start it up lad?" Prompted Albert, as he scratched Woody between the ears.

At that moment Hal emerged from what was left of the kitchen, carrying Nev in his arms. The little terrier was still shaking with fear and patches of his fur were missing, torn off by the taunting cats. But as soon as he spotted Woody he jumped out of Hal's arms and approached the bearhound.

The two dogs stood regarding each other for a moment before ritually sniffing one another. Then Woody lowered his head and nearly drowned the little dog in drool as he licked him.

Dave straddled his bike, turned the key, and swung the engine over on the kickstart. The engine purred into life. He let it warm up for a minute and then blipped the throttle, the engine roared underneath him. The interior of the engine had obviously been treated with the same respect as the rest of the bike.

"How did you get it done so quickly?" He asked Fred.

"I gather it took six months from start t' finish, but I got 'im t' bring it back t'day so it was ready vur you t' ride 'ome." Replied Fred. "Oh, you might want t' take it easy the first few times you rides it."

"You mean to run the engine in?" Asked Dave.

"No lad, it's already been run in. Let's just say the engine's been tuned a little bit, if you knows what I mean."

Dave made a wiggling motion with his finger.

Fred nodded. "It's not as fast as when we rode t' Penhampton, but there's nort on the road in your time that'll catch it."

~~~~~

Aunt Aggie was in a really bad mood as she crossed the square. It had been a complete waste of time, and she had lost money shutting up her shop and going to Penhampton. And that… that young man had even had the nerve to insult her in front of everybody in the court, and everybody had laughed at her! Then there had been the bus. The first bus back to Shoton had been full, and when the second had arrived she'd been elbowed out the way like common riff-raff. That meant she had been forced to wait around in Penhampton for the next one long after paying customers were roaming around the streets of Shoton again. And she'd not been able to do anything about that either.

She stormed back towards her Post Office, muttering under her breath, and nearly jumped out of her skin when a motorcycle roared in the yard behind the Stoat and Ferret. She'd deal with them later.

Removing the locks and chains she opened the door to her shop. Two dozen frightened cats with outstretched claws all tried to leap into her arms at once seeking comfort.

~~~~~

The following morning, Dave was sitting alone in the bar drinking a coffee. After taking his bike out for a spin, he had spent the previous afternoon helping the others to clear up the mess that the cats had made of the bar and the kitchen. They'd had a muted celebration in the evening, but in light of the tragic murders it had been low-key.

Now with breakfast over, and his few possessions packed into the panniers on his bike, he sat watching the clock until it was time for him to leave Lyonshire. Time felt like it was dragging, but every time he glanced at the clock on the wall it seemed to have jumped forward, robbing him of his time in Shoton and heightening his apprehension of returning to his world. There was a large part of him that wanted to stay. After just a week in Lyonshire, he felt more at home here than he did at home.

What made it worse was Albert was nowhere to be seen and Fred was busy out in the brewery, trying to catch up with work that he had let slide over the last few days. Hal and the two dogs were out in the kitchen, and Suzan was working behind the bar, but he still felt lonely.

He glanced at the clock again. He had to keep a careful eye on the time to make sure he left Lyonshire and arrived home last Sunday, or was it the Sunday before that now? It was nearly eleven-thirty. There was less than an hour before he had to leave.

Hal brought him an early lunch, and Fred and Albert joined him in the bar. But all too soon it was time for him to leave, and there was a round of painful goodbyes in the yard behind the pub. Promises to see each other again were exchanged, and when Fred thought he wasn't looking, he slipped a bottle of **** into Dave's pocket.

With the farewells over, Dave put his helmet on and started his bike. But as he rode out through the gates Fred flagged him down and said something that didn't make any sense.

"The next time you see me I won't recognise 'ee." He said cryptically. "Just mention **** and everythin' will be alright." He finished, giving Dave a wink.

Dave rode off towards Hunton, took the turning just past Lord Woods' estate, and stopped at the barrier. He kept a careful eye on the time using the new clock that had been installed on his handlebars, and at the correct time accelerated away. He switched on the lights just in case and passed the barrier.

It was slightly darker on the other side, and a good deal chillier, but not night. At a guess he judged it to be early evening with the sun just setting as he rode his bike along the familiar road towards his home in Tiverton.

As he drew into the parking space below his flat, he could see Joanne's car parked to one side. He put his bike on its stand and peered in through the car windows. It was empty, she must be waiting inside.

Sure enough, she was sat on the sofa waiting for him, a cup of tea in one hand, her attention focused on the television. She hadn't heard him come in.

Quietly he took off his helmet and gloves. He could still feel the pangs caused by leaving the Stoat and Ferret, but they were greatly reduced as he stood for a moment watching Joanne. To Dave it had been more than a week since he had last seen her, and the last time he had heard her voice it had been a recording on his answer phone of her dumping him. But to Jo it had only been a matter of a few hours since they had last seen each other.

He crept up behind her and threw his arms around her.

"Dave!" She cried, startled by his stealthy approach. "Where on earth have you been? I came over to surprise you but you were out, so I thought I'd wait."

Dave opened his mouth to reply but never got the chance.

"And where did you get that ridiculous false beard?" She continued, looking at him inquisitively.

Dave stood for a moment just opening and closing his mouth. As usual he had envisioned seeing Joanne again and ran through various different scenarios in his head so that he wouldn't be stuck for something to say, and as usual she had floored him.

"It's not false." He replied lamely.

Joanne laughed. "What are you talking about? You didn't have a beard when I saw you yesterday, and you can't have grown one that fast! Especially not one as long as that!"

"Try it and see." He replied.

She tugged at his whiskers. They wouldn't come off so she pulled them this way and that to see what was underneath.

"Ouch! Careful that hurts!"

"Ok, so it's a real beard. Perhaps you'd like to tell me how you managed to grow it that long in less than twenty-four hours? And you still haven't told me where on earth you have been?" She said in a slightly miffed tone.

"That's a more pertinent question than you could possibly know." Replied Dave with a slight chuckle.

"Have you been out riding around the lanes again? Did you get lost again?"

"What do you mean *'again'*?" Dave was a little hurt by her remark.

"Sorry that didn't come out right." She apologised. "So did you get lost?"

It was a difficult question to answer. He didn't want to lie to her, she meant far too much to him for that. But how was he going to even begin to explain to her what had happened? Even if he didn't tell her now, he'd have to tell her sooner or later. Preferably much later. Or perhaps he should show her?

Dave smiled and gave her a kiss. "I can honestly say that I was out riding around the lanes and got lost in a bubble of time." He replied.

The End?

Extract from
Quest in Time: A Beginning
Book Two of The Lyonnesse Tales

Ten minutes later when Dave stepped from the changing room he felt ridiculous. He had never been one for going to fancy dress parties, not even joining in for New Year's Eve celebrations. He looked back at the full length mirror behind him, shaking his head as he did so. The sight before him was that of an extra from a low budget Robin Hood television show. A very low budget Robin Hood internet television show. He was dressed in a costume made of green and brown felt, with brown felt trousers, PVC knee high boots and a wooden sword. All in all he looked and felt like a right berk.

"Are you sure this is really necessary Fred?" he shouted in an anxious tone towards the other changing rooms.

"I'm sure tiz not az bad az all that bye. An' you 'eard th' Custodian, uz 'az t' be dressed vur th' part." Reply Fred.

"An' think yerself lucky," continued Fred, "you ain't got to wear a dress."

With that Fred emerged from his cubical. Dave bit his bottom lip to stop himself from laughing. Fred did indeed look like he was wearing a brown dress, a very large brown dress. Fred stood six feet tall in his flat soled felt boots with curled up pointy toes. Fred was not only broad shouldered but fairly broad in the beam as well so the dress like robe made him look more like a pantomime dame than a wizard.

"Why don't you tie the rope belt around your waist Fred?" suggested Dave, still struggling with his composure. "And you could pull the hood up?"

"Humm." Was Fred's non-committal reply.

Never the less he did as Dave suggested. It didn't do much to improve Fred's appearance but Dave began to feel a little less self-conscious about his own ridiculous attire.

"So, what about the other three?" enquired Dave.

"Good point bye. Come on Bert, Suzan, Father Turner, let's zee 'ee." said Fred encouragingly.

Father Turner stepped timidly from his changing room and nodded to the others meekly. All in all he was not that differently dressed than he had been when he had gone in to change. If anything the robe he was wearing was far plainer than his normal multi-denominational one. Granted that what he was wearing looked like something from a cut price costume hire shop, but they didn't have the intricately embroidered, brightly coloured and often clashing runes and symbols of his usual robe. He did, however, have the addition of a foam padded rubber mace tucked into his belt.

"Come on Bert! Suzan!" snapped Fred irritably. "Y're 'olding us up!"

"'M not comin' out." Replied Albert feebly.

"Come on Bert!" repeated Fred. "You can't look any more ridiculous than th' rest 'o uz!"

"I wouldn't bet on it." Replied Albert grumpily as he pulled back the curtain on his cubical.

Both Fred and Dave had to stifle a snorting laugh. Even the timorous Father Turner had to turn away discreetly to hide a smirk. Albert's outfit was as cheap and nasty as the others, though something akin to a medieval soldier; complete with knitted string chain mail, plastic armour and helmet, course canvas breaches and PVC boots. Albert's shorter stature didn't help either, being only five foot in his ill-fitting boots and significantly rotund in the middle. Thus his outfit of knitted chain mail was outfitted by the bulk of Albert's stomach.

"'Ave uz got t' wear this getup?" asked Albert, mirroring Dave's earlier sentiment. "An' will you lot stop ruddy laughin' or I'm goin' 'ome an' leave 'ec to it!" he snapped.

"Sorry Bert." Apologised Fred, trying his best not to laugh. "Tiz part o' th' rules. I'm sure uz all feels like proper berks, but th' rules iz th' rules an' uz'z got t' dress th' part. Now where'z Suzan got to?"

"Erm…" began Dave. "She's behind you…"

Suzan stood defiantly in silence, the hard cold look on her face daring any of them to so much as smirk at her. Like the rest of them, she looked like she had been outfitted at the Thrifty Economy Shoddy Cheap Outfitters' Shop's second's department, but whilst the others just looked ridiculous, Suzan had been transformed. Perhaps it was because she normally dressed fairly dowdily in trousers and loose fitting tops, practical sensible clothing for working behind the bar but not very… feminine. Now she stood with her hair pulled back, her shoulders bare apart from the straps that held a plastic breastplate in place which left her middle exposed, and the short fake chainmail skirt and ankle boots showed off her legs and the plastic greaves strapped to her shins.

"What? No witty remarks or snide comments?" Snapped Suzan after a moment or two's silence.

No one said anything. No one dared. From the look on her face the probable outcome would involve being hit repeatedly with the plastic sword she was holding menacingly.

"Right," began Fred. "let'z grab th' rest of our kit an' get on with it shall uz?"

In silence they crossed the room to a row of hooks where they had left their bags. There was no sign of them. In their place was a line of backpacks and above them were faded and tatty labels in a heavy script that was again difficult to read. Bilboa was nowhere to be seen so without anyone to ask, Fred pulled a pair of half-moon spectacles from his robe and squinted at the labels.

"Right then," he began. "I'm guessin' that these iz vur uz." He read the first label. "Master Cleric. That'd be you Father Turner." He continued, unhooking the pack and handing it to the priest.

"I… I'd…. I'd just like to say.." began Father Turner nervously, "that since we are going to be spending so much time together that perhaps to save time we could drop the 'Father Turner' and you could all use my given name?" he suggested.

"I don't see why not." Replied Dave. "What is your given name?"

"Yeah," agreed Albert. "I've only ever known 'ee as Father Turner."

"It's… It's Howard actually." Replied Father Turner in barely a whisper. "I'm actually forbidden to use it by several of the religions I follow." He continued with a sigh. "And I've had to change it for several others, but since we are technically no longer in Lyonshire I guess it's alright?"

"Howard it is then!" Declared Fred, slapping the poor man so hard on the back that he almost fell over.

"Now where were uz to?" said Fred thoughtfully. "Ah yes! Wizard. That'd be me." He took his pack and a staff off of the peg so marked. "Thief." Continued Fred, peering over the top of his spectacles at Dave and handing him his pack and a toy bow and arrows.

Dave looked at the bow and its saggy string reproachfully. His five year old nephew had something similar with suction cups on the arrows. It had lasted all of five minutes and left the poor lad in tears when it had broken. There were suction cups on the arrows

"Vighter number one." Continued Fred, unhooking the next pack and handing it to Suzan.

"An' th' last one must be yours Bert. Oh." He finished abruptly, and swiftly leant against the wall to cover the sign above Albert's peg and handing Albert his pack and a large plastic double headed axe.

"Best uz moves along I think." He said ushering them towards the door at the other end of the changing rooms to the one they had come in through. "Uz'z still got t' 'ave th' briefin' afore uz goes."

Unsure of Fred's sudden need for haste Dave gave him a quizzical look and waited until the other had all gone through the door.

"Best you don't say ort." Whispered Fred and took his hand off of the label above peg where Albert's pack had been.

Dave squinted at the gothic script. There was one word on the label. Dave bit his lip and stifled a laugh.

"Best if 'ee vinds out vur 'imself." Whispered Fred, shaking his head and led them through the door.

The room they entered into reminded Dave of a recreation of Victorian school room he had once seen at a theme park. The dark wooden panelling on the walls was echoed by rows of dark wooden desks and upright chairs. At the far side, raised up on a dais was a high lectern style teacher's desk and behind that was a blackboard complete with chalk and a board rubber just waiting to be thrown at an errant pupil. Around the room ornate plaques covered in faded guilt script hung on the walls, but rather than proclaiming who had won the house cup or the names of successive head boys, these decreed great deeds of valour or gallantry.

As the companions seated themselves down in the front row desks Dave took the time to study the closest board. It was the most ornate and apparently from the dates, the oldest. The slightly faded gold lettering was again in a heavy script, making it difficult to read but Dave could just about make out the earliest names.

ERNEST GARY GYGAX

DAVE ARNESON

JEFF PERREN

DAVE WESELY

RAY BROOKS

But before he could puzzle over why some of them sounded familiar, a door in the wood panelling opened and in walked the tall gangly gentleman in dark robes that had met them at the reception.

"Ah. Good!" He intoned in a deceptively deep and penetrating voice. "Nice to see that you are all changed and ready for the briefing. No, no please keep all questions to the end of the briefing. Thank you."

Albert bashfully put his hand down.

"I am the Keeper. That is to say I am known as The Keeper." Continued the Keeper.

"I though e' waz th' Custodian?" whispered Fred to no one in particular.

"No, I am the Keeper." Said the Keeper, leaning on the lectern like desk and peering at Fred.

Dave had the feeling that the Keeper's voice would not only have carried to the back of a large and crowded hall, but probably across the playing fields and on into the next county. It was a voice well use to public speaking.

The Keeper pushed his round glasses up his sharp and angular nose and studied the five of them for a moment, waiting to see if there were going to be any more interruptions before continuing.

"What you are about to embark upon is difficult and dangerous, and should not be undertaken with any false pretences. I understand that you wish to travel to the Citadel of Silverman the Wise. Not really the destination of choice for a party of novices. Thus your quest will begin some distance away from your ultimate target and somewhere less demanding to allow you to gain experience. Nevertheless, you will no doubt get injured, possibly fatally."

There was a collective in drawing of breath.

"Should you be mortally wounded then all your experience and everything you have collected up to that point will be lost, you will be returned here and you may or may not get to re-join your companions. However, let me reassure you that if you are killed in the games realm you will not actually die."

Again he scanned the companions.

"As you go you will gain experience. The more experience you get the greater your skills will become and the easier it will be to overcome some obstacles and foes. Unfortunately, the further you get the harder the challenges and opposition becomes. Here, take one of these and pass the rest on." Continued the Keeper, handing Dave five embroidered patches with the number one on them.

"These badges denote your starting level, and since you are all novices, they are level one."

Dave couldn't work out quite what he was supposed to do with the patch. There appeared to be no obvious way of attaching it to his costume. There was no pin or clasp on the back and it didn't have any adhesive on it. It was Albert that came to his rescue, by simply slapping his own patch against his chest. Where, as if by magic, it stuck. The others followed his lead and soon they all had their badges displayed upon their chests.

"Once you have attained the requisite amount of experience then it will automatically increase by a factor of one." Intoned the Keeper. "Your actions will however be limited by the character you are embodying. You may find this restrictive to begin with, but you will soon get used the parameters within which you may operate. Skills you possess in this world do not necessarily transfer across and vice versa. It can be disorientating to begin with. The best way to overcome this is to immerse yourself in the roll and forget about everything else.

"You each have the basic essential in your packs to begin with, bedrolls, lanterns, water and food etc. Anything else you will have to pick or acquire on your travels. And each of you is allowed to take one personal item from this world with you, your luxury item if you like. This is in accordance with the universal law of continuity. However, I emphasise the *one*. Anything else will automatically be assimilated or lost entirely, and taking anything electrical would of course be a waste of time.

"Right. Any questions?" again the keeper peered at them through the round lenses of his glasses. "Yes?"

It was Albert that had raised his shaky hand. "Just what skills will us 'ave? An' how painful iz th' pain?"

The Keeper rolled his eyes skyward. "Clearly you have not read the guidelines on the wall of your changing room that went along with your costume." He said, a slight irritation creeping into his voice. "Your skills are dependent on the character you are embodying." He continued rather forcefully. "And the pain will be real. However, if you die you do not actually die, your slate just gets wiped clean and you will be returned here. Any further questions?" It was asked in such a manner and tone that if you needed to ask anything then you were clearly and imbecile and had no right being there.

"I didn't realise there were goin' t' be a ruddy test on it!" Mumbled Albert irritably. "Ow was I s'pposed t' know uz 'ad t' read it." Obviously Dave hadn't been the only one not to read the scroll on the wall of his cubical.

No one else raised their hand.

"Good." Sighed the Keeper. "If you will all follow me, you may begin." The Keeper ushered them across the room towards another door in the panelling.

"Remember, any slight disorientation will wear off momentarily." He said reassuringly to their vanishing backs as they stepped through. "Anything else is entirely your own problem."

Dave had to admit it was a very disorientating feeling as he stepped through the door. He felt as though he was being stretched, pulled, poked, prodded, shrunk, rolled and squashed whilst simultaneously being dragged at high speed and slammed up against a wall.

"FRED!"

A bellow from Albert somewhere behind Dave interrupted his chain of though before he had had a chance to familiarize himself to his new surroundings. Dave looked around at his companions and immediately wished he hadn't as he burst out laughing.

Father Turner or Howard looked, at first glance, much as they had done before except for their cut-price costumes. The same could be said for Fred. They were now dressed in similar looking outfits but instead of looking like extras from a low budget television show they now looked like they were appearing in a no expense spared block busting Hollywood movie. Even the foam padded mace in Howard's belt had been transformed into something all too real. And Suzan, well she looked every bit the archetypal warrior princess in a burnished steel breastplate and chainmail. It was, however, Albert's transmogrification that was perhaps the most pronounced and had reduced Dave laughter.

Instead of the short and generously proportioned, elderly, clean shaven gentle man with thinning gray hair in knitted chain mail stood a stereotypical dwarf with a long platted beard, wearing very real looking armour and helmet and gripping an extremely nasty double headed axe. What made it worse was the look on Albert's normally good-natured face which was fixed in the most evil, twisted angry grimace imaginable, and gave the impression that he was about to unleash hell on earth. This dwarf was, without doubt, grumpy.

Further information about the author and upcoming work can be found on:
www.lyonnessetales.co.uk
Or follow on face book:
https://www.facebook.com/rick.trivett.18
Or Twitter:
https://twitter.com/LyonnesseTales

R.J.Trivett is a middle-aged Devonian with a love for classic motorcycles, books and writing. He likes the escapism of a good fantasy novel, nothing too dark, but something thought provoking and challenges convention.

He was privately educated until the age of sixteen when he managed to escape a learn how to take motorcycles apart and put them back together. He is self-employed, running his own market stall that sells tools. He thinks life is too complicated and people should be nicer to one another.

Made in the USA
Charleston, SC
22 May 2015